Other books by this author:

Sons of the Rapture, novel
Triumph of the Ape, stories

Shining Man

TODD DILLS

LIVINGSTON PRESS
THE UNIVERSITY OF WEST ALABAMA

Library of Congress Control Number 2019940933
Printed on acid-free paper
Printed in the United States of America by
Publishers Graphics

Hardcover binding by: HF Group
Typesetting and page layout: Sarah Coffey
Proofreading: Be'ana Wade, Nick Noland,Shameika McKinstry,
Jenna Frye
Cover Design: Amanda Nolin

Cover Photograph: Amanda Nolin

First edition

6 5 4 3 3 2 1

Shining Man

TODD DILLS

... we're gonna meet someday
In the crumbled financial institutions of this land
There will be tables and chairs
There'll be pony rides and dancing bears
There'll even be a band
'Cause listen, after the fall
There'll be no more countries
No currencies at all
We're gonna live on our wits
Gonna throw away survival kits
Trade butterfly knives for adderall
And that's not all
There will be snacks ...
—*Andrew Bird, "Tables and Chairs"*

WE ARE OUT HERE.

Dramatis personae
those who matter

Cash: The *I* in the tale, former fry cook, former doorman, former performance artist, former tire carrier. South Carolinian by birth, world citizen by naturalization.

Turner Bascombe: The S.C. born and bred racecar driver himself

Ralph Cash: **Cash**'s father, a phantom who lurks in dreams, around Chicago alley corners, on Charlotte high-rise porches

Nellie Cash: **Cash**'s paternal grandmother

Eula Littlejohn: **Cash**'s beauty-shop-owner mother

Cyrus Littlejohn: **Cash**'s maternal grandfather

Henry's crew:
Bobby Cash: (No relation) Salad man, prep cook, video-sex exhibitionist

Will Theron: Grillman, prep cook

Annie: Kitchen manager, expert gin drinker

Tim Morton: Prep cook, Confederate-flag bandana wearer

Chicago Lark Sparrow crew and associated:
Billy Jones: **Cash**'s closest friend in Chicago, cf. *Sons of the Rapture* (Featherproof Books, 2006)

Eula Banks: **Cash** and father's Chicago landlord

Carl: Lit-rag editor, arts-community fixer, occasional pinstripe-suit wearer

Elsa Triolet: "French-American" experimental filmmaker, romantically involved with **Billy Jones**, also cf. *Sons of the Rapture*

Trey Olden: Photographer, frame-maker, man who would fly

Joe: Lark Sparrow bar owner, pioneer urban gentrifier

V: Friend of **Billy Jones** and **Elsa Triolet**, native of Camden, S.C., hanger-on at the Lark, object of **Cash's** vague desire

Jake: Lark Sparrow bartender, videographer, would-be actor

Mort: Selma's bartender, former theater actor, racing fan

Stephan Long: Aspiring filmmaker, director of cop-show-within-a-cop-show "TV Police"

Eric: Lawyer, hanger-on

Smitty: **Eric's** brother, former marine, BB sniper

Melba: Iowa-raised tale teller, actor, ingester of psychedelics

Jennifer: Close friend to **Melba**

Charles Rinckoff: Actor, shape-shifter

Birmingham players:
Leroy King: Trotsky-specs-bespectacled proprietor of Black Hat Books

Albert: AKA "XoXoZ," AKA "Albee," graffiti artist, skateboarder, smooth jazz aficionado, sometime temporary laborer

Mark Mills: Landscaper

J.R.: Temporary laborer

Team Bascombe Lumber and associated:
Tacklebox: Former tire carrier turned jackman

Charlie Peerfoy: Former jackman turned tire carrier

Sammy Montuck Jr.: Racecar driver, principal competitor of **Turner Bascombe**

Eddy "Hugg" Huggins: Bascombe Lumber crew chief, sports-news personality

Charles Huggins: Tire carrier for Bascombe Lumber, former tire carrier for Bascombe Lumber, "layabout drunk"

Pete Kimball: Team truck owner-operator, bluesman, 6'5" philosopher

Adam Stant: Front tire changer

Judd Winnow: Rear tire changer

Jason: Bacon-eating, apologetic **Montuck Jr.** team member

Briggs Patton: Racecar-driving also-ran of the Cup series

Other Charlotte players:
Rob Rene: Graphic designer, **Cash**'s Charlotte neighbor

Matt Caudill: **Rob Rene**'s roommate, business partner

Bridget Ellis: Supermarket deli clerk, B.A. in Women's Studies, "Down with debt" sign carrier, **Cash**'s significant other

Knox Garp: Marijuana dealer

"Big Bill" Cheeter: 6'8" Cheeter Farms co-inheritor, prospective Team Bascombe Lumber sponsor, energy drink purveyor, biofuels booster

Bob Cheeter: Slightly more empathic, and shorter, brother and business partner of **Bill Cheeter**

Chris: "Nazi" lawyer, city council candidate

"G-man" Gerald: Anarchist bicyclist, personal-space terrorist, environmental activist

Those who definitely matter a good bit (in order of appearance/invocation), or: extras in the drama

Horace: Stool sitter at **McClendon**'s bar

McClendon: Charlotte-area bartender/bar owner

Henry David Thoreau: American author of "Resistance to Civil Government," *Walden,* et. al.

Peter Pan: Cartoon peanut-butter brand mascot

Jefferson Davis: Disgraced former leader of defeated would-be nation

Jim Bakker: American disgraced former televangelist

Danny Cheek: Hobo, Chicago squatter, "adoptive father" of sorts to **Ralph Cash**

Elton John: British singer-songwriter

Curtis Turner: Pro racecar-driving pioneer

Jesus: Blue-eyed savior of legions' imaginations, automobile-malady miracle performer in a race team cap, various

Officer Liebowitz: Chicago police officer

W.J. Cash: American author of *Mind of the South,* et. al.

William Faulkner: American author of the Snopes trilogy of novels, et. al.

Johnny Jones: **Billy Jones**' father, deceased, a man who once drove cattle across the eastern seabord, cf. *Sons of the Rapture*

Alllen Ginsberg: American poet — "Howl," etc.

Little Richard: American singer-songwriter, actor, performer

Malcolm Forbes: American magazine publisher, businessman, motorcyclist

Cassandra: "Cass" to **Cash**, drive-in dry-cleaner drug dealer, past significant other

David Foster Wallace: American author of *Infinite Jest, Consider the Lobster*, et. al.

Roberto Bolaño: Chilean/international author of *2666, The Savage Detectives*, et. al.

Eric Foner: American historian/author of *Reconstruction*, et. al.

Erik Rensauler: Publisher, self-styled "literary terrorist"

Sam Ringer: Writer whose friends write short stories on occasion from the point of view of lightbulbs

Rick Moody: American author of *Purple America*, et. al.

Sammy Montuck: Racecar driver, father of **Montuck Jr.**, deceased

McIntyre: The male of the pair of McIntyre + Feldman gallerists, Halsted Ave., Chicago

Jenny: Toothbrush-taking live-in lover of **Will Theron**

Feldman: The female of the pair of McIntyre + Feldman gallerists

Katherine: Middle-aged office stiff, assistant editor, job interviewer immortalized distastefully by **Cash** in "Dispatches from the New American Economy" as "ASS"

Bill O'Reilly: Rightist TV political commentator stained by past misdeeds, among other things

Schuyler Pelt: Childhood friend of **Cash**, expert cigarette lighter, trucker

Colin "Stonefly" Sanders: Owner-operator of a banana-yellow 1996 Peterbilt 379 with 2 million miles on the odometer, intellectual, hauler of I-beams

John: Loudest among the temporary laborers at 14th and 1st North, Birmingham, Ala.

Bear Bryant: Former University of Alabama football coach

Herman Poole Blount: AKA "Sun Ra," American jazz composer

John Coltrane: American jazz composer

The Birmingham Scream: American noise composer

Beaver Cleaver: 1950s/-60s American "Leave It to Beaver" sitcom character

Dr. Claw: Fictional criminal mastermind in 1980s American cartoon "Inspector Gadget"

Nelson Algren: American author of *The Man With the Golden Arm,* et. al.

J.R.R. Tolkien: British author of *The Lord of the Rings,* et. al.

Toby Keith: American country singer-songwriter

Misty Burlingame: Charlotte AB Bank teller

Jenny Brock: Charlotte AB Bank teller

Albert Ledbetter: Old friend of **Billy Jones** and his family, cf. *Sons of the Rapture*

Stinko: Anarchist, bearer of pillowcases

ℐrologue

Turner Bascombe was wrong about a lot. But when he told me the goons out there wanted nothing more than for me to stand down, remain a basement dweller, a deep-fryer jockey with an occasionally wielded gift for steeling himself against the oncoming traffic, he had it right.

I am a stupid man!—a citizen of a great imperial land slowly on its retreat back to barbarism from the great progressive nature that allowed it to flourish, after all. I *like* to stand in traffic! There is sound, wind. People throw things at me, though they once had more felicitous motives when I'd haul around the front of the yellow-and-black Team Bascombe Lumber Ford to get a new tire up on the front right and squat, ass hanging out into pit road as the remainder of the field flew fast within a foot of my back. Peerfoy might hit me square center of one of my goggles with a rind of peeled-off rubber from tire tests, or Tacklebox, the jackman, whack me on my helmet with his wedge adjuster if he wasn't using it. Tacklebox, man of the bullhorn septum piercing and Hollywood headbanger attitude, now former jackman turned competitive driver himself, was also known to shoot spitballs from the red straw he was constantly chewing on to combat the lingering lure of long-shunned nicotine. But all that's birthday cake compared to the bottles, hats, crucifixes, and plethora of profane insults I received for my efforts farther back in the crucible of time—now, too, of course, when standing in traffic nets me nothing more than the stupidity I crave.

My condition says yes to reading as much as possible, even the drivel; to overworking, occasionally; to drinking too much, most of the time; to abstaining from alcohol when necessary, too; to loafing, day by day just getting by; to being rich, pregnant with industry and purpose.

During my most recent stand out in the intersection of North

1

Carolina 51 and South Boulevard by Henry's, the restaurant that once functioned as my employer and which is now solidly boarded up to keep out the ever-sluggish economy, I happened upon a shiny new quarter and bent at the waist to pick it up just as a large dump truck rattled through on its way to the South Carolina border. The truck's mudflaps passed my hanging head at a distance of scarcely a foot, the driver laying hard on the horn and sending a basso hum of adrenaline through my cells, quickened with vibrato. The quarter wouldn't budge, glued to the pavement by some invisible captain of tomfoolery. I hung there bent, suspended, rapt in that cacophonously blissful moment until the truck, now on the other side of the intersection, abruptly stopped. That wrung another blast of sound from the parade of American SUVs fanning out down the road beyond its back bumper. I stood up, watched now the driver burst from the cab and come stomping my way through the paraders in the intersection. He shouted a barrage of gibberish through the blooming rage of horns. At once, the driver was distracted, between hollers and stomps, by the phone in his hand, which he brought close to his face twice as he got closer. I made out "the fuck out of the street, motherfucker" before he transferred the phone to his left hand, cocked his right fist and punched me in my smiling face.

I was all right, though—I awoke to former coworker and my own half-namesake (we shared a surname, as it were) the great Bobby Cash slapping me awake on the sidewalk.

"I got him good, my man. Don't you worry," Bobby said.

"OK," I mumbled. I stood, sidewalk under my feet, traffic moving again—like none of it had happened.

"You look like hell, buddy," he said, "but I guess you're all right. Let's get on before any cops happen by here."

I said yes, let's, but I didn't worry about policemen. Nor did I particularly care about the state of my face. Bobby Cash, no direct relation to my own Cashes, far as I know, he offered to buy me a beer at McClendon's, a bar just across the South Carolina border and close enough to my hole for an easy stumble home. I said yes. He bombarded me with questions on the way there, as it'd been ages since I'd seen him. I wasn't answering anything that required a negative or any other elucidation, simply yessing him or, alternately, staring dumbly into the street ahead to contemplate the coming drunken night, looking forward to it, really. Bobby didn't stop yammering until we arrived and took our seats on McClendon's ancient stools and I got a healthy look at the red bulge around my iris in the mirror behind the bar, a burst vessel in the cornea.

"Jesus," I said. The minute I saw it, the pain kicked me in the forehead.

Bobby muttered something, and when I chanced a glance his way I could see that he was just as transfixed by his own image, or perhaps he was simply that hard up for a beer. His gaze held hard to his rotund visage, the thick brown mustache he wore giving the false impression he was considerably older than his meager 27 years. Bobby's overall fat face was, if not the very antithesis, at least a topographical negative of my own's gaunt cast. He fit right in, here. McClendon's was a common outpost for the most committed of the region's obese drinkers—like Horace, who was typically just off the bar in a stool at his high table, the man in the same old dirty flannel work shirt day after day after day, a veritable overgrown baby in a high chair with a draft pint and an overflowing ashtray in front of him. I spied him in the mirror looking over my shoulder at my reflection.

"Jesus H, man, what happened?"

I told him, tentatively, chewing my cheek to head off the growing anxiety. Bobby and I ponied up a buck a draft to start the day anew.

"Need some ice? Shit looks bad," said the bartender, McClendon himself, but I demurred.

"I like the pain," I said. The distraction, I meant. I know too well the dark side of Thoreau's goal. The mind can be a powerful, an overpowering thing, holding utmost dominion over the bodies of all manner of day-to-day sufferers. Put me at rest in a close space with other humans, no obvious exit, no alcohol, and watch the panic ensue.

But yes it's likely I "overthink" all of this, my day to day, as my mother might have it: my wont and pastime—I hold no secrets from myself, least of all that there is only a finite amount of time left for me.

"What the hell you standing in the street for?" Horace said, blowing smoke.

"Later," I said, "later," nervous, nodding, and the fat man went back to concentrating hard on the beer in front of him, the smoke in his hand.

Bobby guffawed, awakened from his trance, and got back to business.

"Come on, dude, tell me what you've been up to. Obviously you're standing in the goddamn street again. You back on Turn Turner's team next season?" That's what they called Turner Bascombe. He earned the "Turn" nickname in his first 500 when he sent, "turned," rather, the leader into the wall on the last lap, sailing right on by the poor unfortunate's left rear bumper to take the lead and the win.

"Nah," I said. But I didn't offer the why—inevitably, Bobby wanted to know. He should've been a journalist. The boy may have been as obese as any member of the team here, but he wasn't stupid. I spouted some nonsense about turning a page in life, and he called me on it.

"Bullshit. You're still up to the same old tricks, brother. How do you think you got that big old red eye?" I didn't want to get into it. I wanted to drink. I finished the beer and then another, tried to bullshit my way through the whole thing. Pretty soon, it worked. He dropped the subject of me.

My mistake.

Bobby Cash, the famed line cook of the former Henry's Bar & Grill, told me that he was now trafficking in Internet pornography, amateur stuff, mostly he and his wife doing it on the deck of their apartment-complex unit—more than I needed to know.

My stupidity doesn't preclude the capability of so-called moral judgment, or spot revulsion, as it were.

"That's fucking disgusting," I told Bobby Cash.

"Tell me about it, dude," he said. "Makes good cash, though. Hell, I'm making ten times what I was at Henry's. And all I had to do was get it on with Candace out on the porch a bit with the phone cam on." To my horror, he fiddled with his device as if he was going to show me some evidence. "Even bought 16 acres out in Indian Land. I cut the grass on the cleared portion of it today." He turned the phone to me now with a picture of rolling grassy hills, gulping his beer, a smile falling across his fat face, long-away amazed look in his eyes.

"There's this hill out there," he said. "And you get to the top of it and you can look all the way downtown. I did it today, man. Amazing stuff. Nothing like that feeling! All that fresh mown grass and thinking, Goddamnit this shit is mine and—"

"Enough," I said, raising a hand. I didn't need his lord-of-the-manor routine and told him so.

"I'm sorry, man," Bobby said. "Didn't mean to turn you off."

I tugged on my beer and closed my eyes, thought of Henry's so long ago, of my escape from the place and the days spent out on I-20 in Alabama, back in the spirit of Shining Man, the chance meeting that plugged me back into the economy of fools for a time, my subsequent opting out. Throughout history, individual resistance has often been a necessity. One thinks of grand social movements, of slaves here in the region and their descendants in the northern cities, the 1960s, etc. I am content with my own at this point, though there be increasingly nothing social about it at all. I am in here, in my mother's basement or in this bar, but so far away you might have to squint to see me.

Bobby went on about his recent riches as I receded from view.

I made of this latest attack the confirmation of a knife's-edge quality of outrage in the world beyond my periphery. The attacks had occurred with an ever-increasing frequency since I'd decamped from the pit crew. My usual instinct was to run, though I'd occasionally been struck at a moment of heightened sensation, high trance, unable to muster the will to leave that hot spot in the middle of whatever thoroughfare. Mass protests, peaceful or not, were never enough to suit me. For the endgame toward a lasting legacy, programmatic individual action became a necessity.

It's resentment for this, I know, that the most vicious arm themselves with.

When I got home, it was near dark and lean-mean Turner Bascombe still had his goofy wrap-around sunglasses on, the cheap-o fedora I remembered well from our onetime wining and dining of the would-be sponsors of the racing vanguard. Bascombe looked more like me than any of my drunk compatriots at McClendon's, I thought, approaching him at the back entrance to my mother's house, the steps that lead down into my hole.

He said nothing at first, a statue in a two-point squat on the balls of his feet just right of the steps, a snake coiled to spring. But after a moment of staring, he shook his head as if disappointed at something, lifted now his own routine like the chameleon and told me the world had me where it wanted me, a fry cook no longer and jobless, drunk, homeless but for the basement, a black and blue and red eye and nothing to take the pain away but booze. He amped up the disgust in his face. I wobbled down the steps through his outburst, ending immobile, one hand on the screen door to the basement, grinning at the thought of all that this man had done to bring me here, seething over betrayals and half-commitments and intended and unintended sleights.

He smiled, offered me money, apologized for the sandbagging he'd given my tour through the racing engine. He tried hard love—"You've got no commitment, Cash!" Turner standing now and moving down the steps as if he would enter my little basement straight through my own body.

But I am not invisible, stood my ground as Turner gave pause a foot off the end of my nose. "Come back to the team," he said, simply. "Nobody likes a loser, Cash."

I pushed him, hard. He stumbled back up the stairs, crashing over an old planter on the second from the top, spinning to fall to a knee. What I didn't say: reconsideration of life in the circuit, plugged into the economy of liquid soap dispensers and plastic, overdesigned sunglasses, just wasn't an option after all that had happened. Bascombe takes me for a rebellious sort like himself, and genuine and original as he often is—and right as he may be— again he misses the point. Stupidity has no need for rebellion, for the youthful spirit of originality. It feeds itself on a diet of water and soda crackers and timidity borne of a different kind of outrage or paranoia than what you'll find in *New York Times* columns or right-wing conspiracy theorists' radio shows. Bascombe himself, a man of my generation if not my exact temperament, is afraid, you know, paranoid enough for the both of us. The racecar driver is famous, full of money, pumped up on the self-respect the institution and his upright, decidedly unique place in it has afforded.

Feasting on timidity causes indigestion.

Nobody likes a loser, Cash.

It wasn't the first time I'd heard it, and other than my bit of understated violence I offered no real argument.

In fact, I hasten to agree! No one likes a stupid man! He does not get invited to parties, and must entertain himself in the only economy of which he is distinctly a member: the one that keeps booze flowing out of the taps of wayward barrooms.

"Yes yes yes," I slurred as Turner sprung back to his feet at the top of the stairs, alarmed and, I saw, surprised, "but who's talking about being liked?" I get drunk so better to hear the dripping of the leaky faucet from which I draw the water that sustains me. Listen to it closely and you might find it is trying to tell you something about entropy and inertia, about being alive.

Turner Bascombe conceded my implied point, or resigned himself to the pointlessness of an argument—he nodded, a quick scowl crossing the contours of his stubbly face. He feinted back in the direction of the street, his car, away from here.

"I don't get it," he said. Nor does he have to. Second-guessing is never the race driver's strong suit, though stupid men of my ilk are experts in it, lives spent in struggle to subvert the mind to bring it to harmony with the body, or at the least harness the mind's capacity to accept the body as something other than a foreign agent.

A 19th-century man went out into the woods to find out what it meant to be a human being, or how best to live, in any case, and all he could come up with was this: engagement. Doing one thing at a time and doing it fully. You building *your* house with *this* plank, *this* dove joint, *this* foliage for insulation. I do my best, I sit in my hole. I have a television, at least, to remind me: peanut butter is killing people. A man stands on a street corner tonight bathed in light from some invisible source. He is over-earnest, performing lots of leaning-in, wrinkle-crinkle-brow expressions of an utmost confidentiality. He is talking about peanut butter on the network news.

Midsentence, a psychedelic montage of the prototypical plastic Peter Pan jar's plastic labeling fills the screen, prompting thoughts of experimental writers of 1950s vintage, masters of absurdo-surrealist artistry, left behind, unnecessary, their influence on network news styles unremarked upon in the academic journals, if ever noticed by anyone other than a cretin confined to his mother's basement, a single room deep below ground on three sides with a sink and a collection of weird photographs and pens and paper and that very network news to keep him alive, prove he had existed before the present moment connected to the world from which he was birthed, the suits of the Shining Man veritable coats of armor hung willy-nilly along the walls of his 12'-by-10' cell amplifying the TV's purple glow, or that of the lamp's single low-watt compact fluorescent bulb.

Yes, like those of certain paradoxically invisible men before me, men of intelligence and great capacity for reason, for being, my hole here is full of light, but unlike my forebears the source causes no gigantic loss of electric current: in the spirit of the 21st century, you might even call me a *conservationist* or *environmentalist* and turn me into a god or devil, depending on your nature, and this despite my prior involvement in one of America's most egregious wastes of good gasoline, good oil. I make use of the Shining Man's suits and their reflective properties to cast ever-brighter light onto the minimal squalor of my existence. The suits continue to serve that conservationist's purpose, if they don't allow me here the unadulterated force of their gleaming. Their best use: nighttime standing, the glow of headlights turning the sacred body into a high-watt incandescent bulb. Yes, I am also a sort of shape-shifter, if you like, without antecedent, without any philosophy to countermand the disjointed irony you might find me falling back on as a crutch—I am a product of my generation, after all, confusion of the implied point is expected, experience of the winding route there is king.

But he is playing with us now! I hear you bellowing. Nah. Count me among the great American moralists. I know now your parents and presidents lied—there *is* a right answer, but to get to it requires intelligence beyond the capacity of humanity. Darwin points out that European dog and man alike learned quickly to give wide berth to the North American skunk. When our experiences are limited, so are we. This is sensible and fits a Kierkegaardian outlook: life is what you do with it given your circumstances, the gods mostly indifferent.

It's likely I'll never see Bascombe again except under his helmet on the television at McClendon's, and in his mind I will live on as the scoundrel he believes me to be. You, however, I trust will see my point in the end, which, as once said a man possessed of far more intelligence than me, is in the beginning and lies far ahead.

So, friend, bear with me.

Chapter 1

I got news of my father's death as I stood over an order of our beer-battered chicken tenders.

I was already miserable, a hometown boy living in his mother's basement in Fock's Mill, South Carolina, just south of the North Carolina border, the armpit of the nation on the southeast end of a storied metropolis bursting at its seams with metastatic residential sprawl far and away past the little downtown corner where Jeff Davis heard the news that Lincoln was dead and was said to have remarked, "If it were to be done, it were better it were well done." Cryptic, sure, and maybe more red meat for the peons from the disgraced leader of a floundering, besieged would-be nation. But over the next century and a half those words carried with them a curse on the lands of the fallen territory. There, if anything were to be done, it'd be done in the worst imaginable way.

After the same fashion: my induction into the world of adults followed four years of a lot of overzealous floundering, graduating from the state university in Fock's Mill with a 4.0 and a degree in English Language and Literature, then continuing my many-years-long stint as fry cook at Henry's Bar & Grill north a bit off North Carolina state route 51, near a giant decades-old suburban Charlotte mall.

Will Theron, the grillmaster, himself a former 3.8 in business administration at UNCC, on the other side of the city, and a veteran of the first Gulf War, was my immediate inspiration.

"Listen, man," he said. "You know what you got to do with yourself. Nobody can tell you otherwise." Armchair clichés like this—he called them "truisms," and I did nothing to correct the man—were his stock-in-trade for all my many years at Henry's. At 18 years of age, then 22, 25, 27 and on in the cozy confines of the kitchen, time slipped away from me into the nothing of our everyday, little to get me upset other than the comparably laughable but whip-smart drunk of our kitchen manager, a soup whiz with equally prodigious expertise on the subject of a gallon bottle of cheap gin—the specialization of Annie's knowledge herein could be described as *academic*. Will Theron cajoled and browbeat and laughed and got serious only occasionally, in the last case always revealing his sincerity with a long, almost shy gaze down to his own feet.

I fried on, learned what little there was to be learned, got along.

Then, in the middle of an otherwise typically meager Sunday lunch rush, the news. Will burst onto the line from a break somewhere in the kitchen.

"Hey Honk," he said, using his favorite nickname for me. I didn't even look up from the tongs with which I held submerged the batter-blooming strips of meat. "Annie says to tell you your pop's dead."

I thought he was joking, and actually chuckled in anticipation of whatever cock-eyed punch line he had for this one. I turned his way, but my eyes were drawn to where exactly my friend was staring—he laid a steak the size of a large man's forearm down to crackle its life in death on the grill. Then we briefly met each other's gaze.

He was genuinely worried, and that scared me.

"That ain't funny," I said, attempting a smile.

"I didn't mean it to be," he said, and he screwed up his eyebrows before his eyes shot down to his brown brogans.

My Pop, Ralph Cash, was a test case in hard knocks. The young Cash was the son of a 14-year-old mother in Pascagoula who got knocked up by a step-uncle and then gave the boy up to an alcoholic aunt in New Orleans, formerly betrothed to the crazy uncle, the former shipbuilder of the Ingalls company. He was at Parchman on three counts of attempted murder after he was laid off and held up a Pascagoula watering hole one fine rainy evening in December. The aunt got hit hard by the state of Louisiana after she, drunk, ran over the boy in her driveway during his fourth year, breaking his left arm. Hit even harder when she repeated the accident a year later, this time fracturing his right leg. After a long, quaking period of detox, the woman did time herself.

Rather than see the boy to an orphanage or the streets or whatever awful fate awaited the castoffs of the big river town in those

10

days, whatever family existed back in Pascagoula or in Orleans or elsewhere among the bayous managed to persuade the biological mother, Ms. Nellie Cash, to take Ralphie now to Monroe, N.C. There, she worked as a dancer in a burlesque house operating just under the radar of the nearby Fock's Mill authorities—a barn by an old highway on the future site of bizarro televangelist superstar Jim Bakker's P[raise]T[he]L[ord] headquarters, Heritage USA, it was just the sort of place one might expect to find, in those days. By all appearances just a disused, battered farmhouse, the shiny Cadillacs around back (and their drivers inside come down from Charlotte for a little R and R) told the tale of what was really going on. Nellie danced to antiquated 1920s big band tunes, was said to have been the best of the best, or bust, however you like it.

The boy Cash entered a local elementary school and quickly gained a reputation as a ferocious, if quixotic, fighter. Like a certain boxer of a later era, he was known for biting the ears of the objects of his ire in his first-grade class. The school refused his readmittance after a year, so he spent the extra time under the guidance of another aunt and took a quick shine to the lady's puppy blue-tick hound. The shine didn't last. The hound died a premature death by strangulation at the hand of little six-year-old Ralphie, the man who would later spawn me.

Or so it was told to me by the man himself, likewise that he was sent to a psychotherapist, whom the community in Monroe thought the very spawn of the devil, psychotherapy and its related less-than-disciplines being very recent additions to the general oeuvre of 1960s Charlotte. Though this aunt was a woman of open mind and heart, and Ralphie was done with psychotherapy and back in her care in no time, the upshot was that none of it worked. My father's little mind itched for release—or rather his body: he told me the last time I saw him of a kind of "implicit recollection," he said, confronted by a screaming freight train on the Chicago line banging down the tracks, cityward, a feeling, a tug in the gut that sent him back to the boy at age six, or, he said, maybe he made seven before his aunt's well-meaning commitment to newfangled ideas, her constant lecturing on the ways of fine boys who would become fine men in the new South, made any impression on him a-tall. My father walked away from his Monroe home in bare feet,

11

as the self-styled legend goes, and jumped a rail line from Charlotte that took him all the way to Richmond and thence to Norfolk, where he loses the thread, recalling only the wind and banging and rush of the trains' larger-than-life rumbling in and out of the yard, the bright flash of sky cut in half by the incessant passing whir of boxcars, the blur of the incongruent smokestacks of engine and caboose.

I can retell it all, can attempt to recreate the backward and sideways trajectories of memory, as I've intimated, only because Ralph Cash told me the truncated version on my last visit with him, a year prior to the "news" of his death, like he'd known essentially that his time was up and I needed the knowing. I'd made annual visits to the man's ratty little Chicago apartment, and I'd heard none of it before. His retelling, vague as an after-image at the quick disappearance of something bright, was often rendered in his speech with a kind of lazy but baroque awe. He likened the recollection and retelling to the experience of déjà vu, though I figured it was more simply the combination of his own rage and wonder at the sense of disconnection he felt to what he was telling, harkening the young child of the freight yards he once was.

The story's skeleton: The boy came to Chicago on a boxcar from Norfolk, his newly-adopted father Danny Cheek in tow. Cheek: a transient, his home the rails, an old-school hobo and product of the military.

"He had the look of so many. Scarred," Pop told me, "eyes shifty-scared when he was in place, wild and courageous flying down the tracks. He took pity on me. He wanted to see the world's fair he'd heard about, which had happened more than half a damn century ago as it turned out, here in Chicago. For all that, we made it."

Cheek had friends in the city in the Uptown neighborhood—or whatever might pass for friends for such a traveler. Pop remembered the crew living all in a basement I imagine to have been similar to the ratty little first-floor dwelling where Ralph Cash spent the most recent years of his adult life.

There were seven in the squat: Cheek, Ralphie Cash, and five emancipated residents of a mental ward in the area. Ralphie did manage to win, by the skin of his own stupidity, a job with the city by the mid-late 1970s, at age 20—public works, Department of Streets and Sanitation. He went out to a respectable little nightclub one day the next year and met the love of his life, Ms. Eula Little-john, my mother, as she was on a northern excursion with other members of the then York County Debutantes Club. She saw in Mr. Ralph Cash the dashing figure of a Gentleman in the wrong part of the country. Ralph did lay it on thick, down to a by-that-point-truly-fake Southern accent.

"Your mother was a sweet, good woman," the shape-shifter told me, "which was a thing I took to at first. For fifteen years, twelve of those after your own birth, I loved her like no one should ever love another. Cheek had taught me that terrible lesson, at least—how to give yourself fully and wholly to another, what he'd done for me. I did not love him like the father I never had. Don't think that for a second. He was a scoundrel in most respects, a thief, though a man does what a man has to—a gambler with money, the way of the filthy, this country deserves whatever it gets. The stock market is where jackals go when the cow carcass has long since been picked clean, sucked dry, even the marrow gone. Heed that."

Years on, he followed her to marriage in her native Fock's Mill, S.C., part-place of his own extreme youth, and thence to her soft, beautiful tolerance of fits of depression bordering on psychosis that sent him repeatedly out into the night to the rail yard or the trestle over the town's main boulevard, where he'd sit and await the Norfolk Southern coming up from the south with grain and granite and lumber from pine foresting operations in the mid-S.C. hinterlands. With the yearning, the rock in the pit of his stomach, he would sit on the grating that is the trestle footway, his legs dangling above the small traffic on the boulevard below, heart awaiting the moment when the juggernaut blew its horn hard and loud and screeched its brakes at the conductor's sighting of himself, Mr. Ralph Cash, a grown man monkeying around on a train trestle at 3 a.m.

My mother, despite Ralph Cash's later proclamations about her, held less tolerance than his late-night sojourns—and, further on, hard drinking—required. By the time I approached the years of the teen, Cash had disappeared, only to resurface five years later in Chicago with a new version of his old city job secured, his ratty apartment furnished with the meager thrift-store or alley-score finds he could afford. I began my yearly visits several years on, after my time at Henry's began, after my 4.0 ensured that I might never leave the restaurant's confines.

I did not think of any of this as great Will Theron moved back to the task at hand, flipped the steak, pressed the metal spatula against its flat top, to which it responded with a sharp hiss. He flipped it then again onto a plate, garnished it with a side of our "Heavenly Potato Salad," and put the order up for a waitress.

I didn't believe him, and redirected my attentions to the stiffly floral-looking chicken pieces in my fryer, moving in to prize the crispy strips from the basket. Just as the tongs approached the oil, though, one of the bastards popped, spraying small droplets of grease at 400 Fahrenheit onto my forearm, which brought up blisters instantaneously. I didn't even wince. 'Twas the first episode in what would be a day of little burns, from Annie's hungover answer to my inquiry about this supposed news of my father—"Um, yeah, some lady called the bar phone, maybe your mother"—to my mother's disavowal of the news—"I have not heard the slightest from or about that man in years, and you know that"—to my own unanswered call to my father's apartment in Chicago and subsequent calls to every major hospital in the city, none of which had any record of Ralph Cash's recent admittance, or any pattern of recent admittance that might have suggested ill health. I checked again my old Luddite's answering machine in my basement for any possible message—the caller ID on my home phone showed nothing.

I phoned Will on the early side of night, half-drunk, from my basement. "I can't find any evidence," I said.

Will, more than nonplussed: "Evidence? Man, the word came in. God knows who it was. Who was the emergency contact on your father's medical file? At your pop's work? It's you, right?"

I didn't answer.

"There you have it. Hell, I don't know what you do in that case. My pop died a few blocks from me. Go up there if you need to. Search him out. I'm sure Morton or Bobby one can cover for you. Annie's so screwed up she won't even notice."

14

I would do it, I knew, at the first mention, a tingly little itch shooting up my spine, but still I held the phone tightly to my ear, waiting for words of reassurance, I guess, a more definitive directive. I knocked back the last pull on a pint bottle of whiskey.

"Hey, if you need cash, Cash," Will said, "just let me know."

I called Chicago again—still nothing at Pop's apartment—and began preps for the journey.

My embattled 1990s Ford Taurus could be counted on as a rumbling blue-black steed of the highway, though she had bigger problems navigating the here and now round town. Ninety-degree-or-better left turns were particularly dicey, as they caused the auto transmission to slip fully out of gear, only to fall with a thud back in after you straightened the wheel. My driving was less than aggressive, let's say, as a result.

In the dark of the gravel drive 20 feet off my basement entrance, I idled her and pulled the transmission-fluid dipstick, examining the fluid line in the headlights' blare. I cut the engine and did the same with the oil, watched the place where tires met gravel in the drive for signs of low air. Finding none, I made my way back inside. 9 p.m. on the nose, had to be: My mother, above, getting ready for bed at the sink—water coursing through the pipes above my head. Familiar footfalls, one to twelve, toward her bedroom; the creak of the old mattress; twelve again back to the bathroom and more water in the pipes when she flushed the toilet a final time before sleep. Twelve footfalls above my head back to the bed, creaking, a final silence.

I wondered little at her seeming lack of concern about my other progenitor's whereabouts. Their relationship wrapped just as finally as the quiet dark that enveloped me now. Not for long, I thought, counting the seconds to my own eventual sleep, my eventual waking to, yes, a journey of potentially massive proportions, scratching an itch that hadn't been attended to for more than a year. I am my father's son, after all.

⧗

Skinny-rangy Tim Morton wore an oily-looking, faded Confederate-flag bandana on his head in homage or tribute to no one and

15

nothing, chewed tobacco between cigarettes and otherwise carried on in the prep kitchen like the small-town Southern boy he was—hip-hop-metal and country music fan, hunter of deer and raccoon, fisher of fish, epic prevaricator. Morton was also the primary part-timer who covered the shifts I avoided, my relative seniority (and full-time status) among the kitchen greasers allowing me to do so—Friday and Saturday nights were chief among them. Morton was reared down in Camden, childhood home as well of racer Turner Bascombe. Later I would learn the two had gone to school together and were at odds over the prom queen senior year, something Bascombe had long gotten over (he was the winner and had even married the beauty, divorced after a few years) but Morton had yet to vanquish. He'd sunk into his fate, reduced stature compensated for, perhaps, by the ugly-ass bandana. And like me and everybody else in the kitchen, Morton had once held bigger and better things in mind for his life than spouting homophobic theories to his dirty coworkers, describing the metaphorical thrust of Elton John songs—recently he'd spent an hour laying out just such a theory, the climax of his monologue, the fingers of his right hand emphatically counting out the salient points, going something like "Dude, come on. You know what they're all about. I mean, 'Candle in the Wind,' 'Benny and the Jets.' 'Rocket Man,' for Chrissakes?"

I stopped in for a beer on my way out of town, Taurus auto-shifting out (rev up, pull back off the throttle), then back into gear (*ka-chunk*, throttle, *wheeeeeeee-bang*, *grrrr* ...) upon my left turn off South Boulevard into the parking lot. Morton reminded me of it all.

"Going to Chicago, huh? I can cover for you, sure. Hell, I hope everything's all right," he said, back in the prep room, methodically slicing cantaloupe. "Be careful, though. I know they like Elton up there."

If the black man Will were here, he'd let the little white Morton boy have it, I'm sure, the ensuing tussle erupting in liberally thrown epithets and simmering over the rest of the afternoon. They're good for laughs, I guess.

But since Will was out, fat-faced Bobby filled the good-cop role with swift certainty: "Dude, the Elton John thing is so over."

Morton, without letting go of the ten-inch blade he held in his

16

right hand, flipped Bobby off and in the same motion brought the blade cleanly through the center of a freshly peeled melon.

Morton leveled a great stare at the boy. "This is your brain—after I get through with it."

I laughed.

"That don't work, shithead," Bobby said.

Morton scooped seeds and pulp from one half of the melon into a trash can. "Whatever you say, rocket man."

They'd be at it all day.

Monday was Annie's day off, and I joined her at the bar for my farewell beer. At noon, she was well into her fourth or fifth signature gin-tonic.

"It wasn't my mom," I said.

She just nodded and, her hands trembling, struck a match with the apparent intention of lighting a cigarette that was still stuck behind her ear, which she proceeded to fumble with. By the time she finally fired it, I'd told her of my trip, finished the beer, smoked a cigarette of my own, and risen to leave. On my way out, Morton caught sight of me from his spot in the kitchen window—a server picked up a plate of somebody's chicken wings he'd just put up—and yelled "Yo Cash!" across the patrons in booths between us. He raised his middle finger my way.

"Good luck!" he went on, smiling, before Bobby appeared at his left side and punched him as hard as he could in the shoulder. Morton recoiled and brandished a knife threateningly, laughing all the while, and I shook my head on out the door bound for the open road.

Chapter 2

Eula Littlejohn went to beauty school in Charlotte, after she changed her name to Cash and before she changed it back, after I'd entered the world via her birth canal at a hospital in the great metropolis. I guess that was well done, if I am to believe the stories, or lack thereof. Never have I discussed my birth with Eula directly, never has she offered any anecdote or warning or advice for my own future—though she has to see that at this rate the chances of my further procreation are slim in these Southern climes. It takes money to traffic in "respectable" circles where hope for the future tends to live and breathe. You know, among men who make small talk about racing and real estate investment, developers with their eyes on tracts of land southeast and north of the city who, when they drink too much, generally get loud and get the jones for sitting and watching football games or toodling around a golf course slicing and hooking potshots into the trees; and women whose sense of their own respectability began with the amount of makeup they slathered on their cheeks and around their eyes before setting foot on high school campuses, then at college in their dorm rooms with their hair sprayed up in walls above their foreheads, evermore to get the height advantage on competitors in respectability at the bar. In short, not much had changed since my mother's day and the debutante's club, wherein the process was simply more formalized—the roving activities were group-oriented, less influenced by that sunny cutthroat free-market attitude that has since further entrenched itself in Americans' business circles, societies, individual lives. Selfish fucking jerks.

Back when, though, one needed not to have much money if one was of certain familial connections. If a family's fortune fell today—as did my own in the late 1990s after Ralph Cash decamped—if the pair of young lovers is no longer connected to sequences of large numbers on bank statements backed up by bills stored in some vault somewhere propped up in turn by mythic

18

stores of gold or stocks or bonds, said couple might as well be lost to history. My case: I had friends and coworkers, I had drinking buddies, I had Will Theron and Tim Morton and Bobby and old Horace over at McClendon's and, hell, even Annie. The doubtfulness of procreation, continuation of the line of Cashes and Littlejohns highly unlikely, was a little boost to my lack of regret at pissing the time away in whatever manner I could afford. I did that well.

But one held out hope for love in spite of all, even if I really had no idea what it was.

Eula Littlejohn was the daughter of a respectable pair of Scots-Irish immigrants to Fock's Mill via the North Carolina mountains, where life was hard unless you bargained with the moonshiners for their land and auctioned it off, as the great Turner Bascombe would remind me, to the nearest cabal of timber dealers, like the old racecar legend Curtis Turner'd done in Virginia. It was no accident Bascombe's own hill parents named him after the greatest reckless driver there ever was. Timber: the only legal way to make the land pay, and unless you were careful only once at that. My maternal grandfather Cyrus Littlejohn wasn't so fortunate. He ran a still, and when his particular ingredient wasn't in season, or after he'd long used up what little stock of corn the rocky hills on his property had afforded him during the growing season, it might even have been himself that a timber dealer would approach looking to whet away at what little of his plot remained in big oaks or pines. But the payoff never happened, and after one particularly disastrous season—an early freeze and mammoth snow hampering deliveries and explosions leaving youngish Cyrus scarred for life by his either noble or dastardly profession, depending on your particular thoughts on the matter—he picked up and moved off, setting a course toward the great metropolis only to decamp to the south with what would be his last big delivery to Fock's Mill. Thereafter, he brokered deals between the barrooms of the growing little railroad town and folks he knew better back up in the hills. That got him to a child, anyhow. Eula, my mother, was first-born, and Cyrus got onto a team of construction workers under a man named Colquitt who would become the biggest contractor in the region outside some of the Charlotte families. Cyrus wiggled his way into partnership, and that set him for life by the time Eula was ten years old. In this milieu Eula came of age—with the veneer of moneyed respectability.

My mother was neither home when I left nor at the beauty shop when I stopped in on my way out of town. I left a note for her with the older lady that ran the place: "She's out to lunch," she said. Which I well should have known.

I wrote, *I have gone to Chicago to find the old man. Please pray for me. Your son,* etc. A prayer from my mom was always a little fire in my brain, and I could usually count on it, even without asking. Good to put in a decent word, too. Reassure the lady that her son wasn't as drunk or licentious as I'm sure she figured I was, given how little lately she'd actually laid eyes on me—and we shared a domicile. And I guess she wouldn't be wrong to think it. I walked out of the beauty shop with a smile on my face, all the same, picturing my mother's grandiose visions of the blue-eyed Jesus she prayed to—it made me feel nice, it did.

Jesus followed me all the way to U.S. 74 and a fuel stop in Forest City, N.C., getting close to mountain country, where I let the grandiose silence give way to a little of that old 1990s hardcore I reveled in for so long through high school. I filled the tank all the way for the first time since my last run to the Midwestern metropolis—door open to hear background strains of an old dubbed cassette of the classic San Diego band Heroin—wheeled out (left turn, 90 degrees, rev up, pull back off the throttle) into the lane back to the freeway only to get more or less dead stuck in idle. The transmission never popped back into gear.

Good goddamn, I thought.

I mashed the gas, the engine revved, but the capital D on the auto-shift's mode selector meant nothing any longer. Gear engagement: zero. Times like these I regretted my avoidance of the conveniences of the time. The first decade of the new century was over and I still, miraculously, held off the militaristic march of the cellphone bill, after a brief flirtation, in favor of inconvenience and a reprieve from the annoying ringing and buzzing that characterized the lives of most of my generational (and otherwise) compatriots. Would that such abeyance could be short-lived, I thought, allowing gravity on this slight downhill to edge the car out of the travel lane.

20

I shut it off, closed my eyes and let my chin fall to my chest.

Almost instantaneously, a knock on the window. A white-bearded old man, who wasn't exactly the spitting image of Ralph Cash, but he came close in age. New South version, maybe, in an old Montuck Jr. red race team hat, its little Confederate flag in the center front above eyes that gazed into me from the other side of the glass. The old man smiled. Good Samaritan or devil in coveralls I knew not.

"Need some help?" he offered, finally, as I emerged.

I threw up my hands.

"Transmission," I said. "I'm just guessing, though." My knowledge of vehicle systems was pretty well limited to a basic understanding of the principles of internal combustion, gears, and the placement and operation of the fuel cap.

"That's an auto?" he said. "Mine too," gesturing back to his white pickup truck of obviously recent vintage. "These newfangled things are finicky, nothing like they used to make them, the damned beautiful simplicity of a clutch and gearbox. That old car of yours ain't that new, but damned if I could ever put a bit of work in an automatic transmission, work that would be effective anyhow."

I nodded, mute and dumb. What could I possibly do here? Home was an hour and a half in the rear-view, I had ten hours, at least, in front of me.

"Got a suggestion," the old man said. "You crank her back up and try her again?"

"No," I said, I hadn't.

"Give it a go and see what happens. Hell, worth a shot." And here the old man winked and strode confidently back to his idling pickup and tore off like the entire game was up, the outcome pre-ordained.

Perturbed, defeated, I dropped back into the driver's seat and fired the engine. No problem there. I grabbed the auto-shift mode selector between the seats and pulled her down to D.

Ka-chunk.

My mother was wrong, it turned out. Jesus had white hair, brown eyes, and up here in Forest City the worker of miracles was a race fan.

I drove on in silence, hopeful not to jinx the transmission with abrasive music into another catastrophic failure. I marked time with cigarettes, three drags a minute. A creeping, paranoia-laced doom overrode my mother's blue-eyed Jesus and my own old white-haired savior both there in the Ford, its seats reeking of invisible years. The noxious, blooming tobacco-stink of time marching on brought conjuring of what lay ahead—what lay behind. Recollections of prior Chi-town visits, old friends I'd known in the city, all with only scant connection to the old man I pursued this time around. But for Billy Jones, maybe, the first I'd be in touch with.

Across the Eastern Kentucky mountains on I-75 my mind turned solidly to my father, the nonsensical nature of all of this and the desire, increasingly present, to understand it like a mechanic knows his machine. By Cincinnati, the desire took me off the road—I made five different stops looking for that contemporary holy grail, a functioning payphone, finally finding one at (where else) an old truckstop in Indiana on the far side of town. The pro drivers sat around the counter staring into their tiny computers and the old relic was a disaster just outside the restaurant, the metal-wrapped cord connecting handset to base looking like it'd survived a nuclear war. But 911 eventually got me to 511 or 411 and a Chicago cop, who was dispatched to Pop's apartment on the far-and-away hope that I was simply overreacting and Ralph Cash's phone was out of service or something—or his actual phone was broken, still plugged in and he hadn't noticed the calls coming in these past days. My father led a hermit's life, anyhow, his whereabouts known to but a few coworkers, and then only when he was on the Chicago inner-city highways.

His home was his alone.

I repeated the payphone-search routine a few hours along in Lebanon, Indiana, near dark. The cops dutifully let me know the place was empty as far as they could tell. The landlord had let them in and, "from the looks of it," said an officer by the name of Liebowitz, "nobody's been in there for a couple weeks, at least."

A couple weeks? The department he worked for, surely, would have noticed his absence, the likely source for the cavalry call I received. At once, I sprung and then clung to the notion, smoking a mile a minute, that this was all some weird off-kilter way of Ralph

Cash himself calling me back home, offering up a place and time and dream he could never have given me before.

Chicago, finally, an early-September chill had taken hold near midnight — I stood in front of the outer door to his building hoping for a happy ruse with the two keys Pop had given me long ago clutched in my hand like the last cigarettes on earth. I lit one there in the dim courtyard of the four-story, U-shaped affair, the start of my third pack of the day.

After it was finished I stuck the spare key to the outer door into the lock, turned, and walked into the vestibule and stairway to find the door to his apartment open just the slightest. A woman of maybe 50, dressed in a blue cardigan and jeans, turned my way as I poked my head in the door, startling me dumb.

I nodded.

She nodded back.

"Who are you?" she said.

I didn't answer. Along the walls cardboard boxes were stacked seven feet high, the room otherwise bare but for the old orange easy chair I'd spent many a night propped up in, television set on the floor in a corner, Pop's old mattress.

"You're the son, I've met you," the lady went on. Finally, I met her gaze. She was the landlord. "Eula Banks," she said.

"I remember," I said. "You've got my mom's name."

She didn't flinch. "Where is he?"

I told her I didn't know and she went on to tell me she'd knocked yesterday after coming from her own apartment upstairs and passing by his door to hear the phone ringing and ringing early in the morning at a time when normally Mr. Cash was around—he did things in the courtyard for her.

"We were very friendly," she said, looking away on the last word like she wasn't telling the whole story. I didn't press the issue.

Ms. Banks went on. "I haven't seen him for a week, though, and when the police came earlier today I waited and waited upstairs, watching for him to walk up from the street through the courtyard, that weird stumbling walk of his."

I feared the worst, as did she when I told her my part of the story, the anonymous phone call, the persistent ringing when I called, the remembrance of history. I fell into my father's recliner and the old lady went back up tearfully to her place, promising to check in early, myself swearing to notify her should the slightest information spring forth. I was bummed, but not so bummed that the surprise of meeting the old man's sometime lover and the oddity of the neatly stacked boxes surrounding me failed to pique my curiosity.

The boxes were stamped STREETS AND SANITATION, CITY OF CHICAGO, and with an ever-increasing urgency of motion I began the process of peeling back the upper layers of packing tape to reveal their contents, identical every one: a certain number, perhaps twenty per box, of vests of the type typically worn over the coveralls or work shirts of road workers, each with two broad strips of ultra-reflective material manufactured by the Naperville-based 3M company, per the labels. By the end of the process, with the boxes now mostly unstacked and broken down, flat, in my restaurant-worker's style, and covering the entirety of the apartment's floorspace, I stood positively trembling among them, unable to decide whether my efforts might simply be put off in favor of sleep, perhaps now, at four in the morning with a day's drive and two-plus packs of cigarettes behind me and the boxes strewn willy-nilly, covering the vast majority of floor all around me. But, surveying the carnage, I spied the scrawled script that was my father's customary handwriting style angling up the side of one of the few remaining boxes stacked atop another in the corner. The note read, *"Son! In these boxes may you locate your ultimate salvation—or you might find nothing at all! Just a bunch of orange vests!"*

What I imagined to be my father's last words occupied that place in my mind reserved for the most inspired of late-night musings, and the trembling didn't stop as I lay down to sleep on the old man's mattress, road vests in a pile on the verge of tumbling over at its foot.

I dreamt of light, sight without depth, whiteout conditions on a freeway fading further to white like a trip-to-heaven scene in a film. The dream rattled me, to say the least—so much of life is spent with your eyes closed on nothing more than darkness—and when I woke, the sun casting its glow through cracked blinds onto the myriad reflectors strewn about the room, covering nearly every available surface, the room lit up astoundingly bright, I rose and, trembling again with anticipation of the road I was about to run down, I rehearsed the words I was about to utter. *We found him, officer. Or rather he found me. He came back this morning.* I tried breathless happiness, perturbed exasperation—*We found him, officer. Fucking finally. Or he found me, I should say. Sheesh...*—never so loud as to be overheard by a neighbor. I settled somewhere between a dry, all-business conveyance of information and the first, excitement at a mystery solved.

The old man's past was a story foreign to his own sense of identity. His future would be his, a new story altogether, as his note seemed to suggest. Its stupidity was ultimately deceptive, I thought, stupid like the fox. As for me, salvation lay not far off, and my father's disappearance I saw in the mid-morning sunlight as a mission as potentially willful as my trip here.

I picked up my father's phone and dialed Officer Liebowitz, saying just what I'd practiced. *We'd found him, he came back early this morning, thank you for your trouble.*

"Great to hear," the officer said. "Will you be around this afternoon? We'll come by to finish out the report."

My heart leapt to my throat and I heard myself saying, *Oh, that's not necessary. We'll be heading downtown today, do the museums and stuff since I'm in town, the usual.*

Liebowitz didn't immediately speak, put his hand over the phone's mic and said something to an invisible someone.

I tried to breathe, feared if I had to actually speak again I might not manage it, but then his voice came roaring back over the line, loud and clear. "Routine," he said. "Nothing we can't handle on this end." Let the office know of further assistance needs, if a routine patrol in the area is desired, etc....

I hesitated before making my next move. I sat in the recliner, emptied the last of the boxes, took the cardboard out to the alley bin, its top positioned just a few feet below a tiny square window near the ceiling of my father's apartment—just small enough to discourage a man from attempting to squeeze through it. I returned to the recliner in the close silence, eyes on the other, larger two windows to the courtyard, blinds slit open just enough to see the comings and goings of tenants, of Ms. Banks and her pruning shears working the small trees that lined the walk.

I mustered confidence no new arrivals were in the offing by early afternoon. Ms. Banks was gone from the courtyard, and I walked down the boulevard to a dollar store. I rummaged around in a massive discount bin by the floor until I found just what the Hispanic shopkeeper promised would be there—needle and thread in a sewing kit, a pair of 50-cent scissors. I returned to the well-lit apartment still not quite ready to commit to the task I was about to undertake, but believing in its possibility. I proceeded haltingly at first, paring away the wide reflective strips from an uncertain number of vests until I had an array of them on the floor in front of me, at which point I sewed two together at their longest sides, then added a third.

A door shutting above, footsteps on the stairs in the hallway, a knock at the door. Ms. Banks. I sat, silent, for perhaps thirty seconds before another knock was issued. I shoved my handiwork under the recliner and made an audible show of rising, mussing up my hair to approximate its prior slept-on state.

Ms. Banks was apologetic. "Oh, you must be exhausted," she said, frowning. "I'm very sorry."

"Rough night," gesturing back into the room. "I got into all this, rather flummoxed with what to do about it."

Her eyes went wide as she took in the chaos at my back. "So all those boxes had work clothes in them."

"Yeah, I asked the cop what to do about them. He said call Streets & San."

"But I thought you just woke up?" Ms. Banks called me on my lie.

"Oh, yeah, I talked to him last night. I forgot it was after our meeting," turning my eyes down to the floor to telegraph the coming revelation, just as Will Theron might have done. "They found his body, or what they think might be his body. Washed up at the Point in Hyde Park. I've got to go identify it later."

Ms. Banks' lack of tears spared me any sting of conscience. And the plot's inexorable momentum guaranteed peace of mind, for now. Father, forgive me.

"Will you have a funeral?"

I hadn't thought about this either, and my snap response was to ask Ms. Banks if she'd ever seen an episode of *Six Feet Under*, a

TV series I'd had a guilty affection for in not-so-long-ago, different days, about a family that runs a funeral home. She had not.

"Well, I think I'll just have the body cremated and that will be that," moving back inside and half closing the door before the subject of my father's lease sprung up, again.

"I'll pay you for the remainder of the time," I said. "I'd like to keep the place until I can get all of his stuff out of here."

Ms. Banks, who had turned to walk up the stairs to her place, now faced me and gave me an utterly quizzical look, one that for a split second seemed to say she was wise to what I was doing. It was quick, though, little more than a vestige of something that my own addled state could easily be called to account for. When she spoke she was absolute calm.

"Well, it's not necessary, and none of my business, of course. But whatever you think is right." And she left.

Chapter 3

My father spent his most recent Chicago years in Logan Square, a northwest side neighborhood home to a large Hispanic contingent and a growing white yuppie bloc, likewise a host of artists and punks of all stripes who'd paved the way for the latter in the now familiar American tradition of urban gentrification. The summers I'd spent there over the years had put me in touch with a great number of the last. In short, I had friends in Logan Square. I looked up Billy Jones later that day, after working through the early afternoon on what was turning into a full-body patchwork reflective suit—working with an intensity devoid of mind, mostly, thoughts far and away from anything but sweat and needle and thread. I needed to get out to follow through and make good on the lie I'd told Ms. Banks. Billy was easily accessible via his friend Carl, who kept up a literary sort of magazine-blog online. I found his phone number quickly enough.

Carl didn't remember me when I called, initially, but I reminded him that Billy and I grew up in the same town.

"Oh yeah," he mumbled. "You Carolina people never forget, do you."

"Something like that," I allowed, but reinforced the notion that memory can be awful selective, too—"You ought to feel lucky," I said.

"Right," unimpressed.

"Wondering if he's up for a beer."

Carl gave me the number, then rattled on about what he was working on that very day: an idea for a radio-station launch that I'd say was half-baked, at best. Not pirate, mind you. Legit, complete with license and everything and showcasing exclusively *live* music—or whatever amounts to live performance in the parlance of experimental electronic musicians, among whom Carl could also be counted. I finally shut him up by asking about his mag.

"Ho hum," he said. "I'm still doing it." He sighed heavily.

28

I seized my chance—"I gotta go, man"—and hung up.

Several years my senior, Billy would have to be my anchor here, minus Ralph Cash. He didn't answer when I called, though, so I got in my crappy car and freewheeled around the many left turns on the surface streets across the west and south sides to the Point in Hyde Park, the beach empty in the cool late-summer afternoon, prompting hard thinking to fill the space.

There's something, a gene, some innate tendency, that controls my mind, maybe more, the minds of all Southern people, I thought comfortably—it's that thing in there that facilitates belief in all manner of wild notions about the past. W.J. Cash, as far as I know no relation to me and mine, editorialist for the erstwhile *Charlotte News* and author of the WWII-era tome *Mind of the South*, held that the Southern "man at the center"—by which he meant the outgrowth of the cracker backcountry lineage, the Snopeses and Bundrens of Faulkner, a European peasant who finds himself on particularly fertile land and in possession of more cottonseed than he knows what to do with and a certain amount of human chattel and starts inventing all sorts of romantic stories about his supposed dignified past—that man persists in believing in the very nobility of the "old South," as it is occasionally known, because he/she (yes, "she" too) holds in his/her heart the very incapability of reasoning realistically, thinking about his/her station economically, thinking about things in class terms, and generally evaluating priorities in keeping with what's *in fact* and *very really* good for oneself. W.J. Cash was attempting to obliterate the notion of the old South as the product of people with innate aristocratic leanings, and if it weren't for the very notion he described, he might have succeeded. The propensity to believe self-invented fictions about one's past was too very strong, and Cash's untimely death at the hands of Nazi spies in Mexico City (it's what I believe, anyway— the official story is that W.J. went nuts and killed himself under the delusion that said spies were after him, neatly dovetailing with his primary preoccupation about his heritage) ensured that his message would be deemed null and void in his home territory and even this far north. Chicagoans like Carl, for instance, persist in their belief in the inalienably haughty nature of the Southern heritage, that grand and reliably false story.

My own fiction was taking shape nicely. At the Point, on its crumbling though recently reinforced limestone revetments abutting Lake Michigan, I found myself staring out over the water toward the smokestacks of the steel mills of northwest Indiana and coming to the very verge of tears at the suspicion and/or fabrication, depending on your perspective, of my father's suicide. I closed my eyes and struggled to retain my balance in the wind coming off the water. When I opened them, I turned my gaze to the water below my feet. There twisted my own pale arms, conjured from a pair of floating foam cups, flailing, sinking, with whatever dignity might have once lived in the marrow of their bones.

⧗

Billy got the message. We met out at a restaurant downtown after work hours in a big plaza on Dearborn. It was far above my means, and Billy, who'd just been fired from a minimum-wage job working a bakery counter the last time I'd seen him, I figured must have struck gold or some contemporary equivalent—perhaps his lady, a tall woman with the severe features and the designer-fashion look of a European runway model, to my small-town eyes anyway, was bankrolling his existence. I caught sight of her as I approached. She was raising a slice of crusty rye bread to her mouth at a square table set up against floor-to-ceiling windows looking out onto the plaza. I then took in Billy's bicycle helmet and neon-yellow shoulder messenger bag on the floor by his chair. All made a fine contrast, along with his ropy shoulder-length mop of a hairdo, to his tweed blazer.

"I look like a damn Jehovah's Witness all day long in this shit," he said, as soon as the appropriate introductions had been proffered. His lady, Elsa, a "French-American" as she'd very formally put it (a wry grin dissecting her admittedly beautiful face when she'd offered her hand), raised another slice of bread to her mouth and gazed off into the plaza. Yeah, she had to be the boy's primary money source, though I figured he was at least 32, 34 years old, if not older, by now. I laughed.

"Yeah," Billy said. "I'm a goddamn bike messenger. Love the biking part, hate all the bullshit. Sort of like the view from this restaurant."

Elsa flashed him a razor-sharp look.

"You know, cool plaza, $20 entrees, $8 beers," Billy said. "So yeah, if you haven't figured it out yet, I'm just trying to dress the part, I guess."

Elsa Triolet was the writer-director behind a weird apocalyptic Chicago-underwater-as-financial-crisis-metaphor film then making the rounds of all the big international fests, including Cannes and Sundance—apparently it had secured release and distribution set to begin later in the year, a decent-size payout included, and thus the French woman had quickly readjusted to a lifestyle I imagine Billy had never known. From what I came to understand, she came from stock more moneyed than the lowly Cashes and Billy's Joneses, though Billy wasn't necessarily without family money. He told me a story over a few rounds of $8 Budweisers—on Elsa's part, $10 cocktails of anisette and water—of a sojourn back in the "region," as he referred to our home state, and the South broadly, for that matter.

"Yeah I picked up that particular affectation in Portland, man," he went on, Elsa now positively placid with drink. "There's all these Southerners out there, and the local hipsters, the kids from Washington State and California and like fucking Idaho, they all just call it 'the region,' and all the Southerners are 'the regionalists.'"

"Isn't that a bit—I don't know—racist or something?" I laughed, now, for it was Billy's particular style to absorb the language around him like some teenager. Last time we hung out, I remembered, he'd been referring to an old patched-up Confederate graycoat replica he'd pulled out of retirement as "bling."

And to my surprise, this all got a laugh out of Elsa.

"Yeah, 'racist,'" she said. "You Southerners." I sensed she didn't really get the distinction, but I laughed some more at my own joke—and Elsa's titillation rose with each guffaw I uttered.

"You've got the most infectious laugh I have ever heard," she said.

"Um, thank you," I said.

Billy cut in. "Sounds like a damn retard on speed. So why you're here. Visiting your pop?"

The expensive beers and the foreign gal and the absolutely pristine and predictable Billy had taken my mind off my unique predicament. But I offered much of nothing, really, saying in a tone of mock indignation, "Yeah, Pop brings me here, but you were about to tell me what brought you down South."

Billy exchanged a look with Elsa that asked for permission for something. "My father is dead. He died here in prison after a, well—he got shot by some cops. Long story. I'm sort of surprised you didn't hear about it. I spent some time in Carolina with a friend of his afterward—"

"Which is not true," Elsa cut in. "He left way before his father died." My gaze shuttled back and forth between the two of them, Billy now sighing.

Billy started to say something, but before he could get it out, I said, "Yes, my dad's just died, too. Drowned. I just came from identifying the body." I shook back the last of the high-dollar Bud in front of me and felt my guts rise into my throat as I swallowed. It was a feeling borne of the story, still a lie but gaining credence with every mention, the pull of every invented detail, chief among them my conspiratorial knowledge with Ms. Banks of the boxes upon boxes of reflective road-worker vests in Ralph Cash's apartment.

"That's fucking awful," Billy said, Elsa looking on with unmistakable pity. I pursed my lips.

"Yeah," I said, and felt a distinct regret leading these two, and Billy in particular, along the trail of this lie. I resolved then I would tell him the truth soon as I could get him by himself. An old friend deserved that much.

"At least you're here," Elsa said, slicing Billy open with another of those looks.

Billy then went on to tell the tale of his father, cattleman extraordinaire, whose story I did recall in the manner you can half-remember a dream from a month past you never told anybody about—from news reports, my best guess.

The elder Jones unleashed an untold number of cattle on the inner city near the site of the former Chicago stockyards, long since disused after big beef moved on to rural parts of Kansas, Nebraska, etc. Jones became a sort of whipping boy for a week for the national news media, particularly the right-wing newspaper pundits and bloggers, who made him an example of the degradation of the American left, wouldn't you know it. Jones was known

32

among the denizens of our hometown for an intense animosity toward the "right-wing cabal that has been running our country for twenty years," or some such—it was the quote the commentators seized on, anyhow, to paint Jones as a left-wing crusader and terrorist. Not to be glib or dismissive: It was true, after all, that he'd unleashed 500 or so cows in the middle of the city to go where they would. The hysteria ended with Jones being sentenced on charges enabled by the Patriot Act and Patriot Act 2, but died soon after he started serving his time in the federal pen—as Billy told it, once the man had been sufficiently pilloried and went to trial, the commentators had lost interest. I'd certainly not heard of his death. Billy's chief concern seemed less to do with the old man than how Elsa took it, which was love, maybe, but then he started in with a round of complaints about the old man's finances, which his defense and Billy's willy-nilly pilfering had eaten up. Johnny Jones the cattleman died in debt. Billy did come from money, as it turned out. I guess I should have known, growing up in the very town he did, though since the Cashes/Littlejohns and the Joneses didn't know each other, my ignorance made some sense.

When family came here, to Chicago, Billy told, he fled as quickly as he could—he went home for a little hideout, the inverse of my own residency among the reflective vests in my father's apartment.

"I practiced a kind of mental tennis with myself for more than a couple years," he said.

When I asked what the hell he meant by that: "I holed up down there way out past the paper mill and didn't talk to nobody for more or less the entire time I was there. I got work at that fucking mill. I tried to figure out how to live."

"You can tell he did not get very far," Elsa cut in.

"Ah, you shut the fuck up," Billy said, a bit playfully, but Elsa didn't laugh. "Look, Cash, there's more joy in sitting in silence than drink, conversation, sex—hell, whatever you want to say. I thought I might write my way out of something for a while—and recording your every minute is one way to really sort of pay attention to what you're doing, but there's an anxiety thing that comes along with ultimately unnecessary tasks like that when you're forced by the fact of your fucking empty bank account to work the 10-hour-on-10-hour-off at the mill. So yeah. Here we are, sitting and drinking

33

again. I sort of miss my porch down there"—he gazed then dispassionately at Elsa—"the solitude. Sometimes, anyway."

Elsa leaned in close—her breath antiseptic and lips almost touching my ear—"He told me it was fucking killing him when he came back."

"What?" Billy smiled now, clearly enjoying the conspiracy—and the attention. "What the fuck?"

I laughed. I left with a promise to meet up with them later at a bar back in a neighborhood adjacent to Logan Square, a slightly higher-rent version of the dumpy sets of blocks where my father chose to live out his cursed existence. I really wanted to make it out—here was something, I thought, to keep me occupied. Billy was an infectious personality, at once accommodating and full of fire and bile, standoffish in only the best sort of way. He gave you the feeling he gave a shit about whatever he was saying, outlandish as it might have been.

I paid the lot attendant $20 for the privilege of having kept my battered car for an hour. When I got back to the apartment, bare except for the bed, the phone, and the mess I'd made of the road-worker vests, I was seized by the enormity of the suggested task before me, and quite automatically, it felt, continued with what was taking on the shape of a bodysuit. I haphazardly stitched a tube comprised of the strips of reflective fabric, to approximately the size of my arm, then a rectangular swath to cover my chest and stomach, and by the time I was done it was well past midnight and my eyes were heavy and I'd succeeded, in a way, at banishing my father from my thoughts, so focused had I become on ripping the strips from the vests, threading the needle, puncturing the strips' edges, stitching, tying off the minuscule ends. The last thing I did was to connect the rectangular piece to the arm and insert my own right arm into the cylinder, model the beginnings of my suit in the full-length mirror on the back of the door. The light from the single small lamp in the apartment was reflected off the uneven surface of my handiwork, colossal and bright, leaving various pulsating spots in my vision when I dared move in front of the mirror. I turned off the light, laid down on the little mattress on the floor with the thing still on my body, what little light that seeped through the tiny alley window near the top of the wall above my head bouncing off my chest and around the walls of the apartment, illuminating the area further than would otherwise have been imaginable.

The effect of the concentration of reflective strips was astounding—more than I could have guessed or possibly hoped for. Meanwhile, I lay there on the mattress, thinking, filling the dead space with light, with rationalizations of the task—elegiac light and truth, father, were what I would be/was after.

But through the lens of time, long time: the sadness of this wait, its weight, within the confines of a for-all-intents purloined apartment, I also thought, showed the opposite could just as well have been true—'twas a quest for light that, ultimately, given the task's clear physicality, its mindful mindlessness, blinded me to the possibility of knowledge, of candor, truth.

I fell asleep thinking of the little and quite astounding huge lies of the day, of the day previous, and was awakened by a knock at the door, which I didn't answer. It was Ms. Banks, undoubtedly, as I could hear her feet climbing the stairs from my first floor back to her apartment after a minute or so. I rose, slowly, and set to work on the second arm. Sometime before first light, I pulled through the final ragged stitch in the left leg bottom, sighed heavily, and lay back in my father's recliner to say a little prayer to the man. Not that he'd hear it, though my mother would be proud, I'm sure. Would that he could have seen or have believed in the salvation about to commence! Wrung-out but shot through with a little fire at the thought, I rose, covered upper and lower halves with the two pieces of the finished product and lay down then on the mattress, positioning the little lamp so that its light fell full on my body, filling the little apartment with brilliant light, casting shadows dark and as defined, though I have been known to exaggerate, as those cast by the early afternoon sun. Thoughts swam, began to speed to a blistering pace. I closed my eyes as tightly as I could to keep them all in, falling back slowly into the oblivion of sleep.

I woke slightly startled by the sunlight pouring in through the high little window above me, obliterating what intensity the reflective suit had in the dark hours. Later that day, I found a hardhat in the bottom of my father's closet and with glue affixed a few reflective strips to its exterior. I assumed my father's hermit identity loafing in the suit in the apartment those next few days. I talked to no one excepting the counter worker at the taqueria around the corner, who sustained me with burritos, corn chips, hot sauce. I might have ceased to exist, were it not for a phone call from Billy, wondering if I was in fact still alive, another from Will Theron, who said Annie asked where I was, thought maybe I'd decided to quit the place.

"You figure out what's up?" he asked.

I told him my father was dead, it was true, and I was dealing with all the subsequent mess, give me a few weeks.

"Damn, man," he said, and I had a brief vision of him above the grill at Henry's, eyes dropped to his shoes, to the floor. I didn't give him a timetable for my return, though, nor did I update my mother on my quest.

Though I was slowly dissolving into the memories of my past friends and associates, I attracted onlookers that Saturday night while on the mattress, wearing the suit, lamp positioned for maximum effect.

I was drifting off to sleep when a loud crack awoke me, to be followed quickly by another, which I realized was the product of small rocks being thrown by laughing kids in the alley below the small window above my mattress. I opened the window and donned the helmet, moving a rickety old wooden chair I'd found in the alley to a spot just below the window. Positioned on the mattress, the chair rocked, wobbled when I climbed on top of it, but I yanked myself upright by the window ledge, to full height. I looked out on a gaggle of kids as my helmet shot back the ray of a streetlight positioned next to the building that cast its glow on me.

"Wow, are you him?" said a boy, head tilting right.

"Yeah," another.

"Who?" I said, "or, rather, whom?"

The apparent leader, an older boy in a blue jumpsuit, advanced now through the little knot of children, fifteen feet off in the middle of the alley. One hand behind his back, with the other he aimed and tossed a pebble that ricocheted off my helmet.

"Jesus," said the only girl of the group, as I could see. "You're Jesus."

"I am not Jesus," I said.

"You are," said the leader, who continued his approach still hiding something behind his back. As he moved to climb atop the garbage can just below my window, I saw he held one of those little paper crowns I guess they still give out at certain fast food hamburger joints. I fought the urge to rock back down from the chair, from the window, to shut it against the group, but the boy beat me to a decision and gingerly placed the crown just above the top of my head. He then jumped back down to his friends, who laughed a bit. He turned to appraise his handiwork, me.

"Heil," he said, raising his right arm, then bursting into a big laugh himself.

I reveled in a gathering feeling of notoriety. Perhaps I was meant for Christ-like stature, I thought, staring at my brilliant reflection under the light in the bathroom, then laughing as another pebble cracked at the window. I left the crown atop the helmet, the helmet atop my head, and ventured into the night several hours on, walking the streets in the suit to the outraged astonishment of drunks on their way home from bars, third-shift workers on their way to work, their headlights catching on me at corners and blinding them. On a whim, while crossing the boulevard that cut the neighborhood in two, I stopped in its empty center, waiting, as the streetlight changed. In the distance: the freeway where it crossed the boulevard. From under the highway bridge, heading my way, emerged a pair of headlamps. The approaching monstrosity, the closer it got, revealed itself as a black Hummer H2, trademark conveyance of the wealthy and ostentatious of certain earlier years, typical of the boulevard, I guessed. I remained in the very center of the four lanes of traffic, and as the Hummer approached it veered to its right to miss me, but the sound, the wind, the quick roaring zip of its passing pulled a string deep within me, adrenaline ramping my heart to a cacophonous beating.

I walked forward through the intersection toward the bridge.

Arriving there I listened for a good ten minutes to the whine of its traffic above, looking all the while for a possible entry point. My very visibility as if automatically imparted courage and determination into my brain, or my bones, maybe—I moved somnambulant, robotlike up an embankment adjacent the southbound onramp and jumped the barrier railing onto the freeway apron. I turned back toward the eight-lane bridge, three main lanes and one express lane each side, and walked up the apron.

A tractor-trailer heading my way around a fine curve up the road blared its horn at my form on the bridge, its headlamps illuminating the suit before it roared alongside me with a great blast of air. I stopped walking, my arms and legs now quivering with the rush as cars and motorcycles making up a small pack blew by, compounding the sensation.

Taking advantage of a break in the traffic, after my nerves had settled a bit, I walked as calmly as possible across the three southbound lanes and climbed atop the three-foot barrier separating the main thoroughfare from the express lane, turned my body north, away from the towering hulks of downtown skyscrapers now at my back, and looked all the way down the boulevard to the square, beyond which I'd begun this sojourn. I closed my eyes as a phalanx of rigs barreled by, brakes hissing in response to my shimmering form. I raised my arms from my sides perpendicular to the plane of my body, now forming a bright T as the cars whizzed through, their own brakes squealing, transmissions downshifting, prompting my eyes open to a gathering traffic jam on either side of me, in both the single express lane and on the main highway.

I kept my arms raised through it all—the quickly proliferating barrage of horn honks, the catcalls—only lowering them to catch the gifts the late-night traffickers bestowed upon me: an Hispanic woman in a big old Buick Regal shouted "Viva [something or other]!" and flung me a crucifix necklace fashioned from white pipe cleaners and black yarn.

Then, the inevitable happened. Within several minutes the traffic jam was complete, immobile, and a unit of Chicago's finest, roof lights ablaze, came weaving its way through the stalled hulks of autos and rigs and motorbikes. The two cops in the squad, whom I did my best to ignore, pulled me from the barrier down to the bridge deck, pushed me back through traffic to the apron and pushed my shining form facefirst onto the warm hood of the cruiser. I did not resist. This lead pair was (relatively quickly, considering the traffic) joined by another, and the driver of the first car moved to make do of the rapidly expanding jam of rubberneckers, his arms pinwheeling one after another as headlights, lined up as far north as the eye could see, continued to reflect icily off my suit with intensity enough to prompt one of the gregarious officers assigned to me to don his mirrored shades as he approached.

"What kind of fairy are we dealing with here?" he offered his partner.

"It ain't all that bright," partner said. "I don't think three of us are necessary," gesturing back to the lead driver out in the middle of the four lanes of traffic pinwheeling his arms. "Maybe we oughta tell him he's making it worse." The man in sunglasses agreed, and he and his reasonable partner angled off through the traffic to make a little trio in the center of the expressway.

After the lead officer's persuasive talents worked their way on the two interlopers, they split off from him and took spots between the other two lanes, parallel with the man at the center, pinwheeling their own arms. I couldn't help but laugh.

"It is a little funny, isn't it?" said the remaining officer.

I quickly entered this opening, and asked if I might sit down. He opened the back door of his cruiser, leaving it open even after I'd taken my seat there, fully accepting of my fate—acquiescent, really, to the demands undoubtedly about to be placed on my life. That is, until a genetic predisposition, an inheritance from my father, offered an escape.

Ralph Cash was not a small man. He was short, but his wide torso and bulky shoulders and forearms had instilled in my primary memory of him—cemented when a mere child, before his first disappearance from my world—the sensation of his presence as that of a gargantuan benevolent beast half-covered in prickly black hair: kind, yet unwavering in emotional intensity, fierce yet passive. A life of work had not yet turned me into the hard-fleshed monster my father had been or was yet, but I did share a number of his physical and otherwise personality-type characteristics, likewise the tendency to run from trouble, no matter the cost.

As the final cop sighed and trundled into the traffic to speak his piece to his buddies, I rose from the cruiser, prizing my helmet from its spot on the vehicle's roof, and moved as quickly as I could behind the car, putting it between myself and the sight lines of the improvising traffic cops. I moved quickly to the edge of the bridge. When I reached it, looking down into the boulevard, I caught sight of an old man waving from the grassy embankment I'd climbed to get here. He was scampering back down its slope and gesturing wildly at his truck, parked more or less directly underneath me on the boulevard with its hazards flashing. I turned back toward the traffic, toward the cops. A fat man in a box truck honked his horn and bellowed "Viva Chicago!" tossing a Cubs cap my way, which I quickly donned, pulling the helmet tightly over it.

The man's exclamation also got the attention of the lead cop, who caught sight of me and screamed to his buddies to "get after that little faggot!" But I'd already hopped up on the reinforced concrete of the overpass edge, and the old man 15, 20, 30 feet (I couldn't be sure) below just reaching his pickup and cranking the engine, I said a quick prayer to my mother and Jesus and all my woeful ancestors, and jumped.

I landed hard in the little truck's bed, cracking my finger on its side and nearly fainting at the explosion of pain that ran up my arm from what I surmised somewhere under the dwindling cacophony in my skull to be a break. I fell over on my back as the vehicle sped off down the boulevard, the magnanimous driver's mousy face peering back through the open window at the back of the cab while peeling out and calling, "You all right?" I couldn't manage even a single word. I nodded yes. I must have hit my head, too.

That's the last I remember of the night.

Chapter 4

"We're not born assholes, we have to learn that," Trey Olden told me when I woke early the next morning—after introducing himself properly—prone on a strange bed, my right index finger swollen to the size of a smallish cock, taped to the middle finger. Olden's gravelly voice was muscular and trillingly feminine at once. Truman Capote crossed with Johnny Cash. He'd been up much of the night listening to my breathing, he said, not light or deep enough to indicate a coma of any kind, he guessed—he did want some measure of certainty, because I must have hit my head, he said, pointing out a knot I now found on its right side, below the contours of the helmet. And though I had no idea how he'd possibly be able to know the particular symptoms of a coma, I didn't ask him to elaborate either. Rather, I felt a strong sense of gratitude—shocking, I know—and thanked him for his hospitality.

"You have only time before they find you, maybe, though at the same time I might imagine they're not too worried about it," he said, Buddha-like, through the gap where his left front tooth should have been—a look in his eye and a smile more like a wince, as though questioning the very assertion. "If they've got you on video. Or your photograph. They don't, at least, have this one."

I didn't remember seeing the cops brandish cameras, no body cameras, no ID checks had been made, I told him as he handed me a fresh dark-room print, a negative exposed in his own camera last night, he said, that showed my gleaming figure in the foreground of a spectacular skyline view of the Loop taken, Olden said, out the window of his Nissan as he passed me by in the early, mobile portion of the traffic jam, before sensing something, he went on, something like "empathic fate or just a sense of an inevitable meeting" and exiting at the next street, Fullerton, to loop back under the boulevard overpass before the cops showed up.

"Your finger is broken, by the way," he said.

"This bed sure is fucking hard," I said, pushing myself into a sitting position.

"I've been sleeping on it for 25 years and not a spring loose," Olden said, a little meanness creeping into his voice.

"Sorry. Guess I'm doing a hell of a job," I said.

"You're an asshole all right. Maybe they won't find you. Hopefully not."

I conjured television-show episodes, police cruiser-cam moving pictures of handcuffed arrestees drunk or dejected, embarrassed, full-tilt pissed. Trey moved out of the room and commenced the beginnings of coffee prep just beyond the doorway. I slowly stood to join him, looking from the window—north, I guessed—to the Willis/Sears Tower in all its monolithic glory right outside, it seemed, though really at a distance of a couple miles or more, had to be. This little room, I found upon exiting, was but a drywall box in a cavernous warehouse-like space filled full with row upon row of wooden frames varying in height, most reaching five feet or so, just to my shoulders. I joined the old man by his makeshift kitchenette, outfitted as it was with an industrial-size sink, refrigerator, microwave.

"I've been here since the late 80s," Olden said. "The neighborhood's changed like crazy, man, but this place is a last bastion of the constant. Except for all the new prints." Olden's loft/photo-and-frame studio was on the near south side on the edges of the Pilsen neighborhood, on the south bank of the Chicago River's south branch—almost to Bridgeport, really, he explained, the proximity to downtown very real compared to my father's location to its northwest, but also a trick of the eye made possible by the monolith of the freeway that cut the view from the window in two. Not thirty feet off the edge of the building, said freeway interrupted the middle distance, the stacked neighborhoods—most of them, Olden said, cookie-cutter new construction with a shopping-mall feel to lure yuppies into the former heart of Maxwell Street, present-day ghetto in gentrification. The freeway hijacked the view of the miles to where the Tower and other buildings around it sprung from the earth, whole city blocks of concrete and steel beneath the blacktop.

"We're on the outer edge of new development, here," he said. "If they make it much farther, I can kiss this shithole goodbye."

42

Olden laughed hard, ending in a wracking cough. The man was close to my father's age, maybe, I thought, though when I asked him it turned out he was younger—only a tad over 50, though to have seen him, his missing teeth, the long silver hair and the wizened look the wrinkles along his jaw imparted, you might have guessed he was 70. He lived off his frame business—he made them all and sold them to what he said was a veritable army of fine-art photographers in the neighborhood, plus he did small pet projects for artsy newlyweds and such. Occasionally he sold a shot of his own to a newspaper or magazine.

When it was done, he poured coffee and brought it over to a square wooden table just off the kitchenette. I moved to take it with the wrong hand, the busted one, and Olden pointed out my folly before the disastrous occurred. Indeed, the index finger began to throb at its very mention, pulsing up through my right wrist and forearm and into my very head. The coffee was strong though, a fine antidote.

"Ginsberg taught me that," Olden said. "He knew that being an asshole meant more than just acting like a jerk. People get too comfortable in their bones, their petty little preoccupations. It's folks like us who can strike a blow to their brains."

I was lost, and told him so.

"Allen Ginsberg. I knew him in New York in the 70s, 80s—people were more accessible then. Now it's all staged press conferences, monitored, 'I'll be taking that film,' " Olden miming the grabbing hand of a security guard or celebrity handler. "I've been out of that game for a while now, but I took pictures of Little Richard, Malcolm Forbes all decked out in leather on his Harley—" motioning now across a pile of wooden frames to a spot above his refrigerator, where hung a shot of a young guy in shorts and a tight collared shirt with his fingers clasped around a freshly bitten strawberry positioned just below his chin. Olden let the image sink in. "That's my favorite. 1977. That boy, yes, a boy, as was I at the time. I lived on a boat. That's it over there." Olden pointed across the room to a shot of a big cabin cruiser in a rustic frame hung on the peeling south wall.

"We were docking on the west side somewhere, and we're easing up to the pier and here's this beautiful kid. My boyfriend at the time, Julian, love of my life, I guess—he died back in the late 80s, of AIDS, and yes I live with HIV, but not to worry, I don't, too much—Julian was something like an old perv and he's leaning out over the stern, all wild-eyed crazy: 'Take the boat in! Take the boat in!'" Olden laughed, then formed his hands into a frame before his face.

"But I had my camera out. Click." He pointed back up to the shot.

One of Olden's three black tomcats jumped onto my lap, then, startling me.

I'd never met a man or woman with Olden's particular death sentence, and I guess it'd be right to say I wasn't exactly comfortable with the knowledge. I was dressed only in a t-shirt, jeans I'd had under the suit. I wondered aloud where it was.

Olden motioned by the drywall box in which I'd been marooned, asleep.

"I hung it up in there," he said.

"Hung it up?" I said, incredulous. Its ragged, handmade form I imagined impossible to conform to a conventional hanger. I looked in and saw it now shimmering in the sunlight that fell through the room's little window, draped lengthwise across the wooden horizontal bar of a hanger likely meant for the bottom half of an old suit. *I'm OK*, I thought, memory of the night blazing through my head.

Olden waved my picture now in the space between us. "I've got a good friend at the paper. I can send this and some others to him, if you want."

I hadn't seen that coming.

"But the cops—"

"Your face isn't in the picture. And this is Chicago, old boy. They got more to worry about, surely."

He turned the photo toward me. He was right. My form was awash in white, very little about me beyond my hands in any particular detail whatsoever.

"It might be good press for you, among those who know you, if that's what you're after."

I wasn't, but I was learning quickly—a life could be all sorts of things. I'd have been stupid not to glean that from my father's

44

proffered inheritance.

"I've never done anything like this before," I said in another moment of candor, laced again with gratitude.

"Really?" Olden said, genuinely perplexed. He gulped his coffee and moved back to the kitchenette. I followed.

"You're not an artist," he said. He sat down at the table, pulling a frame from the nearest row and inspecting its joints. In his phrasing there was the twinge of disappointment, of sureties and convictions held with delight stepped on, proved false. But maybe I was, I thought, or could be, if not a messiah, then this.

I recalled my last visit to the city and a night out with Carl and Billy—Carl doubtless forgot all about it, but he was needling me late about Carolina, what he guessed (quite rightly in some senses) about its culturally vacuous nature and my perfect reflection of it. I hastened to agree with him, mean-spirited and blind though much of the talk was. He was tanked, of course, but he was also insistent upon the idea that I'd make one hell of a filmmaker or songwriter or something or other, Carl declaiming I'd somehow "lived" more than most my age, though I'd spent every year since college in the same stinky kitchen with only scant time off and in the same city, for the most part, which I brought up as objection.

"But that's exactly what I'm talking about," Carl said. "You have lived the lives that men lead, quiet desperation, man. Fucking Thoreau, dude. You're the mass of men. We need more among the mass who can really do something with the shit of it. You seem like a smart-enough guy."

Thoreau was far from any regular guy, I pointed out, and we were interrupted at about this point—a good thing. I was sort of manically stewing, brain replaying the gibberish with intercut little excerpts of all the other rushing tweedly-doos it was coming up with in response to an endless kaleidoscope of bullshit, a feeling I knew well and often followed by an intense three-week period of hypochondria over the state of a failing heart—to the point I'd visit a doc and be declared all systems normal and beat a path back to sanity.

I was glad he dropped the talk, that night. I smoked, drank away the mania. But the next day, I was a little flattered, I'll admit. Not that I did anything about it other than ask Ralph Cash if he'd ever gotten a creative urge in his life.

He'd responded with a question. "What does that mean, I wonder?" He didn't go on.

"You ever made anything?" I asked, and felt stupid immediately. I began nodding my head as he looked down the bridge of his nose to indicate, well, me.

"Listen," he'd said, "I've felt all sorts of ways in the long time. I've told you about the trains. If anything in my life might be described that way, it's that compulsion, maybe. I felt like I was on the edge of birthing something new, something from me alone, no cooperation required. Your mother couldn't understand that. She only could take it one way, and that was to read me as deadbeat, derelict, a drunk, maybe, anyhow a man who was not fit to raise a child. Hell, I could see the truth in that, but also the myopia. There's another way. Maybe *the* other way. Some people."

With an eventual ride back to Logan Square in the passenger seat, this time, of Olden's Nissan, I spent the afternoon and early evening half-conscious in the recliner, listening to the apartment creak, neighbors quarrel, sirens blare in the distance. I watched a roach inspect the stapler on my father's little desk. As night fell my senses sharpened to detect the telltale crack at the upper window above the bed, the crack that never came. I imagined, half expected to see Ralph Cash walk in all howdy-doody with the crack of a wry grin, six-pack under his arm. *How you been, son*, desiring no answer, as was his way.

After many hours like this, somewhere below the throbbing finger and roiling monologue in my head, I resolved nonetheless that Chicago would be my home for a time. I would wait for the old man to rear his head, if he wasn't working through me already, not that I believed in ghosts or the mystical afterlife or reincarnation or anything of that sticky nature.

I held out hope that the man was still alive, his disappearance his final attempt at an original creation.

Chapter 5

Trey Olden told me of a bar opening a block away across the river from his place. He'd pointed it out to me on my way home.

"I know the owner," he said. "They need bartenders, door-men." He'd call me later with the man's number. His name was Joe, a veteran of a couple other low-key spots he'd opened in places "just at the opportune moment," Trey said. He laughed. The man Joe was an impresario, a master builder, one with a keen sense for the early stirrings of urban transformation. Olden was a regular at his previous club on the outskirts of Lincoln Park, Meadowlark. "This place will be the Lark Sparrow. I had a loft near there, too, funny enough, until I'd been there ten years and my rent was about to double. If you go there now, there's nothing but big-box house-wares and electronics shops. Crate & Barrel, suburban-looking mothers pushing their kids around. Which is not to say Joe's a bad guy. He's made a shit ton of money doing what he does, I guess, and he always gets out just before the place goes sour with money, selling for a fine take before he can stand it no more."

I met him the next night, an unassuming man in his mid-50s. He sized me up casually, across a table in the bar's dusty interior—a workman was putting red vinyl covering over a set of custom booths along the south wall, and the place had yet to be cleaned, though Joe claimed that weekend would be the grand opening.

"Can you start Saturday?" he said. I told him I could.

"What's with the finger?" he asked. I still had it taped up, though it wasn't broken, contrary to Olden's diagnosis—jammed, I guessed, it had already begun to heal quite nicely.

"I jammed it playing basketball the other day," I said. I hadn't played basketball since I was 16.

Joe went on, then, asking about my background, what brought me to Chicago. I told him I came from a place where change hap-pens slowly, that I was probably a product of this idea, in spite of it all.

"You'll be here a while," Joe said.

"Yeah that's right," I said.

"I get it," he said. "People sometimes accuse me of opportunism, of thinking of neighborhoods as speculative investments, the city as a malleable whole. But look around this place." I did. Even in its unfinished state, it was a beautiful old bar. I let my gaze wander around the dusky interior, falling along the old cherrywood bar and the cheap cocktail tables before finally settling on the workman by the booths, who nodded.

"This place has been a bar in some permutation since the thirties. My father used to cash his factory checks in the back there," Joe said, pointing past the booth to the rear of the place, where now stood nothing but empty space, an old piano, a photo booth, and a couple cocktail tables.

It'd been a stop on a streetcar line that brought men from the factories in after work to drink away their paychecks. The rails, weedy and disused and in some places paved over, ran along the east-west thoroughfare just outside the bar's front door.

"For me, all this, opening this place," he said, "is simply a return, you know, a return to the roots—that's what it's all about in the end. Improving upon your progenitors' mistakes."

I wasn't so sure, but at that moment I felt my employment here was contingent upon an appropriate response. I don't really know why—Joe leaned back in his chair and folded his arms across his chest, quite calmly, casually, but there was something in his gaze that bore into me, and the necessity of retort or concurrence bumped me right into realization.

"My father worked for the city," I said. "Streets and san, I think. Traffic. Road construction. He lived on the north side, in the very apartment I'm in now. Carolina's my home, I guess you could say, but I came here looking for him, too." Joe slowly nodded his head, satisfied.

I started two nights later.

Carl and Billy and Elsa came along flashing their IDs at me with exaggerated grins and sarcastic winks, the latter two peppering me with facetious and overblown bits of outrage at blowing them off, days ago now. It was grand, over all, if nothing more than a soft opening—no flyers, no radio announcements, nothing

48

to suggest the Lark Sparrow hadn't been here for the last 20 years. Other Logan Square kids, and folks from all over the city, really, had heard about the place and flocked to fill the seats at the bar and the booths and the tables. I moved from my doorman's chair only to pick up glasses, wipe down abandoned tables.

I'd called Will Theron and Annie and given them my notice the day before.

"You'll be better off," Will said, but I could hear the sadness in his voice and imagined that his eyes were aimed paradoxically straight into the sky.

I told Billy of my plan to stay in the city a while.

"It's obvious, brother," Billy said, sweeping his arm out at the packed bar. At that moment in walked a plain-looking girl who transformed with a wild expression and a giggle at the sight of Billy, who in turn introduced her as V.

"Like the Pynchon book," I said.

"Like the 23nd letter of the alphabet," she said.

"You mean the 22nd," I said, after brief calculation.

Her brown hair parted loosely along the center of her head back into a low ponytail. Thin-lipped, severe features, familiar in a way. She hugged Billy and marched off in search of a drink.

"Camden," Billy said.

"That's her real name?"

"No, she's from there. And not New Jersey. Our fine home state."

A Carolinian. I watched her as she wedged through the three-deep crowd at the bar, leaned in and raised a hand like she'd been coming here every day in her life—calm and confidence coupled in the first sip, a quick turn of her head to take in just as much of the place as was necessary, then a slow turn back in the direction of the door, the direction of me. And Billy.

"Be careful," he said. "She might not look it, but she breaks hearts."

My own beat faster. "Be careful yourself."

"Holy shit!" he said, laughing, then going quiet as we watched V snake her way toward the back of the bar.

I was near breathless with excitement, in spite of myself.

Around 11, Trey Olden stopped in and immediately unfolded

a copy of the *Sun-Times* in my face to reveal a photo feature with the caption

SHINING MAN—Unknown male in suit made entirely of reflective material walked into traffic on the Kennedy two nights ago, causing a traffic jam and a bright sight to motorists.

"Not very grammatical, is it?" I said.

"I went ahead and sent it in," he said. "Your anonymity is secure. I told my contact I shot it from my car while in the traffic jam, which is true." Trey smiled that gaptoothed thing at me. "Nothing else."

"It is a beautiful picture," I said, marveling at the stark newspaper reproduction. Trey moved into the space, and I held tightly to the shot, the newspaper, thoughts racing.

He had another copy of the paper with him, and between my duties—checking IDs, picking up empty glasses and kicking people out, all of which I did a prodigious amount of this night, but for the last: 'twas a gloriously subdued, if massive, crowd—I watched him ping from table to table, open the paper, talk, gesture my way and nod solemnly. He seemed to know everyone, and sure enough, eventually he got around to Billy, to Elsa and V. Billy jostled me as I stacked a pile of empty pint glasses at a just-emptied table next to their own. Midnight by then, I was pretty well exhausted.

"I see you met old Trey," he said. "Well done," a solemn nod like he held some new measure of respect for a man of meager origins.

"Crazy ass story," I said.

"I heard indeedy," he said, and I moved too quickly for him to follow to the bar, then back to my chair up front just as a hammered older couple waddled in, IDs out and ready.

I waved them by.

Billy lingered. "Your old man worked the roads," he said.

"He did," I said. "Listen, I didn't tell you the absolute truth the other day about what happened to him." Billy's eyes shot wide. "He just disappeared, man, and that reflective suit thing, well, it just came out of me—he left behind all that shit, these boxes full of those road-crew vests, the reflective stripes on all of them."

"But so he's not dead?" Billy said.

"I'm assuming he is, Billy," I said. "But I just don't really know, you know?"

"That's tough," he said, and he pulled a Will Theron, eyes on the floor as he sipped a beer.

"Hey, listen," I said. "Keep this to yourself. I'm getting on, you know. No need for pity, that sort of stuff. My pop was a strange bird, I think you know a little."

"I met him once when you were around," Billy said, "and actually saw him occasionally on the train in the neighborhood, though *very* rarely. Very long time since then. We never really spoke."

"Shit," he said.

"Yeah," I said. "Go on, man, have fun. I'm all right."

And he did. I watched him collar Trey in a little headlock at their table, sit down and go deep into conversation. Some kind of first night for the Lark Sparrow, and by the end of it, as folks began heading out, the bartender, Jake, and I got our crew together with Joe's blessing by the end of the bar for a round or two. Elsa had left earlier to get some sleep before a trip to L.A. the following day, and Billy and V were now arm in arm next to me as Carl toasted—"To the South!"—and everybody nudged each other and sniggered.

I added, with a needling glance Billy's way, "To love among comrades in traffic," which he seemed to get, maybe. V did, anyway, as she moved away from him, the crowd readying for the drink, and placed her arm now in mine.

"To the Shining Man," Trey offered, "may he shine forever with the light of a thousand halogen headlamps," holding aloft the newspaper—all had by now heard the story.

As I wiped down the tables in the bar's empty interior 15 minutes later, Carl followed me from edge to edge with an idea of his own—so impressed was he with Trey's photography and my budding eccentricity—a gallery show of Trey's photos of me, in the suit, in various locales throughout the city. Always at night, but of course. The show would be attendant to a happening out on the Halsted Street gallery's corner, just north from the bar.

"We could make 20 or 30 of these suits, get a bunch of people together and form a phalanx across the street, or up the street," he said. "*Occupy* Halsted."

51

"I don't think I have enough material for that many," I said. I'd dismantled perhaps half of Ralph Cash's vests for the first suit alone.

"This is Chicago," Carl said. "Maker of the world. Surely we can buy the stuff in bulk. This is America, for that matter."

Which was a perfect name for a show, I thought.

Trey overheard the whole thing and signed on right there. Billy said he was down for helping with logistics. He knew the owner of the gallery Carl had in mind, anyway. The enigmatic and decidedly coquettish V, as well, offered her services.

"I can document," she said, pulling out her phone and snapping a picture of me and Carl leaned over a table in the back.

"I'm good with a needle, too," she said, "which from the looks of the suit in the picture, you'll need." She did a little twirl out into the bar, snapping pictures in panorama as she spun. The place was officially closed for our own little private party—again, with Joe's blessing.

The caveat: "Under no circumstances will this be a regular event."

V cornered me by a rear table once Carl and Trey left me alone to finish my work. I looked away just before she snapped yet another picture.

"Why do you turn away like that?" she said. "I'm not going to bite," laughing.

"Sorry," I said. "I just work here."

"Why did you come to Chicago?"

"Why did *you* come to Chicago? Billy says you're from Camden."

"Got a parrot on my hands."

"My father died," I said.

"Yes, Billy said so."

"Why'd you ask, then?" I looked over to Billy, who was watching us. He smiled.

Now she looked away. I fixed my gaze hard on her.

"Yes, I'm from Camden," she said.

"Yes, Billy said so."

"Do you like being a parrot?"

"Do you?"

It was Will Theron's game—repeating, answering questions with questions, implying answers. It was one way of saving face when greeted by a curiosity as insatiable as V's; another was to simply match it.

"You know the Camden Mortons?" I said. I referred to the family of the self-same Tim at Henry's, then mentioned him.

"No," she said, "but I know the Bascombes—ever heard of Turner Bascombe?"

"Racecar driver, bad seed, or so they want you to believe on the TV," I said.

"He went to my high school. Comes from money and money more," she said.

"Then Tim went to your high school too, skinny guy, wears a Confederate flag on his head, makes gay jokes like it's going out of style."

"Rings some bells."

"I worked with him at a restaurant in Charlotte," I said.

"So do you know the Camden Mortons, then? Did little Timmy come from money?"

I had no idea, not that it mattered, really.

"I know Tim," I said.

"But weren't you curious, Cash? Follow the money and all that. It's important."

She was drunk, she was smiling, aggressively cajoling.

"I got no excuse. I'm a dolt." And I was back in the hot seat.

When the night was over I drove her home—windows down, we screamed along with "Bad Romance" on the radio. When she didn't invite me in, I didn't protest—maybe Ms. V was the 21st-century S.C. debutante, an updated Eula Littlejohn (as crude as it may be to cast your would-be lover as your mother) on an extended sojourn up North. I knew the types back home. Believe it or not I'd come close to marrying one after she'd finally come around to the prospect and pleasure principles of sex. That took a while. Cassandra (V looked a little like her) had dealt drugs since high school—selling dimes and quarters from the drive-through window at the strip-mall dry cleaner where she manned the counter alone—though she came from a new-money family of land developers, high standing in the community, etc.

The dealing continued on through my time in college, when we likewise continued to date and, eventually, go at it in the backseat of my little 1980s Ford Mustang four-cylinder in a cul-de-sac her father owned that was as yet unpopulated. It wasn't the dope, though, that pricked her inner debutante's conscience. The sex went on for maybe six months—say a few times a week, at most, before she insisted that we marry and just get on with the business of life with children, drug money and what would surely eventually be my professorship or, as it were, managerial position behind the line at Henry's and a long, fruitful life dedicated to hard liquor.

I acquiesced, at first, then we had it out one night, high as kites and me half-drunk and ornery as hell, my tendency in those days. She broke it off, and I was in the end utterly relieved.

I thought of Cass as V bounded up the front steps to her building and disappeared. I smiled to myself, too, at the possibility that I might just be wrong—quick anticipation of what the future might hold.

The next night couldn't have been more different at the bar. Jake brought along a stack of magazines and two empty notebooks.

"Your friend Carl told me you were a writer," he said, handing one over. "You might use the time to purpose."

"I'm not a writer," I said, "but OK."

I took my seat on the stool at nine. By ten I'd carded exactly two people, and they'd long ago finished their drinks and left. The only people in the bar were two old drunks I'd met the previous night.

I grabbed a pen from Jake, opened the notebook, and made my first entry[1], a response to a spam email I'd gotten via a nearby

---

[1] *Dear Generation20something.com,*

I did receive your emailed solicitation re: stories about the trials of we saps snug in the craw of twentydom. I am indeed twentysomething (though I find it hard to remember exactly what age, as I tend to drink quite a lot of whiskey). I have just the story for you: Last night, sitting at my post as doorman at a bar in a depressed area of town, a drunk lady fell unconscious at the feet of her boyfriend (here I am making assumptions, and I'll have to admit it's occasionally difficult to determine who is with whom in this place) as they drunkenly approximated what appeared to be the tango. She—bangs ruffled and unkempt and the rest pulled up in a bun atop the rear of her head, be-jumpered, absolutely trashed—fell right out of her slightly less drunk boyfriend's arms, and I, being the door

Mexican café's Wi-Fi earlier in the day on the ancient but functional laptop computer Carl'd loaned me. The email was generated, I could only guess, by my late inclusion on the editor's lit-spam list, which he said was massive and I assumed he sold for a small profit whenever the opportunity arose.

Nonetheless, textually interrogating the notion proffered in the missive made me a little more than giddy with the anticipation of everything—crafting a new self, the artifice behind the task.

You can be whatever you want, really: I hadn't understood this until Chicago gave it to me. And not just through these near nightly entries, as a certain routine emerged from them in the subsequent weeks of what would become my summer of traffic—nights like these, followed by early morning stands in neighborhood thoroughfares, away from the expressway. I crafted myself in the streets, on the page—my selves, rather. They're muddled in memory their characters are so close, one a two-dimensional jack of all trades with no expertise but a knack for getting into embarrassing situations, the other a philosophical nobody with a bar job, a physical body, and a pen. What I didn't realize yet was that, ultimately, my choice would not be between the two.

You can contain as much as your guts can bear—five pounds of beef, for instance, a case of beer—before you pass on, or less finally, pass out.

---

man—stone sober, you see, and genuinely worried here that I would have to throw someone out—moved across the dank room to the two of them, herself in a red, crumpled pile at the boy's feet, like so many cast-off undergarments, while he stood dazed for a moment. Need some help? I said. He only nodded stupidly at me, so I bent down and pulled her into a chair by her armpits. Dropping her there, though, I felt her body give a small jolt, her red self coming to life, so I backed away; she rose, turned to me (at which point I caught sight of the now absolutely nonplussed boyfriend, eyes wide, looking my utter reflection there—shag haircut, denim jacket with a little pin on the flap on the left breast pocket) and lunged at my face, catching my lips in her own in the sloppiest kiss ever achieved, at which point she passed out again. I did not catch her. I wiped my face with the arm of my jacket. The boyfriend made a small attempt at it himself, without much success. Then: "Get her out," I said to him, but he stared at me, perhaps ten, twenty seconds. And passed out himself.

These two were born in 1984, I say. I know. I am the doorman.

I do not know if this is a story to "keep you from falling down," as you say. If not, the coffee I forced down the throats of these two might warrant a short tale of its own.

Please advise. Yours...

I woke Trey occasionally for the excursions, and he'd come by my father's place in his pickup. The first night he was there, I caught him staring down my father's parting message, which I'd unmoored from its box and tacked up on a wall in a prominent place to remind me where I came from. I told Trey where it originated—I told him the truth, that it contained for all intents and purposes my father's last words, far as I knew.

"Sorry," Trey said, simply, but he was clearly transfixed by the text. "I can see more of what it is you're doing here, and why."

As he gathered photos, some 35 mm, other nights with a large-format view camera capable of producing mammoth prints of my shimmering, suited form, momentum built behind our camaraderie. This was work of a kind, certainly, but also a fulfilling war—beneath our pith helmets brilliant notion after brilliant notion raced, or I liked to imagine so.

One night as we were walking through yet another neighborhood, searching for an appropriately lit spot for a shot or two, Trey told me a story culled from an old cartoon about a Ping-Pong match between Zeus and the mortal Perseus. Nearing the terminus of the match, score 21–20, advantage Zeus, a long uninterrupted back-and-forth ensued, neither the father god nor the leader of the Mycenaeans able to capitalize on the other's perceived weaknesses, the Ping-Pong ball shuttling over the net at humanly impossible speeds. Finally, Perseus popped the ball up with a misplaced backhand, and when finally it came down, hours later, and took its bounce on Zeus' side of the table, the god rammed the would-be winning spike with such fury as to split the ball in two. In the aftermath, a rat that Trey Olden called by his own name found his destiny in one half of the little ball. He used it for a motorcycle helmet while he toured North and South America on a big Harley.

"And Trey Olden's adventures were many," the old man said, snapping a picture of me beneath a streetlight out front of a mean-looking housing project.

"So we're all just picking up after the big guys," I said.

"You got it," he said. "The trick is in the picking, of course.

What's really going to make you happy? Ask yourself that."

I garnered from the moment some kind of connection beyond the everyday between myself and the old man, looked him in the eye and in my imagination began the tale of my father's disappearance as I'd told it to Billy, minus the prevarication I'd filled it full with to date.

Trey caught my inner distraction in his camera lens—these the first of his Shining Man portraits that featured more than just the human-shaped blob of light. In the photographs I look pensive, melancholy—or as it were elated, dreaming, the recollections' contradictory inspirational qualities shown right there on my face.

When it was all done he just looked at me.

After a minute of silence, during which I lit a cigarette, he said, "You're picking, gleaning well, far as I can tell." I wasn't so sure. "Now let's get the fuck out of here."

In the daytime—my mornings, usually noontime—I took to setting forth on a steel steed, an old Chicago-built Schwinn, had to be upwards of 30 years old. Billy plucked it from the junk at his messenger service's station and cleaned it up for me: "Take it, man. It's good exercise, and if you ever need another job." I wasn't cut out for such hard riding, I felt sure. I more naturally maneuvered the machine due south from my father's apartment for the curved thruways of Humboldt Park, lapping them up to 20 times at a clip, slowly and surely. The curves and small rises of hills cut a nicely contrasting picture to the rigid brutality of the Chicago grid. The rides calmed me, set me smoothly and contentedly within the limits of my own body, my own skull.

And as the Shining Man show approached, I took this new-found calm experimentalist's approach toward life and tried to pass myself off as an editor. I figured, with all the writing I'd been doing at the bar, I might just make it. (Reading, too, of course: anything I could get my hands on, the entire oeuvre of the somewhat recently deceased David Foster Wallace, Roberto Bolaño—loaned by Carl; Galeano's *Open Veins of Latin America*, a history of Euro-exploitation; Eric Foner's *Reconstruction*; lesser-known quantities of prose and verse, some written by the bar's very customers.) V had cornered me one lonely night in my doorman's chair, on her way out, and flashed her lovely sarcastic smile as she capped a conversation about the mirage of the future with this: "You can't work in a bar the rest of your life."

I needed a job. Joe cut one of my nights to make room for a former employee of his. I'd promised Eula Banks rent, of course. The first of the month was almost upon me. I had enough dough, but barely.

I picked ten job ads out of the paper one Sunday and sent a doctored-up résumé to all of them. I got three calls back, amazingly, considering the long doldrums of the entire economy—much less the tanking publishing business—thanks in large part to the Wall Street cheaters and their dupes, but when I started going in for interviews a week later I had a bit of trouble playing the part of the respectable candidate.[2] Transformation was possible on paper, at least: I certainly had more fun scripting the interview scenes at the bar afterward, embellishing wildly, than bullshitting with the authority figures at the various publications and organizations I visited. The last of them, the city Traffic Management Authority, had their eye out for a night-shift copywriter for their hourly broadcast updates. Their main office was downtown, up a flight of stairs through an entrance sandwiched in the center of a sub shop's storefront and unmarked but for the address stuck on the glass door. I took it as a fine omen that the man to greet me when I reached the stairs' precipice was wearing a TRAFFIC MANAGEMENT AUTHORITY-emblazoned reflective vest, but I spent a flat five minutes really attempting to pretend that I wanted the job before I told my interrogator, a bespectacled man with a Ditka mustache whose

---

[2] *I declare: I am the Candidate.*
CAST:
CAND — Candidate for the position of Assistant to the Assistant Managing Editor, a man of perhaps 28 years, shaggy-haired and short, wearing a pressed business outfit.
ASS — Assistant to the Managing Editor, a woman of perhaps 40, perhaps 25, a woman of indeterminate age in a pressed gray pantsuit.
MAN — Managing Editor, a woman of, perhaps, 60, but more likely 70 or 80 years, wrinkles deeply set along her jawline and brow, allowing for a gaze of interminable consternation, in a gray pantsuit near identical to that of her apparent protégé.

CAND: Hello.
ASS: Hello.
MAN: Yes, well, Hello... Mr. Cash, is it?

CAND: *Uh-huh.*

ASS: *OK.*

CAND: *Yep.*

MAN: *Tell me, Mr. Cash, have you read Melville's 'Bartleby the Scrivener,' the short story?*

CAND: *Many times, Ma'am. I have read much and often, in my time. I can't remember most of it, but this I can.*

MAN: *Call me Asshole, please.*

CAND: *Yes, Asshole, well. My pleasure. I have preferred many times in the past to read Melville's fine short story entitled 'Bartleby the Scrivener.'*

MAN: *And have you read the famous* Rubaiyat?

CAND: *I have, Asshole, but would prefer not to have to...*

MAN: *No matter, it is none at all...*

ASS: *Mr. Cash, what I believe the Asshole means to say is that the position of Assistant to the Assistant to the Managing Editor, the Managing Editor being of course Asshole here and her Assistant being me, and do please not hesitate to call me by my given name, Ludy.*

CAND: *Thank you, Ludy. You were saying.*

ASS: *Yes.*

MAN: *[*clears throat for a full minute as CAND and ASS look on in horror, and at the terminus:*] Do please forgive the interruption.*

CAND: *Certainly, Asshole.*

ASS: *Do continue, please, if you must...*

MAN: *[*another round of throat clearing followed by a brief fainting spell, MAN's head lolling back, her eyes twitching up into her head so that only the whites show, at which point ASS and CAND begin to exchange certain pregnant glances, raised eyebrows, until MAN revives and says:*] The position, Mr. Clash, is very much akin to that of Bartleby, i.e. that of a scrivener, a copyist, if you will. I will have to refer you to Ludy for the details.*

CAND: *Thank you, Asshole.*

ASS: *Yes, well, you basically will operate a Xerox machine.*

CAND: *I've done that before, certainly!*

MAN: *And a very important operation it is! Without the—* [another fit, this time of coughing and a fainting spell, prolonged, at which point ASS's hand moves abruptly to CAND's crotch, but quickly pulls away, as MAN revives...] *Excuse me, Mr. Crash.*

[MAN exits stage left. Makeout session, near slapstick, with CAND slapping the ass of ASS and ASS howling. At the terminus:]

CAND: *So.*

ASS: *You don't really want the job, do you?*

CAND: *Of course not.*

ASS: *Because you won't get it.*

[EXEUNT]

name I can't remember and who also wore a reflective vest, of my late father and my new preoccupation with standing in traffic. I stressed my experience out in the streets of Chicago's neighborhoods, likewise the expressway, as proof of my potential worth to the TMA. The guy thought I was making it all up and laughed at me, and I returned the gesture, or rather just laughed with him, at myself. Five minutes later I was out the door.[3]

I crafted my fanciful versions of several of these, typed them and sent them in to Carl, who a few weeks on published a collection of the mini-dramas in his online mag under the title "Cand/Ass/Man: Dispatches From the New American Economy."

Carl talked it up—"Just fucking genius," he said. "It's like we're sitting here and looking at this absurdist set-piece-type thing but feeling the burn of shame and the generally humiliating nature of the 'job interview,' " fingers describing air quotes around his head, "particularly in this day and age."

He'd come by the apartment, where he laid the title on me and continued to talk about the little scribbled series for the majority of

---

[3] *I cannot hear the birds chirping, for today I am again the Candidate, as follows....*

CAST:
CAND — Candidate for the position of Owl Editor, Traffic Management Authority, a male of perhaps 28 years, shaggy-haired and short, wearing a pressed business outfit.
DIRE — Director of Traffic Control, Traffic Management Authority, a man of perhaps 60 years who can only be described as burly: thick, grey Ditka mustache, wire-framed spectacles, salt-and-pepper buzz-cut head of hair, fat.

CAND: Hello.
DIRE: So who are you, then?
CAND: I am the candidate.
DIRE: What makes you so confident?
CAND: I stand in traffic. Daily.
DIRE: Well, don't we all. This city's got some fucking problems, that's sure.
CAND: Rats.
DIRE: Tell me about it. You wouldn't believe the sight of the garbage bin out in my alley.
CAND: Oh, but I would.
DIRE: Well get the fuck out of here.
CAND: OK.

[EXEUNT]

an hour. He talked so much, in fact, that by the time he left I'd come to the conclusion that he was doing a pretty good job of convincing himself he wasn't making a mistake in his thinking.

"I told you you had it," he said, finally, and I could do nothing but laugh. He grimaced.

I bet a total of three people read the page in the week following publication. I heard from none.

"Good response, man," Carl said at the bar when I asked him about readers, though he didn't elaborate. I probably could have done just as well reading them aloud to the alley kids.

Editor I wouldn't be. I resolved to spend less. I spent more time in my father's recliner, hoarding every cent I could in hopes it would be enough.

Two weeks prior to the show, V visited me at my father's apartment for the first time (I continued to think of the little place this way, not yet having done away with the majority of his boxes, or any of his clothes—in fact, I'd taken to wearing them) to scavenge the reflective material from my remaining vests. She and I would be lead seamsters for a marching cadre of Shining People attendant to the big show. Carl had found the city's supplier and then their nearest competitor, a vendor based in Milwaukee who beat the other's price, but he figured we'd use what we had first.

Before V and I got to work, though, we headed north at her behest to a screening of a film out several years before from a couple locals about the Weather Underground, the 60s/70s armed left-wing propagandists. "You know the group," she said along the way.

I didn't—yet.

"So think Chicago 1968—plenty-well-off white kids take a mission, self adopted, to fight the U.S. government in solidarity with the Black Power people, third-world liberation movements, etc."

We were sitting back in the apartment, surrounded by vest fragments, needles, thread, a paring knife V wielded like a dagger. Some beers into it V was on a tear with her talk.

"Weather – blew – shit – up," she said, emphasizing each point with the knife. "What a story. Makes what we're doing seem, I don't know."

"Useless," I offered, though I was at least somewhat convinced we were on to something.

"But hey if they never hurt anything but property—"

"But that's not true, remember. What about those armored-car guys. What about their own idiots burned up in the New York house."

"Their bombs never hurt anyone," she said. "But them. The upshot—considering the ignorance of many of our 'compatriots,' no, 'comrades' on their story—in America we are reared, indoctrinated early, at least I was, to look at any kind of violence at all as either criminal or insane, right?" And she giggled, deflecting her serious tone, working at one of the reflective strips on one of my father's purloined vests with the knife.

I took up where she left off, haltingly, as if channeling some high-toned theorist or other, "And thus symbolic violence fails to impress upon the American mind any particular message," warranting only minuscule attention, buried articles deep in the interior of the *New York Times*.[4] But then I turned tack and argued that she was well off the mark.

"America's capacity for killing people violently is unmatched in human history," I said. "Just look at how easily people like us forge war that continues on in Afghanistan, Iraq, Syria, etc."

She shook her head sadly, like she'd hoped I were someone else. For a moment I wished the old man was there so that I might ask him for his memory of Weather, for his thoughts on violent symbolism.

But then I attempted to lift V's spirits, saying, "If something as elemental to the human experience as violence ultimately fails interpretation in a symbolic context," again the hopped-up theorist within, "then by extension all symbolic action will necessarily fail to, like, *coagulate* into any kind of desired rhetoric."

Her eyes lit up. "*Coagulate*. Fucking exactly," she said. She then

---

[4]*Remember Paul Auster's Benjamin Sachs, the "Phantom of Liberty," as Sachs dubs himself in Auster's novel* Leviathan. *Sachs stirs up little trouble or sympathy with his explosions of 40-plus replicas of the Statue of Liberty across the wide Americas. He accomplishes nothing other than his own accidental, lethal detonation not in a New York town home, but in a car by the roadside in rural Wisconsin.*

knocked back her third beer, and I mine, the last of a six-pack she'd brought along. This was the last of the vests, anyway.

"Yeah I don't know why we're doing this," I said.

V nodded, shrugged her shoulders as if to question the very questioning of what reasoning might be behind any and all of our tasks.

But then she said, "People like Weather were after *sort of* clear goals, you know. But that was a long time ago, and we're not wannabe revolutionaries." She put on her best low-country S.C. "This be a fine metaphor, I think. Standing in traffic—doing nothing, but lighting it all up. I mean, do you not think of it like that?"

She stood and moved to the window onto the U-shaped building's courtyard, futilely tipping back the empty beer.

"A kind of failure," I said, "willfully explored."

She turned to me, glint in her eye. "*Valiantly* explored. Commit to that."

And then I did something I might soon regret, rather automatically. She picked up the little box we'd deposited the reflective strips in and moved toward the door. I moved toward her and, when she turned back my way, I grabbed her free hand and pulled it up to my lips, softly kissing it.

"Thank you," I said, "for coming over." But she just stared at me. Then she laughed. And she left.

Chapter 6

Carl was hard at work through all of this promoting the show, which would be held at McIntyre + Feldman, a gallery in the long-upstart, dilapidated arts district just north on S. Halsted from the bar. Trey and I both began getting emails from all manner of folks interested—press people, Carl's friends who wanted to tell us how much they liked the idea, though I got the impression again and again that they were just going through the motions of human contact, getting ready for a social upheaval of an affair, a big-ass party.

Among those whose inquisitiveness arrived with an understanding that eclipsed even my own was Erik Rensauler, "literary terrorist" and leader of a cabal of misfits pursuant of that same self-imposed label. They'd spent the past three years crashing readings the nation over given by the cream of the younger half of New York City's literary establishment. Rensauler himself actually engaged in fisticuffs with none other than the great Sam Ringer after loudly questioning the "social relevance" of one of Ringer's friends' stories (one told from the point of view of a lightbulb). The primary recipient of Rensauler's rhetorical attack—"let there be no pussy-whipped New England trust-fund babies in our army"—was Rick Moody, who with all his obvious success was still the landing pad of largesse from our government's arts endowment.

Rensauler's overall point was airtight as he saw it: there's serious injustice in this, and someone like Moody should not be the one applying for these grants, and to top it off then a couple years later doling out the awards himself to others like himself—award-winning, financially stable, etc.

Rensauler's tactics, however, didn't always achieve their desired results—cf the above-mentioned fisticuffs, from which he walked away with a black eye, much the worse for wear of the pair of combatants. What little press cared enough to pay attention to this sort of adolescent mumbo-jumbo held free rein to paint Rensauler and his organization as no more than, of course, a bunch of dumbass goofball thugs. But I thought he was interesting, not to mention funny, and agreed to meet him when he was in town for a Sunday-night reading put on by his organization to benefit a writer of a photocopied fold-and-staple zine. The guy was sent to a coma in Milwaukee via head-on collision with a city bus while he was riding his bike.

We met at Ronny's Steak House downtown and ordered their fried pork chops, over which we talked.

"An activity normally reserved for mass protest," he said, squeezing chop grease from the ends of his handlebar mustache, "not normally something one does for personal fulfillment."

"Maybe we can take it to your town if it goes well," I said, and a number of the assembled nodded in agreement. He had a crew of other aging writers/bloggers/punks/zinesters from his Philadelphia home base in for the show, which might have been a contradiction, or simply further reinforced the east-coast industrial hegemony in the American lit world. Not that they looked or acted like the snot-nosed-overgrown-rich-kids-got-old Rensauler decried, but I couldn't really see the difference but for the money that came along with the effort. In any case, Carl was the only local on the bill at the woefully underattended show that night—in a Greektown bar whose stage would normally be reserved for traditional bands catering to overweight tourists from all over the Midwest—and he just looked puffed up, fat and flabby as he droned on in pseudo-diary format about a Floridian bigfoot called a "skunk ape." Mildly humorous, little else.

And there were no performers from the felled zinemaker's hometown an hour-thirty up the road in Milwaukee.

I watched from the bar, where I sat with V. She'd shown up in a strapless black dress and bright red high heels. We drank voluminously through a performance poet whose overwrought, half(though only, tragically, half)-sarcastic delivery of a particularly bad sex poem left me feeling sick to my stomach. We sat quietly, but inside I fumed at the stink of a world where even the insurgents reveled in useless mediocrity—a thing I might have known well, of course, but that evening, that concentrated, the valiant nature of our failure was absolutely embarrassing to see.

Yes, *our*—I could still consider Rensauler and his crew as of a piece with the dynamic I projected. We'd made a flyer a few days prior and I had a cache of them in the bag I'd taken to carrying. At the night's terminus I walked out into Jackson Street in front of the place, the few remaining showgoers exiting there.

"I stand in protest of general filth!" I shouted, fist raised high. A passerby muttered that he was hungry. "Join me! I entreat you!" adlibbing to beat the band. "Join the Traffic Report. Weather, traffic are all that remain to us of optional venues. We are washed-up! Washed-up versions of ourselves with leaden brains!" A small, squinty-eyed crowd sort of shuffled around in front of me, V laughing among them. A dump truck rattled by at my back, the driver working the truck's horn. I turned with a pile of flyers from my arsenal, walked further into the street and tossed them into the wind of the truck's wake. Turning back to the crowd, now quickly breaking up, I found I recognized the looks on those faces: expressions normally reserved for turning on men at the borders of sanity, or bums in the street.

I flashed a wide-eyed smile at V, lone among them in being quite as drunk as me tonight, and the rest of the crowd backed or turned away.

Erik Rensauler's handlebar mustache materialized perched above his own grin, moving toward me out of the middle of the mass, saying, "That was all right, man—you scared them good!" He joined me in the street, shook my hand and took a copy of the flyer.

"'We are out here,'" he read. The line was a reference to a performance artist Carl brought up weeks back who everybody around here seemed to know something of, who'd done something similar to my own traffic-stands back in the late-1990s. His own stands were conducted nude, and indoors—in lobbies of office buildings downtown or in neighborhood hospitals, at dot-com and weapons-tech conferences, even a police station once or twice. I had not the necessary chutzpah for all that. To hear Carl tell it, this guy spent no small fraction of the five years he was active on this project in such stations locked up with who-knows-whom.

Rensauler stared down at the image of the Shining Man, drawn with a fat marker, short lines extending from the human outline to represent light reflected in great beams from his body, the dotted black line of the highway receding in linear perspective behind him. I stuffed the rest of the flyers in my bag, and the remainder of the cache now on the street began to blow in the strong west wind down Jackson toward the Loop, to be picked up by derelicts and criminals, others out this late. People like us.

Rensauler, slightly upset (in contrast to his Philly cohorts, who positively fumed) over the low turnout but determined to make something of the night, left behind his bitter crew and joined V and I at a bar at Halsted and Grand called Selma's. The bartender there was an old guy named Morton whom I'd met with Billy a week back. Mort watched a lot of auto racing, particularly the big guys, Indy and the Charlotte-based stock-car premiere league, and he was an ex-theater actor, characteristics which made him one of the more persuasive personalities I'd met in my days.

"I've got proof," I told V on our walk up Halsted.

"Oh yeah? Of what?"

"You absolutely *can* work in a bar your whole life."

"Are you two an item?" Rensauler said. I stumbled over a crack in the sidewalk. V giggled wildly.

"Um," loping along as steadily as I could manage, "why do you ask?"

"We're absolutely not," V said, still laughing.

"You talk like you are," Rensauler said. "Or were. What's your name again?" he said to V.

"V," she said.

"Like the Pynchon book," I said.

"Like the 23rd letter of the alphabet, usually with two *e*'s after it," she said.

"Yeah," I said.

"You mean the 22nd," Rensauler said, "V."

V smiled. "Oops," she said, looking at me.

"Not the first time she's heard that one," I said. "Eh, V?"

Rensauler, cool, kept his eyes aimed straight, no smile gracing the space below his mustache. We'd almost arrived. Near the precipice of the gigantic Halsted bridge over the train yard north of Lake Street, as V and Rensauler began to chatter aimlessly, I looked out away from our city's skyscrapers and west across the relatively meager lights of the neighborhoods, where my post-midnight life had happened these past weeks. It was a look of longing, maybe, strong enough anyway for me to urge my compatriots onward—"It's just up at the next big intersection," I said—as I was overcome by the feeling of required action. V and Rensauler talked their way down the bridge's other half, under a commuter-train overpass, and out of sight. I walked into the street and straddled the center double yellow line, arms high, body thrumming as a sedan passed, calling out with its horn and swerving. After: nothing. It was unprecedented for my Chicago stands, which I tried not to take as an omen. I closed my eyes, said a little prayer for traffic to my mother that went unanswered. I shrugged, turned back to the sidewalk and down to rejoin the crew.

"This your proof?" V said when I walked into Selma's, pointing down the long bar to Mort's stooped form, his bald head visible just above a trashcan behind the bar.

"In the flesh," I said.

"We just met," she said, raising her bottle.

I nodded and she and Rensauler went back to whatever conversation they were having. I backed away slowly, moving for the bathroom. On my way down the length of the bar I gently waved Mort's way when he looked up. I was surprised he remembered my name when we shook hands.

"I'm good at this," he said when I asked him if he were telepathic or clairvoyant or what. His index finger went to his temple. "All up here."

I disappeared into the bathroom and when I came out highlights from the day's race at the Indianapolis "Brickyard" track were playing above Mort's head.

"You see this? They're calling him 'Turn' now," Mort said, sliding a beer this way and making reference to Turner Bascombe, undisputed "maverick" on the circuit. Bascombe hadn't yet even won a race, as Mort told, but still the commentators seized his every move on the track as opportunity to glorify the beauty of his persona, that of the rebel. (He was good enough that he stood at ninth in the overall points standings, with a clear path to making the final 10-race playoff among the top racers, Mort told.) Bascombe on the surface seemed to resemble so many of the younger drivers—clean-cut, a devotee of tiny oval sunglass lenses in wildly overpriced plastic wraparound frames. He counted as a rebel primarily by virtue of a reputation for hard partying he didn't try to keep in the background—something of a lush-bastardized throwback to the rough-and-tumble roots of the league's early-early days—and a complementary style of competition. What's more, his team was virtually alone in employing a black guy and a man born to Mexican parents, and Bascombe, though just as Southern and white as so many participants on the circuit, was thus also seen as emblematic of a new era. Pressmen, even the good-old-boy network among the racing press, were so hard-up for a novel approach to bolster their sport's historically newfound and at once floundering popularity on the TV networks that they latched onto Bascombe like he was God's gift. All they were doing was going around in circles, "turning left," as went the derisive old adage of nonfans.

I wasn't acquainted with the young driver's hard-nosed sincerity at that point, so I half-rolled my eyes in comic dismissal of Mort's mirror-gaze preoccupation with him.

I drained the beer, scoffing, saying "he finished fucking 30th in a field of 40, Mort." A horrible showing in today's event.

Mort waved me away.

"He's the real thing," he said. "You watch." His new nickname was acquired via a move he'd made on Montuck Jr., son of the great and all-powerful—and dead—Sammy Montuck, a few weeks back, Mort said. A feud developed, subsequently, as young "Turn" Bascombe had gotten the inside run on Montuck but didn't manage to clear the young man's left bumper on his way through the pass, thus "turning" him right into the wall at Pocono. You weren't supposed to do that, of course—not to mention that it was borderline damn homicidal, suicidal at that—but on account of his popularity, members of the chattering class were saying with no small amount of derision tinged with that balls-to-the-wall trainwreck glee, Bascombe got off scot-free.

"He's done it every week since to somebody," Mort said. "He'll be getting death threats soon, if he isn't already."

He'll be drowning in debt back in the pack, I thought, rolling my eyes a little for Mort's benefit before gazing down the bar at the lovely V and the mustachioed interloper, who were prattling on in what appeared to be absolute enthrallment with each other.

"She's a catch," Mort said, nodding compulsively, running his hand over his bald head as if through the phantom of his hair. "She means something to you. Let me tell you something here. You'll never get anything done without trust, old boy." Mort nodded some more.

"Yeah," I said, and I tried not to think about that.

"Jealousy is useless." He asked me about my show—again, big surprise he actually remembered that—and I was drunk enough to grant him the assumption that I was a working artist, not some guy who'd stumbled into his shit. I told him it was coming along.

"Standing in traffic," I said. "A fine metaphor?"

Mort smiled, and I remembered who'd given me that line. I turned and found she was watching me as Rensauler, his back to me, talked on. Now I smiled and looked away. She grabbed my elbow a minute later, bringing me back from the TV.

"You're ready to go," she told me.

Something in my face, I guess. I swayed a little on my stool.

"It's true," I said. But I was too drunk to face Rensauler without a little bad blood seeping into the interaction.

"What was with the crowd tonight, man? Why so small?" I said. Not that I didn't like him by now: for the failures among us, the defeated had infinitely more charm than the victorious, after all. Rensauler was just a guy.

But he surprised me.

"Hell," he said. "I was expecting as much. You realize that no one reads anything but their own blogs and web-stats reports anymore, don't you?"

I was incapable of confrontation, in the end, so I smiled and kept shut and let V lead me out—"We are out here!" Rensauler screamed as I left, raising his fist high—and back down Halsted to my car, which was parked in the Greektown lot. Rensauler stayed behind.

"He likes you," V said.

I kept my eyes focused hard on what my feet were doing.

"Is everything OK?" she said.

"He likes *you*," I said. "But yes. OK. I'm just drunk and confused."

"About?"

"Just general," I said, stumbling on another sidewalk crack. "General confused, generally."

We walked on. V insisted she drive. Though she'd never driven my car, the dilapidated Ford Taurus that had surprised me by making it all the way to Chicago from S.C. one more time.

"Be careful," I told her. "You can't really gas it through 90-degree left turns, like a full left turn, you know? It slips out of gear."

"Maybe you *should* drive," she said.

"I can't," my head hung low. I could hardly think.

"It's the transmission," I said, "stupid fucking automatic transmission." We pulled away, busting a left-turn U on Jackson back west (*ka-chunk*, throttle, *wheeeeeeee-bang*, *grrrr* ...) to take the city streets instead of the freeway. She moseyed through remaining left turns like a grandmother, prompting enraged horn honks and the ire of even a bicyclist or four out this late, two of whom, their helmets and wraparound night-shield glasses flashing reflections of streetlights and headlamps, menacingly hurled insults into my open window. I only nodded at them, raised my palm, stupidly, in the universal gesture of greeting, of goodwill.

We didn't talk. I realized at one moment that V was just cruising near-west- and west-side neighborhoods, passing various spots I reckoned from my many stands with Trey these past weeks.

"We were out here," I said when we rolled east by the scant remnants of the Cabrini-Green project. V nodded like she knew what I was talking about. "Here too," when we passed Halsted/North, "and here," as V pulled into a covered lot for an all-night diner at North/Ashland.

"Let's sober you up," she said, and we ordered plates of eggs and hashbrowns and grease.

"What is it you want from me?" she said, her gaze boring into me as my own settled somewhere just past her shoulder.

I didn't answer.

I was hungry.

I smiled halfheartedly.

The syrupy Southern-ish waitress—"Here you are, honey"—

71

brought the food, and as I concentrated and knifed into the cheap tube of breakfast sausage on my plate I felt V's hand on my shoulder and looked up in time to catch a distorted sight of her puckered lips before she planted a kiss on my forehead, like a grandmother. It woke me up. She sat back down, smiling furiously. I laughed nervously. I finished the plate off in five minutes.

She drove us then in what I imagined as great figure eights through the city neighborhoods, and I was reminded of a story I'd read in Carl's little magazine in which an astronaut, emboldened by years of experience and his recent coronation by a board somewhere, somehow, as "Astronaut of the Year," orders his driver, the teller of the story, around the city, demanding that he be taken to strip clubs, expensive French restaurants, all the while wearing a giant silver space helmet, drunk, passing out intermittently as the driver pines over his long-lost height-challenged-women's-clothing-model ex-girlfriend. Both men are astoundingly sad, and the story ends in a moment of empathy near as syrupy as our waitress' voice.

"I always wanted to be an astronaut," I told V as she turned toward my neighborhood. I put my left hand on her shoulder, ran my fingers up into her hair, gently stroking her head like we might have been the very vision of an old married couple on a long run. She stopped in front of what I quickly realized was her apartment.

"Is that a good answer?"

She shot me a truly confused look, then: "Can you drive home?" she said, turning in the driver's seat to face me. She smiled, now.

I blinked.

"Yeah," I said.

She lingered, smiling, and I smiled back at her, then made to get out of the car. She got out, too, bounded up the steps to the three-flat and blew me a kiss from the doorstep.

I stood there for a moment before motoring away.

It was verging on 2 a.m. when I arrived at Ralph Cash's apartment, and, smashed though I might still have been, I did not hit the mattress immediately. I sat at my father's desk and peeked through the blinds into the courtyard for V, who was not there. I wishfully imagined her overcome with emotion, trekking the blocks that separated us to save me from my bashful stupidity. Yes, stupidity, or something like it. I pushed back Carl's laptop and placed my hands flat, palms down, on the desk, closed my eyes, conjuring my squat-bodied father here, in my place. The image would not resolve—he never sat here, used the desk for absolutely nothing, as I could tell. Its drawers were empty. *You may locate your ultimate salvation* tacked up on the wall to my left. Salvation was an immeasurable quantity, I thought, inscrutable, really—I'd never been one for religious feeling or thinking but for a faint edge of fatalism in my dealings. Any prayer I ever uttered—and only in moments of high fear—was to my mother.

I moved to the recliner, anchored my hands on the armrests and laughed at myself, at my father, long and loud, eyes closed, body swaying in the chair no matter how hard I held on. Would that I were a detective! An heroic sleuth! Capable of gargantuan feats of deduction. A clue, a signal, a sign. I opened my eyes to the weak light of the bare bulb hanging from the ceiling in the room's center. I donned my suit and lay directly under the light, which doubled, tripled its intensity. Maybe my dreams were peaceful on the floor. Maybe they were tumultuous.

I don't remember.

But I did sleep, that much is certain. I woke in the light reflecting off my body and the increasingly familiar sound, slowly becoming more and more insistent, of pebbles hitting the little portal window above the bed. I quite automatically rose, put on the helmet, climbed onto the rickety chair, wobbly atop the mattress. I waited, another pebble cracking the window before I opened it. Below, in the alley in comparable dark, stood a youngish man with a crew-cut head of hair and a black suit and tie.

"Son of Ralph Cash?" he said, all business, reaching into the inside pocket of his jacket.

I winced. "Yes," I said. A flash of light erupted in the relative exterior darkness.

"Here is a piece of paper," producing a small envelope and moving to hand it up to me.

"It's an envelope," I said. I did not take it.

"Please," he said. He looked away.

"Are you embarrassed?"

73

"Yes, well ..."

"I'm sorry," I said. "I didn't mean to embarrass you."

"It *is* a piece of paper, don't you know?" He flipped it over now twice in his hands, inspecting its structure excited, agitated. "In fact! It is even continuous! Or contiguous? This piece of paper is merely folded and glued to itself to create this structure!"

"Yes," I said. "It is in the *form* of an envelope."

"Well done!" he said. "But also there is another piece of paper inside, isn't there. I'm sorry," now letting out a big sigh, his body deflating just to perk back into its formerly rigid posture. "Here are *two* pieces of paper!" he shouted, delighted again. "Please." He thrust his hand up to me. I took the envelope and lost balance on the chair, nearly falling backward into the apartment. When I righted myself and made to open the envelope, the well-dressed young man in the alley below let out a distressed yelp that sounded so distraught I nearly lost my balance again.

"There are instructions!" he cried.

"OK, OK."

"You are not to open the envelope—the outer piece of paper!—until, well, after your show, until you are home, in Ingalls."

"Ingalls? What the hell is that? I'm not going ... Who are you?"

He looked up and down the alley, then, flustered, scurried off then to the south. I opened the envelope as quickly as I could, and inside, to my absolute astonishment, in a hand closely resembling the angular scrawl now tacked to the wall on the side of a piece of a box meant to house reflective roadworker vests was written, "Stupid men are given to exclamation! To be sure!"

Chapter 7

Trey and I were in the McIntyre + Feldman space, a wide-open expanse of blondwood floor but for a single white drywalled column in the center. Hung in a magnificent array on three walls were oversize prints of pictures Trey had taken of me these past weeks, arranged by neighborhood. On the center column: four shots taken in the Loop, each named by the nearest intersection. In the black-and-white "Madison/State" I stood in front of the famous former Carson Pirie Scott department store display windows turned slightly to the side with arms out, forming a blank 0. On the south wall the various neighborhoods of the south side were represented, on the west wall the west, north the north, and across the length of the picture windows at the front of the east-facing storefront were pasted outward-facing five-foot-high posters with a gigantic letter each in stark white against a black background, spelling out S – H – I – N – I – N – G   M – A – N to the streetwalkers. Viewed from behind, it made sense long as you could read backward.

"That's a shame," Trey said as I looked on, east.

I shrugged. The totality was impressive. There was plenty to admire. We'd been at it, setting up, all day long, under the watch and subject to the frequent suggestions of McIntyre himself, who thought Trey was pretty special, I'll say. He thought I was insane, I think, after I told him the story of how'd we'd met, my dive into the back of Trey's truck and the busted finger, the newspaper photograph, the bar. It was fairly unbelievable, I can see now, though my thoughts through most of the interaction—the entire day, really—had been elsewhere.

"I got a problem," I told Trey. The night previous a disastrous bar shift[5] and fifth consecutive day of no contact with V had sent

---

[5]*Thirty minutes in: Blitzed by a girl who came flying by me into the bar before I could even raise my head from the latest issue of* Harper's*, grabbed a half-empty bottle of* Lite *beer from the nearest table (to the astonishment of a yuppie customer), brandished it and motored back my way with the bottle held high just as two young dudes in jeans baggy enough to convert to togas or perhaps capes walked in and I stopped them, their eyes going*

my mind reeling—with the persistent annoyance provided by the drunks, I couldn't bear the suspense: V hadn't answered my two calls to her since our late Sunday night, though she was the lead seamstress on our mass production of reflective suits. I'd tricked myself into believing in the businesslike nature of our relationship the first few days—Carl told me how hard she was working, which told me she was coordinating with him, anyway—but I'd come to a different conclusion over subsequent days.

"What'd we forget?" Trey said.

"I think I'm in love with the girl," I said.

Trey stared at the back wall, his hand going to his chin. He smiled a little, but finally he frowned, lips pursed in concentration. When he spoke he didn't so much as look my way, and his voice conveyed a shocked gravity.

"We have to learn that, too," he said, moving back to continue sliding a leather love seat to a position with other oddly-placed seats around the post in the center of the space. "There's two kinds, the assholes and the lovers. Occasionally, as was the case

---

wide now at the specter of the girl with her glass weapon held high, a furious, enraged and perhaps pained cry escaping her I realized bloody and swollen mouth as she followed the boys back out the door, bringing the bottle down on the head of the lead guy repeatedly, though not hard enough to shatter it and do the damage she wanted done. I followed them out into the street, pulling the girl off of the guy only to realize that her injuries included more than just her mouth—her face was gashed, swollen, and bleeding, in fact covered in blood, various angry welts.

"You knocked out my fucking tooth!" she screamed at the lead dude, a young white kid with a would-be mustache. He sorta looked down at his shoes. "Call the cops!" she screamed at me. "Call them now!" and she wailed in pain and anguish and god-knows-what and the boys ran off down the street, only to swing back around in a gigantic 1980s-model Cutlass to entreat the girl to come with them before the cops showed up. We had a big crowd out in front of the bar by then, and our heckling of the boys and support of the girl cheered her up enough that she laughed wildly at their powerlessness, now. I memorized the car's license plate.

"Stolen," the lead cop among the six that showed up told me, after he'd run it through the computer. The fire department rescue guys joked about the girl's lost tooth, telling me she said she'd had it in her hand when she came in here, one later bending on his way out of the bar and picking up a tightly wadded piece of paper and shouting "Eureka!" and turning my way. "You got any ice to put this on?"

"What?" I said.

"The tooth, man!" he said. And I scurried off in search as they laughed away.

with my longtime mate, though not me, let it be known, the two are joined in the same body."

And I'm one of these?

"He was a player," Trey said, "and he got what he deserved, I guess, but he was an asshole capable of sincere feeling. Problem was he felt too much of it, for too many. Time goes by, my realism won my other side over." He paused. "Actually, yes, I think we've all got a bit of both people in us—we can learn."

"I don't think I've much learned either," I said.

Carl burst in the front door all business as usual, beard wild and unkempt above his rumpled red pinstriped suit. He quickly laid out an itinerary for the night. The suits would be distributed to the gatherers in the alley by 10 p.m., at which point the gallery would have been open for four hours, plenty of time to build excitement, to sell some work, Carl raising his eyebrows to Trey.

He lectured for fifteen minutes, Trey and I nodding along stupidly, and when he was gone we wandered out to the street and picked up the thread like he'd never been here. Trey told me the ways of love were despicable, the cult of need quickly asserting itself over the pleasure or any usefulness of the feeling.

"We need each other to get by, it's sure," he said, "but people think too much about it and worry takes hold and next thing you know you're pondering imbalances of affection and things like this. It's insane."

I remembered Will Theron's lady, Jenny, a white girl who, according to him, had bouts of jealousy matched by none other in human history. His code for these fits, when she'd up and leave him after incidents, the details of which I had no knowledge, was to come into Henry's and announce that it's serious, she took the toothbrush. I remembered my jealous reaction to Rensauler the weekend before.

"Tread softly," Trey said, bursting into a fit of his trademark coughing.

"You oughta get that looked at," I said.

"It's nothing," he said, coughing some more and lighting a cigarette.

He went home down the street a few minutes later to "grab some things," he said. "Be back soon." I lit a cigarette myself and sat out front of the gallery in a tobacco trance to watch the cars go by. At the end of the second smoke, Billy rode up on his bike with a box containing various bottles of wine strapped to his back. He was a splendorous vision, clad entirely in partially reflective yellow, hair tangled, windswept out in gigantic wings from under the sides of his white helmet. I hadn't seen him for a couple weeks, had to be.

"Where's Elsa?" I said, following him inside. He dropped the wine bottles in the rear of the gallery and McIntyre started setting them up.

"Remember the Alamo!" Billy finally said, exaggeratedly huffing and wiping his forehead before forcing a smile. Meaning: The war is not over. "I haven't heard from her for a couple days. She went out to California for some meeting or something. She said she'd be back yesterday." He threw up his hands.

"I hope she's all right," I said.

"Nah," he said. "She's fine. Probably just messing with me. She does that shit all the time. Little games. She's probably with V waiting for me to find her: I never figured her for a needy type like that, but you learn things. Living with someone."

Trey huffed and puffed his way back in, carrying a television and a detachable antenna.

"What time is it?" he demanded, and proceeded to plug in the set.

"Wait-wait-wait," McIntyre, now in his gallerist's black suit, rushing out to intervene.

"It's 5:30," Billy said.

"Just hold on," Trey pushing McIntyre back, "it won't be on for long, trust me." And when he plugged the antenna into the TV's back the local news was just starting.

"Check this shit out," he said. He smiled, eyes fixed on his own image on the screen.

"I want to fly," Trey's picture said, there, as the announcer went on to describe an upcoming report on an event sponsored by the station's affiliate radio station and a well-known energy drink at the main north-side harbor in which participants built homemade flying machines to compete to see who could remain airborne the longest. Here was a quick flash of Trey, his missing front tooth, wiry gray hair pulled back into a tight pony tail, coughing, standing next to a three-wheeled, pedal-powered glider with four propellers mounted on wings. Trey wore a top hat, too, on the television.

"Damn, old man," I said, genuinely amazed. "When'd you find the time?"

His gaze, in thrall to his own image, didn't move from the TV screen, and the subsequent segment focused on Trey's machine, calling him the "only Chicago resident" in a field of mostly regional participants.

He'd spent ten hours or more of every day for the past week, he told the reporter, working on the wings. The contraption did not look particularly air-worthy; the propellers were cut from scrap aluminum. The reporter remained appropriately hokey and skeptical up until the final moments of the segment as he, the anonymous-looking TV man, walked around Trey's loft space—he did finally come to the ultimate question, the response a teaser already heard in the introduction.

The newscaster leveled a serious, inquisitive gaze at Trey as he asked, "Why do this? Why take the time? The prize is not much, really, a couple hundred bucks. But you've devoted all this time...." He gave the impression he really couldn't understand, and he did it mighty well, I say.

The editors prolonged the delay before the response with a further pan across Trey's frames, his little kitchen, before snapping back to the old man.

"Well," Trey said, and the cameras cut hard again across the expanse to focus close onto the grimy window where I'd stood and looked downtown that psychotic morning those weeks ago: you could just case the outline of the skyline through the glare cast by the sun falling on dirty panes before it came into a hazy kind of focus with a continuing zoom effect.

The shot cut back to Trey, and, the old man appearing a veritable sage in his top hat, he said, "I want to fly."

Billy let loose a war whoop that jolted me from the trance of television, then clapped furiously.

"All right!" he screamed. Trey let his gaze be sundered from the box and smiled now at us all, taking a bow. Even McIntyre dropped his pretension and slapped Trey on the back for a moment.

"That's tomorrow?" I said.

"Yeah," Trey said.

"I'm there, man."

"Me too," Billy said, just as the main program anchor announced Trey's show tonight, looking at her watch and saying, "That's 'The Shining Man,' photos by Trey Olden, at—" struggling for the name, "—McIntyre and Feldman."

McIntyre's eyes widened in fright.

"We've never been on TV before," he said.

Trey smiled as the gallerist rushed to the back for final preparations and Billy rushed on home to get cleaned up before making his way back. Everybody was doing something, here. Chicago was an electrifier—I'd become another person, but the line cook in me kept me from fully participating in the endeavor. McIntyre didn't seem to mind, nor Feldman, a middle-aged lady with a stiff demeanor and beautiful red hair, who showed up shortly. As gallery-goers ambled in, Trey did most of the talking—and Carl and McIntyre, and Feldman to a lesser degree. She chatted with the drinkers over a table at the back, pouring wine and jotting down purchasers' information when one or another materialized.

Trey's approach was to simply answer questions, whereas in the first two hours McIntyre and Carl both had told my story ten times each, amping my character into something of a downbeat superhero grotesque, an eccentric for the people, shedding light on the plight of the late-night prowlers, the streetwalkers, the third-shift workers. At the end of each telling, they'd contrive to be in my vicinity, feigning surprise at the fact that I happened to be standing right next to them, yes, here he is, the man himself. *A touched stooge*, it felt like they were saying, a Neanderthal who, under the veneer of imbecility, had the capacity for astute insight, wildly brilliant thoughts. I wasn't comfortable the first three times, but as Trey began securing sale after sale, I warmed to the role. I didn't speak much, put on a docile humility that, rather needless to say, wasn't necessarily an integral part of my natural character. Though that might not be entirely true. *The region*, as Billy would have it, mandated at least an outward show of politesse of all its children, something none of us are quite unaware of.

I began to see Carl's approach to me—he was that convincing—as nothing other than sincerity, and maybe it was. The bearded freak exuded the excitement this night of a ten-year-old on a particularly bountiful Christmas morning.

He pulled me aside during a brief lull in the gallery-goers' unceasing momentum—some had left, others surely yet to arrive—and confided, "This is what I live for, man," his hands planted firmly akimbo, eyes full of the stark unreality of the place. It was fun, I had to admit, and in the face of extremes even the most original of us resort to speaking in clichés. But Billy then sprang my way and he was looking glum.

My mind shot to an image of V, her delicate hand covering her eyes as if a child playing peek-a-boo.

"You heard about the free publicity," Billy said to Carl, who nodded vigorously.

"We've done good," Carl said. Carl was next to incapable of speaking in the terms of marketing and PR. It was his greatest strength, though it occasionally left him tongue-tied in casual conversation, searching for a way to describe the latest Motorola cellphone, some way other than using whatever silly name they had given it—or as in this situation, he simply let the act going on around him speak for itself.

"I took the box of suits out back," Carl said.

"Is V here?" I asked.

"I have not seen the lady," he said.

"Showtime's almost here," Billy said, holding up his watch for me.

"I've got one, too." I smiled and gazed at my own wrist. I was looking forward to the streets, if for no reason other than that it afforded the opportunity to see V exploded, all lit-up with light. A well-made-up lady in a leopard-spotted faux-fur coat strolled in at that moment and Carl bounded away.

"Still no sign of them," I said.

Billy just shook his head as he watched Carl's progress to the front door, and I felt a little twinge in my heart and with a shocking pull of memory turned to the leopard-spotted lady myself. Her face, prominent if not too-round cheek bones, wrinkles forming at the outside corners of her eyelids, a pointed and slightly upturned nose.

"Ass," I said.

"Huh?" Billy whipping his head around to me, utterly confused.

"The lady who just walked in," I said as Carl started in on her with his painting of me as a midnight savant. "She was in on the interview I had at the magazine, editorial assistant."

"Oh. 'Dispatches from the New American Economy.' You made out with her, didn't you." And Billy snickered now and turned to the back of the room.

I was surprised he'd actually read it.

"Hell yes, man! Carl told me about it. Funny stuff!"

I hadn't made out with anyone—one line's worth of a slapstick makeout session in the brief bit of silly theater was my little fabulist paean to my own repressed vanity—and I told Billy as much.

"She is pretty, though," I said.

"She's fucking hot," Billy said, "though in the overly-made-up-trying-to-look-ten-years-younger kind of way. I'd do her, with opportunity. I like old ladies." She might've been 40. Probably not even quite there yet.

He shrugged, then looked hard at me.

"You're blushing. Dude, so she's here. Who cares."

We both pivoted to the entrance in time to see Carl pointing me out in the crowd and (I think her name was) Katherine's jaw dropping open in recognition for a slight moment before she re-assumed cool and affecting attention on Carl.

"I saw that," Billy said.

"Fuck," I said. "Let's move. Are folks out back yet?"

"I ain't been out there," Billy said. He tipped back his plastic wineglass. We started walking that way. "I'm pretty fed up with this, man."

"Tonight?"

"Elsa—women. Several years ago I thought I'd figured everything. I swore them all off, man, no shit. That's why I went back down south—for some time away. And here we go again, a distinct tilt in commitment, you know? The seesaw is off motherfucking center." He shook his head some more and stopped to refill his cup. I walked out back to find them, Elsa and V both, donning their reflective suits.

"It's going to be hot in this thing, maybe," Elsa said. She pulled it down over her top and tied the legs like chaps around her leather jeans. Meanwhile, V giggled at every pull and tug of her own, before buttoning it up the front and raising her arms high over her head, tramping toward a streetlight illuminating the alley.

She deepened her voice, "I am the Shining Woman. And I"—a seam at her shoulder ripped loudly—"a-and I'm not a very good seamstress." I congratulated her on the buttons—*nice!*—and she laughed some more and strolled back over to us.

Now that she had it on, Elsa inspected her own suit, frowning. There were maybe ten others out here, folks I didn't know, and they multiplied exponentially over the next twenty minutes. V seemed to know everyone, the eyebrow-pierced boys on bikes fresh from the Friday Critical Mass ride and the women who looked like they had just come from office jobs in the Loop. She made the rounds with the box of suits. Heads swiveled, sizing one and another up in the circle of light falling from the streetlight and reflecting from them a shimmering island in the alley out here. Calming yet energizing light, its power in its association with the self—this is me, this is us.

"Billy loves you," I told Elsa. I tipped back the last of my glass and she laughed. As did I. I had no idea why I said it and I didn't care.

"I know this," Elsa said. "He tells me all the time."

I felt like Carl feels, maybe, in that moment—cool, unaffected by any melee of products and services and their attendant nomenclatures, full-fledged languages.

"I suppose you want something from me," Elsa said. I let the situation speak for itself, my eyes firmly on V as she snaked through the crowd. I said a little prayer: Maybe I'd been wrong about her debutante leanings. Maybe not.

"V likes you," Elsa smiling now. "I don't know if I'd call it *love*. I know she wouldn't. She likes a lot of people."

I couldn't hold the pose. My head fell and I busied myself with my own suit.

"Billy's looking for you," I said.

"As is he always," Elsa said with a little upward lilt.

She moved away and I snuck back in and poured a new glass of wine, no sign of the leopard-spotted editorial assistant, the few gallery-goers left I imagined amazed by the explosion of light with my entrance. A trick of the suit—you were only really aware of your own presence by act of imagination outside of the lit-up countenances in front of you, the strangely off-kilter shadows cast by objects in front of and to your sides, depending on the orientation of light coming your way. Billy was by the wine table, Feldman long gone, with a bottle of red in his hand. He raised it high in my diffuse spotlight as I approached and then poured into my own plastic cup. He took a deep breath as if for a grand toast, but then just deflated without saying a word, tipping back the bottle in an outrageous gulp.

"She's here," I said, taking a sip with him and gesturing behind me, to the alley.

"I don't think I can do this, dude," he said. "Too drunk." He tipped the bottle again. "They'll arrest me for sure and it'll be drunk and disorderly."

"Get out here," I said, grabbing him by his shirtsleeve and pulling him onward. He held hard to the bottle. We were outside before I could persuade him to put it down. Elsa came over shaking her head.

"Billy Billy," she said. He smiled like a dog caught with its mouth in the cat food. He put the bottle down and hugged her too hard, too long. I backed away, gazing on at Elsa's unsmiling face above his shoulder.

Carl directed the proceedings, herding me up front for a "speech, man, speech"—which I did not give—herding everyone else down around the end of the alley and onto Halsted, on which we simply walked. A marching band of shining men played its romps—trumpet, trombone, tuba, bass drum, snare drawing the residents of this strip of Halsted out of their third-floor windows. The traffic lined up behind us, quietly idling or turning down side streets we passed. No horn honks, the lot curiously placid, accepting of its fate. We marched, the band played. There was by design no chanting, no talking. Billy joined me at the point in solidarity, he said, but really he just wanted to gush.

"She's threatening me!" he yelled over the drumbeats bouncing up from behind us. "Jesus Christ!" He spat as he weaved along. The glimmer of tears shone in his eyes. I put my right arm up over his shoulder and we wobbled on in embarrassed silence.

Our shimmering phalanx had made its way up to the business district at Roosevelt before the cops showed up. The band quieted, and we slowed our march to a crawl as three squad cars maneuvered up ahead to block our passage on Halsted.

84

Soon enough we were stopped, hearts aflame, beating out of our chests—of mine, at least. I tamped down the anxiety and skipped up a little ahead of the long lines of the Shining People now stretched out for the better part of a block down Halsted. I jumped atop a stone planter built into the sidewalk but minus any particular plants. I channeled fear and elation into a single breath— "We are out here!" I screamed, then again, and again, nothing more, raising my fist high—the small horde came on, responding with a roar so exuberant, so very boisterous, it brought chills with its vibrations through me. I smiled and continued standing as a man in a business suit came strolling my way up from the direction we'd come. He was just a diagram at first, a white, vertically bisected V surrounded by the black of his suit, but as he got closer I felt a shock of recognition. When he handed me the note the recognition banged its way up my spine with the chills I already felt. The note read, "He is watching." I felt very conspicuous now in my ill-fitting silver suit. The little man strolled confidently away, invisible in his uniform. Carl had begun herding everybody back the way they'd come, but I turned and, paradoxically, inconspicuously gave chase—constituting the main thread to the evening. I was out here.

But so was Billy[6] , who was cognizant of the Suited Man and

---

[6]*When it was over, this time we disappeared and left V and Elsa to whatever method of invisibility they preferred, and Billy cried, I swear. After it all, he cried—like a depressed man, he seemed to revel in it, I couldn't believe it, I couldn't deal with it, I couldn't. We got rid of our suits near the end of the parade route and after a rendezvous with the Suited Man followed the path Rensauler and V and I had taken to Selma's after the bike-accident victim's benefit. Mort opened bottles for us and I tried to comprehend the tears in the man Billy's eyes.*

"He OK?" Mort wanted to know, confidentially, ever the bartender, assuming Billy was blasted out of his skull though genuinely worried, sure, attempting discretion.

Billy heard it. "Remember the Alamo!" he wailed, now, and Mort threw up his hands and walked away.

I only put my arm around the boy and smiled down the bar, knocking Billy on the back and loudly—too loudly, garnering the disgusted looks of the old men down there—proclaiming him drunk and sappy over a woman—a woman!—who loved him and was hard on him.

"Hard!" I bellowed. "Just hard, that's all!"

We were drunk.

As the place filled up, Billy increasingly wanted closure.

"Let's end the night, man, but we've gotta hash this shit out before it's over," he said. "This is the night, man, this is it." And in more than one way he wanted it done, out.

my interest, and I soon found him following me up Halsted at a small remove. I waited for him, keeping the little Suited Man in my sights. Carl, back behind the bushy-headed Carolinian, had paused his herding efforts and watched us. Billy caught up.

"Who is that guy?" he said.

"You see him, too?"

"Do I *see* him? Of course I see him! Little bald guy dressed like he's a fucking banker," he said.

Billy, brow furrowed, walked on—I watched him, then followed. But he then motioned forward excitedly. The Suited Man was gone.

"He went into that alley," said Billy.

It wasn't an alley, though, it was a street—a tiny street off this row of cookie-cutter shops on Halsted. And when we turned down it, the little man wasn't there. "That fucker," I muttered.

"Who is he?"

"A messenger," I said. I began disrobing—removing the suit, anyway.

"Listen," he said, tears clouding his eyes again but quickly drying as he laid his less than carefully considered case, "dude, I came back here for her, because she wanted me to, for her and her idiotic short-film-making career, for her eyes and ears, tits, for her pussy, man, and I know it sounds fucked-up, but what do I have for it? She's playing power games with me, or seems to be playing—what is that? A gal takes off and leaves you for two weeks though she claims to love you, doesn't even call or email or text the whole time she's gone. Fuck, man."

I was silent. Mort was a statue six feet down the bar, an old George Washington just after the cherry tree, maybe—all disavowal, incredulity ... I didn't hear that. I was silent.

Billy went on. "I know it's shitty of me, I guess."

"No shit, man," I said.

He turned to me: "You think so?"

I knocked back my beer. We could be anything. We could be assholes readily enough, as Trey had learned so long ago.

"Not just shitty—infantile, I guess, which is probably what you're thinking. You let it get to your sense of manhood. Your self-interest won't let you be happy for her success, maybe? It's ugly, yes, and you know it is but you can't help but feel it. Rationalizing her 'power games'—calling them that, even, coming up with an armature under which to talk about it and make yourself feel better in the end. It's baby shit, that's all. You, my friend, are a baby."

"Here here," he said, shaking his head now, wiping his eyes.

Carl pushed open the door to Selma's and raised his arms high, howling when he saw us. "What the fuck happened to the very life of the journey?" he screamed.

"Who the fuck is this?" Mort said, though he was smiling as Carl put me in what

"What are we marching for?" Billy said—he began ripping the flimsily stitched thing from his body.

"Unanswerable questions," I said, still scanning the street, which dead-ended not a block away. "Besides, we're standing now. For beer, how about that? We march for beer."

My eyes darted over every crevice here, but then a couple cops on foot stopped at the corner on Halsted behind us, where we'd just been. The taller of the two muttered something to his partner, motioning our way, where we were by now out of our reflective suits—they sat in a crumpled pile at our feet.

"Walk," I said, "for beer," and Billy understood and we proceeded to the little street's dead end, at which point Billy looked back and saw that they were coming after us.

"Run," Billy said, but I didn't. There was nowhere to go.

"Run," Billy repeated, grabbing my arm and pulling me into a space between two buildings barely big enough for a man. We were no men, though, and we fit. He ran, and I gingerly began to allow my feet to propel me through the darkness. "C'mon! There's

---

amounted to a sleeper hold that *Nature Boy Ric Flair might have been proud of. I hoped the figure-4 leg lock wasn't going to follow. Billy didn't bother to look up from his beer.*

On Carl's red-pinstriped coattails came striding a crew of formerly Shining People, Elsa and V among them, and the music on the juke seemed to crow even louder. Carl began a dance in the center of the room, Billy stood, making a point of not looking in the direction of our friends or foes, and I focused my attention on Mort.

"How about a shot of Beam," I said.

My brief time in Chicago had been a gold-plated dream I didn't know I had with this ever-so-enthusiastic set of people—a secret wish gilding the muddle of the ho-hum: that long-away look in the eyes of folks passed on the street at all hours. It's vacant, steely, inapproachable. These cats were different. They were all here now, but I focused on Mort.

"Is that your real name, anyway?" I said.

"Morton, of course," he said.

I conjured the little boy in the bald old man, or tried to, a reckoning complete with bronze-cast baby shoes and everything.

"Morton it is," I said, absurdly. I knocked back the shot and asked for another. I told him—haltingly, as he scampered around serving the growing coterie of patrons this night—the story of my lost father, the short version that included only his disappearance, not the resurrection.

"I had no idea," Mort muttered, giving pause.

It seemed like it might have happened years ago, now.

Thirty minutes passed with the world roaring around me and then I wondered what

87

space," I heard Billy say up ahead. The two behind me now I could hear, grunting and shouting for us to stop, but as I plunged from the tiny alley into the square by the bookstore at Roosevelt and Halsted, the blockade two hundred yards off to our right, an unseemly curse rang out from the little alleyway.

"I'm stuck!" one of the cops said to his partner, his voice then rising in hysteria. "Oh shit, I'm stuck, man! Help! Help!"

Billy smiled, then pointed across Roosevelt, where stood the Suited Man, beckoning us. We marched, following the shadowy figure into the dark of the University of Illinois campus—*Did you see him? Where'd he go? Oh, he's behind that bush. Bullshit!*—and finally lost all trace of him at the exit of the campus this side of the freeway across from Greektown and its little main drag of shops catering to tourists in what once was actually a Greek immigrants' community. Before we got to the joint where Rensauler's party had taken place, we stopped in Pegasus, perhaps the best of the restaurants on the strip, Billy said, and wolfed down

---

we'd got out of our time—I remembered fondly a recent Friday at this Greek joint downtown. Pegasus, it was called, and everyone was fresh off work at five and I don't even remember how it happened—likely Billy said he knew a place, and that was that—but we ended up all of us but V hunched over the bar mulling over the finer points of the flyer in progress for our show, and Billy had some line illustrations he'd done of the Shining Man, of me, thick marker lines jutting off said Man's form, a cartoon freeway receding in linear perspective to the top of his head. Elsa scratched T - R - A - F - F - I - C in bold script with a Sharpie across the top and Trey Olden produced the photo he'd taken of me in my silver suit out on the expressway, framing its placement on the page with his thumb and index finger. We must've talked for hours about paper types and a screen printer Billy knew and we were doing this, however small and whatever it was—which is not to say Billy didn't lament his sore knees, the daily woe of the bike messenger, or Elsa her back, tied up in knots from the monotonous at-the-computer editing she'd been at, Trey his burgeoning framer's arthritis—this isn't me, we all said, but whatever was we'd not know but for these short few moments at work, a unit—not to say even that we didn't go on and do the thing that kept us regular and get trashed on the hospitality of the Greek men behind the winged horse's bar.

I called for another whiskey and when Mort came over with it I knocked it back.

"Morton sir," I said, "what the hell gets you through? You know, the day and all that."

"It's just work," he said, smiling. He liked his name. "It ain't nothing," he said.

An old guy, a regular, entered. As Mort moved to pour him a beer, the man looked over the melee in the center of Selma's and moved to the jukebox himself, dropping a few quarters into it. And though I can't swear he played it, a song from another era arose, a simple slacker-pop riff over an ever-more simple, shuffling drumbeat. More than thirty years young, the song, but its particular style and impressionistic poetry had accompanied me these months

plates of chicken, pita, salad. I told Billy the story of that strange night—what purported to be a note from my father delivered through a window from the alley.

"And that little guy is your delivery man?" Billy said.

"Yeah."

"Creepy." He shuddered, though our small chase seemed to have left him in better spirits. The night wasn't over yet. Once we were sated, the magnanimous bartender here upped the ante and brought out a bottle of ouzo he said he'd smuggled to the States, pouring the clear liquid over ice in three small glasses, where it quickly transformed to a milky white.

"You're Greek?" I asked him.

"Turkish," he said. "Efkaristo! Salud! Cheers! Thank you!" nonsensically lifting his glass, we ours.

"To love," Billy said.

I couldn't commit to it. Billy shot his, knocking it back in one gulp—I sipped. The bartender gave the boy a wide-eyed look.

---

around the city, really. All over town in the new century. If it was on the juke old women and little boys alike seemed to flip to it. Every bartender or DJ in the city played it, too, if happen there wasn't a box around. You know the one. "Planet Queen," T-Rex, it's got it all, really. Space aliens in flying saucers, dreams of daughters, chorus: absolutely ecstatic.

"Love is what you want."

Man, I knocked back yet another whiskey now as the vocal soared through the dumpy little place, waving to Mort for another. He poured it.

"Yeah," I said, nodding. "Thanks, Morton." He laughed.

I'd spent weeks here wasting time with the boys—Billy and Carl and Trey, others—the girls, hour atop hour whiled away as the real thing, the winged beast to take our collars between its teeth and carry us on to happy times, might have been right under our noses, right here with us, alongside the griping and moaning about jobs and the lack. I mean ... I turned in my chair and caught Elsa holding up her phone as video camera, its lens focused on the now swaying Billy, and I hoped against hope for a reconciliation. Trey hobbled in through the front door wearing his leather airman's cap, which he removed and put on my head.

"Happy birthday," he said.

"You're not giving me this," I said. It'd been his father's, a Korean War-era navy pilot.

"You're right," Trey said. "It ain't Christmas." And he took it back, but not before I'd caught my reflection in the mirror on the back bar—my hair curled out from either side like a bumpkin's, like Billy's. But I thought for a second that he was wrong: it might well have been Christmas, cause I had it here with the lot of them, love—if it's just the truth, like somebody wrote long ago. They were it for me. And before it all went sour with sorrow, as it most certainly would by the end of the night, as it so often did, depresssingly, on my way

89

"I don't think that stuff's safe to shoot," I said, laughing now as the cool fire put ice in my gullet. Billy's eyes crossed—he feigned a swoon and then burst into a fit of laughter.

"Oh God," he said, sorrow filling his face.

"Don't think about her," I said. "Don't even let it bother you. 'Love is whimsical and brutal,' Trey says."

"Fuck Trey. I came back here for that girl."

"She came back here for you," I said. "A lot farther than you came." Elsa hadn't ostensibly come back for Billy, but rather a job with a filmmaker. She'd told me the story one night at Selma's. It'd been years ago now, she said, her return just in time for Billy's father's bovine assault on the city, after which Billy left for South Carolina.

"It was the leaving that's done it, ultimately. I'm killed in her eyes, I've got nothing behind me but bloodlust and balls, only in the sexual sense. I'm an unjust, unfaithful asshole. That's what I fucking am, man."

"C'mon, buddy, c'mon," I rapped him hard on the back. He was repeating the old adage—nothing worse in a woman's eyes than a man with no spine. His trips back and forth over the course of years between here and Carolina he simply couldn't pass off as enterprise, whether or not he'd plotted bombings or networked with fictitious rural-south bike messengers—bearded and tattooed to the nines—or had a change of political heart and signed on with the administration of a Republican governor. Billy, fast approaching middle age, that time when youthful panache and effort

---

to the foul bathroom I dropped some change into the juke myself. By the time I was done in the john that chorus had reared its head and electrified the air. Billy and Elsa were dancing on the bar, now, Trey nodding along with Carl distracted from their deep discussion on stools just below the pair. Mort, even, that old cool man, held an empty glass in each hand over his head and was swaying behind the taps, eyes closed. Elsa aimed her phone down at him as they all danced on.

I smiled, felt like I might cry, maybe. I tapped my foot a bit, then decided to leave them to their bliss for the moment. I wandered into the night outside for a smoke, a little fresh air to keep the burning brighter.

A hooker wobbled up on a pair of disastrously thin heels.

"You know how to get to ..." she began, but I didn't catch the rest of it. The bass rattled Selma's windows at my back, and buoyed by its weight I flew, a great wind, a mythic beast disappearing into the night.

just isn't enough to engender respectability, Elsa knew, was indecisive, unsure about direction, and though I knew this was unlikely to be the way the fine lass might articulate her budding distaste, if it indeed was a budding distaste, I couldn't help but trust in the growing anguish in Billy boy's voice.

I badgered the bartender for two more small glasses of the special swill for our contentment, and we were to have them. We were getting tanked. I longed for a great many things, now, as Billy fought off tears. The drunker he got, the less he could manage. I longed for Trey's cool presence, for Carl's cool magnanimity—we needed talk of world tours, here, of Shining People for savior politicians holding up the traffic of megalopolises the nation over as defense of the soft line on things. Yes, while I was preoccupied with the disappearance of my progenitor and parading for not much more than whimsy, elsewhere a movement was growing, fast approaching and imprinting itself on the minds of the young, funky, and depressed—constituting if not a majority anywhere in 21st-century America certainly a sizeable coterie in Chicago—as a wide and raucous lobby for nothing less than the continuation of the human race. (It may yet prove a decisive historical reinforcement of our direction on the road toward the inheritance of hell, but as of that moment at the bar of Pegasus in Chicago, summertime, it still stood as little more than a mistake.) Billy descended into self-involved mind-funk, and I was slowly captured by much of the same—I watched Pegasus' door, attempting to will Carl into the place. The master of ceremonies might lead us on to greater heights. Or at the very least he might deliver into our greedy little paws the women we so longed to possess on the tails of his trademark red pinstriped coat. Ah, the best of circumstances—to hold emotional bliss and intellectual engagement between thumb and forefinger and drink simultaneously of each. But don't think for a second that I'd mastered this, or mastered any disinterest in self-preservation, either. Here, tonight, I was as worried for Billy, truly—I feared for the boy—as I was worried for myself, for my own happiness. Empathy is crushing.

Just as Billy wanted to cry, my eyes fought their wont to let pour the gushing stuff of self-pity. But before things got too out of hand, I began to write. And write and write, and therein I discovered a few things. One of which was that the Suited Man had settled the matter and it was time for me to leave. The other had to do with synchronicity, symmetry, parallelism, or whatever else you might have called it, between mine own and Billy's stories.

"The last time I was out on Halsted marching it was among a crowd of cows," he said.

"Nothing's too much different this time, eh?" I said.

"My father had plans for me. I still don't really know what they were. Seeing him again after years was too much. I left the next day."

I could feel it there in my bones that I was in for one hell of a mindfuck to come. All the same, a parallel upwelling stretched my tear ducts looking at Billy Jones in the seat next to me all puffy-eyed and pursed-lips. I knew, no matter that how I really wanted my exit to go down would never be possible now—*love is what we want*, we humans, before all—if my father had plans for me, I'd give them a chance.

Chapter 8

Yes, I might have more than a little of that tendency integral to the mad mind of the Southern hedonist to elevate myself to mythic status. A rather swaggering sort of impulse, I know, and I apologize. Yes, I've got that defeated land's impulsive apologetic tendency, too—I'm sorry for everything, forgive me.

My disgust with the shiteating attitudes of Presidents past, present and future as well as the leaders of armed revolutionary collectives is a sort of self-hate, in the end, just as the worry and sickness I felt for my Carolina compatriot, the lout Billy. All the great, truly great or, as it were, fantastically rewarded people over the ages have been full of self-hate. Just look at disgraced broadcaster windbag Bill O'Reilly! Look at Turner Bascombe, a man who played the game a while but who, secretly until I came along, harbored a resentment of his upbringing exceeding in intensity even that of Mind of the South Billy Jones. It was probably him, Turner, who engineered the bombing of the State House monument, the sacred Confederate flag incinerated, become dust carried away by the breeze off the Broad to be shortly replaced with an identical flag unremarked-upon in the newspapers or scholarly journals—until they took the whole thing down those years later.

Here's a toast to forgetfulness, drink up.

Then again, it's true I love myself like any good narcissist would, and as such couldn't think of actually fulfilling my mental pledge to be dust in the wind right off. The next morning in my father's apartment I was reminded of Trey's impending flight before my own. I was dreadfully hungover. How very much ouzo had we drunk? With pounding head I rose from my bed at 10 a.m. and picked up the ringing phone.

"Have you gotten the message?" said the voice on the line— the Suited Man. The hangover lent a devil-may-care confidence to my newly wakened thoughts, so I interrogated the voice as to the whereabouts of my father, and it boomed into my ear the ingratitude of the lot of two-bit messengers of eras gone by—the

93

demand for more specific directives by the humanity on the receiving ends of these would-be Hermes at the same time betrayed our own primary weakness, a disgusting lack of courage to drive the chair farther down onto their throats. The messenger was thus a broken record, skipping back to the same simple directive over and over and over.

"Get thee to Ingalls!" the voice hissed. "Two pieces of paper, one folded and glued so as to resemble an envelope, await your attention outside your door." The connection died. The door from the building to the courtyard banged shut and I flung open the mini blinds behind my father's little table to see the little man turning the corner onto the sidewalk. I was too hungover to give chase, too hungover to bother with the latest message.

Sunlight poured into the apartment, this morning, in any case—real light, unreflected, though refracted, intensified in greenhouse-effect by my apartment's windows. I zombie-walked, heart pounding, to my kitchen to make coffee. I tramped into the bathroom and washed. Only then did I grab the messenger's envelope, inside of which was a map, "Ingalls" marked on it just next to what appeared to indicate the intersection of several large highways, marked only by numbers it was too early to contemplate.

I called V, who agreed to meet me at a coffee shop from which point we might head out to the triumphant end of Trey's saga. Carl had told her all about it last night.

"Where were you and Billy?" she asked, a near-trace of regret punctuating the syllables.

"On another planet," I said. Somewhere between elation and doomed fatalism, happiness at a deal done well and sickness on account of an anticipated future—fat mediocrity was our American inheritance. But let me show you what the aggrieved petulance we imagine love to be can produce.

Turns out I *was* wrong about V.

When I arrived at the coffee shop Carl was sitting across from her.

I wasn't prepared for the impresario's presence, to say the least.

"Well, you're looking plump," I said, grinning sardonically at the unnaturally-skinny Carl. I could manage this, at least. Their faces were smudged with bad sleep. They'd spent the night together. That much was obvious.

94

"Good showing last night, old chap," Carl said.

"We were missing you," V said. Again, the regret. "We went to that old man's bar ... what's it called?"

"Selma's."

"A town near Montgomery, Alabama's," Carl said, grinning smugly. He leaned back in his chair and crossed his arms. "It was a riot in there, brother. Full of people with reflective suits. We need a series, performances in Rome, London ..."

"Goose Creek," I said.

"Goose Creek," said he.

"South Carolina," V explained. I was silent. She smiled a little, then chewed on her nails.

Carl grinned, again, quite aware of V's growing unease, my own.

"Well," he said, finally, beaming Cheshire Cat-style. "You two have interesting things to talk about. I can sense when I'm not wanted." There was nothing to laugh about. He laughed anyway. V didn't beg him to stay, after all. I nodded and wished him a good day.

"Trey is flying today," I said.

"Oh, I know," he said. "I'll see you there." And before he was off he asked about my little suited Hermes. "What was he, FBI or something?"

"We went after him," I said. "Lost him, long story."

"Another time," Carl said, and he departed, he said, for a long morning of thrift shopping. Carl's many ill-fitting (mostly on the too-slim side) suits were all famously west-side thrift finds—straight from the closets of Chicago's skinny mid-20th century players, too small for the rotund men who tended to run things these days. When he left, after escorting V out to the sidewalk for a small goodbye peck on the cheek and a hug, I took my time moseying back to the small table where she now waited. When I did I carried a big coffee and half a muffin I stuffed in my mouth before I began talking to her. It was an asinine way to conduct oneself, but desperate times call for ...

"What's this about FBI?" she said.

"So you and Carl, huh? Somehow I never would have figured it," I got out, crumbs flying. V rolled her eyes and sipped, slowly. "Absolutely *not* FBI. Long story, like I said. So what do you want to do?"

95

She didn't respond, immediately.

"Did you see the paper?"

I hadn't seen any paper, but still I said, "Which one?"

V rolled her eyes as if to quash my question—a paper was a paper and thus facile, painting pictures in brushstrokes of sentences even a first-grader could read. She opened wide a copy of the *Tribune*, in fact, laid across the table right in front of her—there was a small article about the Shining People. The writer didn't cast our march in any particular light. It was a very small item, terse sentences.

A large group of young men and women in reflective body suits stopped traffic on Halsted briefly before police arrived. The leader of the group, whom sources say is a native of South Carolina on the run from charges brought in his home state, is being sought by police for questioning ...

Charges? I sensed Trey working a sensationalist's magic—the item accompanied one of his pictures of the march, after all. And it went on, mentioning a veritable "stampede"—I couldn't help but think of Billy—that followed the police blockade, at which point I looked up from the paper and grilled the apparition across from me (a ray of sunlight had peeked through the riotous late-summer vines covering the shop's storefront windows and alighted upon the sleep-riddled frizz on the top of her head) about the names the story mentioned among the injured. I didn't recognize a single one, though I wondered at the fact that no one had told me of any of this.

"Carl thinks it's a small stain for such a big success," she said.

"*Carl* thinks?" It was something he might say himself, big-picture, third-person, self-interested.

"I think, too," she said.

"I can't believe it ..." I didn't know where I was going with that and so trailed off into nothing. Responsibility weighed on me, though as I continued to scan the piece I might have turned toward Carl's point of view, the succor of 15 minutes and ten copy lines of notoriety so very seductive. My mood perked, and I insisted to V that she accompany me to the lake for Trey's flight. She pursed her lips and grabbed at her paper, still in my hands, but acquiesced eventually. She didn't want to do it, truly, but she felt sorry for me.

I could tell.

"You can't think, really, we've done something important," I said.

She looked at me, wide-eyed, before prizing the paper and moving to pay up and check out. There was no music pumping through the café.

⌛

The energy drink's "Flying Day," as the event was descriptively dubbed, took place in the sun on Belmont harbor, a 30-foot platform nestled in the water at a turn in the concrete-and-steel shoreline so that the audience, lined up on aluminum bleachers on the shore beyond the turn, could get a view. I didn't see Carl anywhere. Nor Trey—crews didn't mingle with the rabble, apparently. But the Shining Band was here, the shape-shifters today decked out in white-bone-on-black-skeleton bodysuits. With every new ascension to the launching platform, each team going through its own version of the theatrics that brought the "style points" that won the perhaps most important award of the competition—showmanship, the $1,000 prize being the only cash payout on the docket—the shining/skeleton band let roar a caterwaul of dissonance that effectively muted whatever the team up on the platform was doing.

They were here on behalf of our man Trey.

Maybe not. Judges or "Flying Day officials" were effectively mum on the shenanigans, so perhaps the Shining Band was on official payroll.

An hour or more into our time there, still no Carl in sight, our moods had improved after consumption of a number of tiny 10-ounce beers a vendor sold for $5 apiece and that I paid for with door cash. I tried to laugh at V's jokes. She was playing with me, telling whoppers derelicts from back home in Camden told her the summer after her senior year of high school, the last one she'd spent there. A joke about a country boy taking his first trip into town and coming upon the splendiferous neon lights of a bar blinking BILLIARDS, BILLIARDS, BILLIARDS and which, upon country boy's entry into the bar's dank climes, reveals nothing of the excitement its exterior had inspired in his bones. Nonetheless, country boy pulls up a stool with inappropriate eagerness and signals the at once sanguine and cynical barkeep, who carefully wipes down a glass on his way to country boy's spot.

97

"What'll y'have?" he says.

"Glass of billiards," says the country boy, and here in V's story the perspective shifts slightly to the equally myopic perspective of the barkeep, who mutters small insults for the country boy to himself thinking he's got a joker on his hands, trolls to the back room whereupon he pisses rather haughtily into a frosty mug, wiping the edges clean of steamy dribble, finally setting the glass down in front of the boy, smiling sideways.

"One glass of billiards. That'll be $2.50."

And then he steps back as the country boy takes a long draught, wincing at the bitterness.

The barkeep swallows his astonishment, which over the next 20 minutes will dwindle considerably as country boy continues to sip, and sip, and sip, until finally he rams the glass hard onto the bar with a fake satisfaction he might have seen in a movie if he'd ever been to the theater—but country boy is country through and through, tipping the cow might have been an entertainment, or catapulting cow pies, stealing watermelons ...

"Will y'have another, good sir?" barkeep genial now, though flabbergasted and genuinely full of wonder at the will in this man.

"You know," says the country boy, "I'm gonna tell you something, sir, and that's that I've had many a glass of billiards in my life"—pause, chuckle, back deadpan—"but if I didn't know better I'd swear that was piss."

The punch line. The kind of joke you have to really oversell, accordingly V burst into forced laughter after the line just as the skeleton band let fly another big volley of noise, a team of men in what looked like marching band uniforms pushing a neat little red-and-white pod, outfitted with just a small black propeller at its top, off the edge of the platform. The thing nose-dived into the water.

"Surely Trey can stay up longer," I said.

"You didn't like the joke," V slurred, pouting a bit. She was drunk.

"I liked it," I said, trying to smile. "I think maybe I've heard it before, though."

She punched me hard on the shoulder.

And now the band burst into the "Battle Hymn of the Republic," embellished with a hip-hop bass drum beat, and old man Trey and his crew ascended the platform, the lot decked out all in skin-tight yellow uniforms like Mexican wrestlers without the masks. Aided along by the band, the crowd cheered. The old man, his long gray hair wildly extended from under his protective helmet, took a bow, and V and I leaned forward, ever forward in our seats.

The hard fact that he would plummet 50 feet into the water stood high in my mind. The impact was sure to rattle his bones and brain. But Trey strapped himself and life jacket into the lawn-chair cockpit of the flying machine, a pedal-powered glider with dual makeshift propellers that began to spin with his mad pedaling, the four members of his team all raising their fists, high atop the platform, crowd bursting now into a fervent chant for the old man. The band marched on.

Trey had crafted an at least slightly propulsive craft, if nothing else. The flying machine inched forward, miraculously, without the help of the crew members. But then the four-man crew grabbed the wings, two on either side, and pushed the contraption to a start as Trey's pedaling reached a frantic rate and the lightweight bicycle tires of the three-wheeled mechanism left the edge of the plat-form, soared out above the water—the crewmembers all left tee-tering at the edge of the platform to watch the impossible occur.

"I want to fly," Olden told the Chicagoland television-viewing audience. I was with him, in that moment, with V: the two of us pigeons dropping bombs on traffic jams, beholden to nothing but whimsy—no schedules, no holier-than-thou so-called impresario friends to get between.

I smiled. And Trey's contraption did soar, there's no doubt, hovered there 10 feet off the platform above the water as time stopped following propulsion from the valiant, running push of his crew—Trey smiling beneath his helmet, whooping, too, un-moored from the ground, unencumbered by daily responsibilities, in task, flying—before the inevitable happened. The left wing wob bled mid-air, snapped from the main body of the mechanism. Trey careened to the right and down hard into the harbor. A skyrocket-ing groan set forth from the crowd, and I smiled, and V cheered, for with the fall, the crew raised their right arms in unison. Trey's own arm shot up from the water of the harbor, where he bobbed, as if even this were a victory.

And maybe it was.

I saw him later at the Sparrow, where V had joined me for my shift. She commiserated with Carl in the front booth, just next to my chair, and when Trey came in looking like he'd been hanging out in a wind tunnel—what hair was left up there stuck in a wall that rose nearly six inches from the top of his head—V warwhooped like an Alabama college boy at a football game, like Billy, and the bar came to a standstill, before joining us in laughter.

Trey mechanically produced his ID for me, though, before he even realized who was sitting here in front of him.

His beard was matted up like it'd been doused with ketchup and blown dry.

"Wow, old man," I said. "You been celebrating?"

He just looked at me for a long moment and smiled.

"I didn't win," he slurred, "but I got close. A crew of goddamn Australians, engineers, actually flew 40 feet." We'd missed it, I guess: after his flight the Shining Band left and with their bombast went any excitement. But so what, I thought, as Trey shuffled toward the bar: he may not have sailed far this afternoon, but the man was well on his way to the clouds tonight—waltzing about, requisite Guinness in hand, in quiet shiftlessness. Trey was gliding behind his glasses, though, his feet shuffling just above the level of the floor, hair rising higher and higher away from his skull before !BOOM! breaking the sound barrier.

The old man eventually ambled off to his place, leaving the public and Carl and V and I, along with a crew of Carl's boys and girls, among them a host of young actors and Stephan Long, their director, an aspiring filmmaker at work currently on a television pilot called *TV Police*, a cop-show spoof detailing the all-very-meta attempt of a bunch of young urbanites to make a cop-show spoof called *TV Police*.

"We're almost done," Long, as everyone called him, told me. "Next weekend, Saturday, we're having a sort of unveiling at Jake's place." He pointed toward Jake the bartender, who was busy doing nothing by the taps this evening.

"Jake's in it, briefly, though he doesn't play the bartender," Long said. "Plus he's the crew's camera tech. The workman behind the art of the magnificent *TV Police*. Think *Chips* produced by and for early-21st-century hipsters. You can imagine the bar scenes, I bet—and the sexual drama."

100

Long was a Carl-type player, but with his hands in only one pie—more focused on himself and his work than the world around him. The two men got along famously. "You're Carl's artist, right?" he said. "I missed the show—or happening, or whatever it was—yesterday. Sounded rad, though."

"Mmm," I said. "It was interesting."

There were a host of characters associated with Long's show arriving, among them a lawyer whose ID I'd neglected to check a number of times these past weeks as he walked into the bar. He aced both age and respectability tests—priestly grey hair, grey suit, stiff handshake. His name was Eric, and tonight his much-younger brother, a less obviously respectable gent named Smitty, or Smit, Eric told me, was coming in as well. Smit was fresh from a rotation of a marine brigade in Afghanistan, and when he came in he was obvious. He had a three-day beard, glasses, and little hair on top of his head. He was taller than me and looked slightly wide-eyed addled, like he was on something.

I checked his ID, what doorman's surveillance instinct I'd developed presenting itself in full as he trolled across the mostly empty front space to the table in back where Eric, Long, Carl and V and others had moved and were holding court. Smit stood just to the rear of his brother for a long moment, while no one said anything to him, before moseying over to Jake at the bar. He quickly downed a brown shot and a beer like an old Chicago drunk.

A pair of farm girls-cum-hipsters, 21 and 22 respectively and carrying Iowa IDs, joined the party shortly, after which I lost track of Smit for a time until he appeared right in front of me.

"You know those two?" he asked, now pointing where I'd just been looking. The Iowa gals stood smiling up at priestly Eric. "They seem to know my brother."

I introduced myself.

"I know him, too," I said, though truthfully Eric and I had talked little.

"They're fresh pieces of ass," he said, "clean." He didn't smile. It was an interesting introduction—the Lark Sparrow was anything but a hard-ass' bar. Though corner joints in the neighborhood two and more blocks farther into the west side, where many of these "pieces of ass" lived alone in apartments formerly occupied by large new-immigrant families, might have been tough as nails, this sort of open assiness was well outside our norm. I squirmed a little in my seat.

"It's like prison sometimes, right?" he said, looking back at me—he was wearing thick prescription glasses, and the low light in the bar glanced brightly off the lenses. "It's a cliché, but true. It's all ganging up and taking down—those out of line get it best."

"How old are you?"—all I could think to say. Smit/Smitty seemed young, much younger than his brother.

"You checked my ID," he said.

I hadn't really looked at it much, in truth.

"I'm 30," he said.

At once Smit's outsider bona fides pulled a string in me. I nodded.

"Ever stood out in traffic?" I said.

He looked closely at me—I could tell by the skepticism in his pursed lips, his eyes however invisible behind the shifting reflections on his glasses.

"I've heard of you," he said. "Good to meet you." He backed away slowly, before he turned and, after stopping by the bar for another quick shot and a beer, resumed his spot behind his brother and was surely introduced at some point or other. I missed it, lost as I was for a time in my notebook.[7]

---

[7] *EXT SMIT's back porch, twilight*

Dressed in combat fatigues and a furry hat, laughing, sitting in the twilight on a chair on a back porch open to the backyard, SMIT holds a cheap air rifle. Now he aims at a saw horse in the backyard perhaps thirty feet (tops) off, on the top of which are perched small G.I. Joe and other figurines. He continues to aim, holding the sight for a full minute, camera angling closer into his face while alternating with individual figurines, then shoots.

SMIT: *Bull's Eye.*
[Enter ERIC dressed for business from the backyard, walking up and stopping briefly by the saw horse and shaking his head at the expressionless SMIT, who begins to count down his brother's approach under his breath.]
SMIT: *10, 9, 8, 7, 6 ...*
ERIC: *Ho, brother!*
SMIT: *5, 4, 3 ...* [raising the air rifle, training it on ERIC as he approaches SMIT's rear porch...ERIC shaking his head] *2, 1 ...* [SMIT abruptly moves

When I looked up Smit was commiserating soundly, or at least making an attempt at sound commiseration, with the two Iowa farm girls Melba and Jennifer, the latter of whom, as far as I could gather, was Eric's current love interest. He and Jennifer sat close and pulled cigarettes from the same pack during their few trips past me as the night wore on. As I made the rounds at the end of it, I caught what I imagined was the latter half of a story Melba, Jennifer's more or less exact replica (though they were not sisters), was telling their table: "Two Saturdays in a row, or rather two weekends in a row, since it happened on a Saturday and, last weekend and the one before that, on a Saturday, I have been right next, like in the immediate vicinity or whatever, of a *fatal shooting*, a killing. A *murder*. Two weeks ago I was out with my friend from Charlotte, who was here for her silly bachelorette weekend. We were all going nuts over at that Redhead Piano Bar?"—Long, Jennifer and Eric, Smit even, laughed. "The downtown place was a veritable 1930s-Chicago caricature peopled by wealthy suburbanites and greasy Italian mobster wannabes who were kissing the bachelorette and trying to get her to show her tits and other nasty shit like that. Anyway, I was ready to go and Charlie showed up with his beater and whisked me away to a wonderful 5 a.m. dinner. Shitty diner up on the north side" — Melba pointing to the rear of her open mouth— "Anyway, we're getting ready to put in our mouths whatever crap we ordered—I don't even remember what it was—when the waitress, very Chicago broad-shouldered and gum-popping, comes up to our table

the rifle to his left and fires past ERIC's head. ERIC doesn't flinch, mounts the porch steps and extends a hand, which SMIT doesn't take.]
ERIC: *Target practice, huh.*
SMIT: *I ain't talking to you, boy.*
ERIC: *Listen, I can help you.*
SMIT: *I don't need your help, traitor.*
ERIC: *Leave off with the traitor shit. You don't have the U.S. Army to thank for this apartment, you know.*
[pausing, SMIT's head going down]
SMIT: *That's Navy, dumbass.*
ERIC: *That's right, now. You got a cigarette?*
[ERIC sits. SMIT rolls a smoke, passes it.]
ERIC: *Do you remember the day Ronald Reagan was shot? For some reason I was thinking about that earlier. What was the guy's name? Hinckley, right?*

103

very excited and says 'Dyou guys park in the lot?', which we did, of course. 'Well, yer not gonna be able to get your car. It's a crime scene.' and she even winks at us, I think?"

The table here chuckled, a little, the collective response little more than signal for Melba to continue on, continue on ...

"Well somebody *had* been shot, and killed I might add, in the parking lot?"

Melba drank.

"And everybody in the place, particularly the people who worked there, were totally excited. Charlie was hopping mad because of his car, which he didn't end up getting till like 3 the next day—and he may have been lying but he said there was a dark stain right off the back bumper?—after we'd gone home and slept all day and he took the bus all the way back up. But the place was humming, I say, and the sun was coming up, and detectives were all over the place, and we were drunk and there was *a dead man*, right next to our car. I couldn't believe it! Then ..."

Melba drank. People shifted uncomfortably in their seats. Jennifer held up a flat palm to her friend, who smiled wanly, and jumped up to go to the bathroom.

I followed Long to the bar, where he scoped out the identity of young Jennifer.

"I think she's with Eric," Jake the bartender said before I got the chance. Long didn't pay me much mind anyway, I thought, but when I looked up from wiping down the west end of the counter he was staring at me. He was drunk.

"You coming with us, compadre?" Slapping my back a bit too hard for comfort. I stepped out from under his arm as Smit appeared on my left, ordering a beer and a shot.

"Last call!" Jake bellowed through the place.

"I'll have one of those, too," I said. Late night it was OK for the shift workers.

"You coming with us?" Long repeated.

Smit piped up: "Coming where?" he said.

The two men glared at one another as I tried to smile. I nodded for Long and backed away slowly to wipe down a newly evacuated table. As he and Smit talked—tersely, each man refusing to look the other in the eye—I learned Long and crew were having a late-night viewing of a rough edit of the *TV Police* pilot at Jake's apartment tonight, after the bar closed. Smit just nodded.

"Nobody told me that," I said, downing my shot and prizing my beer out from under the two. "You told me next week."

"I was trying to a minute ago, you jackass," Long said. He shot angry eyes Smit's way. Smit visibly fumed, eyes narrowing to slits.

"Smit, you going?" I said, tipping back my beer and winking.

He didn't answer.

"Let's hit the late-night traffic on Fullerton," I said. "Then we'll catch the last half."

"It's only 45 minutes," Long said, moving back to the table—"you guys are weird"—where he pulled a chair into a small chasm between Jennifer and Eric, Eric scowling obviously.

I laughed. Smit smiled, at least.

Melba brought her story to fruition wrapped in the cloak of omen and superstition.

"OK, so a week later, after the diner shooting, which was all over the news, by the way, I was at the YMCA, of all places, running hard on the treadmill with maybe three others total in the gym, and in comes this guy, who very casually says, 'Is anyone here a doctor?' I didn't even really register the guy's voice at first, but he repeated it, and even then, after I heard it, all I could think was that someone like as not had had a heart attack out on the basketball court or something, or somebody passed out, because here I was running and 30 minutes or more into it—very, very tired (I'm not in good shape, to say the least)—but now one of the other people in the workout room was grilling the guy for details and, as I'm continuing to run and run and huff and puff, I hear the guy say, 'Someone's been shot.' !! Jesus, right? Have to say my first thought was that the shit was in the locker room, which would now be of course a 'crime scene.' But that wasn't it, so on second thought I was *relieved*. I mean the dead guy's at least *on the basketball court* and not in the women's locker room, so I'll be able to get my stuff and go from here, eventually, without having to wait to change back into my regular clothes and whathaveyou ..."

"And they always happen in threes, eh?" Jennifer said. She laughed. Clearly, she'd heard this before.

Melba was not amused. "Let me remind you, young lady," she said, "the third night would have to be tonight, the last day of the third weekend—it's after midnight, after all."

She looked up at the clock on the wall behind the bar, catching my own eyes for an icy second.

"So watch out, girl," she said. "Watch out! You're with me. I am the marked woman."

"But do you really believe in it?" Long said. Nobody spoke for a long moment. Glasses were raised to mouths. "Man, all you guys are weird."

Melba lifted her cocktail back again and turned deep into her melodramatic interior. "I don't know. I don't."

The place emptied. Smit hung around while Jake and I closed up. At the end of it we sat around the end of the bar drinking, Smit calling for shot after shot and toasting his health and the national disease. Jake went into the back to cut the lights.

"To the cancer at the heart of the nation," Smit raising a bourbon.

"Hell yes," I raised my glass, too, but put it back down as he turned his up.

"Smit, let me ask you this," I said. "You got a BB gun?"

"You didn't drink," he said.

And so I drank, sipping slowly. The lights went out and Jake returned, bag slung over his right shoulder.

"Finish up, boys," he said. "You drunks gonna be all right getting home, or wherever you're going?"

Smit nodded.

"We're going the same place you are," I said. "Eventually."

"We're gonna be at it all night—stream on a constant loop," Jake said.

"Show up anytime, then."

"Yeah."

My eyelids were struggling there in the moment, fluttering and twitching with dehydration and need of sleep. I lit a cigarette as we filed out the back door and Smit and I jumped in my ailing Taurus, myself wishing I had my bike tonight, anything—wind on my face, the rush of automobiles next to me—to keep me up, awake.

"I do have one," Smit said, smiling, and before I knew quite what he was talking about he was directing me to his brother's place in Bridgeport, where we picked up his air rifle before we proceeded northward.

At Fullerton and Clark, the cars of late-night downtown party-

and bar-goers poured into Lincoln Park from Lake Shore Drive. "Ever stand out in it?" I said, cramming my car into a space too small for it back on an otherwise deserted residential side street. The front bumper raked across the edge of its rear counterpart on the car in front of me, producing an absolutely horrifying sound. Smit's hands went to his ears.

"Shit," I said. Better motor.

Carl had tried to warn me about drunken late-night parking. We were in his tiny apartment, a three-room railroad unit stuffed with books and records and computer gear, talking about one among many of the impresario's harebrained ideas, a grand plan to capitalize on the as-yet-to-be-realized death of ad-based commercial radio to launch a raucously low-budget FM station showcasing the city's artistic ne'er-do-wells. He was fucked with drink and spun to the subject of snow.

"It's crazy, man," he said. "You haven't seen the snow here. Just wait. I once waged a war with someone I never had the pleasure of meeting. The guy kept leaving messages on my car after I parked in 'his space,' as he put it," Carl's head turning, mind fogging over evidenced by the stupid unfocused cast of his eyes before rallying, his lungs surging into a maniac laugh and "the motherfucker broke my windshield after a while. See, people will hold their spaces with chairs when it snows, chairs or milk crates or old Coke crates like you'll see at the junk shops off the freeway in Alabama or Mississippi—I mean, this place is just as ass-backward and vindictive and mean as any smiling Southern jackass. And hey! Don't ever leave your car in a space you've hit the bumper of the guy in front of you or behind you. You can bet those sons of bitches are doing everything short of taking paint samples from their bumpers first thing in the morning. Best you might come out is with a key line down one side, worst— Well, I once had what looked like a baseball bat taken to every window, the hood in numerous places, trunk. Terrible fucking violence, man."

I hit the gas too hard and scraped and banged out of the too-small spot, leaving now an actual hole in the bumper of the Volkswagen in front of me. As we tooled slowly away, through Smit's open window appeared a fist that narrowly missed the man's chin, the fist's owner's arm getting yanked with us as I hit the gas. But Smit was mad.

"Motherfucker," he said. "Turn around."

In the rear-view mirror I saw the dude—baseball cap, polo, jeans—standing now at the back of his car shaking his head and yelling in our general direction.

"No fucking way," I said to Smit, who held the butt of the air rifle propped on his right leg, the stock in his left hand, devilish grin on his face. I couldn't help but laugh.

Then: "All right," I slurred, making a quick U-turn in the next side-street intersection.

"Roll down your window," Smit said.

The guy railed, still standing by his car, as we crept back up the street.

"Hey!" he shouted, approaching my now-open window as I rolled sleepily up to him.

"Sorry, man," I said, and Smit leaned across me with the rifle aimed out of my window, just as the guy leaned down and reached out to grab my shoulder or wring my neck—we'd never know which. Smit fired, the BB hitting the guy square in the back of his hand.

He yelped and jumped away from the car, but his pain or surprise didn't last long as he flung himself then at the door and I gunned it, the laughter bubbling up from my gut quashed quickly with the sharp thud and bump I felt rocket through the driver-side rear. I scanned the rear-, side-view mirrors both to allay the blood-rush of fear that welled up in me—no such luck. I stopped the car, jumped out and ran toward the now crawling, wailing man. His right leg bent out at an odd angle behind him, eyes peering up at me through black slits for a brief moment there in the streetlights. What had I done?

"I'm sorry," I said. "I didn't, I didn't mean it, to hit you," but it was like he didn't hear me.

He moaned a little, long-away look in his eyes, his head falling forward as he managed to sit up against one of the other parked cars here, letting his head now rest against the passenger-side door, breathing heavily. "That motherfucker shot me!" he yelled, to no one as much as me or himself.

"Yo," I heard Smit yell back at me, "let's go."

"The guy's really hurt," I said. I couldn't well just leave him, I felt, truly. Could I?

108

"C'mon, pussy—what are you out here for, charity? He got what was coming."

"You drunk fuckers," he said. "I swear to fucking God," more quietly now, hard-focused look in his eyes and well out of Smit's earshot up the street. "At least I got a good look at you, piece of shit. Go on and do it—I don't fucking care, I'll find you."

He had his phone out and was punching in numbers as Smit finally made the scene.

"I'll take that, bitch," he said and ripped the phone from his hand, combat-boot-heel down on its screen on the pavement. He removed the battery and put it all in his pocket. "Now let's go," he said. I was escorted back to the driver's seat by my elbow, a veritable child—I was shaking like one when my hands took the wheel.

"Get it together, Cash," Smit said like it was his final word on the subject. I could hear sobs now from the dude down the street above the engine, now punctuated by increasingly weak calls for help. More than one light in apartments up and down the block had blinked on following the scuffle, and I don't know if I actually saw or just imagined blue lights flashing down the street a hundred or more yards now in my rear-view, but I didn't stick around to be sure. My trembling hands held hard the wheel and I hit the gas and put as much distance at as much speed as I could between ourselves and the scene. I thought about using Smit's phone to call an ambulance out to pick the guy up, but by the time I'd decided to do it I had no idea where to tell them to go.

"That was fucked-up, man," all I could muster when finally I could breathe, about halfway now toward Jake's place.

"Nothing," he said. "BB wouldn't kill him, don't worry."

"My goddamned car might, man." I hadn't checked the side yet—there was sure to be evidence.

"That's on you, man," he said. "But don't worry, he'll be all right. Probably won't remember half of it. A guy like that out this late—got to be drunk, traffic man, 'Shining Man,' whatever the hell you are."

He wasn't smiling, just staring straight ahead, almost like he was talking to himself more than me. I bucked myself up against whatever was to come, resolve on the bubble up to be rid of the town in spite of all my yearnings after certain of the people in the place.

109

"If you can't take the heat," said Smit, "stay out of the fucking street." And here he laughed a disaster, as we proceeded shortly in silence to Jake's, taking Fullerton west to Kedzie and turning north up the boulevard, circling the square at Kedzie and Wrightwood and rolling west. Jake lived blocks back into the center of this neighborhood on a street known for its dealers, Smit said. It wasn't all that far at all, really, from my father's apartment.

"How do you know?" I asked. "Haven't you been in like Iraq for months?"

"Afghanistan, man," he said. "We're out of Iraq. Almost. Trust me. I grew up here, bitch."

Despite the unstoppable tide of gentrification, the razing of ancient bungalows and three-flats to the southeast of this neighborhood, things moved slower out here—a measure of stability evidenced, when we turned finally onto Jake's street, by the young man standing on the corner beneath a pair of what looked like mid-80s Air Jordans strung by connected shoelaces over a power line.

"Sure enough," I said. I conjured the dealer in a reflective suit, for a moment, which led to a false feeling of solidarity—*my people*, though the guy was likely to kick my ass should the sentiment be voiced within earshot. I was more scared of my companion now than I'd ever be of a Chicago corner dealer, and I nodded as we passed him, receiving a cold nod in return. Smit nodded, too, the BB gun's stock resting on the floor of my car now, the muzzle propped between his legs. He pointed to Jake's place—light pouring from the third-floor windows of a three-flat. There was nowhere to park on the street, so Smit directed me around back, where I squeezed the Taurus between two lines of trash bins against the back of a building, light spilling from a little window just above us reminding me of my late-night encounters of the tiny suited messenger. I watched the window for a helmet.

"Go on," Smit said, and I rose from the car. "Jake's is back that way two lots." He pointed the BB gun north up the alley.

"What are you going to do?" I said.

"Go on," he said.

I told him to not fucking forget to lock the car and he nodded and I moved as fast as I could up the alley, turning into the riotous garden of prehistoric-looking foliage planted in Jake's backyard and up the four steps to the first-floor wooden fire-escape landing. Lights were off in the first-floor unit. I was seized there by waves both of fatigue and fear, nausea. Above me, on the third-floor landing, partygoers were gathered smoking cigarettes. I lit my own here and sucked it down quickly, no yawns now, recognizing Melba's voice telling her story of fateful proximity to death at the YMCA and the late-night diner, ending "and if the third time's the charm, today would be the day it would go down," Melba a natural storyteller, really drawing it out and now laughing wildly in spite of, I imagined in the optimistic half of my brain, theatrical shudders from her audience, "right here, tonight."

"Ooooooo," I said as I finally walked up the last flight of stairs, predictability, familiarity lightening my mood, and was ignored by the lot of the folks on the landing. I moved to a corner, finished my smoke and went inside.

The place was hot, packed. Three guys moved slowly out of the way, pressing into the mess of bodies here in the rear kitchen to let me in the door. The party hadn't been going on long enough for any spectacular mess to accumulate, but I imagined it wouldn't be long—everyone was drunk or getting there, late as it was. I scanned the faces and bodies in the rear kitchen for V but found Long, who showed me the pilot, on a loop in the front common room. Few people bothered watching.

"The production quality's so-so," he said, and no shit it looked like something a couple teens could put together with decent-quality cellphones. I didn't make much comment at all, but then a horribly-directed car chase turned into a bar scene—they'd used the Sparrow as their set. In the middle of serving the two main characters, one based on Long and the other, an actor also moonlighting as the show-within a show's director, the actor playing bartender, I thought looked oddly familiar and must have been some guy who filled in at the bar as third man on busy Friday or Saturday nights or otherwise only worked the odd weeknight. But the more I watched, the more I truly cased the association he sparked in my brain.

"Who's the bartender?" I said.

"Guy name of Charles Rinckoff," said Long, "sort of came out of nowhere—he saw one of our ads, I guess."

"Give it up," the bartender was saying, now, to the Long-based character as he lamented the amateur nature of his show-within-a-show's actors. The Long character raised his glass and the bartender poured a shot and smiled, and it was that smile, laced with brutal sarcasm, that was the final clue. I looked around the room for the Suited Man and, when Long noticed my attention to the pilot flagging, he muttered something about it being just an experiment, in the end, embryonic, and stuck his nose up in the air in an unconvincingly masculine head-nod. I laughed a little inside.

"Is the guy here?" I said, scanning the room behind us, beyond Long's thick head. I was now wider than wide awake.

"You mean Charles," he said after a time. "I don't think that guy gets out much. V knows him, though, or seemed to."

Screams erupted from the back of the apartment and Melba blew into the room a storm of hair and bile and with bodies, some still attached to their back-porch cigarettes, at her back as if ready for a schoolyard brawl.

"What the fuck, Jake!" she roared. "This neighborhood is off —the—fucking—charts—some son of a bitch just shot BBs into the back porch!" She paused then to gaze quickly around the room, fixing on me before I had a chance to give away my knowledge of the shooter's identity. "You, what's-your-name, what are you smirking at?" Melba pointing at me. I guessed the knowledge did get out. "You heard my story, so you're presumed guilty!" Then I saw none other than Smitty himself looking quite innocently poker-faced just beyond Melba's right shoulder, gleam of outright fucking insanity in his eyes. I went into a full-throated laugh, then.

She charged and jumped onto my back when I turned away, her legs scissoring my waist and little fists—she really was quite small, Melba—pounding playfully yet sincerely on my shoulders. I exaggerated a scream and buckled my legs so we came crashing easily onto the wood floor. Melba rolled off my back, over my shoulders and into a sitting position facing me on the floor.

"How's it going?" I said.

"You know," she said, "that was a dirty trick out there," and she seemed to deflate a little.

"I wasn't the shooter," I said. "I didn't have anything to do with it, besides."

"But you know who was."

"Not exactly." Smitty's presence in the house so quickly, Rinckoff's absence, the connection of both to this entire crew, including

112

V, who was likewise absent: the whole thing seemed scripted for the benefit of a secondary player in the urban drama, a pawn to be moved about at the whims of the other actors.

"Well, who do you think it is, I guess?" Melba said.

"The bartender," I said, gesturing back toward the T.V., next to which Jake stood commiserating with Long and a very young girl.

"Not Jake, no way," Melba said, now smiling.

"The bartender in the show," I said.

"Ooooohhhh …" Melba said. "He's always seemed a little creepy to me. For definite."

We rose from the floor as one, revising our outrage and disbelief to include our shared secret knowledge. The Suited Man was the shooter, evidence or no. He was creepy. Maybe we were drunk enough to accept this rigid thinking—the presumption of guilt.

Then we sat back down and remained sitting after tabs of LSD had been passed around. As the sun began to come up later and the whole rig of the room began to rotate around us, it felt like we were the ones moving. I continued to scan the place for V, little chance though there was of her showing at this late, early hour. My new friend, somehow appropriately, spoke my mind for me.

"Listen," Melba said as we spun, morning light framing her childlike face, "never lose hope that you'll get what you want. She could show up anytime, we could all drop this charade and confess that we are what we are, actors, and"—Melba smiled big and put her arms up around my neck and then gave me a sloppy kiss. "Yeah," she said, "we could tell you you weren't wanted or that you were just too weird for us all but look, it's not true, it's in fact just the opposite, you have become a, a quite goddamn vessel for everything *we* want. I don't know what the others think, really, but me, watching you and marching, marching, marching I think it's the … Nevermind, yes, maybe you should take that vessel and distribute that message—take V with you, I think she'll go along with it, depending on where you're going and what the plan is. I know I would. If I was her. But then I'm not her, I'm just a southern Illinois farm girl whose friends have BB bruises on various parts of their bodies." And she smiled and, as I stood slowly, uneasily to leave some time later unsure if she'd ever spoken at all, Melba clutched my right leg and refused to let me go until I agreed to take her with me. So I did and I didn't tip my nonexistent hat goodbye to Smitty on the way out and Eric smiled knowingly my way, I guess, though I'm not sure what he felt like he knew as paranoia crept up in my mind and Melba's friend Jennifer hung on Eric's arm and she smiled, too, and Melba and I roared out of the party's lifeblood to become something else, together, on the floor of my father's apartment in the morning light, in this sex-starved age, humanity's greatest pleasure also its potential annihilator, the ultimate paranoia that entailed. And though I knew, my knees digging into the boards that made up the floor, that I would never see her again, it was A-OK, as my father might have put it. If one couldn't exactly be anything without the empathic desire of those outside the mind, one could certainly try. The Suited Man, Trey, Carl, Melba, V, they taught me this.

And Melba she seemed clean, disease-free, and as far as I ever knew she was. I guess I was, too.

Chapter 9

Rinckoff's map was clearly the work of a creep, crude and embellished with miniature skulls for markers that were only evident as skulls with the aid of a magnifying glass—my father kept a wallet-insert-size one in the medicine cabinet of his little bathroom. I once lit a cigarette with a magnifier of the type, focusing ambient sun's rays in a point on the cigarette's tip during afternoon break from high school marching-band camp, where all of us high-school marchers began to learn our show, and I learned to smoke, the summer prior to the marching season. Me and Schuyler—who sort of reminds me now of Long or Carl, I guess, or Long or Carl reminded me of him as he was then, always the one behind whatever collective motion or progress was made among your friends—we got the magnifying glass because Schuyler refused to accept the dead lighter he brought to the N.C. mountain college campus as the definitive wrench in his, and by extension our, plans to smoke the Virginia Slims cigarettes, absurdly, I'd nabbed from my mother and brought with me. Schuyler knew the magnifying glass would work, somehow, though we were anything but Boy Scout types. He knew where we'd come closest to finding a glass—the college bookstore, called the Cubbyhole after the mountain college's Bears mascot. I remember well the suspicion of wrongdoing that crossed the face of the old lady behind the register: what did a couple Kurt Cobain-wannabe teenagers in Axl Rose-type bandanas want with a wallet magnifying glass from a college bookstore?

But hey, it worked like a charm, just out of view of the front windows of the bookstore where we scorched a tiny pinpoint into the end of the smoke from which to get the embers going— Schuyler would later be suspended for torching greater vegetables, or cash crops, in the parlance of our southern upbringing, when he got caught in the act of lighting a joint in our high school's A-building back stairwell by the faint magnified light piercing the only window in the stairwell. At the high moment of incineration, in walked none other than Schuyler's nemesis, the vice principal known as "Coach Mac," a fat and balding fortysomething whose merciless bullying of the nonathletic coterie of young males at the school was legion.

After sleeping most of the day after Melba left, the next morning first thing I called Fock's Mill information on a hunch and, sure enough, they had a listing for S. Pelt in a subdivision off U.S. 21 I knew well. A surprise, indeed, I never ran into him at McClendon's.

"You got a map handy?" I said when he answered the phone.

He did. I was lucky to catch him at home, he said. Thirty minutes and he was off on a run to the northeast—"I'm an O – T – R driver," he said. "Over the road. 'Trucker' in your layman's lingo."

"You might not even need the map. Where does I-65 cross I-20?" On Rinckoff/Suited Man's map "Ingalls," marked by one of the man's infinitesimal skulls, was situated mere blocks south and a smidge west of the thruways' intersection, assuming these were interstates and not just state highways.

"Downtown Birmingham," he said. "Alabama. I know it well. I load out of U.S. Pipe on occasion well west of there."

"Well," I said. Birmingham, straight shot south on I-65, reverse trail of the Great Migration, back into the fold of New South empire.

"Yeah, well west," he said.

"I've never been there," I said.

"Got plans?" he said.

I guessed I did, and he then finally asked me why the hell, after all these years, I happened to be calling him.

"We still live just a few miles from each other," I said.

"But you're calling from Chicago. Up there with your dad or something?"

I was surprised he remembered. I had forgotten the very fact of cellphones and caller ID, too, I guess. My powers of recollection were centered around stories told and retold, like that of the magnifying glass, which I'd shared countless times with Will Theron over the years as a parable for teenage ingenuity, for national ingenuity to evil purposes, the American Way, the folly of New South upbringing, you name it. I could remember nothing of Schuyler's own family lineage, so I just said yeah.

He gave me his cell number and email and said to be in touch.

I said I would.

I packed the trunk of the car with the little I'd brought—added to it several Shining Man suits, some of my father's less-battered clothing and not much else, really. The bike Billy gave me I stowed in the backseat. With the exception of all the purloined traffic-worker vests, which I'd minced long ago by now, my father's apartment reflected an existence even more spare than my own. The man ate out, always, so there was nothing in the way of kitchen equipment to be rid of, and little of value anywhere in the apartment. Everything that I hadn't already left in the alley for Chicago's army of trash-pickers to appropriate or ignore—the phone, the television, his twin bed, his desk, the rest of his clothes—I did so today. I then left Eula a note and two months' rent, which left me $500 cash to work with. I walked two blocks to a café on Milwaukee Avenue with Carl's loaner laptop and emailed him, first, to let him know I was assuming ownership of "this overcomplicated typing machine," in his own expository style, unless he needed it back. I wrote Trey, then Billy, then Joe at the bar, to tender my resignation from all my temporary gainful, and not so gainful, employments. I emailed a fellow door guy I knew wanted my shifts, telling Joe in turn that I would be doing so. I emailed Eric to relay a message to Melba—"see you around," essentially—and to his brother, Smitty. "Tell him I said, 'Nice shooting, cowboy. Watch your back.'"

I scanned crime-beat reporters' dispatches from the last day or two, in my brain the pained face of the guy under the ballcap (Chicago-Cubs *C* right above his nose) and above the popped collar of the polo, head back against the anonymous vehicle on what might have been his own damn street, for all I knew … All for naught, or for the best I could have imagined, no mention of a manhunt on for the driver guilty of a hit-and-run, a Ford Taurus with S.C. plates that could be connected to the disturbance on Halsted Ave. care of the so-called "Shining People" and, yes, I'd checked on my way here, with a big-ass dent in the driver-side rear quarter panel and scrapes along the front bumper. Staring hard and scanning through the unrelated words on the screen the room tilted a little around me and I had to close my eyes tight for 10 seconds to stop it. My heart skipped a beat, shouted out in pain at me, then I was at peace, a little. Dalliance with Melba brought on that dog-eared regret, the come-down blues. And reckoning with what that meant for what I might (might not) have felt for another didn't sit well either.

Finally, I wrote she-whom-I-had-not-seen-these-last-days.

Vivian, Vera, Vee, V, Wanted to extend invitation to escape with me, but you've not been around much these past couple days. No big deal, but if there's not much keeping you here, consider the invitation an open one. I'm on the road today, but I can always turn around. I've got nothing if not time. Don't ask me why I don't just call. I guess email's easier for me at this point. Yours ...

I almost typed *I'm sorry* before I decided that I wasn't and closed the screen and almost made the decisive move to walk the two blocks back to my car before I sat back down and opened it back up. Just as I was about to start a new message I noticed a fresh one for me:

I can't believe you. You put me in your little drama and basically rake me across the coals of your insidious bit of self-congratulatory B.S., and you know it and you run from it. I got fired, did you know that? I'm not exactly sure how it happened, and you'd figure somebody—my boss—who went to the fucking Iowa writers workshop would have a little more appreciation for what FICTION is, but I wanted you to know and carry around in your little mind the fact that I got fired on account on your reductive humor! "Creating a situation inside the office that was untenable" were her exact words, as if I'd actually done anything! I mean, a couple of suggestive glances is one thing but Jesus. And you wrote it! And you don't even work here! I would laugh but for crying. I haven't found another job yet, though I have a mind to apply to that shithole bar where you work and make your daily life a living hell, chieftain.
Your buddy Carl gave me your email address. I told him I wanted to screw you. I didn't specify what I meant by 'screw.'
Fuck you.
—Ass

There was enough truth in the lie to reveal the sad reality—the thought was at once exhilarating and crushing. More reasons to get far away from here. "I'm sorry," I typed in a reply to Katherine (my memory was correct), and meant it, then quickly left, walked my two blocks, scanning the front of my father's building for signs of activity: no cops, no Eula to be found, fortunately, so I started the

118

car. Tried to, rather, for it didn't take immediately, but on the third effort something fully turned and the increasingly-antique-bull-of-a-car's electronically calibrated emissions system whined to life with the engine. I dropped it to D (*ka-chunk*) and pulled the wheel left with the throttle (*wheeeeeeee-bang, grrrr...*) and a little under five hours later, the sun low on the horizon, I was broken down in Indiana, just north of Louisville.

It wasn't the transmission, maybe something even worse. I thought about flagging down and then didn't have to flag down a rig, whose owner-operator took one look at the car, the check-engine light blazing when I dared attempt to crank it, a curious burning smell emerging from the engine block, and pronounced it FUBAR.

"I got nothing to fix it with," I said, knowing the cost of the repair would probably just kill all the cash I had.

"You hitchhiked before?" said Stonefly, as he then formally introduced himself.

"Your CB handle," I said.

"Colin Sanders," he said, "and yes, you're right."

Sanders, in his upper 40s, lived in a little town named Wabash and ran steel I-beams out of northern Indiana to the southern states, mostly to a distribution point in North Carolina but also to Florida, where he was headed today, to Georgia and occasionally elsewhere. "Yeah, I've hitchhiked," I lied. We stood side by side in front of my car's open hood, our gazes locked dumbly on the block, from which wispy fumes rose.

"Where you headed?" Sanders asked.

"Alabama," I said.

"I can get you as far as Birmingham, maybe farther, depending on where you need to be," he said. And so it was that I came to rest, minus one dead car, minus the old Schwinn, in the passenger seat of Stonefly's Peterbilt 379, a bright-yellow 1996 model closing in on two million, he said, in the mileage category.

"I take damn good care of her," Stonefly proudly reciting then a list of custom add-ons he'd installed over the years, the custom coding of the "technicolor banana" yellow paint job on the exterior. The cigarette lighter, though, was broken, and as Sanders went for what he said was his last match to light a cigarette, I tensed with anticipation. The beautiful moments in this life are so very few and far between, though in retrospect I ought to have been happy for my Chicago time, happy for the missed opportunities, the brief fucked-up sex, the gainful employment, the wonder of the entire story—the ultimate mystery of my father's fate and the fool's errand Rinckoff or whoever else had me on now, the mistakes I'd made and the people I'd hurt in the meantime, made me feel more victimized, for good reason, than anything else.

Beat down and run around on a leash.

I dove for the ecstatic moment this sunny late afternoon: as Sanders struck his match, I rolled my window down, the resulting rush of air into the cab causing a disturbance sufficient to fizzle the matchstick before he got it to his cigarette's tip.

"Shit," he said, as I rolled up my window.

"Sorry," I said. "Needed some quick fresh air."

"I hope you got a light," he said.

"No, but I've got the next best thing," producing from the pocket of my jeans my father's magnifier.

"Shit," he said, laughing. "Boy Scouts it is."

We stopped for a lighter an hour later, when the sun had disappeared and rendered the magnifier "patently useless"—those were Sanders's words. I mentally christened him the most erudite individual I'd ever met. Sanders seemed to know more about American life and letters than the most well-read and -traveled professor you might come across, much less any of my old or newer friends.

"We see the best and worst of it all out here," he said, fueling at the same stop, just off 65 in Kentucky, halfway between Louisville and Nashville. "Living a majority of time on the road, we've got time, too. It might seem like we don't, but we do, or I do, and if I don't I damn well make some."

Sanders read voraciously, finishing a book or two a week, he said, and in his truck's sleeper, big enough for a pull-down desk, a small shower and toilet, and much else besides, he read on a small tablet computer capable itself of the library of Babylon—before electronic systems made interlibrary loan programs a simple reality, Sanders said, "the enterprising among us were already some of their best customers. It was hard sometimes to find a place to park to get to a library, but ask around and you'd find the town alleys and old lots the other guys used."

Sanders showed me to his tablet and I checked my email. A message of fond bon voyage from Carl, telling me to take the laptop and pay him back some other way later. A note laced with barely concealed outrage from Billy—"If you are going back to SC, don't tell me I didn't warn you. You'll find much of nothing there but the exact reason you left staring you in the face every day." Two slightly melancholy-feeling messages of hope from Trey Olden, Eric and Melba, respectively. Nothing, as might have been expected, from V. Nor Katherine, not that I hoped for that.

When we strapped ourselves back in the front seats I asked Sanders why he did what he did.

"I always have," he said. I guessed I meant to ask how he got into it to begin with, and he said, "Hell, the same way anybody gets into much anything. I had an older cousin who drove truck and it seemed like a good idea at the time." Mentally I asked myself the same question, mulling over the answer as we rode on through the evening, a cup of coffee and a cigarette never far from my lips. I'd later warm it up from a mammoth thermos Sanders had filled at the last stop. It didn't keep me from nodding off close to midnight in the middle of a conversation about Decatur in north Alabama, where Sanders wanted to move for reasons of economy, he said, and personal ambition for winters that were bearable.

"You wouldn't believe the snow in Indiana," he said. He knew I was a Southerner at this point, just as he knew the exact map coordinates of where I was going, a whole host of things about my sojourn in Chicago and so much else.

I'd told him the story of my father—the real one, as I saw it by now.

"I don't know what to make of it all, really," he said. "Parts of it sound implausible, for sure."

"I'm not making up a word," I said.

His eyes stayed hard on the dark road, but before he continued he allowed them to turn my way. I imagine Sanders saw hope in my eyes—and no small measure of fear. The telling left me anticipating rebuke at my own stupidity or some other fearful sentiment, a dismissal of the folly of my relative youth. But Sanders, plenty wise for his years, just reflected back the ultimate confusion inherent in

121

the play-by-play I'd offered. Father apparently dies, son travels to settle his affairs to find no evidence of his death only to hear from him via a crew of people his own age, mostly, who son ultimately thinks are playing him for sport or something else, ultimate reality unknown. When Stonefly—a name he'd picked up when living on a boat most fancifully stoned in the late 1980s in Key West—turned back to the road, he sighed.

"So I do think there's probably some validity to the idea that the people you describe in Chicago are jerking your chain," he said. "To some degree they are. But if 'the suited man' by some chance is not this Rinckoff character, then I don't know where to take it. Your blood is your blood. And a man's dying wishes might best be heeded. Of course, if the suited man is this guy, this Rinckoff dude, then my guess is your old man's not out there."

At once, I wasn't relieved by his empathy, if you could call it that, like I yearned for him to really turn hard and tell me I was certifiable, check yourself into a nuthouse, son, you're not long for the realm of the real. Next thing you'll be telling me there's a codriver in the bunk who's the ghost of your dead mother ...

I sighed, if not audibly over the roar of wind on the rough edges of the rig and of the big diesel motor, at least mentally, a kind of sigh much more than a marker of time or a paltry thing to fill the space between words. I felt it, down to the lining of the stomach of this weary traveler.

And just where the hell was I going? With nothing more than an address and a psychotic map, whatever resolve I started the trip out with had to be little better than a kind of religious faith in following things through. There was, of course, little in the way of fact to go on. Or was I just wrong again, wrong as I'd been about so much so far.

"So you don't think I'm crazy," I said, simply.

"No," he said.

It was a fact—he didn't think it, or if he did he wasn't saying. I stared out the window into the black bewilderment, not exactly content that either interpretation would have been equally disappointing.

Chapter 10

Birmingham presented herself at first meeting as a perfect inversion of the old Southern stereotype of the lady so concerned about keeping up appearances you'll never see either side of her mouth turned down, unless she has a debilitating stroke. The city's hulking buildings, even at central points in the old downtown business district, flaunted windows burst and makeshift scaffolding covering facades to shelter from falling stone the shuffling maniacs walking by below. Redneck bikers at the brewpub at Five Points South commonly posted up to throw sick jokes past perky college-student bartenders. West of I-65 and south of I-20/59, in my new edge-of-things domain, drug-trade bullets flew at elevated rates, their shooters playing the largest part of all the city's residents in claiming the crown for the town of "most dangerous southern jewel east of New Orleans," as ran a newspaper headline around the time I arrived. I would come to know all this in the following week in conversation with an array of humanity as bizarre as I'd ever come across. Even though time was short, I managed to scare up more than enough in terms of employment. At the intersection of 14th and the freight tracks business was to be had for most who bothered to stand there typically three days of the week, folks told, and on the others all gave up if no employer (dudes in pickups, really) showed by 10 a.m., blasting out then on their respective searches for diversion. For most that meant gathering back across the tracks around a fire fueled by whatever could be mustered and a communal bottle or two of, again, whatever could be mustered.

For me, it didn't mean any of this, as it never happened, but disabusing myself of first impressions would nonetheless be my primary occupation in the magic Alabama town. My Suited Man, Rinckoff, my father and/or a cabal of ne'er-do-wells arranged behind him/them had sent me to a building whose unofficial lack of positive attributes were many and quite officially tallied on the fading warning posts tacked to the chain-link fencing, in several places compromised, that surrounded its mass.

"I've seen this joint from the freeway," Sanders said when he dropped me off, "been closed forever and hell. Damn sure does look like you've been sent on a goose chase. Sure you want me to drop you?"

I'd already offloaded all my stuff from his improbably yellow truck in preemptive answer.

"Thanks for all your help," I told the man. I was learning gratitude, I guess, if I'd never been taught it. The former home of Ingalls Steel was a Superfund site, the warnings said, and could contain all manner of environmental pollutants making it unsafe for human traversal, much less habitation, etc. I reconsidered, briefly, felt the fear wash through me in a shiver despite the continuing heat. But I bucked up and sent him on, waving goodbye as Sanders pulled his horn and rolled away. I scanned the dimly-lit plane at the top of the knee-high grass for movement, for indentations indicative of recent activity. I saw nothing, really, though paranoia worked its way around my skull as I set off through the fence into the void where a double doorway once stood at the side of the building. Inside, a hallway that let into what looked like the main reception or office area. The walls, if not crumbling old plaster of paris, were otherwise wood-paneled and dark and, turning from a spot that might have been at the center of the building, I stooped slightly under just barely visible cobwebs hanging from a doorway and into a massive hangar-like space. Opening three and more stories upward, many of its panel windows long-ago shattered, tiny glass shards providing shimmer to the gray sand/dirt floor here, where there weren't massive parts of formerly massive machines left to rust to no purpose. Rinckoff's map had a breakout map of Ingalls' interior on its backside, which I took the opportunity to peruse in the scant light—from what I could make out, the southwest corner of the place held particular significance.

I made my slow way there, away from the whine of the north-south freeway, across the pulverized glass and concrete and gravel. I periodically stopped and listened. Above the low freeway roar now came something else—jazz, smooth jazz the likes of which I will forever associate with Ada's Lounge nearer downtown, the perhaps dumbed-down descendants of Birmingham's own Herman Poole

Blount, or Sun Ra, left on this earth to bounce around with bass guitars playing slap syncopation and soprano saxophones trilling Kenny G notes. I heard the music loud and clear upon my entry to Birmingham, and as I approached the Suited Man's lair, divided from the main room by four old wooden doors propped precariously against a support beam near a corner, I cased the source—a local college radio station, a DJ soon identified, slipping out of a box of the type you'd have seen on the shoulder of say the biggest Fock's Mill neighborhood wanderer in the crowd in the late 80s. This one evidently ran on A/C power, plugged as it was into an outlet attached to an ancient electrical conduit running up the wall of the hangar, on up past the broken windows near the top and into the main electrical system. Next to it: a slightly rusted hotplate showing evidence of recent use in vague splatters along its outer edges; an upturned saucepan, clean; four not-so-dirty blankets folded just so and stacked neatly on the gravelly floor, with a new-looking pillow on top; three cigarette butts lined up lengthwise in a row a mere six inches from the blankets. I spun around and cased the environs in total, 360. I turned off the music, repeated the turn, listened to the pounding of my heart in anticipation of something.

But there was nothing.

Home sweet home?

I'm no forensics expert, but the otherwise white butts had gone yellow with age. They looked like they belonged to last year, if not another decade. I soon added a bright-white fourth to their number, no magnifying glass necessary, thankfully, it'd have been useless in this light. I deposited the collection in the paper cup that formerly housed my last coffee of the night. The top blanket—the dirtiest one, as it were—I unfolded and spread on the floor in the partly enclosed space, laying my head down on the pillow at the end of this most strange sequence of days. I turned the jazz back on, then off, listened for a long time to the hum of the highway, the brittle and constant and comforting, even, sounds of the building—paint chips falling, electricity humming, wind whistling softly in quick bursts through the old window frames above—and eventually slept the sleep of the damned.

I woke soaked in a sticky sweat that gummed every corner of my naked body. Combined with the grime of the interior of the former Ingalls Steel, God-knows-what falling from the ceiling of the place, what skin I'd not managed to wipe down at a Waffle House nearby—under my t-shirt, maybe—carried a layer of grit like sandpaper. I was back in "the region," to borrow Billy's parlance. And my bearded, bespectacled Birmingham fellow regionalist Leroy King I met the next day just over the train tracks from downtown on 21st Street. I was looking for Wi-Fi. His "anarchist bookstore," as he called it, according to the screen of my overcomplicated typing machine, had just the portal.

"*Leroy* doesn't fly with my people," he said, introducing himself just as *King* when I walked in. "You know, punks, artists, communists, fewer and fewer of them around lately anyway. You'd figure the antiquated feel of it would rate, but I usually just get the proverbial blank stare when I say my real first name."

"I'm looking for the world I left in here," I said, sitting down and pulling up a page on the laptop screen devoid of anything new in the way of emails from the land to the north.

"Ain't that just fucking deep," King said. "Welcome to Birmingham." With a wide sweep of his arm he indicated the space, a veritable cavern of a building filled with utility shelves lined with books, mostly secured at estate sales of deceased *B-hammers*, as he called the denizens of his town. Significant in his gesture, there was no one in the shop. I rose and searched the stacks for a while and sat back down with him at a coffee table in the space's open center to thumb through a 1960s academic text about the international regulation of civil wars, the beginning of the postcolonial historical era, the seeding of the Weathermen—I recognized much of the talk of popular revolt in Africa, South America and elsewhere.

We smoked cigarettes over the next several hours as I continued to read, and King asked not a single question of why I might be visiting him this day. I asked him where I might find work, and he said I was welcome to put in hours in his shop.

"Whoever's on the clock takes 50 percent of the till," he said, "not much, as you can see, but if you've got time ..." He allowed the words to hang in the air.

"How about tomorrow," I said.

"No dice," he said. "Got a few others vying with your obviously entrepreneurial spirit. But I've been looking to cover Saturdays."

I thanked him, and he pointed me to the spot on 14th seven blocks to the west and across the tracks from the store.

"You're probably too late to get on a gang today, but get out there early tomorrow," he said. He once supported himself that way, after moving back home to Birmingham at age 25 from a five-year walkabout through New York City, Boulder, Colo., New Orleans and points between with a touring experimental theatre group. King was writer, director and actor.

"No money in it at all," he said, his Trotsky glasses flashing in the sun out front of his shop. "Or laboring, really, but you'll get by if you don't have expenses, and though we haven't talked about it, I'd guess you don't."

Did I smell that bad? It occurred to me then that I appeared just what I was, a man who'd slept on dirty blankets laid over gravel last night.

I gave King the information of my true living situation then out there in the hot sun, and he offered to put me up in the store.

"There's usually some sort of show going on upstairs here nights," he said, "so we're all around pretty late. Come in anytime. You're welcome to a shower here, too. In the very back of the store there's two bathrooms, one for customers, the other one locked for me and other employees. Let me know if you need it."

I walked downtown and found a coffeehouse on 2nd Avenue North next-door to an art gallery next-door to a shop filled with 20th-century kitsch for sale, and I posted up with a small coffee I sipped ever so slowly and let my imagination wander in the manner of a travel writer[8] around the idea of the power vacuum that had,

---

[8] *I have met the man who resides at the corner of 1st Avenue South and Richard Arrington Blvd, or 21st Street. He should be Birmingham's next mayor. Leroy King's Black Hat Books commands a view from its front door not only of the parking-garage-construction site across the street but the old business district across the viaduct over the tracks on Morris Avenue, a pristine row of shops on a cobblestone street that might suggest New Orleans in architectural character if not in vital business activity: much of the street appears deserted as one walks its length, if not the storefronts, many occupied by professionals like lawyers and architects, then certainly the sidewalks ... Both at Mayor's Black Hat shop and up on 2nd Avenue North, though, the life of the city thrives in shops run by kids with funky hair-cuts and hats indoors in contravention of the old politesse and even as the South's humidity and heat weighed them down. All the same, you're just as likely to see them huddled around a television watching the Bristol, Tenn., race as any punk or indie band playing live in a corner...*

King said, apparently left Birmingham the little potential Boho paradise that it was—*potential*, mind you, not even close to reality. Most of your artistically or intellectually inclined Alabamans still fled the town for points north and east, but the weak-kneed mayor and city council combined to leave long-abandoned, prime real estate downtown, like King's store, open to occupancy, if not renovation, for a pretty small price.

And though the promise of a shower was tantalizing, I didn't immediately head back to Black Hat. First, I needed food, and toward that end ordered a bagel with a second cup of coffee, sat down and looked up to a wall-mounted television on mute to find none other than Turner Bascombe leading the Bristol race on a rain-out Monday running. He was well through the lapped cars by this early afternoon point, and he passed several before I realized what was going on. His arch-rival in the series those days, dynasty boy Montuck Jr., was chasing him through the field, and there was no other racer capable of catching them in the remaining 25 laps without some miracle of an accident.

I stuck around the shop and read the news—no warnings of "October surprises" in the off-election year but a commentary on them from some hamfisted conservative columnist, wishing hard for the fruition of indeed some October plan some months to come to save his perspective in an increasingly weak-kneed liberal age (if only)—as by a hair Bascombe pulled out a win, something of a photo finish, he and Montuck side by side on the final stretch, Montuck held in check only by Bascombe's expert blocking of the former's Chevy as he tried the pass into the path of a slower lapped car. When they crossed the finish line, a clearly angry dynasty boy gave Turner Bascombe's Ford a hard bang on his left side, sending him glancingly into the Bristol wall. It was the inevitable culmination of several of "Turn" Bascombe's incidents of dubious intentionality, Montuck on the losing end of at least three, as the commentators no doubt proceeded to spell out the rivalry and ratchet up the drama for watchers.

Mort would have appreciated the race. I wondered whether he was behind the bar at Selma's and seeing it right now. Talladega was next week, one of the commentators said, which I found out from the middle-aged hipster running the place was a mere 45 minutes east of Birmingham, and Alabama undoubtedly held further possibility for the battle's continuation.

I got directions from the same hipster, then set off on my way to the nearest grocery. Mental shopping list:

—loaf bread
—tub hummus
—several cans spinach, collards, sliced beets
—canned ham
—carton Marlboro Lights
—3x 22oz. Miller High Life* can
—sewing needle, thread

Food enough to last several days in the end, I thought, cigarettes longer. Tobacco was but of course miraculously cheap in Alabama, after Chicago's $10-plus a pack, and the canned vegetables and meats were dirt cheap themselves. I said a little prayer of thanksgiving to my mother, then the Suited Man, who couldn't have led me to a better place, financially speaking.

I made my way back to Ingalls through the Five Points South business district, where the freaks and weirdos met with the town's shuffling old guard, as Leroy King put it, a clash made manifest for me today as I descended the large hill into the district from the grocery in the presence of both protesting peaceniks (from middle-age-looking soccer mom types to your more typical young folks with weird hair) on one side of the circle where met 20th Street and Magnolia and 11th avenues, and directly across from them a slightly larger coterie of anti-abortion types. Among the latter was a decidedly demonic-looking cross between Abraham Lincoln and Gandhi (with the latter's trademark spectacles) preaching from atop a milk crate clad in what I could only assume was Amish garb, floppy farm hat a'flourish. He was flanked mostly by women bearing signs that read gorily and variously, some including pictures of the bloody mess of aborted fetuses and such.

I watched them all warily, grimly the latter crew as I strode by on the other side of the street.

WHAT DO WE WANT? /
Peace! /
WHEN DO WE WANT IT? /
Now!

"Peace my brother!" Lincoln/Gandhi, of the anti-abortion party, attempted to boom, though the peaceniks were surely louder. I was close enough to make out his message. "Peace indeed for the unborn souls of the world's wicked, who blaspheme the teaching and the omnipotence of God. Only God gives life, and only he taketh away, in the name of the Lord!" There was a guy in a Harley-Davidson shirt next to the street preacher holding a piece of poster board printed with a red, black and brown blob of an image of what would have been indeterminate content if it weren't for the "GOT A SMOKE?" tag at its top, "Tobacco is the devil's killer of choice" in smaller lettering below the picture. I pulled hard on my cigarette. The guy holding the sign then did the same, incongruously, with his own, looked me square in the eye, then turning his gaze to his poster, his cigarette and back to me again. He shrugged, puffed, and smiled.

I felt my head expand.

I was conspicuous, after all, one of the only single bystanders not rolling through in a car. The man in his Harley shirt shrugged again, extinguishing his cigarette in the gutter, breaking away in short order from the preacher.

"Is that blob supposed to be a lung?" I asked him.

"If you're out of work," said the man, "there's money in this poster." He got paid for what he was doing. The anti-abortion types tended to limit their appearances here, thus every time they showed up the television newscasters followed, ever to make on-air references to the 1990s clinic bombing by crazy Eric Rudolph of a still-extant abortion clinic just a couple blocks from this very place, I learned.

Who exactly paid him? I asked.

"It's cash, man, how do I know?" he said. He pointed over to Lincoln/Gandhi. "Does it matter? They want us to help swell the ranks, make a good show."

I nodded to the peaceniks across the square. "They do the same?" I said.

"No way," he said. "They've got real balls and blood behind them. They're out here every freaking day—not a new crew every time, but rotating members and a constant swell of new folks. No money in it, as you could say about most such things, but hey they've got a real war at their back. See? Got a smoke?"

Lincoln/Gandhi took final notice of us talking and turned his bible and bile in our direction. "... and we were talking about sin, yes, and even among our own here today are vile prognosticators, fornicators and partakers of the vile weed that is the tobacco plant and worse, most surely," he said. "Take the example here, of Winston Grubbs, 50-year-old homeless cancer victim who continues spreading the message of the destructiveness of his habit while continuing to engage it, proselytize it to the youth community as only a Promissory[9] member can." I took it he made reference to me as a member of the "youth community."

"I'm nearly 30," I said, loud enough that he could hear, and lit another smoke for myself, passing a fresh one to my companion, whose eyes lit up as if prepared to offer a profuse Southern message of thanks and, perhaps, an apology. "Don't sweat it," I cut him off, and schlepped my groceries on down the street. Lincoln/Gandhi never skipped a beat.

Back in the Suited Man's lair I combed the environs for clues, messages from Rinckoff or signs of my father. Whomever it was I was chasing was long gone, though clearly the bed had been laid for my existence here. I took it as a matter of course for a Shining Man, and laid groundwork of my own for some time in Birmingham, enjoying the beers and a hot meal of sliced bread, one can spinach warmed on the, thankfully, fully functional hotplate. A background of smooth jazz served musings on a Southern networked cabal of radical-right mercenaries known as the Promissory well before it took me off to dreams upright at the computer.

---

[9] *Unlike their predecessor organization the Promise Keepers, the Promissory offered the mainstream right-of-center political world unprecedented legitimacy in the Internet-fueled hyperdrive of conspiracy-minded rightists, beginning in the first decade of the 21st century. Their most common tactic was the staging of demonstrations with paid "actors," often laborers picked from the local homeless shelter, though the use of violence was not unheard-of, as the organization's name implies, the implied promise directed not to its members but to its enemies. In the digital age, it remained website-less, but an internal communiqué estimated to be from the period of 2001-02 (as the Sept. 11 attacks are referenced in the text as being of recent vintage) spoke to this point directly: "We promise to rip out the hearts of the baby-killers, blasphemers and devil children, whether that be by hand, mind, or bomb."*

131

Then I woke, having slept sitting for several hours, and the radio was off, and the smell of a freshly burned cigarette was in the air, and I listened closely to the sounds around me, gaze darting over every crook of the immediate, walled-off area of the lair. Heart quickening, pounding, I sprung to my feet then and peered into the darker greater space, now fully lit over on the other side of the cavern. I picked up the nearest weapon I could find (the hotplate, ripping its plug from the wall) and slowly crept toward the light ready to swing the plate by the power cord into the head of whatever beast or apparition jumped out at me.

It was quiet but for my own slow footfalls, and when I reached the light it shone on a beautiful sight. As if emerging still from dreams, laying eyes on the stark image of the shining suit, cast in spotlight so very dramatic that it seemed to float in midair, I nearly collapsed with at once elated and terrified excitement. I shaded my eyes from the sight, gaze darting about the dim recesses in every direction, listening further intently for sounds of the Suited Man around me. There was nothing. I finally moved closer to the suit and recognized in it a similar design to the original pieces I'd constructed, though its seams were of an industrial rigidity that bespoke factory, or at the least professional, more-competent-than-I production.

I found the fishing-wire lines that kept the suit suspended and ripped them down, all the while expected the Suited Man's squirrelly voice to catch me up at my back or ring out from the darkness ahead of me. I unplugged the single aluminum floodlamp that had illuminated it, then carried all back to my corner. I felt a familiar tug—though I left Chicago, flight from the routine wasn't in any way the bedrock of reasoning behind the move, after all. I let it pull me out, here. I donned the suit—no doubt about its quality, more race-worthy firesuit than the claptrap constructions I'd crafted to this point. I examined myself as best I could in the glass on an interior window, then made my way out of Ingalls and into the night, bypassing I-65 or 20/59 for the emptiness of nighttime downtown. I got little from the square blocks' desertion, though at the top of a parking garage attached to what appeared to be a mixed-use residential/commercial building, down 1st Ave. North, I could see up the hill to the mountain ridgeline just south of the

132

Five Points district, and the city lights no doubt caught my suit and sent a little pinprick of light back into the minds of those among the souls sitting awake this late gazing from windows in apartments and homes along the hill, where the city's neighborhoods were most densely concentrated.

The most insignificant star on the night's horizon.

I gave a silent thank-you to my now invisible messenger for motivation, and stood stock-still on a small riser under the garage roof's edge, nearly seven floors up, closing my eyes against the soft wind that blew across me. This was a loner stand, though I was not entirely alone. When I opened my eyes a single flash of light as if from a camera's bulb winked out from a rooftop several blocks distant beyond the train tracks. I smiled. Otherwise, Birmingham's empty evening didn't even prove a spectacle for my fellow street-walkers, proper to the core, I guessed. The night belonged to the truly devilish here, perhaps more literally than most anywhere. Did "Promissory" members cruise the avenues, I wondered, God's vigilantes armed with machetes like death themselves? It was a nice little image to conjure, particularly combined with the absurdity of Lincoln/Gandhi's 19th-century style. I made mental note to ask King if he was familiar with them.

And I postponed my first day fishing for work on 14th Street in favor of sleeping in, such as I could (considering that by 10 a.m. the Alabama sun was overhead and scorching the pates of the hairless, heating up my little-big cavern of a home here again to near unbearable levels). Plus, it'd be much less hot out the day next, the radio told me. I idly wandered from Black Hat Books to the grocery store to a taqueria I discovered nearby where no one seemed to mind that all you ever ordered the two hours you sat there and scarfed down free tortilla chips and salsa was a single beer.

King wasn't around all day long, but the volunteers working the counter past noon told me right—he'd be in by sundown. A punk band from New Orleans called Monocle was warming up when I strolled over from my second $3 visit to the taqueria and found King out front of the place in the street arguing with a city cop. They stood next to one of three orange cones said cop had used to block off the roadway in front of Black Hat, one of just a couple surface routes over the freight tracks and into the down-

133

town business district. King removed his glasses and waved them around, smoldering cigarette in his other hand, which he jabbed at the cop to emphasize his vulgarity.

"Fucking city bullshit," he said.

"Deal with it," the cop said, then made like to walk away. The second he turned his back King picked up the cone that had stood between them, then walked deliberately to the next one, parked in the center of the middle of this three-lane one-way street. He'd grabbed the last cone before the cop even noticed anything was amiss, then the two waddled at King's lead down to the end of the block, where King deposited the cones, turning around and doing his best to pretend the cop didn't exist.

It wasn't easy, as the black man was now shouting at the bookstore proprietor, threatening all manner of civil and, as it were, more personal action.

"That motherfucker just told me he was going to kick my white ass," King said, when the small altercation was finally done and the cones were back in place. "Guess we'll just have to deal with it."

When he got here earlier this evening, as it turned out, King had immediately moved the cones once and come a hair's breadth nigh of causing a wreck on the other side of the viaduct, where road crews were resurfacing 1st Ave. North, the cross street at the bottom of the hill across the tracks. Or so the cop said. I wondered whether he'd figured there might have been a reason they'd blocked it off.

"Well yeah, but the principle, man. I run a damn business here."

The cop was just as unforgiving as the anarchist businessman. Though the cop left for a brief period immediately after my arrival, he parked outside for the duration of the night's show, Monocle loud and brash, another local crew known as Alabama Rivertown less so—unruly-headed folk music for the loud and brash among us, I guess you could say.

I got my shower, the main reason I was here, and plenty of cheap beer from the Black Hat fridge. I read more about the international regulation of civil wars and learned a little from King about content management systems for websites as I stood over his shoulder asking questions to his posting of news of Friday night's event—"big noise show," he said.

"Loud guitars, that kind of thing?"

"Nah. Laptops, old modified amplifiers, mixers. *That* kind of thing," in addition to extreme low-tech, he said, bricks on the bottoms of aluminum trashcans. "It's basically jazz improv toward the achievement of ugly, maybe? Though some of it can be beautiful, too." He shrugged.

I knew the movement toward this sort of thing in the early '00s among indie-rock types, but my awareness had fallen off long ago among the Skynyrd- and Prince-loving set in the back kitchen.

Finally, I got around to the subject of the Promissory.

"I know exactly who you're talking about," King said. He didn't know the Promissory name—the group's ID was little more than guess on my part—but he did know the "preacher."

"That guy's a theater dude, a little crazy, wanders in and out of here occasionally, actually. I think he practically lives at the shelter in the church in Five Points."

I wondered aloud whether what the non-smoking sign holder had told me about the whole charade was true.

"Could be," King said. "This is Birmingham, Deep South USA, brother."

In the final analysis, the guy wasn't much different than me, just with a more lucrative pastime.

I would have bed down on the couch in the center of Black Hat's main space among the dusty words of the last century, but the show upstairs went on late into the evening, still blaring at midnight; I promised King I'd be back with the weekend for my first shift and, with last night's walkabout weighing on my eyelids, trudged the mile to Ingalls and crashed out with purpose to meet the new day. At 6 a.m. I trundled on to 14th and 1st North by the train tracks to join the mini-horde of five men—all denizens of a group encampment over the nearby railroad tracks, they said to my "Where you guys live?" query.

"Just watch it when the motherfuckers pull up," said John, the tallest and loudest of the lot, all of whom knew each other too well. "You'll be the first to go."

"How do you figure?" I said, held hope against the thought that I knew what he meant.

"Look at you, man," he said. I was white, young, he went on, and though I didn't exactly look the model of the perfect employee, I could command a degree of cleanliness these men could not.

"You've had a goddamned shower," as John put it. "You can tell by the fingernails. We slept on the ground on the other side of the tracks, digging in the dirt in our sleep. Except Albee," John pointing out a young man who'd just arrived maybe five years my junior, who nodded coolly.

"These motherfuckers look like they spent the night in a coffin and dug their way up just in time to go mow some fucking rich woman's grass, pull them stinking weeds," Albee gestured out over his compatriots, laughing to encourage them. They scoffed, to a man. I grinned uneasily. The power dynamic in this crew would be proven to my delight when the first crew pulled up, a rust-red pickup carrying two rust-red-bearded white men who looked like brothers and who picked off John first, then one of his friends, and left me and the growing cohort of shufflers to our shame.

"Proven wrong," I said, pointing John's way as he silently jumped into the back of the pickup.

"He's an asshole," Albee, or Albert, as he introduced himself, said, "but everybody knows him who comes by here." He went on. "Safety in familiarity. I've been out here just a few months. Shit's pretty dry, generally. John says it used to be better, before the Mexicans came. They hang out at a spot across town. If you get desperate, you might go hang with them, try to pass. You know any Spanish?"

"*Burrito*," I said. "I guess I'm hoping it doesn't come to that. Got a gig at a bookstore lined up for the weekend, maybe ..."

"Black Hat?" he said.

"Hell yes," I said, impressed.

"This pays hella better. Might sell three books a shift at that place."

"I was afraid of that." A black pickup clattered to a stop in front of us and the driver claimed me and Albert and another man I hadn't yet met. We rolled out west through old industrial Birmingham, empty-seeming husks of factories and sheet-metal-lined buildings dotting the space beyond the freeway, which we crashed down at speeds surely too fast to take safely with three guys, all manner of hedging shears and a lawnmower and weedeater un-tied-down in the pickup's bed.

Where we were headed was less industrial though no less der-elict. The house on the lot was once a near palace—a large old columned thing in the style of Tara of Southern literary fame and the old mansions of Main Street in Fock's Mill, the well-kept-up gigantic homes of Sharon Ave., Myer's Park, Charlotte.

"Ensley," Albert said when I asked where the hell we were. "Technically it's another town, but it's almost functionally a part of the city. I know people anyway who write *Birmingham* as the city on return addresses on their envelopes, though technically, you know, this ain't B-ham."

The driver was also the boss on the job, and showed us to our mini-headquarters on what was ultimately a sizable urban plot of land, in this mansion among row houses some blocks, bungalows others.

Mills had described the work as some "landscaping" when he picked us up, "longer-term if you're available." He now described it at least partly as clear-cutting; he wanted all the old-growth shrubs, included well-rooted boxwoods, gotten rid of, the intense tangle of vines in the several trees in the backyard dealt with, and those were just two of the things that needed done. We'd be at the old gem of a house a while.

"Gonna be a long haul," Albert said, who with myself on as-sist tackled the overgrown, well-rooted hedges along the sunny side of the house first off.

In addition to being a temporary laborer, Albert was a recre-ational/aspirational skateboarder and, more interestingly, maybe, an artist whose media was spray paint on concrete, brick, steel. From the yard of the house, if one walked around the front and to a particular spot out on the sidewalk at the corner of the T intersection where it sat, you could see the left edge of some of his work, as he was proud to point out—skulls with elaborately stylized *X*s for eyes and exaggerated smiles. His tag was XoXoZ, a wonderfully whimsical touch, I thought.

"Not enough of that around," I said.

"I try," Albert said. "Beyond the gangsta shit my friends are about."

I'd lucked out on work partners, the third in our crew being a black man likely in his 50s or 60s named J.R. who kept to himself unless he had something absolutely essential to impart, such as the news our driver's remark about a basement "infestation" actually referred to roaches, not rats or mice or other large creatures.

"I seen the bait," J.R. said. "Asked him about it, too, said he'd been using the gel. That shit works."

"You're the expert," Albert said, and J.R. laughed. They knew each other pretty well, having worked on jobs over the past year Albert said he'd been doing shit like this. J.R. looked like he could have been out here all his life: wiry untrimmed mustache a speckled silver and black, back beginning to stoop, curve forward to the ground—he wore a mesh ball cap like my contractor grandfather Littlejohn had when I worked his construction sites a mere child in the 90s, after the mess of my father hauled ass back to Chicago.

When five o'clock came round, both J.R. and Albert took off on foot for places relatively nearby, they said. I had no idea where I was, so I jumped in the pickup's passenger seat for a ride back downtown.

"You live down there?" said our foreman, Mark Mills was his name.

"I might not call it living," I said, "but that's where I've been most."

"Funny," Mills wheeling his pickup back onto I-20/59 past U.S. Steel back to Birmingham proper, "I didn't take you for one of these homeless. You don't have the right skin color, for one."

I didn't know quite what to say. "You can drop me off—"

"Not that being black is like a death warrant or anything. Anybody can have bad luck."

"—by where you picked me up, that's fine."

He considered it for a bit, spit a loogie out the window that trailed back into the truck's bed in a 70-mph collision.

"You don't want to tell me where you're staying," he said. "That's fine. I don't begrudge you your pride."

"It ain't that," I said, but didn't go on. If I could have told him how wrong he was, how pride might never have had anything to do with it, much less now … I was a pod in the throes of movement, of action, of the outward-rippling effects of my own mindfully puny force. I was learning how to be, simply, and arguing about it with this middle-aged workingman could very probably have made no purpose whatsoever than to leave him with a series of sadnesses or a bit of righteous anger to flood back into his country home, spoil his dinner.

When he dropped me, I said only: "You'll pick me up, same spot, in the morning, then?" I was tired, besides—it had been a back-breaking day.

Mills did pick me up, though, the next day and we went and did it again. Albert was back, as was old man J.R. XoXoZ told me more of his childhood, in particular the elementary school where he was mostly left alone, the West Side high school where no matter what he did to keep on top of it all there was always a new boor laying on him, essentially, yelling all sorts of *motherfuckers* as he strolled by. We went at it long and hard and, when it was over, I took the walking route across the west side Albert and J.R. recommended. Took almost an hour and a half, but its traversal past a famous old baseball field—Rickwood, the oldest standing park in the nation, as J.R. had it—and through the main old city cemetery with its Bear Bryant football mecca gravestone and its lesser known lights, like the aforementioned Mr. Herman Poole Blount, cosmic jazzman extraordinaire.

The walk was long and mostly uneventful, with the exception of a catcall from an Oldsmobile whose long denouement I didn't hear, just the first birth of "Mother..." with the T – H – E – R sounding more like *three*, maybe, pitch-warped with the speed of the passing car. I got a little jolt from it, though, and I got the idea, the notion, the little prod of movement there on 6th Avenue South that would lead me to new heights of awareness—one needn't a shiny suit down south or particularly in Birmingham for people to stand up and take notice. They're going to yell at you, be up in your business, any old way, whether you give them reason or not.

Next day, Friday, Albert and I talked more about it over beers in the neutral territory, as he called it, of downtown and Five Points—a pre-show beer at Ada's Lounge. "Get there, get in early enough," he said, "we won't pay the cover."

The boy was right.

We walked there all the way from Ensley for the better part of two hours, arriving sweat-soaked and stunk up outside in time for the place to open its doors at 7.

"You might be the only white guy in here at first," he said.

"I've gotten used to it," I said, not that it'd ever been too much uncommon outside of Chicago, in any case.

And indeed I was, though the graffiti artist seemed to know the dolled-up middle-age women manning the bar this evening. They treated him like a friend, with a tinge of condescension to his youth and ragged stink: when he ordered a rum and Coke, one remarked that that was a good ladies' drink. But he held a rapport with them that might have been expected of a much older, more well-dressed man. And when an old man Albert eventually identified as the owner of the joint sauntered in and welcomed "Little Albee" back, Albert nodded cool and calm as if he'd been coming there all his life.

And a life it was, marked by all the successive successes and abysmal failures any guy in his 20s could half expect. Albert could have been the Shining Man himself, had he ever been prodded enough to leave the post-industrial wasteland that was the town of his rearing. The accents of speech in Birmingham were woefully familiar to my brain, after all, but the place had been walloped by the collapse of its industrial base of employment from the late 1970s onward. The evidence was everywhere, from my abandoned home at Ingalls to the myriad of closed-up mechanics' and small manufacturers' shops that were the scenery of the walk downtown from Ensley. Farther east, a famously mammoth old iron smelting operation was a protected historic monument, park and very occasional concert venue, Albert told.

After high school Albert was the beneficiary of a scholarship to the state university in Birmingham to study art—painting concentration. He finished with flying colors, building his alternate ID on the plethora of left-behind and otherwise exposed concrete and brick walls the city offered as canvas. He then long made his plugs for gainful employment in town, but found all the city's universities' departments stuffed full of people just like him. He worked in restaurants—smoking ribs, tending flat-top cookers, prepping coleslaw and potato salad—before he found something he could well feel beyond the occasionally errant knife-slice of his fingertip

140

in whatever kitchen.

"I got an itch, man," he told me there, a couple moderately priced drinks in.

"I know it," me, nodding vigorously, thinking about my father, runt of the railyards, the drunk on the train trestle and alone in that Chicago tiny-space where I unearthed the few clues he gave to his present or near-present tense, cried a little over memories of other times. My pop could be a damned hoot. He came home with a baseball glove for a birthday somewhere around the time before he disappeared. He'd never played hardball once in his life. Rather than waste money on his own glove to throw around with his slowly learning son, he went straight for the throat.

"Go on and hit me with it," palms out, right fist into left hand producing a slap to rival the best gloved coach on Camden Yard, at Fulton County, the best catcher you'd ever meet. I hurled the rock hard as I could, Pop jumped, spinned, dove, did whatever he needed to catch my wild-ass pitches—with his bare hands.

"Harder, son," he kept on, "keep it coming. No other way to live, no other way." How I reimagine it, what I felt like I'd heard from the man, if I could rationalize my own addictions, predilections, tendencies, itches scratched till they bled to become something new.

I tried to better imagine my father's final moment, the one of which I had any clear evidence. The squat old man in his deliberate manner writing that black-marker-on-cardboard message that spent so many weeks staring me in the face. How long had he thought about it, pen in hand, son in his mind's eye, visions of reflective salvation dancing in his head?

Very little, very probably. The answer was right there in the text itself. The speculation, conditionality of *mights*, the exclamation points. The realization of one's own willful stupidity in the writing, tamping down paralyzing analysis in favor of things, of action. *Live that life, son! No tomorrow! Be a vessel! Be a mirror!*

Stupid men are given to exclamation, very probably, run out of new ideas, get an itch, scratch it.

"I got it," Albee said, "scratched it out to 14th and the tracks there and, the first day some asshole redneck white man picked me up, no offense—"

"None taken."

"—I loaded big trucks with old furniture all damn day long. Did a few of the new downtown apartments after that, moving people in from up north who God knows why they came to Birmingham, but they did. The papers say they're coming in droves here taking banking jobs and such but it's a bunch of bullshit. They want it to be like Charlotte or Atlanta, man, but it ain't. This city and those people are living on the backs of all the motherfuckers you see out there every morning. And the Mexican guys I told you about. That's about it for honest work, I guess, unless you want to serve the people in the restaurants, the bars, such as their presence is, I guess, and the honest work don't pay worth much of a shit ..." He drifted off, took a long gulp to finish off his drink.

"Take this place, for instance," Little Albee/XoXoZ now lowering his voice several decibels. "Later, it'll be not exactly full of them, but they'll be here peppered around the crowd of your everyday Birmingham and thinking they're getting something creative and authentic and cool from whatever 1980s smooth-jazz knockoff's playing tonight. Granted, I love this joint, but you get my drift."

Lessons to be learned one day, I thought, and at once that I'd already learned them at war with the patrons of the Sparrow, maybe stood to know even better "around the corner from here," I said. "You know the Black Hat, you said. I think there's a show there tonight."

He nodded.

"Pretty white crowd," I said, "but not exclusively. You get it. You'll dig it."

He nodded again, and so on we went in time, as the band set up to play. I noted the leader's metal-mouthpieced tenor and soprano saxophones resting on chrome stands and thought of John Coltrane, thought further of a group I'd seen at the Lark Sparrow—a free-jazz combo with a woman on flute, a man whose name I can't remember on Coltrane's instruments, if Trane could be said to have infected our culture so widely as to have owned the tenor and soprano outright, not to mention the alto. This guy had played alto and soprano, again if I remember. They had a bassist who did some indie-rock playing, too, bartender Jake told, and a drummer who could do funky-beats bombast as well as more typically slippery free-jazz propulsion.

Albert and I talked about this on the short walk to Black Hat. "Albee," a nickname he said he shared with his grandfather, whom he was named for, a big blues fan and a sometime blues guitarist.

"Used to take me out to joints in the middle of nowhere," he said. "You'd have guys and gals, some dressed to the nines, pulling up on these country roads all the way to Mississippi to hear folks play blues in rickety old shacks with unfinished plank stages. Larger than goddamned life in my head. I might remember it wrong."

He got viz-art from his grandfather, too, who painted houses in his off time, from old-time yearly whitewashing to more creative work.

"Sometime let's take a walk west from Ensley and I'll show you one of his more well-known places," Albert describing a red, white and blue house with, on the roof, the map-outlined image of Africa tying it together. "It's a crazy-looking joint, no doubt, but impressive—kept up by the community down there like totally voluntarily."

His grandfather wasn't in well-enough condition to do it, or he'd passed on. The latter turned out to be true, and Albert got quiet after he divulged it. I came within seconds of telling my own sob story, felt on the verge of a connection beyond just idle chit-chat, but we were turning onto the rise to the viaduct on 21st that led to Black Hat, and the cops were "out again," I said, laughing in spite of myself. "Stubborn dogs never learn."

I briefed Albee on the situation of the cones, here again parked in the roadway with the police. King learned his lesson, absent today on the street. We ran on in amongst the shelves and the people, kids with bad haircuts and cigarettes attached to their fingers. Not a suit among them: I continued to half-expect Rinckoff to show his face.

A monolithic drone like an amplifier on the fritz blew in from the upstairs performance space. We followed the march of boots and chunky-soled shoes and vintage sneakers upward and were greeted at the top of the stairs by a fat knot of 30 or so spectators 10 feet off a solo performer behind a table piled with equipment of obscure character but for an easily identifiable laptop at its center.

This was the "Birmingham Scream," Albee yelled in my left ear: "I know him!"

I listened, though "listening" probably doesn't do the experience justice. I could better feel than hear the waves of sound rippling through the space in my diaphragm with each slight move of a mouse The Scream had hooked to his main unit. I closed my eyes for several seconds, opened them and scanned the growing horde of the crowd to find others in similarly meditative mode. Albee tapped my shoulder, held up an index finger and said something I couldn't hear. I nodded as he traipsed downstairs, then closed my eyes and let the sonic power pass through me.

After several seconds it was as if my sense of balance was gone for a moment and I tipped right, stumbled and slowly made my way to the far side of the space, sitting on the floor with my back propped against a brick wall. I closed my eyes again to the continuing cacophony.

When I was brought back to the din, Albee was standing a couple feet off holding two beer cans and looking alarmed. King was gripping my right shoulder, his mouth moving.

"I'm OK," I tried to say, and stood up as King backed away. I'd fallen asleep, I guessed, and told them as much. I laughed and threw up my hands, but they couldn't hear me. I grabbed a beer from Albee in attempt to quench an uncommonly strong thirst.

"Water?" I mouthed. King grabbed my right arm and led me down the stairs, Albee following.

"Wow," I said, when we were back downstairs with plastic cups filled, half-empty beer cans and cheap cigarettes in our hands. "Good sleeping music."

"You all right?" King said, fiddling with something on his computer. "The cops." He gestured outdoors.

"Long day, right?" I looked to Albee, who nodded. "Hey, you said you knew the guy up there."

"The Scream," King said, still not looking up. "Travels around the city with a boombox on his shoulder like an old-school corner hip-hopper. What you hear up there is what's coming out of his boombox. When he's not touring."

"Yeah," said Albee. "I've run into him by the train tracks downtown, painting. Know him only well enough to say hi and be done

144

with it." A squeal pealed through the ceiling, and Albee began to tell of a friend who'd moved to New York to pursue D.J. work and came across his hometown Birmingham compatriot there. "'Noise is the new punk,' Will says, or the punk that never was. He said he was wasting time by the East River and thinking over climate change with a beer or something else weird, and the Scream came walking around the corner with his boombox and just sat down."

Albee gazed up into the ceiling, searching for the story.

"Will, he likes to say things like," Albee's voice assuming his best mock-gravitas, "'When I see climate change in the local news, in the plants growing in my little patch of Brooklyn earth, I think the only solution is for meteorologists to become politicized.' Dramatic shit like that. The Scream is more or less the same. They got along famously."

The Scream did not stop playing for the hour and more we were there, during which time we ventured back upstairs and swayed and swooned with the rest of the crowd. In the intensity of one particularly rumbling moment, I studied the Scream's face—he looked like Rinckoff a little, I thought, and continued to think as the old nervous anticipation grew in my limbs and I moved to leave, bumping fists with Albee and King, who said he expected me there bright and early, 11 a.m., when they opened in the morning.

"I'll be here," I said, and off I went back by Ada's, down 6th and all the way to Ingalls and the Suited Man's lair, minus any Suited Man other than me, as I pulled the Shining Man's getup over my sweat-sticky skin and trod out into the night feeling the power of visibility, of reflectivity, recent buzzsaw muscle memory of the Scream's sonic variations humming through my bones. My first real stand in Birmingham, little did I know, would be the last time[10] I truly felt the suit's physical power—the reflections I got here were much too loud, garish for even my eyes to bear.

---

[10]An exercise in firsts and lasts, tapped out around this time on Carl's loaner laptop, one of the final bits of scribbling I did before the fruits of what you are reading came into focus: *The first time I shoplifted I got away with it. Hell, the second and third and fifth and eighth and tenth times, too, candy at the corner fuel station, anyhow, nothing to be too worried over if you weren't a man of principle, particularly, and in our lifetime a*

I brandished the thing like a weapon, this night.

I trudged north in the dark on the route west of and parallel to I-65, aiming for the mini cloverleaf bridge junction of 65 and I-20/59. I'd only really seen it from Sanders' rig, from Mills' pickup. Heart pounding quick with the effort, the anticipation, I scaled a 10-foot fence in the dark at the bottom of an embankment that rose to 20/59 just west of the sharp left turn of bridge that through-traffic took before snaking into downtown. I got to the top of the embankment awash in light, finally, the traffic density not near what I'd seen on 90/94 in Chicago, but dense enough that my inner sense of my own exposure was driven to high alert.

I hurtled into a dead zone just off the rightmost lane after an exit split—not quite to the true beginning of the curving bridge, not so far away as to relinquish to cruising by with little worry at my presence the approaches of tractor-trailer rigs and a lesser number of autos. The vehicle I first took notice of, a rig, noticeably slowed as it moved closer to my bright form before jake-braking

---

precious few of those are left. So I've got excuses.

My first-ever drunk was out back of long-haul trucker Schuyler's parents' place when we were a mere 15 years of age, tops. His parents were out of town and we were nothing if not wild and experimentally free of regret or worry—or in our state we were, tanked out on multiple shots of bargain-basement brands like Everclear, Lord Calvert Canadian whiskey, God knows what all else. I wonder to this day at the unconscious mind, what it chooses to transfer to the conscious part for memory. I was forced into a shower fully clothed by the drunk and disorderly that night—after cops showed up and Schuyler took it upon himself to rescue the more wasted among us back to sobriety—but I have absolutely no recollection of it but for my slightly damp attire upon awaking the next morning. What I did remember—the hole in the bathroom floor, in which I sank thigh-deep at one precious moment.

The first time I had sex was after work at Henry's with the 30-year-old bartender Lucy—against the cold silver doors to the walk-in cooler and freezer. It was difficult but exciting. I came quickly. I'd been working there only a couple years. I was 17.

The first time I had my toothbrush stole was also the last, which probably says a great deal about my lack of success with the female sex. Whosoever ransacked the Suited Man's lair during my fateful Birmingham I-20/59 stand was the culprit, and unlike Will Theron's case, the toothbrush was undoubtedly not the most significant thing that was taken.

The first time I smoked a cigarette was at Henry's, out the back door to the greasebins, take a right, walk three steps, sit down on the pine needles between the rear sidewalk and the building. From there you could see progress in the raw, in the flesh—a late 1990s monstrosity of a mall with its perimeter road dotted with gigantic boxes of retail repositories. The last time I smoked a cigarette: a few minutes ago.

its slow away around the remainder of the curve. I stood almost a full five minutes without police intervention, so I closed my eyes and turned my back on the traffic, walking with the flow up onto the bridge, where a mere four feet of shoulder between traffic and concrete-and-steel bridge abutment was my path. The dopplered horn-honks really got going then. I trod on, the shoulder opening up on the other side, where I turned back to face the traffic, extending my arms from my sides in Christ pose.

Near-instantly, astoundingly, really, the traffic died. I counted *one – two – three – four* until I got to 30 and another pair of headlights shone from behind the bridge curve—*thirty-one*—and a magnificent pair of headlights they were, bright halogen bulbs on one hopped-up refurb'ed 1980s-vintage sports car that, when the lights caught my suit, jerked a little left as if in response before the high-performance engine in the machine—an old Camaro or Firebird, I thought—revved high and guttural, burning by faster than any had previously.

But the hot-rodder, speed freak out for a joy ride, didn't keep the engine gunned to a veritable blast-off. Rather, after I closed my eyes to bathe in the engine's vibrational hum, the well-tuned machine quickly down-shifted, reverse-throttled. I spun to see the car careening right quickly toward the exit ramp I stood just ahead of, decelerating to a stop not halfway down the ramp and beginning to spin in reverse my way. I watched the car come, thinking it too old to be a detective's or other cop's, likely, wondering just the same whether to make a break back the way I'd come. But when the car stopped 30 feet on, a short man in a familiar racer's uniform stepped out. I froze and watched the apparition come on as a small black car flew by and three quick bursts of camera-flash came from its passenger side. I smiled, only slightly distracted from the apparition walking my way on the highway apron.

"Turner," the man said when he reached me, offering his hand.

Goddamn Turn Turner in the flesh, it was, and I couldn't help but be stunned into a moment of silence in which to ponder the extent of the race man's stalking of me and mine these past months. Well, me and my own mind, in the bar at Selma's, downtown on the coffeehouse television, Birmingham, Alabama. Talladega, I thought to the background music of air-brake hiss, the whine of 22.5-inch tires. Turn was decked out in his yellow-and-black bumblebee firesuit, grinning, eyes wide.

"You always wear your racing suit in your personal vehicle?" I said.

"Do you?" he said.

"I don't drive," I said. "I stand."

"And walk," he said. "I passed a while ago while you were crossing the bridge, then doubled back. You're bright, man, but not that bright. And we're not talking about professional drivers out here, either. Not exclusively, anyway," gesturing out to the road as the next rig whined by, the driver pulling an air horn that dopplered its cacophony by us. Traffic had picked back up quickly, to the point where Bascombe the racecar driver had to shout to be heard, not that shouting would have been out of the norm for him.

"Come on!" he said. "I was out joyriding. Get in the car."

And so I did.

Turner Bascombe didn't talk much on our drive to the airport, a masterful set of maneuvers at speeds approaching the upper limit of what the Camaro, it turned out, could handle. We toured the relic of downtown that night in a 1979 model that was often enough ensconced in an enclosed car hauler running alongside his racing machine when he was, more typically, flying, he said when I asked just where in the hell he spent his time in transit. Our trip in the auto ended with our disembarkation, two bright-suited men walking across an airfield at an airport that was dark at this hour in large part, critical functions finished after the end of a business day. Security was on hand, though, to let in Turner and myself, after a quick pat-down of our suits, ID checks for Turn's clearance through a door at the far northern end of the passenger terminal that let almost directly onto a taxiway, across which he directed me to a small hangar he said was the area's main private hangar. He and a couple other teams had rented space in it this week.

"Qualifying was today at the track," he said, by way of a final explanation of his suit. He'd carried a duffel from his Camaro and, as we walked into the mini-hangar, he pulled a pair of jeans and a plaid button-up from it and threw them my way. We were about the same size, he pointed out.

"You could use a little sprucing up for where we're going," he said.

Where exactly would be divulged at a later time, and I gave no argument in the whirlwind of movement, of momentum, Turner now proud to introduce the amphibious Cessna 208A, interior converted for maximum in creature comforts with a side wet bar and refrigerator, coffee maker, all of which he seldom used, including sleeping space enough for three men, everything tied down and ready for flight, as it were. There would be no sleeping tonight, he said, not for a long while anyway. He commandeered a vehicle to pull the aircraft out of the hangar under the night sky. After I changed, and he did the same, to a pair of jeans and striped button-down that left us looking like near-identical twins, he motioned me into the aircraft.

Curiosity got the better of me now with the fear of high speeds, high altitude.

"Where are we going?" I said.

"Sit tight," Bascombe said, and I began to strap myself into a jump seat just behind the pilot's chair. I waited for information. The engine rolled up to lit.

"It's stock," Bascombe yelled, "Whitney something or other. I do know the particulars, but I'd spare you. Just like a driver, right?"

That meant little to my ears today.

"Where are we going?" I repeated above the growing howl of the engine, whine of the wind, and words were exchanged over the radio and we began to move, quickly, runway lights appearing to my right and left out of the Cessna's windows, the dim beacon of the airport itself now in the distance beckoning familiarly with its covered passenger walkways at gates drawn back like the warm, folded hands of a sleeping giant. We continued accelerating.

"Here we go!" Bascombe looking back at me, and we were in the air and rising quickly, Bascombe screaming then like a delighted banshee at the controls. We were moving west, back the way we came, as just off port of this flying mini-boat I could see the downtown cloverleaf where we met far below.

"Come on up front," Bascombe said when we were over dark rural terrain some 10 minutes on. I did, and he gave me the scoop.

149

"We're over Hueytown now, or outside it, I guess. Tuscaloosa in another 10, 15."

I knew nothing of it but for its college and football team and the memory of online videos of the somewhat recent high-powered tornado that ripped through town. I told Bascombe as much.

"You'll see it tonight," he said, and the plane dropped in an airless pocket and my stomach lodged in my throat and my heart raced, pushing a fog into my brain whose persistence over the next several minutes had me leaning forward, hands lodged under my thighs and eyes closed tight.

"You OK?" Bascombe said, and I recovered by telling of Trey Olden and his flying machine.

"I've heard of the Flying Day!" Bascombe said. "Did he win?"

Not exactly, I told him, and made to elaborate, but Turner Bascombe suddenly let fly another banshee scream, hit the throttle then let the engine calm slightly before turning in a wide arc to our right, easing then back left to correct the course. I felt as if led by Trey or maybe rambunctious Billy, had no idea how he was navigating the course here it was so dark on the ground. We passed over like death in the night.

Small display screens in the cabin suggested good altitude monitors, but in my slightly worried excitement I failed to find any kind of radar map or GPS pinpointing our location.

But then the suburban neighborhoods giving way to strip malls and the dark swath of the tornado's path and then the college and miniature high-rise dormitories and the stumbling scant few blocks of downtown Tuscaloosa all made themselves visible in stages, and I realized just how low we were when we flew past a crowd of people standing outside a bar who actually looked up and waved at us.

"Jeez. You do this sort of thing every day?" I said.

Turner laughed. "Not hardly," then exaggeratedly leaned hard right with a turn now that went near a complete 180 degrees.

"Are we landing?"

"Yes."

"Where's the runway?"

Turner gestured off port. I stood halfway up, about as far as was possible in this thing, and looked and could see the river that

150

cuts through downtown. We were coming up on a couple of large bridges over it, the bridges brightly lit but the river under it a black cast iron frying pan, its wide handle extending into the distance. Bascombe was taking her down fast; we were no more than 50 feet above an old train trestle whose functionality looked like it might be a toss-up. I strapped myself in and we splashed her down quite smoothly, really, as a crowd of well-dressed, mostly white people watched and clapped and waved from a pier that looked to be connected to a restaurant or bar built on stilts on the shore across from downtown.

Our destination.

"Need a drink?" Bascombe said when the Cessna was parked.

We made our ways through the small throng of people on-hand to greet him, Bascombe introducing me as "a friend from Birmingham," and found the bar. I was about to order when he appeared at my left shoulder.

"It's on me," he told the bartender before I could order. "He's one of the team."

I ordered a whiskey, rocks, and a water that was served in a nicely hefty pint glass with lemon. When I turned around an even shorter man with a bent rod maybe an inch in length stuck through his nose's septum like a bullhorn was offering his hand. He was pretty obviously drunk. Bascombe had disappeared.

"Tacklebox," the nose-man introduced himself, part of the crew of the Bascombe Lumber Ford, pinching his nose in what I would come to know as his signature gesture. He was a tire carrier, sometime mechanic, but the crew chief had lately talked about making him the anchor of the team as the jackman, but wouldn't he like doing the tire carrying more, wouldn't he prefer stability to the stress of leadership? It's a fucking jackman, he said, not President of the United States, answering his own afore-seeming rhetorical question, which he would continue to do as I gulped and was otherwise silent. His extended monologue ended with us drinkless on the pier, yards from the amphibious aircraft.

"How's it on fuel?" Tacklebox said, a drunken blank stare leveled into but at once beyond the plane into the black nothing below the surface of the water.

"20 miles a gallon," I said, grinning.

151

"Not bad," he said, not batting an eye.

"I'm thinking we'll put that hybrid in it next time."

"Sweet."

"I like diesel fuel for it, too, man."

He snapped out of the ridiculous reverie he'd entered, finally. He squeezed his nose with thumb and forefinger of his right hand, again, flipping up the half-bullhorn with his thumb just slightly at the end with a smile and then a laugh and "Were you just saying something about a hybrid fucking plane engine? What. The. Hell"—his fist rapped me on the back and his arm stayed on my shoulders as we walked through the crew of well-dressed folks young and old on the pier back inside.

"So what is this, anyway?" I asked.

"This place is called the Cypress, but all this"—he stepped back and threw his hands out from his sides—"all this is us. We do it every year down here—Turner got so damn happy a few years ago when he was able to do the water landing that he's made it a tradition." Plenty of locals involved now, too, he said, both Talladega races each year.

"Does he usually fly solo?" I asked.

"He does," said Tacklebox. Which reminded him: "Where the hell did you come from, anyway?"

I figured I might for once leave my story to someone else. I told him as little as possible—Birmingham boy, but not originally, met Bascombe by chance out on the street and he offered me a joyride down here. What I still didn't know but would soon find out was that Tacklebox's likewise drunken teammate, a fellow tire carrier, was much more drunk than even he, and:

"Word has it, don't you know, that Turner wanted something new, that the crew chief, Eddy Huggins—we just call him Hugg— wasn't about to give, see, as the tire carrier in question was his son, and did I mention one hell of a layabout drunk, look who's talking, but he's volatile as all hell and Turner he has a way with his team, a way of taking shit into his own hands."

I couldn't exactly see it with the clarity that might have been provided by a flashbulb on a man clad in reflective material repurposed from reflective roadworker vests, but the vision was at the least somewhat in focus. My traffic stands had prepared me for

152

the high-balling brushes with metal at extreme speed to come. I gave ghost and told Tacklebox there and then how I met Turner Bascombe on 20/59, of the noise show and the anticipation it breathed into my very limbs, my entire body and soul.

"Goddamn fate and fucking hot dogs," he said, snapping from a passing hostess' tray the last two miniature gourmet sausages wrapped in some sort of dough. Tacklebox was as a ghost himself confirming a congruity—Suited Man of a different color I would be.

But I wasn't in the clear yet, by any means. Tacklebox disappeared into the loud crowd and I visited the bar for a beer. Had to be going on 3 a.m., the place legal only with the implicit, or explicit, blessing of the local cops. By the time I made it back onto the pier with my beer word had gotten around of Mr. layabout drunken fighter and tire carrier Charles Huggins' replacement and Chuckie himself came out to join my solo sojourn in the dark night all arms extended in exaggerated hugs and "Yeah man, yeah," he said, "so fucking good to meet you," at first.

I started to laugh but hadn't fully committed to it before the drunk Huggins changed course. He sort of stumbled back from me, caught his rearward motion on his right foot and lunged hard, right fist clenched, with a distinct swerve at my face. I dodged and took most of his body's momentum on my right shoulder, following him with my left into the pier's railing and mustering, beer splashing out of the glass into my face, every little sap of strength I had to get him as far away from me as possible.

His wail as he fell over the rail before the water engulfed him, a sound reminiscent of the Cessna's engine, really, brought the attention—with a splash, of course—of a gaggle of revelers standing on the restaurant/bar's riverfront porch.

"Holy mother of god!" I heard one dame exclaim, and as Huggins emerged from the black water below with a stream of curses that would have been vile even for a sailor, much less a racecar crewman, some applause chattered out from the crowd. Turner came leading a reconciliation party of his crew down the length of the pier to where I stood, pulling Chuck Huggins out, Tacklebox the newly anointed jackman and Charlie Peerfoy, the only dark-skinned member of the crew, far as I could tell by then, and current/former jackman (though he likely didn't know it, yet), serving as anchor to keep the enraged, wet man idled as Turner spelled out—quite simply: "you're done, Chuck"—the terms of the end of his employment:

"Eddy will approve," the driver said. The elder Huggins wasn't out here tonight, rather with the cars and skeleton crew of mechanics at the track discussing and performing last-minute adjustments ahead of the Sunday race. Likely sleeping, at this hour, a thought for which I spent a moment conjuring envy.

"Bullshit," said young Huggins.

"It's not a bluff," Bascombe said. "You're through, after Sunday. I got a replacement here. Shoulda seen the man out on the road tonight. He's born to do what you do, and though I've known him just a few hours, I've got better confidence in him, which should tell you an awful damn lot about what I think of the recent shit I've been putting up with."

The crowd up at the porch railing didn't exactly cheer, but here on the pier I got the feeling of being back in a parade, on public display for an unsuspecting audience. The plaid shirt and jeans covering me positively chafed, my shining suit hung on a peg just above our heads in one of the Cessna's windows.

Huggins cursed Bascombe, his family, the entire team and the spectators up at the railing, who, on a sliding scale depending on their ages, rolled their eyes dismissively, clapped and laughed, or placed hands over their mouths in exaggerated horror. Through it all, the offender's body convulsed like an angry baby's. Peerfoy and Tacklebox strengthened their hold on the drunk man.

Turner "Turn" Bascombe turned to me, finally, as they dragged Huggins back up the little dock indoors to an unknown fate, and said, "Ready to fly?"

We boarded the Cessna. Tacklebox came running out to join us after Turner got the engine humming. The water takeoff started off choppy but the run was ultimately smooth, the dark flight back to the airport at the edge of Birmingham a silent endeavor but for the roar of air.

Chapter 11

Chuck Huggins disappeared then into some distant haze at the crown of some nearby mountain. He didn't show for Talladega racing the Saturday day before the main event, and I got my training on the fly that night, Tacklebox running through the essentials of carrying—"squat, lift with your legs"—careful not to over-exert the new guy.

"We don't want you feeling like a dead mule in the morning," he said.

If only he knew what I'd been doing all week. The cleanup in Ensley took its toll, and the long night previous hadn't helped the stiffness at all.

I practiced throwing my legs quickly over the pit wall, a move Tacklebox said wasn't necessary.

"Most guys they just get up in a crouching position on the wall, like this," hopping onto the balls of his feet atop the small wall.

I closed my eyes, sat with my back to the pit road, trying hard to sense Tacklebox's motion, sound, behind me. "I'll do it this way," I said, kicking my feet high and pushing off my right—I raised my body onto my left hand and threw my feet over the wall with the rest.

"Ta-da!" he said. "That's slick, but one misstep and you're toast. I'd suggest extreme care. And remember, it might not be exactly easy with a tire in your hands. Speaking of which," and we ran through the motions with the surprisingly heavy tire-and-wheel assembly, Tacklebox playing the part of tire changer, the man with the ratchet gun who would follow my setting of the wheel in place to tighten the nuts. We did it all on a car jacked up on pit road like it was a real raceday, Tacklebox eyeing my exit from setting the tire.

"Nah, look, you're stepping back too far," he said, freezing me mid-stand, my left foot's arch centered squarely over the white-painted barrier between the pit box, where the change happened, and the pit road, the speed-limited highway of the track.

"Again, asking for trouble like that," he said, and he demonstrated a technique with very tight movement, limited range of motion, before we called it a day and walked through the garage area, something of a party scene this evening after the "junior" series race, teams celebrating small victories and ignominious defeats in groups on folding chairs set up at the back of big team trailers, lined up in two big rows ass to ass like slicker versions of the rigs at the truckstop I'd seen just a week ago with Stonefly Sanders.

Montuck Jr.'s team, Tacklebox pointed out, were "drunker than skunks. They rolled the little Chevy today." Montuck and several other premiere series drivers moonlighted in the junior competition as a way of getting more track time, I guessed aloud, but Tacklebox disagreed.

"Every car's different," he said. "Practice with one won't do shit for you with the other. They do it for the money. Not like they need it so badly." Montuck, he added, speaking softly now as we strolled down the aisle between the two trailer rows, you wouldn't find imbibing with the junior series team, one of the many indicators of his particular character. "Turner's a party man, which makes him great for building camaraderie, see—'team love,' you could say. You'll see these guys up here and the most relevant point of comparison you might want to make you saw coming at your face last night. Most of us can keep things in check because we like the job, you know. We like our driver. These guys here are just stiffs. Like fucking factory workers or temp slaves, they tend to overcompensate in the off time. I have doubts about whether any of them have even talked to Montuck."

He motioned their way as we passed—three guys, part of Montuck's team, still in their red-and-black suits, milling about the back of their trailer on folding chairs and looking as if they would fall asleep at any moment. We walked on for 30 seconds or more.

"That doesn't mean we don't like them, of course," Tacklebox laughing when we were out of their sight. "A friendly prank is friendly, in the end."

He turned a 180 abruptly, then, and motioned for me to follow as we doubled back and slipped into the three feet, tops, of lateral space between Montuck's trailer and the Canadian whiskey logo-emblazoned team house beside it.

We stopped halfway to the front of the trailer, at which tires were stacked high in several columns under a canopy: "For the race tomorrow," Tacklebox said, then stopping, turning with his index finger firmly to his lips, before we continued on to walk through the space. In all of it, I could catch just the hint of grin.

When we reached the stacks, he hoisted the top tire and passed it back to me. Each tire had M-O-N-T-U-C-K written in fairly large yellow capitals and in repetition around its circumference. Tacklebox pulled two yellow paint pens from a pocket somewhere and, devilish grin spread over his face, directed me in the tires' defacement. The difficulty was in morphing the C to a K without a black pen, but otherwise the joke was fairly simple. As it turned out, it wasn't the first time Montuck's team became the P-O-K-E-M-O-N express.

The sixth tire in for me, giggling, maybe the eighth for Tacklebox, we were spotted by a team member from the rear of the trailer, who gave pursuit. We exited at the front of the rig, by the tires—Tacklebox sprinting left, me right, divergent paths back to the main garage area off the South row of trailers. We convened inside the Bascombe trailer, Tacklebox already popping a beer when I entered.

"To a long and productive day," Tacklebox raising the can, sounding like Trey or Carl or one of the many artists and/or sarcastic-ass ne'er-do-wells whose IDs I'd memorized at the Sparrow. That was where the resemblance stopped.

He leaned from his chair and hit the play button on a stereo system's CD unit, the opening cello strains of an old Anthrax record swelling through the team "lounge," this 10'-by-10' compartment near the front of the rig.

"You like noise, you said," Tacklebox raising his right hand, fingers configured to the horns of the devil, and banging his head a few strokes when the guitar and drums came in.

"Euphoria," I said, "State of…" remembering the record's title. We sang along at the chorus. "Be all, and you'll be the end all / Life can be a real ball / State of mind: Euphoria!"

I popped open my own beer and reveled in the languid fatigue growing in my biceps, at the back of my thighs, calf muscles. I attempted to resist the urge to break back in the mind into

157

my childhood's dirt backyard and the ancient little cassette player and its C batteries, nothing near the Scream's surely more worthy D-powered behemoth. I nonetheless caught the thread of something fascinating there in the trailer. Tacklebox continued his ridiculous headbanging—ridiculous for his lack of headbanger hair, his 'do close-cropped over the ears and above the eyebrows and tucked under a ball cap—and I channeled the present aggression of the music, closing my eyes to feel the tinny speakers' whine, dirt on knees and elbows, and my muscles in the memory of flailing around the yard, kicking up more dirt, alone and content and full of undirected rage ultimately false in its very conception.

"I fucking love that shit," Tacklebox said when the song was over.

"Me too," I said.

"Now let's get back to it a bit."

We practiced with our own tires till the sun set on Talladega and drivers slept and teams turned away from alcohol in favor of soda or electrolyte-boosting sports drinks and ate big meals of grilled meats and vegetables and complex carbohydrates at the backs of their trailers, preparation for the coming day of contest. I was exhausted, and fell asleep in a folding chair out back of the Bascombe rig listening to the rig's owner-operator, a 40-something by the name of Pete Kimball, hum trucking songs to himself like a Clarksdale delta bluesman.

I woke to all 6'5" of Kimball attempting to hoist me up from the chair, whereupon I started and stood as tall as was possible.

"Sorry," he boomed. "Tacklebox couldn't wake you up and took off to the hotel for some rest. You can sleep in the rig, I guess."

"Shit, Pete," I said. He motioned me around to the entryway to the 10'-by-10' box. Muscle fatigue had become a stiffness surprisingly pleasant. "Where'd you learn to play like that?"

He laughed. He'd already told me the story in brief, he said, in response to the same question I guessed I uttered about five minutes before I passed out in my chair.

Kimball grew up in little-known Hamlet in N.C. 30 minutes by car from my own hometown. A black man played for passersby on its little Main Street through the 70s and early 80s, he said, taught him the craft, along with black women who worked as maids and nannies to him and his brothers in his decidedly white-upper-middle-class household.

Four Murphy-type beds pulled down from the walls in interlocking patterns from either side of the box, Kimball pointed out, so I lowered one and sat, before I got too far with messing with sheets and pillows and such stored in overhead bins that looked oddly reminiscent of flight-bins. He laughed when I told him so.

"I never get over pulling the thing," he said, having started out his long trucking career in the dirty business of hauling cattle and pigs and other livestock, then the back-breaking business of hauling steel and anything else that can fit on a flat deck. This was relatively clean, if not exactly simple, work.

"You like heavy metal?" I said then, hitting the play button on Tacklebox's vintage Anthrax CD and watching Pete shake his head ruefully as the cellos ballooned into head-banging beats and crunching guitars.

"You're fitting right in with the pit boys," he said. "And that's just dandy, but I'm more of a country-blues sort."

"Robert Johnson?"

"Well sure," he said. "Let me show you something." And the tall man stooped and stepped down from the side door of the trailer, leading me to the door of his rig. He climbed in and, when he emerged, carried the dobro hung out in front of him. Pete then sat on the bottom step of his Peterbilt truck and slid his way through a joyous blues about love loss, conflict, redemption. The song's approach was timelessness, rang a strong contrast to the strains of Anthrax's "Out of Sight, Out of Mind" overlaying its major chords with minor power dissonance from the open door of the trailer bunk, but I clapped a little and smiled when he was done, trying hard to appear sincere in my praise or at least not in any way dismissive of the small performance, which was itself genuinely accomplished and strange for a middle-aged white guy, in the end.

"It might send you off to a rousing sleep full of nightmares." He grinned.

He'd be a good man to keep happy, as Trey Olden might have said, with the keys to our movement and clearly several entertaining tricks up his sleeves, invaluable for all manner of escapes. And

I did sleep, and when I woke I donned the yellow-and-black Bascombe Lumber team's suit, found a disposable razor and shaved
in the little bathroom off the sleeping quarters. Damn the past for
that tight moment. I was flying. I stared at myself in the floor-to-
ceiling mirror adjacent to the toilet and sink and felt the electricity
of a transformation, the furry anticipation of being birthed again.

Chapter 12

Early in the racing league's final 10-race "playoff" system, the P-O-K-E-M-O-N team and our own were neck and neck, along with 8 other of the points leaders. We were only a couple races into the playoff, and though at least one team had blown an engine in an earlier competition and put themselves virtually out of contention, the balance of the "playoff" teams all had plenty opportunity to close Montuck's lead, if they didn't get tangled with any of the 42 other cars on the mammoth Talladega track.

Race morning, Bascombe himself gave me the rundown before moving on to the first of his myriad of television interviews—more than any other driver out here, Tacklebox said, "you can be sure of that, but you know that already, if you watch this shit on TV, which I suspect you do. He loves it, and they love him."

I didn't tell him of my relative unfamiliarity with the sport and its celebrities, that I might have been better acquainted with the players of the late 80s, when before my father went away he had a brief love affair with motorsports and educated his little boy on Pearson and Petty, Allison and Bodine, and a then young Montuck Sr., running down competitors on the track.

I would get better or die. Maybe I exaggerate. Already, the workaday feel of the spectacle we were central to held within it a fair amount of team-to-team isolation, competitors cut off from each other in the focus on individual performance. We ran through the paces as a full seven-man crew, the lot of the team members pushing me to perform but at once welcoming me, some going so far as to offer a derisive anecdote about the man I was replacing.

"Good to have you" was their simple message.

And it was not exactly stunning, but surprising, nonetheless, to witness the steely demeanors of the lot of the crew, race day, the men focused on the tasks at hand, speed and efficiency. Tacklebox ran me through my carrying technique, with no mention of my swinging-legs wall pivot of yesterday in favor of re-emphasizing the standard, least-motion-to-the-explicit-point route, today.

"This is the way," he said, hopping straight down ahead of the car, tire held ahead.

I had perhaps the easiest job on the team, in the end, others stepping up to fulfill the ancillary former duties of the young Huggins, whose father didn't say word one to me. Such was the pull among the team of the star of the show, who was ultimately paying the salaries, if, technically, he didn't preside over the rest of us throughout the race.

Bascombe threw back to the history of racing's premier league—his operation that of an owner-driver—when enterprising driver-engineers brought this all into being in the broader region of my upbringing on the strength of their racing and mechanical prowess, and their audacious salesmanship. Not that I knew much more than the skeleton of this story at the time. Turner himself, to a point, would impart it to me in stages over the next several weeks—and months, years. Maybe not years, but let's not get ahead of ourselves ...

The run-up to the big show included some terrible radio-country music on a large stage set up ahead of the grandstands on the front straightaway. Right ahead of pit road, too, where we did our pre-race run-throughs. After all the rigmarole—"Make it happen," Turner said to me on the way to his car, staged on pit road in his No. 8 qualifying space, helmet under his arm—and the ceremonial starting of the engines, relatively quiet in the mammoth expanse of the bowl of a two-plus-mile Talladega track, the big go of the green flag hit me right in the gut. Cars all lined up and roaring around the final pace lap and the race announcer rattling on, getting lost in the roar even with the loudspeakers, when the green flag dropped in front of us and the 43 drivers all put the hammer down at once, flashbulbs from the stands popping a constellation of no doubt too-wide-terrible pictures of all of the cars and crewmembers on pit road, the hiss of the crowd combined with the absolute scream of the engines reverberating off the stands in a noise that was bigger than anything I might have been able to compare it to, or even imagine. Bigger than the loudest Chicago rock band in the city's smallest club. A lightning strike and subsequent thunder at close range.

Humanity's conquering of the natural world.

The shit put a smile on your face in spite of your topside, rational better judgment.

Ecstatic moment.

Tacklebox, standing at my left behind the crew chief Huggins' control station off the pit box. He must've seen the awed, slightly horrified look on my face. He quietly—no other way possible in this din—handed me a pair of earplugs.

The first pit stop was a quixotic fuel-only stop during a debris caution period when the rest of the field changed tires, too—Turner had shuffled toward the back of the pack in the early going after getting loose coming out of turn 4 with another driver tight on his back left bumper. I wouldn't get my first taste of speed just yet. He came out of the stop with the race lead.

"He'll hope for the caution flag to come out again," said Tacklebox, "before those tires began to really lose their close grip."

Though his lead initially expanded under green, you can't run out there ahead by yourself for long at this track without a group of drafting drivers catching up with you. A six-car pack coming up on his back bumper was led by Montuck Jr., and he soon passed Bascombe, with the rest of the pack following him around the Ford into the third big turn on the track.

"Need that caution," said Tacklebox. We were huddled around the broadcast feed on a little monitor stuck in Huggins' station. "Watch this."

It was turn time. Just after the fifth of the six cars made its way under and around Bascombe, Turner feinted to the left, coming very close to rubbing sides with the sixth car, whereupon said sixth backed off and Turner jumped in line with the rest of the them, catching the draft and holding on for dear life on those worn tires around the rest of turn 3 and then 4 and, coming out on the front straightaway Turner gave it everything he had and got the car in front of him loose, its grip on the track cut in half by aero downforce taken off its rear spoiler—the driver, a former Indy Car hero turned stock for the big endorsement cash most of these drivers hauled in at levels far and above their actual race winnings, he lost it, spinning out into the grass of the infield. Caution flag, here we go. I put my helmet on, through which I could hear the driver-spotter radio and the crew chief's instructions—*fresh four tires and fuel, boys, four tires and fuel.*

But what I heard first was a blood-curdling scream of delight from Bascombe at this turn of events. He kept it up for the entire lap he had to get back around to the pit road entrance.

I poised on the pit wall as the second half of the field came roaring into pit road at 55 mph, the large majority of the teams just getting splashed with fuel before jumping back on the track. Once the first half of the field roared back around the track and into pit road, Turner came squealing into the box, tires smoking, and I did my duty—for mere seconds with my left foot on the pit road marker line, hanging onto the tire as three-four cars motored by within a foot, mere inches.

The buzz and burr of the tire changer's custom-as-all-get-out ratchet, the handoff, repeat, and I was back on the other side—it all lasted just several seconds, really. In this world, there was no time for the revel, the full sense of stasis surrounded by the controlled chaos of fast-moving chess pieces. The bodies of the crews at this close proximity to speed themselves danced a rapid ballet. The stasis between stops was akin to distracting oneself in front of the tube, nothing like the Kennedy Expressway in early morning.

Turner may have given up his ghost a little too early—he came back onto the track having slipped to 16th place and, though his tires gave him some advantage when the field got back up to top speed, the rest of the race he more or less stayed in line, no more of the shenanigans he'd pulled out early this fine Sunday.

When the day was through, though, we'd done what we needed to—not exactly won the race, but cashed in on the P-O-K-E-M-O-N team's misfortune at a critical juncture. Montuck had to come back into pit road for a penalty pass-through after a stop in which the excess-fuel catch can remained attached to the back of his Chevrolet when he took off, a crucial pit-crew mistake we wouldn't make today. Montuck finished an unimpressive 20th place. We finished in the no. 7 spot.

Turner Bascombe was happy. I hummed excited, wary, scared shitless all at once—a late-race pit-road scare saw a competitor come within an inch of taking off front tire changer Adam Stant's rear end and breaking my left leg. We were in the middle of the handoff at the right front when the driver was bumped by yet another car just shy of our station and nearly lost it.

Stant was all wide-eyed as I stood back safely over the wall with my face in my hands—"Close, I do say," he said, all Mississippi redneck drawl, "too damn close." He slapped me on the back, my heart pounded, and all was right with the world.

But it didn't last.

I was driven back into Birmingham by Bascombe himself to the lair off 6th Ave. that night, where I figured aloud we might at least partake of a hot beer among my stash.

"Like a goddamn airplane hangar in here," he said when we emerged into the main space in the old building. "How long have you been here?"

I answered tersely, coming upon my corner and stopping cold in my tracks when I peeked around one of the old doors that demarcated the living space.

"What's the problem?" Bascombe must have noticed the surprise in my eyes.

Carl's laptop was plugged in and glowing, as if it'd been recently used. On the screen, in an open word document, screamed, in fifty-point type:

we

are

out

here

165

I had not left it this way. The laptop, meanwhile, was the only of my personal effects that remained.

"So much for that beer," I said, closing the computer, rolling up the power plug and moving to get out of there, Turner all the while verbally head-scratching, muttering "well well" and other uncomfortable yeah-yeah-yeahs and battle hymns under his breath as he scanned the big space with his eyes. Paranoia is contagious, I guess, however accustomed to it I may have become the last months. We left quickly.

And I directed the racecar driver, my heart racing now, breath coming in quick gasps, where I figured there was little chance of him being recognized. Out back of the Black Hat bookshop, a loud punk show blaring on upstairs, unwashed youth drifting into our alley periphery to smoke cigarettes in little knots around us before drifting back inside uncertain of our very existence, we drank PBR tallboys and waited for King to show in order that I might at least offer a word of apology for not appearing the previous day.

We talked.

I told Turner of the Shining Man show at McIntyre + Feldman, the WE ARE OUT HERE message explained away as remnant of the show. He didn't mention the paranoia of the Suited Man or other's presence in the hangar with us, the computer's lack of screen saver. He didn't know the Suited Man as yet, and I was glad for the fact. I wasn't protecting Turner Bascombe from the drama of my life so much as I might have been protecting myself from the same in his, instinct borne of my father, Smitty, Billy-boy and a myriad other bad dads.

"You did good," he said.

"Thank you."

"For a first day out."

"I think I've got the carrying. The rest of the—"

"Everything else will be intuitive. You've worked before, you know what the shop/office is like."

"I spent the majority of the last years in a kitchen, then at the door of a bar."

"Perfect. You'll fall in," Turner said. "Naturally. Not to worry."

"OK," I said, though I can't say I actually, fully, believed him. Then a series of flashbulbs went off in the room somewhere off over Turner's shoulder, and I peered into one of the knots of

166

youths to spy between the shoulders of two guys in hoodies a pair of eyes framed by the beginnings of crow's feet that darted away from my gaze as instantly as they'd delivered the recognition I supposed they were meant to. Rinckoff turned on his heel and walked, clad himself not in his more typical suit but in a black hoodie and a pair of jeans.

I watched him go, zigzagging slightly at the center of the store around shelves devoted to the latest in hip lit mags, and though it felt nice just to sit, with the very fact of the Chicagoan's presence here confirmed I finally couldn't bear the lack of an explanation for it all.

"Turner, we gotta go," I stood up and grabbed the driver's arm to pull him to the front of the Black Hat and to his car. I managed just to see Rinckoff diving into the passenger seat of a black hatchback farther along the block from us. I was fairly certain Rinckoff didn't realize that, as we jockeyed down the road behind him, the follower had now become the followed.

The black car, a little Ford compact, hit the freeway going east for several miles, taking the offramp to a suburban commercial strip dotted with gas stations and auto parts stores that quickly gave way with Rinckoff's left turn into an obviously 60s neighborhood of houses with well-manicured lawns and near Orwellian sameness from lot to lot. Whomever Rinckoff knew in Birmingham, their milieu was a far cry from anything I'd ever pretended to.

"Who the fuck is this guy?" I said, mostly to myself, though Turner chimed in with "Nice neighborhood. Sorta reminds me of my old place in Charlotte. You know Dilworth? It's not quite as cookie-cutter, though, for sure."

Turner eased his Camaro, definitely not the best tailing car—and if Rinckoff hadn't seen us by now then the man was a blind fool—into a short, empty driveway seven houses or so down from the bungalow Rinckoff pulled into, he and a much larger, maybe even older, man wearing black sweats head to toe emerging from the little Ford and entering the house quickly, with nary a look our way.

I backed up and explained just whom I thought we were after. "What do we do?" I said.

"You said it yourself. Who is this guy? Do you want to find out? Only thing to do is wait. I'm game. We've got some time."

And, trailing off at the end of it, "This is kind of fun."

Turner, in love with the cloak-and-dagger. If only I had a spider man's premonitory sense to know whether someone was in trouble, here.

We waited. The lights in the house where we waited were off, but after a short time the front door opened and a disheveled-looking old man peered down his front steps at us. Turner waved, started the car, backed out and pulled on up the street in front of the house Rinckoff disappeared into. We idled in the Camaro, every ten minutes or so pulling off and circling back around the block, returning to sit in front of a house a few doors down each time, our lights off. After four or five such circumnavigations, Turner said time was up, we ought to be on our way—he'd scheduled to fly the Cessna back out toward Charlotte and I was on a commercial flight with Tacklebox.

"Hold on," I rose from the car, too close to let it go now, and it was getting on 10 p.m.—if Rinckoff was sleeping he was unlikely to emerge from the house. And I couldn't have blamed him. I was tired, too, foggy with the long, long day and so much else besides. It was as if difficult to remember where our journey began, just what the reason he or I had for being in the city of Birmingham. There was the continued mystery of my father, but I truly didn't expect Rinckoff to have an answer for that. I'd have had better luck in that department with a long discussion of history with Billy Jones, or Turner Bascombe. I had a vision, standing on the small front porch of the bungalow where he should have been, of my first night in the Shining Man's suit, arms wide at the sides, eyes closed, atop the freeway barrier surrounded by traffic, Trey Olden's camera somewhere unseen along the roadway and his little pickup then awaiting my eventual escape down below—I looked back at Bascombe in the Camaro a few houses down. He was watching me and nodded as if to say, "Go on."

I knocked on the front door, and Rinckoff opened it, easy as that.

"Hello," he said. He still wasn't wearing a suit, rather a white t-shirt and jeans, black socks, no shoes. The sarcastic hiss of the voice I'd heard to date seemed far off, hard to recall as any of it. He sounded like he might've been a Midwestern version of Tim Morton or Bobby Cash or Turner Bascombe himself.

A car door shut in the near distance and I turned to see Bascombe now up standing next to the Camaro, stern look on his face like he might run up swinging any moment. When I turned back, Rinckoff smiled.

"Took you long enough," he said.

"Jig is up," I said. "Who the fuck are you?"

"Is it?" he said.

"C'mon, man, just come clean," I said, impatience boiling my blood for perhaps the first time since long before my traffic stands, long before my history with the imp standing in front of me, who was not even an imp so much as a guy about my age, with any luck as hopeful of getting this over quickly as was I.

"We're renting this house," he said, gesturing back inside.

"Who the fuck are you?" I insisted. "C'mon!"

Rinckoff held up his hands. I could hear Turner now moving around his car and up the walk behind me.

"You know us, man, Jesus," Rinckoff with a nervous little laugh, gesturing again back behind him where emerged into the hallway's light from a dark doorway the old man in black we'd seen shuffling into the house earlier.

The mad instant, ecstatic moment, psychotic break from the real, whatever humanist professors, artists, psychologists might want to call it—I remembered with crystal clarity not a particular vision or anything important but rather a story, which socked me on the crown of my skull, minus its necessary pith helmet: blunt force trauma of the mood, the psychologically grounding variety.

There he stood, Zeus, in his black getup, smiling a woefully familiar gap-toothed grin. "Shining Man, how goes it?" the old man said.

"Motherfucker!" I said, and we were at war, Rinckoff's measly frame blocking me, his arms groping me as I lunged my way head-down into the house, a massive force then knocking us from behind as Turner seemed to actually dive headlong into the hallway himself. I rolled to my right, Rinckoff following over me, and I kicked him into the wall. Pain in my head blossomed, and Zeus, old man Trey Olden, sat on top of me the instant the brief melee was over, virtually as soon as it had started—"You've learned well, asshole," he said, huffing and puffing, that gap in his teeth gaping widely.

"Hold off, Turner," I said, raising my battered head to Bascombe, whose well-placed maneuvers we could thank for our prone status. Rinckoff was up. Turner had both of the man's arms pinned behind him. Trey had pinned my own, of course. "Get the fuck off me, old man, before I hurt you," I said.

He did.

I feigned punching Rinckoff in the nose while Turner held him, Bascombe wincing hard with the faked punch before letting the man go.

As Trey and I talked, Rinckoff disappeared into the house.

Turner Bascombe: "You cool?" then "I'll be outside" with my quick nod.

We didn't have much time, and I told Olden so.

"We didn't want something like this—we really wanted to save the knowledge for your return to the city," Trey said.

"My return to the city?"

"We figured you'd be back in time," he said, "considering the business of your father."

I'd not told Olden of my father, though I could well guess the identity of his unwitting informant. Trey could see the wheels turning in my brain.

"Billy, of course," he said, his tone suggesting the man's loose tongue should have been self-evident. I couldn't remember the point-to-point chain of events, but it didn't matter. "And I've been using the royal 'we,' but really it's just that, royal. It's just me. Cary is my nephew," the old man gesturing back into the house to the invisible presence of Rinckoff, "an actor, stage hand, that sort of thing. He owed me, so I put him out there to catch you, to bend you, as you can see it."

"I thought his name was Charles," I said.

"It is. 'Cary' a sort of weird shortening." Trey Olden seemed as if to have all the answers. I remembered then with absolute clarity, like it was yesterday, the old man's fixation on my father's final scrawled words on cardboard, another source of inspiration for him, no doubt.

But why the fuck was I in Birmingham? The night of the conception of the Shining Man show, he said, as ... Billy and I were no doubt blowing our minds in the Pegasus' bar, he and Rinckoff pulled out a U.S. map pursuant on continuing this little misguided project in the art of psychological manipulation through subterfuge, through photography, as it were, closed their eyes, and both laid their fingers down on two separate locales.

Birmingham, said Trey, was preferable to San Diego. "We figured you might actually come here, given where you're from. I want to show you something."

He led me to a room at the back of the house outfitted as an old-school photographer's darkroom. Prints lined the walls, telling the story of my time in Birmingham—and before. Here was Rinckoff, Charles, Cary smiling for the camera next to the dumpsters the neighborhood kids in my back alley used to crown me Logan Square Shining King. I well recognized the trashbins off in the background of the frame, dark but for the little square of light above the middle of the bins in the otherwise nondescript brick wall. Here I was as if moments later, helmet in the now-open window, Rinckoff on the ground, envelope in hand, talking up to my bright form. I marveled at it all—scenes from the night of the Shining Man show itself, down to a print of me and Billy, disrobing from our Shining Man suits before plunging into dark space in flight from the cops.

I shivered a little and looked to the room's exit as Trey pointed up to a high line strung from top corner to corner along the low ceiling, 8-by-10s clothespinned there for drying. I felt again like charging the old man, hunched over another pile of photographs on a low coffee table across the room and with his back to me. So skinny, Trey, so frail-looking, his weak submission maneuver in the foyer notwithstanding. He couldn't deserve it.

The scenes hanging from the line showed Birmingham action—I recalled the flashbulbs that followed the Shining Man around the last week as I gazed onto a downtown evening vista with one little swirl of light atop a roof this side of the mammoth skyscrapers, my virgin B-ham stand.

"How the fuck did you get that one?" I asked the old man, pointing out the picture.

And he had an answer for this, too.

"A little coordination is all," he said, describing a process by which Rinckoff tracked me on my late-night sojourn, cellphone at the ready to log and pass on coordinates for my rooftop stand, Trey on the other end attentive and watchful in the red-eye night, long lens amplifying the glimmering pinprick on the horizon.

He didn't have it all, however, the trail going dead with my air voyage southwest to Tuscaloosa for Turner's party. I moved away from the final portrait, a motion-blurred swath of white at road-side, a slightly more in-focus, knowledgeable gaze shot from a car a little farther along, back up the road to mine and Turner's high-way-side meeting. The Camaro figured darkly, prominently, the left portion of the frame, my bright form and the receding highway lines illuminated by distantly oncoming traffic to the right, Turner in his bumblebee digs stock center, back to the viewer—unidenti-fiable, I guessed, to Olden. The puppet master's power was limited. He knew not what had happened at all between then and the pres-ent night's light—the roar of the track, the blood of competition. My breath quickened, pulse shooting through the roof in all the excitement. It had been right there all along in his assumption that I would return to Chicago at all! Truth stood that my places were falling away at an ever-more-rapid clip, and for now I liked that. Charlotte still remained to be confronted, conquered, its roadways built by the hands of mine own father, that ghost as yet to be vanquished along with its living, breathing ghosts, I felt, and facing it required more than courage or determination or resolve or any of the ridiculous qualities that in those days were being associated with whatever was admirable about successful Americans embark-ing on wars of choice, dispatching robot planes to kill people, etc. Nonetheless, I had a suit of armor just perfect for the battle, and Trey Olden wasn't about to penetrate it. Ultimately it was he who had no idea what the hell was going on, his transgressions in a way forgivable.

"You don't hate me," he said, watching me closely and as if reading my little mind.

I didn't, couldn't hate Trey Olden, Zeus, mouse, Perseus all in one, puppeteer of Shining People the world over.

Indeed I didn't, though I also didn't give him the satisfaction of a verbal confirmation, and though I had the two of them to thank for this next chapter, of a fashion, I couldn't allow him to go unpunished for the runaround he and his little nut of a nephew had put me through.

"These belong to me, old man," I said, finally, and jumped to grasp the overhead line and pull it from its moorings, pushing him back when he came my way as if he would stop me. "Get the fuck

172

back!"

Rinckoff appeared in the doorway.

"Call him off, Trey," I said, and when he didn't immediately respond: "Do it now!" I scooped up the stack of prints he'd been hunched over and saw on the top one of the originals of our first encounter on the Kennedy Expressway before brandishing the entire stack like a weapon and staring between the two men. Trey nodded and Rinckoff backed into the house and shut the door.

"I want them all, negatives too," I said, and after a brief bit of protest on his part, I threatened to bring Turner back in here and we'd settle the score once and for all. "Two against one and a half. I don't like your chances."

"Fuck you," I heard Rinckoff beyond the closed door.

"Shut up," Trey yelled off into the invisible space, "just shut up and get on!"

Footsteps down the hall, receding.

"OK," Trey breathed, and we cleared the walls. I found negatives in a drawer of a desk wedged into the corner, struggled with and then directed Trey in the rewinding of the spool in the camera on top of the desk. He popped out the canister and handed it over.

"Thanks for everything, Trey," I hissed, sarcastic and pissed off as any Suited Man should be, but at once relieved with my new, weighty burden of paper in tow. "So long."

I could feel his eyes following me to the door, but I didn't look back.

"What the hell, Cash?" Turner said when I dropped the stack in his trunk. He read something he didn't like in my blank gaze, I suspect less blank than it felt, I guess. He just shook his head.

"Fuck it," he said. "Let's roll."

I was free for the time being, free from one mystery, or one small part of a larger mystery, this life. I never saw Trey Olden again.

Chapter 13

I missed my commercial jet. After a bumpy hop-skip-jump of a flight through three different minor airports between Birmingham and Charlotte in the Cessna, the majority of the team's crew long aboard the U.S. Airways direct and landed, Turner took me to his bachelor's house north of town and I slept on a giant antique four-poster bed in the guest room. "For now," he said. The next day they put me through the paces in the team's local garage, where I would serve as go-for (*gofer*, as the men of the team pronounced it) monkey. As Turner had half-promised, I fell in easily. It was mostly silly and tedious work, if at least diverting.

We were paid three days after a race, so what little bank I could expect wouldn't come till Wednesday. Tacklebox was kind enough to lend me his car for the time being—his wife was picking him up, he said. My disbelief, I imagine, showed in my entire being. Not just the fruits of gratitude, either.

"You're married," I said.

He just nodded, chewing on a straw he told me earlier in the day was his answer to nicotine addiction. Back on the home front, as on race day, Tacklebox was all business. He kept distinct vigilance, he said, through it all to keep from lighting up. "No worries," he said when she rolled up and he handed me the keys, the couple's two-year-old screaming at me from the backseat of the family Ford, not even a full-size sedan.

I lit up a smoke and loaded my collection of strange photographs, film negatives, computer and what little else I had and drove his near-identical car through downtown south and blew off the freeway into the parking lot at Henry's to find it more or less empty in anticipation of whatever meager Monday early-dinner crowd the place could expect. Autumn in the South! 'Twas fine respite and positively magical for anyone reared with the oppressive heat as foreground of nasty summer. It was no different for me, sitting out there, windows of Tacklebox's unfamiliar Ford down, eyes intent on the much more familiar brick front of the place, dead leaves swirling between the vehicles. The hostess was a new gal, likewise the bartender, from whom I ordered a beer and waited for a familiar face to pass before me. I could see the cooks' line from my vantage at the bar's corner—no one there as yet. I'd finished my second beer before a family of four trotted in and sat and ordered—I vaguely recalled the mouse-nose and high forehead, the dark eyeliner of the waitress taking their order, though she didn't register any recognition of me when I waved. She walked by to the cooks' line to put the order in. I stared for several minutes at the piece of paper, hanging just west of the grill on the familiar spring-loaded wheel from which Will Theron had pulled so many orders in a former life. I ordered a third beer from the bartender, and after I'd drained a quarter of it in one big pull—only after—I looked back to the line and the paper was gone. I rose, walked over to the big open window and saw two steaks sizzling on the wood-fired grill, an order of wings in the fryer and a big salad half-done on the long cutting board, an empty container that formerly housed diced hard-boiled egg next to the salad bowl, its romaine contents sweaty with humidity. The walk-in containing replacement eggs I knew to be on the other side of the back wall of the line from the fryer. This afternoon's line worker could be expected any moment now to emerge from the rear kitchen onto the line through a swinging doorway no more than 10 feet from my eyelids. I stared at the top of the door and waited, pulling from my beer, soaking in the déjà vu of the place's gummy stink, heat from the grill radiating slowly up and out.

Distracted by a bottle tossed into a trashcan full of other bottles over by the bar, I just missed any opportunity to duck out of eyeshot of Bobby Cash as he flew through the door from the rear kitchen and bellowed "He's back!" with every bit of budding-redneck gusto he might ever have contained.

"Aw shit," I said.

Bobby ran the line now afternoons, occasional Saturdays, but business was down and there were rumors Henry's was to be shuttered. The other two locations, one way out in Gastonia, the other in Concord, were rip-roaring small-town cash cows by comparison, without the same level of competition from most of the big chain restaurants and the relative few more high-end eateries catering to well-heeled city clientele as they crept ever southward, and "You can be sure," Bobby said, "if they're going to close one, it'll be this—and do you think they'll find *me* a space at one of the others?"

I didn't leave the place when Bobby and others had quickly blown through what little news they had to offer, rather went back to the bar and drained a couple more in hopes Will Theron would show his face.

Bobby said he wasn't due in today at all, but you could never tell when his girl would take the toothbrush and leave him blissfully, as Bobby saw it, taskless and inert. "She leaves, man, and it's all Will talks about for his first couple hours at the bar, that's why he's here, after all, but by the end of it he's always glad the girl is gone and is loudly hoping that the bitch never comes back. She always does."

Tonight wouldn't be one of those nights. I sat at the bar alone as the meager dinner rush came and went with the small kitchen crew, minus Will, gathering around me when there was time and spotting me drinks—all excepting Annie. It was obvious she held my long absence against me for the shifts she had to cover.

"Tim's no better than you," she said at a moment near the end. "We had to fire him, too. Guess who got to play with the fryer?"

"I'm sorry," I said, "but it's OK. I have another job now."

"Asshole."

At once, drunk Annie remembered the initial reason for my departure and asked about my father, her scaly right palm resting gently on my left forearm. It gave me the chills, and I recalled a similar gesture offered on a long night in the city of my father's rough-and-tumble rearing. I thought too of the serendipitous weirdness of the past week and more in that instant and closed my eyes as if to let it all drain out of me into that tough lady's palm. Soon enough she was gone and I left and drove along my father's streets, letting myself in the back door to my basement hole at my mom's place, quietly as I could as drunk as I was, though I was certain she would be down to say hello within minutes of my entry. The hole, though I did not yet think of it as such, was not as I'd left it, strewn with clothes and empty coffee cups, beer bottles, the detritus of an uncomplicated life. My fastidious mother had put a sheen of organization on the entirety, which I could newly appreciate, and I quickly closed my Shining Man's suit off in the little closet on an empty hanger next to a business suit my father had bought me when I graduated college, and which I'd worn perhaps three times since. Had there been more than just scant ambient light in the place, I would have been able to see the dust gathered on its shoulders. I gravitated to the blue light of my laptop, which I opened on the bed, connecting to the neighbor's Wi-Fi and typing out a note to V.

"I can fly," I wrote. "Or: I have flown, with one of the nation's pre-eminent speed demons. Remind me to tell you about it next time we meet. Trey Olden is an asshole. There's that, too. Thinking about you tonight. Yours ..."

Like clockwork, my mother appeared at the top of the stairs. I heard her, the door opening, before I moved to the bottom of the stairs into the beam of her flashlight.

"The light switch is to your left," I said, "but I imagine you know that. It's your house."

She bobbed down the staircase and into the dark.

"You haven't turned on any lights yourself," she said. "Leave me alone." My mother loved the dark, I should say, a quality that, given the history of the man she chose to hitch her fate to those many years ago, might seem incongruous or just plain foolish. But fear is elemental, not to mention contagious. Staring into the flashlight bulb she now held aimed into the carpet in the basement, I could feel it bubbling out of her.

"It's OK, Mom. I'm OK," I started. "I've got a job now with a racing team, can you believe it, doesn't look like Henry's is going to be open much longer anyway—"

"Save it—"

"—and have you heard of him, maybe, Turner Bascombe? Ford team, very Charlotte, though he's cut from different cloth than the other drivers. Met him in Birmingham—"

"I said save it for another time."

"—and ..." I stopped. "OK."

"Did you find your father well?"

She wanted to know, Annie wanted to know. Will Theron I

177

imagine would want to know, too. They were decent people, after all, and I was connected to them. They were afraid, and their fear derived from not knowing.

I resorted to the truth. Though it would not set me free, it might help push me closer.

"I did not find him," I said, "well or otherwise."

Eula sat on the bottom step of the staircase. She held the light in both hands so that it now shined upward into her chin, her nose casting an inverted pyramid of shadow over her eyes.

"Well," she said. "I guess I'm just glad you're back. There's sandwich stuff in the fridge if you need it."

I listened to my mother methodically getting to bed. Another trip to the bathroom, just off the top of the stairs—the brushing of teeth, the spitting of toothpaste, the footfalls above my head toward the bed, the creaking of the mattress, the ensuing silence. Tomorrow would be a long day at the beauty shop full of calculated, careful conversation about the black sheep returned from the land of the even blacker sheep with no knowledge, no education whatsoever, to show for it. I recalled the lessons learned from the women summer days long after Ralph Cash left us and I assumed my position in what stands in my mind as the biggest little wooden armchair in human history, at the end of a row of similar chairs lined up in the downtown storefront window where my mother plied her trade. I read comic books, later horror novels, then more upright stuff—literary novels, philosophy, literary theory—and they talked, the women did, their voices growing louder and louder as the years went by. Their stories, about the shameful behavior of a husband or friend, longing to let loose once in a while, escapades in which they did just that quite tame in retrospect. All amounted to a single lesson for me. It's no accident that "take care" was Lula May's departing greeting, Shirley's too. My mother was less effusive. Fear wasn't necessarily in my DNA so much as learned, the outcome of the repetitive rhetoric of the beauty shop, my own learning by the experience of failure.

Had I failed my mother? To the extent that my journey had been on her behalf, and that I failed to *take care*, to be careful, certainly I had. But after the relative firecracker of Trey's revelation as master of Cash puppets, the question about my father's fate was put to rest—or at least I chose to put it down. And if that only offered a partial sense of completion—did it matter for instance that I didn't know truly what happened to him, now that he was at least for my purposes most definitely gone?—it would have to be enough. My mother could deal with it however she liked. I wouldn't be around here to remind her of our shared failures.

Charlotte wasn't exactly all open arms and jubilation for me, in essence. It remained a haunted place—my father was in the very roadbed on which the asphalt of its thoroughfares had been laid. All the same, my return afforded a glimpse into a world I'd never known there. The ramshackle structures into which I was thrown as member of a race pit crew made meeting and greeting non-existent, a man made a man not if he had the wits to outsmart Zeus but rather if he had the physical strength or petro-chemical-and-steel force to best whatever foe happened to be standing in his way, whether three-foot concrete wall, rival for a woman's affections or unemployed former tire carrier. The job then carried with it enough *a priori* respect from members of the general public to make it somewhat more bearable to go about the business of life, worrying about keeping oneself fed and clothed and suited. Not that the last required much worrying.

By the end of the week I was signing a $900 month-to-month lease on a small apartment in a mixed-use building downtown overlooking two major roads. My neighbor to the immediate south on the hall was a young lawyer I only saw once or twice the entire time I was there. His apartment was also his office. Down the hall were a pair of former college roommates from Rock Hill, just past my hometown on the south side of the N.C./S.C. border, who'd gone in together on a graphic design business, building websites and designing posters and such. The elder of them—Rob Rene was his name—was the artist of the pair, and I found out he was a race fan when I ran into him as I offloaded some stuff Friday: bed from my mom's, which I tied closely to the roof of Tacklebox's Ford for a surface-street run downtown, some clothes.

After I gave him my brief intro spiel, he sort of exclaimed, "I'm standing here in my own apartment talking to a bona fide member of a Cup pit crew whose background is in performance art?"

"Fryer art, too," I said.

"My life just got a lot more interesting." And he was off to find his roommate/business partner, Matt Caudill, who was strangely less outgoing than Rene.

But Matt was a fan, too, and came at me with a myriad of questions I had no answers for, other than those directed at sussing out the real qualities of the job. Yes the tire carrier does only that during the pit stops, usually, front side anyway; no there aren't any pit-crew groupies far as I knew, unless you could count the mechanics in that department ...

Many of those questions, too, I couldn't answer, still so new I couldn't know it all. I could sense his disappointment.

"Check back with me a month from now," I said.

"Dover this week?" Matt knew the schedule.

Indeed it was—I was getting on a plane with several other of the guys tonight for Baltimore bound ultimately for Delaware. After the mammoth Talladega, the relatively short track presented great opportunity for Bascombe to shine, to hear the crew chief talk about it all week long as a sort of pep-talk refrain to team members: "Team Bascombe rules the shorts," Huggins echoing himself on a sports talking heads television program two days prior to the race that I caught at a less-than-lively but not quite lonely downtown bar, down the street from which the mini tent city of demonstrators who'd been parked now for weeks outside the AB Bank headquarters loomed as reminder of the teeming mess I'd recently driven out of. When Huggins came on the feature program, the bartender, in response to the shouted pleas of several men at a big table in the back, shut down the house music so all could hear the man's strategy talk, which consisted of less actually talking strategy so much as talking around strategy with platitudes like the reliable "rules the shorts" one for the host, who joked and cajoled his path through the majority of the interview. I didn't think much of the silliness, but did perk up at the mention of "personnel changes, particularly in the pit crew area" in a question from the interviewer about Bascombe's perceived good chances on Sunday.

Huggins, from whom I'd only gotten a sort of all-business attitude to date, here turned on some performer's charm and "didn't exactly regret the decision to fire my son, since we've really shuf-

180

fled the team around for the better, with an addition of a fantastic young tire carrier—who's also quite a good driver, I understand, great addition to the team nonetheless, not the error of judgment I may have thought it was at the get-go."

This was me he was talking about, goddamn! I was probably better at standing than driving, particularly in the kind of traffic the boys would see Sunday. The crew chief was a liar, but he could hope he might make for a fair takeaway himself on this night's program. The facts or falsehoods of my existence were little more than filler material. Veracity held little bearing on whether the team or Huggins or both got what they needed to get out of talking shit on a television show.

After the Dover race Sunday there was a big party a two hours' drive west in Baltimore where the pit team got drunk and trotted out at a big club rented for the night for fans and other dignitaries after Turner's impressive third-place finish behind two non-competitive cars. Which all meant he now had the points lead among the ten final tourney contenders two races in, just what we'd all hoped for.

Chief Huggins was there, too. He was drunk as the rest of us.

I found myself suited and wobbling next to him in the lights on a stage meant for rock bands in full yellow-and-black Bascombe team regalia, white-hot in the moment. I hadn't said word one to him all day long.

"What was that shit about my driving ability?" I muttered to him as Turner loudly ran down the merits of rear tire changer Charlie Peerfoy a few men down the line from us.

("He ain't the only black man in the league today, but he damn sure is the oldest!" Peerfoy was a rare breed among pit crew members, at least 10 years my senior.)

"And 'error of judgment'? I figure I might deserve better," I said.

My attempt at good-natured ribbing of course fell flat on its face and broke its nose. Huggins didn't even look at me.

"Hey," I said, a little more loudly.

"I heard you, Cash," he whispered. "Didn't know you owned a TV. You shouldn't watch it. Just shut up and enjoy the moment." And he turned to me and put on a wide, shiteating grin, making a show of slapping me on the back as if we were sharing some joke.

Talk about an error of judgment—I *was* enjoying the moment till this.

"And our newly appointed jackman!" Turner shouted into his microphone, reaching Tacklebox at my left. "Some of y'all may know the man by a different name, but we figure he's got every fishing tool we could need down by Charlotte on Lake Norman, eh Tacklebox? That hook in his nose included, of course." Tacklebox gave a dramatic bow, then waving with one hand—pinching his nose with the other—into the lights as a diminutive roar rose.

Turner had little to say about me. "To the final two, getting along quite famously down here, our newest crew member"—Turner pointing and passing me by—"and our oldest, Eddy Huggins." Couldn't do it all without these guys, we're taking it one race at a time, etc. etc.

I shed my suit and blended in with the crowd as much as I could, skinny in black t-shirt and jeans among the overweight, polo-shirted minions. A particularly rabid fan, a young guy about my age, recognized me from the stage and corralled me at the bar with talk of Baltimore and Charlotte, the latter "destination city," as he said, for all manner of race-heads. Several of his buddies had moved there with the express purpose of gaining employ among the many top-tier teams headquartered there. That'd been years ago now. Most, he added, worked in restaurants today.

I told him the truth. I was from Charlotte, "more or less. When I was a kid," I said, "I guess I thought I wanted to teach English at one point."

"So you like to read old books." You could see the disappointment in his eyes. "How in hell did you get this job?"

"Long, winding story," I said. "I met Turner out on the highway one night in Birmingham. What do people come to Baltimore for?"

"They don't. Maybe government stuff, I don't know. There is *The Wire*, though. You know, the old TV show."

I told him I'd never seen it, to which he expressed no small measure of disbelief.

"Long off the air now," he said, "but people call it the best T.V. you'll ever see—set here in projects and government buildings and police stations."

"I guess that shows how far out I've been," I said. It was a fact of my life I would have been more acutely aware of given a different set of circumstances, more downtime to reflect on the life I wasn't living—that of a character of the sort of ideal of fathers and mothers everywhere, if not exactly my own, the one where the kids are top achievers with stable home lives and real property, industrialists or software engineers, anything but overpaid gearheads, underpaid cooks, broke-ass performance artists. Or, conversely, the ideal of the teenage budding hipster who should know just exactly what his/her friends are listening to. I'd done better on that one, but it'd been a long while since I could care to keep up.

This kid then didn't seem to give a shit himself—he didn't miss a beat by pondering my (or his own, perhaps) failings.

"You ain't missing much," he said, "though talk to some people and it's like you've missed the biggest thing since sliced bread. Ain't nothing more than cops, guns, and drug dealers, you ask me."

He was signaling his end-of-the-night to the bartender.

"Keep an ear out for something called 'TV Police,'" I said. "Out of Chicago. I hear it's gonna be good."

He gave me a weird look, settled his tab and hit the streets. I remained anchored at the bar, my eyes and then mind finding old man Huggins across the space chatting up Turner about something or other. "Chatting up" is probably not the right way to describe it, more *engaged in hushed conversation with* or *godalmighty-damned pissed off at and making his personal point of view as clear as can be with squinted eyes and that mustache of his all cockeyed on his upper lip as he scowled*... Huggins finished a thought, lip curled, waved out over the bar like to stress his point, and Turner rejoined all calm and fortitude. Huggins shot back in with more of the same, this time pointing square in my direction, where they both turned. When they locked eyes with me—I had just enough booze in me to not look away myself—they turned away quickly and Turner placed his left arm over Hugg's shoulder as if to lead him somewhere more private.

But Hugg resisted, and now he was hopping mad, and spoke up in a near shout for the benefit of his perhaps intended audience—"Goddamnit, Turner! I do not give a rat's ass who hears me

183

or what you say. That boy has no business in this…"—but not so loud that I caught the rest as the two disappeared behind a bank of vintage Golden Tee videogames.

My snug position in the team could not best be described as *snugly ensconced,* as it were, in the manner say of a restaurant reviewer declaiming on a particularly homey, comfortable corner booth. That's tortured as all hell, I know, but appropriate, given my own state there, considering Hugg's rage, protruding forehead vein and all. Damn. When Turner emerged from whatever back room or *ensconced ensconcement,* as it were, behind those vid-games, I was playing one myself, trying somewhat unsuccessfully to remember half-forgotten South Carolina barroom nights with Will Theron amid squalling poker machines.

"Yo!" I put out as the racecar driver walked on by me. Turner sort of jumped, uncharacteristically un-cool, wound-up.

"Shit, man. You scared me." His turned his eyes back to his left, behind the games, then.

"Who's coming?"

"Nobody," he said, visibly relaxing. "Listen, man, I got your back. Don't worry."

I wasn't worried, exactly, I told him—and told myself. "Stakes are low for me here, Turner. You've got to know that." I moved as if to turn my attention back to the Golden Tee, self-preservation. Conflict. Shit, I couldn't give a good goddamn …

He shook his head, disappointed. "If there *is* a problem, that's it." He put an index finger into my chest. "Get off the Mr. Cool routine or whatever you want to call it. I've seen it too many times. Whatever you do between now and next Sunday, you've got to raise those stakes. Or, I'm afraid, Hugg will raise them for you. I call the shots around here, ultimately—I own the team. And I've got your back here. But if I don't give him some rein, and know that to this point I have, and we've had success. If I don't let him make up his own mind, his own decisions and all that shit, he'll go somewhere else."

Last thing he needed, he said, was crew mutiny.

"Don't worry too much about it," he said, "but take this shit seriously. I've got no real indication you don't take it seriously, till now, which is what I told the man, and he's got no damn performance-type problems with you. Yet." He put his head into the air. "It's the attitude, maybe, got to be. I don't know. Think *all business*. No nonsense, but serious, commit to it."

I told him I heard it, and back home in Charlotte on my father's streets I gave it what I could, never quite sure if my definition of *all business*—which had something to do with quiet, careful routine, engagement—was quite up to par with what Turner had in mind.

It was exhausting, that's sure. I spent the best of what dead time I did have slovenly sleeping. I dreamed post-fried chicken nightmares in the parking lot of a supermarket near the South Charlotte Team Bascombe headquarters. The dreams were as quotidian as you'd expect, what little time I had during race-weekend preps spent sifting through the recent realities during the lunch-break stupor that followed eating half an eight-piece of supermar-ket-counter fried chicken—this place did it surprisingly well, how-ever, good enough to rival my mother's iron-skillet-cooked variety. I had enough time to reflect on the picture I made conked out in Tacklebox's driver seat in the virtually empty lot. Plus, the girl who worked the deli counter was the spitting image of V, my Chicago maven, the girl who got away or who'd never been caught. Bridget Ellis had more pluck, probably six fewer years, and was much less ironically unhappy in general. I entertained all manner of fantasies of behind-the-counter hookups that never quite found their way into those car-borne fall nightmares.

"What do you like?" Bridget cockeyed coy on her side of the counter.

"Well," I said, my own left eyebrow high, a wink, and we were going doggy-style on top of the counter and in front of the midday supermarket crowd.

I'd never seen her anywhere away from the grocery, guessed she lived in my old neck of the woods south of town, closer to the supermarket than me.

Meanwhile, with the tide of protest and ongoing economic malaise in the radio news broadcasts my nightmares were increas-ingly occupied by demons resembling a marauding crew chief Eddy Huggins or Turner himself in a Wall Street banker suit interrogat-ing me mercilessly as to the true cause of my father's death, ask-ing for information I didn't have. By then, off-and-on protest vigil around the AB headquarters had grown considerably with street upheavals in bigger cities around the nation—I may have partly lamented missing out on the potential reality the Chicago Shining Crew's numbers could well have been, a chance to Shine with light and volume, pure spectacle with at least some underpinning of political or social meaning. All the same, every time I thought about it, half-awake in the supermarket parking lot in Tacklebox's driver's seat or, less often, half-drunk at the bar, existential dread, fear took hold, manifesting physically as my pulse raced and I pondered heart attack, tucked my hands under my thighs and held hard to whatever seat I was on against vertigo.

Stand up, then, quick walk around the perimeter of the parking lot, cigarette at the ready, or a trip to the bathroom, a quickly popped piece of chewing gum or a cigarette, alternately seemed to tamp down the anxiety, and as the weeks went by and I settled into an all-biz routine, the episodes lightened up, gave way to a minimal sense of care that I may have mistaken for the seriousness Turner had so urged.

My neighborhood bar's television, as well as the laptop and newly acquired overly elaborate cellphone (lit up with invitations to "Take Back"—from whom?—the Charlotte tower's lobby on a date not far into the future, a weekday between the Charlotte and Martinsville Chase races, three from the end), kept me well plugged in to the new national reality.

People were pissed and wanted other people to know it. My building neighbors Matt and Rob, for instance, badmouthed Wall Street tycoons in the abstract, their Charlotte corollaries in more personal terms.

"Have you joined in?" I asked them, the three of us wedged at odd angles around a corner table that next week.

"Hmm," said Matt.

"Who has the time?": Rob Rene.

We were midweek at the bar after the Kansas race, the television was tuned to a sports channel, and as the broadcaster turned to racing, detailing Team Bascombe's unlikely win there, I suggested we do just that.

"We have time now," I said. "I'm drunk enough."

"You mean those people haven't been kicked out yet?" Matt said.

"You live around the corner from them, man. You mean you don't know?" Gesturing back over my shoulder down Tryon to 5th or 6th, a distance of just a few blocks, after all, from where we all lived. "They're there, man."

"I might not be drunk enough," said Rob, and we ordered another round and talked of nothing and wandered out of the place by 10 p.m., the boys opting for sleep over the low but dense hum of downtown, which called me out. I'd need to be down at the shop off Westinghouse at 7 a.m. the next morning for final preps for the hometown race that Saturday night, but I opted for caving to curiosity. I pulled out the Shining Man's suit, wished for the helmet and stood staring at my reflection in the big west-facing window in my apartment: a column of light to someone looking in, suit held with each hand at a limp shoulder in front of me. Now, I didn't need it. I smoked a couple cigarettes along the slow way to the vigil keepers at Tryon and Fifth. It was like the late shift was arriving, replacing those who'd been standing outside bank head-quarters since the place closed up in late afternoon—I confirmed it after striking up a conversation with one of five guys I joined ranks with trudging up Tryon.

Then I slowed, falling in behind a knot of unwashed humanity, my heart skipping a beat or two when I caught sight of a recog-nizable sprite carrying a DOWN WITH DEBT sign. Walking with a couple other gals, Bridget smiled a little when she passed me but clearly didn't recognize her serial fried-chicken customer.

I stopped, caught my breath and turned around, calling her name.

Her friends turned to look before she did, one of them obvi-ously older than her, closer to my age. I was uncertain about the other.

"Um, I buy ..." I started to say, but she finished the thought for me:

"Eight-piece, baguette on the side," she said. I always ap-proached her counter with a skinny baton of fresh bread from the bakery. "What are you doing up here?"

"Could say the same to you."

She raised her sign high. "I didn't make it." Neither of her friends carried their own messages. "A guy from down in South

187

Carolina who wasn't going to be coming back gave it to me." She knew some people who knew some other people who knew the organizers of all this, she said, as much as it could be said to have a single group of organizers, in the end. "Sort of like a big party, in a weird place, minus the booze and the pressure to spend a lot of time talking to people about nothing."

The women she was with silently begged off of the conversation, turning to continue their way away from here. I smiled and made like to turn to go my own way, but Bridget didn't move herself.

"And what the hell are *you* doing here, anyway?" she said as I stalled.

I smiled. "Want to stay a while?"

She walked with me and the giant posterboard-and-broom-handle sign back up to the scene. A speaker with a whining, feedback-squelch-peeling megaphone blared something unintelligible just outside the AB building's main entrance and was solidly ignored by the huddles of mostly cross-legged men sitting here and there around the late scene. The cops on hand milled about almost in a casual way, megaphones within reach, smoking cigarettes or staring into their phones.

"C'mon, you didn't answer my question," Bridget tugging on my arm.

"I live right over there," pointing back the way I'd come. She nodded for me to go on. "I'm drunk, I guess." She laughed. "Some friends of mine were too scared to come by and check it out, so I came myself."

She was glad she ran into me, she said. We sat down lateral to a crowd of others 30 feet or so off of the headquarters' entrance. Bridget was a year out of college, she said, a degree in Women's Studies from Chapel Hill, back home now and looking around seeing little for an appropriate next thing to put herself to.

"I may apply for grad school to start next year," she said. "Then again I might just keep serving chicken and making sandwiches, or move to coffee at Starbucks or something."

Had she read *The Handmaid's Tale*?

"Of course," she said.

Cambodian Grrrl?

She surprised me by knowing the book—one by a writer I'd met in Chicago who wrote it after an extended period of conducting zine/self-publishing workshops among young women in Southeast Asia.

"So what brings you here?"

"Seriously?" she said, rolling her eyes.

"Other than the sign, I mean. I know that sounds …"

"Like the beginning of a pickup line." She laughed. "You meant it, didn't you."

I asked about her two friends—the obviously older of whom was her sister, who'd been the primary instigator toward bringing her out tonight, the other a friend of the former.

"They live pretty close, Annie and her boyfriend, up North Davidson in a funky bungalow the two of them have put loads of work into. It's a nice place"—she pointed off to the northeast—"and Annie's great, she is my sister, but he's sort of a turd, works for these guys right here."

We both looked up, up, up to the top of the tower, which in my youth had been the Nations Bank building I think from the time it was built in the 1980s. It'd since undergone more than one name change over the course of merger upon merger upon merger resulting in what was now the biggest too-big-to-fail institution in the nation.

"My mom—my parents are divorced …"

"Mine too."

"Oh joy, right? My mom bought her place out in South Charlotte, close to where I live down in Pineville, I guess it was in 2006 or so. One of those loans given to somebody for way more than they could afford for an amount of house that was just off-the-charts small for what she was paying. Guess who?" She looked up again. "Not that mom's not without fault, I guess, and my sister she's motivated by some kind of insular- and ungrateful-type personal rage given Josh actually works for them. Me, though, I didn't need much persuasion to come on out."

She picked up her sign now and pumped it twice high in the air before letting it rest on her right shoulder.

"I don't have anything better to do other than maybe search for a job, though that's about as hopeless a fucking task as sitting around downtown Charlotte holding a sign."

I nodded, began to tell her about the Shining Man. Magnanimously sarcastic Bridget or maybe the several beers I'd had encouraged candor, encouraged truth among the off-and-on loud, close rancor here. Just as I really got into it—the beginning of the part about the crime or disappearance or ruse or whatever it ultimately was—a cop maybe 10 yards off opened up through his megaphone with orders to disperse now or face an unspecified terrific fate come midnight. I put my hands over my ears.

"How old are you?" she asked, laughing, then taking off before I could answer: "They've been doing this every night—pretty much everybody takes off at the end, not sure what law or rule allows them to kick everybody out at midnight, but the shit seems to work. A few people have gotten arrested, for sure, though. Something of a scene when it happens. I was here right up to the end a week ago and it was just the second night they'd actually kicked everybody out, you know, by force and all that. Cleared out pretty quick that night."

"Getting up on 30," I said before she could catch her breath. "A couple years left."

"You're not dead yet."

"Good thing." I lit a cigarette.

The cop charged ahead through his megaphone again and, the minute he stopped, Bridget belted out "We fucking hear you!" Then, lower, "My dad was a cop before he took off in a big truck and my mom left him. I guess I understand these motherfuckers. With him every reaction came with like this cool aggression, you know? Like a schizo housecat sitting there all silent waiting for you to just go ahead, try and pet me and see if I don't put a hole in your goddamn face."

The cop reminded me a little of Ralph Cash, something about his face. Bland, noncommittal expression. All business, no bullshit, sneak-attack billy club at the ready. "Yeah, so my dad ..." I wouldn't get another word in.

"Hey, check this out," Bridget gazed off over the assembled squatters. "See that guy over there with the black beads?" A hippie-dippy-looking sort with long light-brown hair that covered much of his shoulders and, yes, a necklace of shooter-marble-sized

190

black beads that, if it was in fact made of glass shooter marbles, probably weighed 10 pounds. "I know him. Like to smoke weed?" Her eyebrows shot high.

I nodded, but reflexively looked at my watch.

"Ah come on! You don't need to be up early."

"Six a.m. at the latest."

"Well how about you don't *want* to be up early." She smiled, grabbed my right wrist and we stood to mosey our way over to ...

"His name's Knox," she said. "Wait till you hear his voice," eyes flashing.

"Well hello, Mr. Garp," she mock-drawled when we got to him.

He was with three other dirty-looking guys sitting around a rolled-up tent. The voice that came out of him was somewhere between Andy Griffith and aw-shucks Gomer Pyle, with more of the latter's utter-and-total-dumb-ass inflections, I guess you'd say.

"Well if it ain't little Bridget and—hey man, I'm Knox." He thrust out his hand like the salesman he was.

"Call me Cash."

"I likes me the sound of that." Then to Bridget: "Got you a nest egg here, don't you."

He wished.

Though in the dim light I couldn't well tell it, by the sound of her voice and the relative heat in my own face, I'd say brash Bridget blushed.

"Knox grew up down the block from me," she said, turning away.

And she pulled him aside very hush-hush and the three of us walked away from the crowds around the other side of the AB building and down another two blocks, where he handed her a small plastic bag and she rifled through the pocket of her jean jacket for some bills. I started to pull out my wallet.

"No no, man," Knox caught my arm before I could produce it, quietly adding, "y'all settle later," and taking her money and scanning the distance in a sort of forced-casual way, then again behind me, behind himself, and off across the street.

He smiled, "Much obliged," bowed slightly, and made his way back to the vigil. We kept going.

"Your place?" Bridget asked.

"Up with cash transactions!" I pumped my fist in the air and we switched back the way we'd come, then veered off Knox's trail toward my apartment. But on our way to the elevator we passed a well-heeled couple in formal attire. Both man and woman grimaced at the picture of me carrying the sign, and Bridget burst into full-throated laughter scarcely five feet beyond them. No one had said a word otherwise.

I heard their footsteps stop down the hall behind us.

"What are you kids doing in here?" said the man of the pair—he might've been 45.

"I live here, man," I said. "421."

"Can I see your key card?" he said.

I reached into my back pocket to produce it when Bridget blurted out: "What are you a fucking Nazi or something?"

I put myself then between the man and her.

"Jesus Christ," she muttered.

I held up my card, which showed my picture and everything, right next to my face, putting on a big goofy smile for him. He nodded and turned on his way.

Bridget wouldn't let it go. She'd probably been high all night.

"You people are the problem!" she bellowed. They just kept walking. "Yeah, go on. Get the fuck out of here. We live here too, banker trash!"

They didn't skip a beat.

The elevator opened.

"Jesus H," I said, and we entered.

"That was awesome."

"That guy probably lives next-door to me."

"Maybe you should move. Better yet, maybe he should."

She got high on the tiny balcony and I popped open a beer (dope could cost me my job—the league's banned drug list is longer for crew members than it is for drivers, go figure: money can go a long, long way toward getting what you want) as Bridget talked and talked and talked a stream of belligerent dissatisfaction that was, ultimately, quite familiar. I was enjoying it all, frankly, the slight unreality of the night, Bridget's incoherence somewhat infectious, *here's hoping any contact high makes its way into the toilet before the next official sampling, thank you Knox Garp, if that's your actual name, Bridget*

192

on the couch across a little coffee table I'd found at a thrift shop up on North Davidson, myself down on the floor taking in her image in 3-D Technicolor relief yes the resemblance to V was uncanny minus the talking and talking and talking on. "… is the main problem. I mean, just what the hell sounds good to anybody about sitting at a little desk and punching the numbers in elevators or climbing stairs for your coffee from the fucking Starbucks in the lobby, man. I just won't do that job, whatever it is in some office building or teaching snot-nosed brats like myself at a college or worse some little fucking urchins like my little brother in a high school"—and here she cackled wildly. "Man that was hilarious. You should have seen the look on that guy's face when I called him a Nazi!"

I had seen it, of course. It was an expression of impatience more than whatever disgust may have lurked beneath his skull. Empathy is crushing.

"He didn't know what hit him," she said, laughing, then talking on as my focus turned to the kitchen, where a loaf of sliced bread I'd bought at Bridget's grocery store awaited my best efforts at mastication atop the refrigerator. Or had. It wasn't there anymore.

"… man I don't know maybe I'll just move. Move to fucking Europe or something, maybe out to California or Miami, yeah, Miami. Where did you come from again? Birmingham or something? …"

I stood and walked past the couch and toward the kitchen. The bag the bread had come in sat against the wall on the kitchen floor lateral to the refrigerator, half torn apart.

"Hey Cash. Are you listening to me?"

She was right behind me now.

"Did you eat my bread?" I pointed dumbly to the bag, obvious for what it had included, a squared-off loaf of the cheapest white bread money could buy.

"Dude, you should really be eating whole grains. That stuff will kill you."

"…"

"No, I didn't eat it."

I scanned the kitchen as she murmured and put her arms now around my waist, making short work of my belt and unbuttoning my pants. "Hold on a second," I said. The cabinet below the sink

193

was open by a couple inches, and a corner of one piece of bread's crust sat on the empty bottom shelf. I pointed to it.

"C'mon," she said, "let's do it."

I finally looked at her—her shirt was already off. I was for a moment unmoved, for reasons that still aren't altogether clear to me. My body resisted flight-into-sexual-bliss mode, brain revved the blood to readiness to fight.

"I've got a problem," I said, and kneeled down to peer into the cabinet, where off in the darkest corner was a gaping hole big enough for a small cat leading God-knows-where back off into the innards of the building. I don't know how long I stared at it—it smelled fucking feral down there up close, dirty and alive. Midnight approached. I popped open another beer, putting the remainder of the almost-full 18-pack of cans firmly in front of both bottom-cabinet doors. Bridget had put her shirt back on and was on the porch with her rolling papers.

I ultimately buttoned my pants and sat down on the couch, where I guess I passed out. It was my father who woke me when he walked in from the porch carrying one of the little chairs and pulling it up directly across from me with a stern message: "The fairer sex has got your number," he said, he laughed at me, he smiled, he reached across the distance between us and grabbed my shoulder.

"You're not real," I said, a shiver passing through me as if to belie the conviction.

"Maybe not, but did I ever tell you about the repaving project out here—Church, street of gods, of weak-minded men, devils and dipshit disciples, too. Soon as we pierced the ground with pavers the street called back with a blast howl, my God! It was something—the animals just came bursting up out of the storm drains like nothing I'd ever seen."

What kinds of animals? I wondered.

"Alligators," Pop said. "Fucking been living off the trash and human feces and what all else down there after being flushed by little kids. New York City was a crazy town, man, holy Lord Jesus."

I opened my mouth to remind the old man of where we were, why we were here. But why were we here? The door to my porch he'd left open and I wanted to ask him to close it, God, the animals that could get in if he didn't, how many bread loaves would be sacrificed for simple laziness, nonchalance. But I was struck immobile, just as suddenly struggling to raise my head from the spot on the couch cushions where it rested. Summoning the breath to speak was impossible.

My father rose, leaned over me and grasped my shoulder again. "Don't worry, son, I'll close it on my way out." He repeated, "Don't worry, never worry for me," and he turned and walked, not looking back.

I tried again to call out against the giant weight now as if holding me in place, as if keeping me from the thing that it was my very destiny to do. Pop shut the door behind him, climbed onto the porch railing, and jumped.

Chapter 14

When I woke at 5 a.m., my pants were open, cock half hanging out, flaccid and pinched just below the head by the elastic waistband of my shorts. There were three empty beer cans on the table in front of me. On the balcony the DOWN WITH DEBT sign stood tall, its message broadcast out to whoever could see it from the street or other building. Bridget was long gone.

A blistering headache announced itself when I stood to peer off out over the edge of the railing, shaking the sleep from my eyes and moving back to the kitchen. Bridget had put the beers back in the refrigerator, probably thinking she was doing me a favor, and the door to the bottom cabinet again was open, this time just wide enough say for a squirrel or other small rodent to get through. I put the beer box back where it belonged. I called down to the shop off Westinghouse Boulevard and left a message on the reception voicemail that I was sicker than a dog, and prepared for battle.

I'd need my energy.

Better, hopefully restful sleep called.

But I was awoken by Turner himself, who started in with "Where the hell are you at, man?"

I took it he didn't get the message.

"Sleep it off," he said, once I gave him my story. "Here's the thing—qualifying tomorrow, as you know. Be at the track by nine. And after, I've got this dinner with some potential sponsor types—they wanted me, solely, no Eddy, no wives, girlfriends, that sort of thing, but I told them I wanted to bring a pit team member, give them an idea of what we have. Tacklebox has something going on. Want to come along?"

I didn't know whether to accept or run like hell, though if it was just Turner, it was just Turner—a simple hang, easy to talk to, easy in all things long as you were serious. He had my back.

"Do you have a suit?"

"Um, yeah, I don't know."

"You sound like shit warmed up, man. Listen, go out and get a suit and give me the receipt. It'll be fun—it ain't like we really need these people, and my policy's always been I'll just be my damn self and if they take it, they take it. If not, they can go to hell. Too, though, we could all use a bigger payday."

"I meant I don't know if I can do it. My mom—"

"All right, Cash, figure it out and get back to me. No pressure or anything like that. Get better. We need you this weekend."

He hung up.

When I appeared at Rob and Matt's door some 30 minutes later (showered, hair combed, aspirin taken) asking about potential vermin infestations, their immediately downcast reactions told the tale.

"Not squirrels," said Rob, though I was thinking something bigger.

Nor blue jays or cuddly little cartoon raccoons or possums.

"Rats," Matt said. "Yeah, we've seen them around, never in our place."

"The guy who lived in your unit before you moved in there," said Rob, "Nice guy and all, but the place was a wreck."

"How much you paying in rent?" Matt said.

"Nine hundred," I said.

"We pay almost twice that," Rob nodding conspiratorially, "same space," his hands out to his sides as if to say, take a look around.

"They wouldn't," I said.

Neither Matt nor Rob would definitively allege anything, claiming they'd never heard of such, but it definitely struck them as odd. To my way of thinking the discount could have been the buildings' owners' way of giving a man a break for the possibility the beasts would return to scenes of former crimes. I don't know. Rob had seen them in the hallway, he said, in the corner-of-building stairwell, in the lobby, on the elevator.

"The elevator?"

"So look up next time you ride, there's some fluorescent lights behind the plastic grating up above your head, and I'd say two-three inches of space."

"Holy shit."

197

People complained all the time, he said, but most of the truly rich folks who kept places here did just that—kept places, only visited off and on, or owned spaces and rented them out half the time to folks like us, given to nonconfrontation, less than apt to complain until immediate space was invaded.

I recalled some of Billy's tales of late-night forays with an accidentally-acquired pistol, potshots in his favorite back-alley-behind-restaurant shooting galleries. Rob Rene had advice that took into account the particulars of what I'd seen.

"A friend had a bunch of them living under his kitchen floor—he lived in a Brooklyn basement-type apartment. They were coming in through the tiny little water-heater closet just off the kitchen, squeezing under the space between the door and the floor to the smorgasboard."

Getting rid of them all he described as a gruesome exercise in isolation, patience, vigilance and discipline. "The man spent three months transporting dead beasts from the boxed-in space of the closet to the dumpster," Rob said.

Three months? Oh joy.

Kills came first in rapid succession at one or two a day, then more slowly, one a week, finally an odd kill every other week or so. Rob mixed his metaphors to emphasize the task at hand: "Dig your fortifications and pack for the long haul."

I commandeered Tacklebox's Ford bound for the nearest hardware store but got an unexpected text along the way:

Having lunch today? Come see me, cowboy

Bridget. I bounced my head on the steering wheel there in the garage before, ultimately, pulling out and steering the wheels southbound on 77 for the world's best grocery. My late-night distraction wasn't enough to, morning after, banish the now-splendiferous vision of Bridget topless in my rat-infested kitchen, and I could supply plenty of justification for making the drive, given a hardware store stood perfectly adjacent to the grocery. This was a moment of outreach, of meeting halfway—an olive branch of an easy-if-embarrassed quick return to normalcy in my dealings with the woman, however exceptional the day itself would or would not be.

I bought six large snap traps and three glue boards after a brief conversation about poison with the store sales clerk.

"They eat the poison, typically, and go back somewhere you have no control over and die," she said, matter-of-factly. "If you're willing to risk one dying somewhere within nose-shot, I guess you'd say, go for it. Otherwise, the snappers are the best, quickest remedy. Some things never change."

The glue boards were for the smart ones, as she told. Some will get wise to their comrades' mistakes in taking the snap-trap bait, eventually. When kills level off, place a board so that they have to walk across it to get out of the hole.

"Bam, you've got another."

The store shared a vast parking lot with the grocery and several other attached shops—strip mall, more or less. In the several weeks I'd made the parking lot the place of daytime dreams and nightmares, I'd never seen a coworker, and today it was well earlier than typical for the lunch breaks of the men of Team Bascombe. But here was tire changer Judd Winnow making his way across the parking lot from the Chevy pickup he drove, moving toward the grocery. I moved quickly as I could to the car, repositioned the Ford and its cache of rat traps with a view of the grocery's entrances across the lot. Ten minutes later, Winnow emerged carrying a plastic sack bulging with a familiar geometric shape—eight-piece fried, more than likely.

I chuckled. Winnow I liked. A man of few words, a benevolent practical joker. A close call, though—the entirety of the team knew where I lived, nowhere near this little shop. If I needed groceries, Pepto Bismol, antibiotics, whatever, it made zero sense for me to be here. He pulled out and surprised me by wheeling his pickup directly this way, either making a bee line for the hardware store or cutting the lot off to take the east exit. I sunk down in my seat as low as I could go, praying he didn't recognize Tacklebox's "GO ___ OR GO HOME!" bumper sticker, the car itself. I heard a vehicle pull in two-three spots away from me, a door open, shut, and 30 seconds later I dared take a peek to see him walking into the hardware store.

My luck was running out. I wheeled back out onto the roadway downtown-bound, blood pumping. Bridget could wait.

Night arrived with no small amount of trepidation—if I

couldn't be expected to hear the stirrings of my furry cohabitors I could definitely anticipate the noise of a catch, the *thwonk!* of the killing bar rotating with velocity around its sprung axis too fast even for that oh-so-speedy of animals to beat out. I whiled away the time smoking on the balcony overlooking my father's paving handiwork somewhere down below the top layer of asphalt, my DOWN WITH DEBT messenger at my side to remind me of so much chaos. But by the third beer I was quite upright and proud and thanked Pop for his financial tutelage, or lack thereof—he did once impress upon me the usual reality of the notion that if it seemed too good to be true, you'd be justified in hoping all you wanted but always keep the boomerang's return in mind. I congratulated myself for coming out of a rearing amidst the easy-credit juggernaut with nothing unwieldy to show for it, not exactly for lack for interest, in more ways than one, truth be told. The couple credit card offers I'd responded to over the years were for premium, low-ish interest Amex and Gold MasterCards that were sent to people like me, I ultimately concluded, just to tempt us into denials that came with hopeful strings attached in the form of snares. *While you ultimately don't qualify for this standard of credit, pre-approval notwithstanding, try one of our special Bluish-Black-and-Grey-Green-Limpopo options—we'll take anyone at a reasonable variable APR of 37.97.* No thanks, grifters.

Maybe I was special, I could hope with a reasonable amount of certainty of the boomerang's eventual trajectory, proudly displaying Bridget's sign, an exemplar of the improbable in the New American Economy, a man with high standards and low potential and equally low expectations. More likely I'd just been broke and somewhat resigned to the fact—even still, though my stock-car-racing sojourn had proved lucrative beyond what I'd previously known, putting down a payment and assuming a massive debt on a property or vehicle or anything else was in no way an appealing fate. I'd join the ranks of the pissed and dispossessed protesting on the streets in earnest on behalf of the real losers before I did anything of that nature. If rat-death became too unbearable: decamp to my mother's basement, gladly suffering her footfalls and toothbrush-swish-and-spit leaking through the flooring as punishment for my weakness, if I had a choice in the matter.

What I did have, today: a brand-new black suit, 30 regular, hung proudly soaking up every visible spectrum shining down from the apartment's overhead lighting. Yes, I called and confirmed with Turner, though putting on the dark suit would deliver me into likewise dark, uncharted waters I had trouble visualizing a commitment to. Then again, what had I ever truly committed to? Ever a man and boy open to suggestion, a sponge lapping up the needs and wants and desires of those elder or with hard-won experience beyond familiar bounds.

If Turner had plans for me, I'd give them a chance.

Chapter 15

I did not yet operate with the full benefit of knowing the brilliance of my pristine stupidity, you see. The people around me were beginning to know or had always in some sense known it. Turner could hear it in the tone of noncommittal reticence with which I accepted his invitation, Bridget in my inability to respond to the buzzing machine in my pocket, lit up with her notes of invitation since that first message. My lack of response did nothing to deter her—*cowboy* I was, star pit crew newbie capable of hobnobbing with those who held fast to the keys to what amounted to a collection of individual fortunes, well made. (*Look out for the boomerang, Cash, look out.*)

As for Turner, the man had opened a window for my view into something elemental about the team's greater operation, its financing and long-term scheming, its future, and I wasn't sure why or I didn't feel up to the challenge of understanding it. As far as I'd known to that point, Turner was an uncommon member of the 1 percent of Americans capable of living not by his wits but by the interest from his forebears' savings accounts, gains made from a logging and lumber business too old and cash-rich to really fully flounder with the hit taken by the late macroeconomic plummeting of the construction business. I'd never considered him less than indestructible, which I was beginning to see was folly—Turn Turner would have to hustle like the rest of us to get by, the amounts on the deposits and tendered checks just naturally larger than the array of, by comparison, piddly numbers that amassed around a life such as mine.

Still, why he would involve me in that hustle was an unanswerable question. I thought about something he told me the night I met him out on the highway in Birmingham. *Unclouded*, he said, *your eyes are clear, and you don't know just how damn important that is to me at this point.* Tacklebox, for his part, and Peerfoy and Winnow and old Huggins and even the young drunk of old Hugg's son, though his father's team involvement made him something of an outlier and probably more entitled in Turner's mind than the rest to whatever precarious position he held now that I'd replaced him—regardless, all of them were of Turner's world, men of the inside, aspirational to a fault, their very existence maybe an implied threat to the race-car driver at the head of their team… I was far from certain of this, and hoped there was something simpler going on, some more intuitive reason I would be joining a dinner happening with money enough on the line to pay my rent for months—if not decades.

I sat silent thinking about it all in the common area of my apartment, shifting between the couch and the smoking porch listening alternately intently and not at all for any evidence of activity in my kitchen, a copy of *Naked Lunch* Rob Rene lent me at the ready. A chair on the porch afforded a view to the similarly constructed mini-balconies of units on the higher floors. Near 2 a.m. I was surprised to see Bridget's Nazi businessman propped on his elbows leaned out over the railing, himself with a cigarette stuck in his mouth. He was still, sucking, for a long moment as I watched, his eyes full of the view into the knot of buildings that was downtown Charlotte, before a long tendril of ash dropped and his gaze followed its floating progress down, down to a resting place on my knee. I smiled grimly and waved it off as he registered recognition.

"Sorry," he said.

I thought of what Bridget might have told him and felt like rolling my eyes.

"Me too," I said, sincerely, brushing the ash from my knee.

He nodded and thumped his cigarette out into the street.

My wide-awake vigil, I suspected, kept whatever vermin were out and about this evening far away from my unit. (Though they'd stolen enough white bread to feed a veritable rat army just yesterday, so perhaps they still grazed on it in a massive improvised ratking in den central.) When I woke I was on the couch, 6 a.m., phone alarm ringing away in a pocket.

I examined the under-sink cabinets, no evidence of further activity, got dressed for racing and was off, running with the windows open to the track north and east of downtown. Qualifying was nothing like the high-intensity race days, though there was plenty to keep even a lowly tire carrier occupied. When I wasn't playing right hand to the engine or body man or running through double-checks on equipment maintenance lists in prep for the Saturday-night race, I hung with Pete Kimball by the truck, quizzing him further on his history, exceptional in the new-ish century, the brand-new decade, though he was the last man to view said history as such.

Was he aware of the musical legacy of a giant of a jazzman who grew up in his North Carolina hometown?

He was. He loved Coltrane.

How does a kid who grew up in a house with full-time maids and nannies and such end up driving truck?

It was how he'd made his money for 15 years, he said, more or less. There was an attraction to the freedom of the road, variability of schedule, all that, in the early days, when he ran long-haul, "irregular route in the lower 48," as he put it. "Thankfully this gig came along"—none of the initial attraction remained beyond a few years. Though "it can be a good paycheck if you know what you're doing and you enjoy the life."

Five o'clock rolled around and it looked like Turner would command the sixth starting spot. Sitting half-asleep in the passenger seat of Kimball's Peterbilt listening to his CB crackle with staticky voices from I-85 just north of the raceway and the hordes of RVers camped out in the infield, I finally took the time to translate the maybe 10 text messages Bridget had bombarded me with throughout the day:

is the Charlotte race this weekend?

Translation: I already know the answer to this but I need to make sure you know I'm actually interested in what you're doing this weekend.

c'mon cowboy, bait the hook, sink it

In case the former note wasn't enough to make the interest clear in your mind …

a lady just ordered an eight-piece here … Where you at?

I'm feeling a little desperate, maybe, but again maybe it's more that I want you to hear the ringing gongs of a familiar situation— warm-fuzzy gongs, not the ugly clanging kind of recognition that might come, say, with a reminder of the state of your penis when I left you the other night. About which more later.

how often do you see this ... an elderly man wearing elderly clothes pushing a double babystroller with what looked like infant twins in it just wandered past

Not done yet…

the counter to the flower section: 'I need something for a gravesite…"

Yeah, that might be the coolest-weirdest thing seen all day, maybe even for you—don't you wish you were here?

down with debt! Heh …

Interest, connection—that, little boy, is the coolest-weirdest thing you've seen in the last week.

big march next week downtown … we're going inside!

ab building, I mean …

Involving you, Cash, involving you. You must be there.

You said something just before you passed out the other night—something like, 'I am in here' or 'we are in here' or 'out here' what the fuck?

That penis I mentioned earlier. You should at least feel a little shame w/r/t the state in which I was forced to leave you two nights ago, so here's a reminder of it. I'll soft-pedal it nonetheless with a question I am genuinely curious to know the answer to, or at least one behind which I suspect you might have a moderately interesting story.

And the last, received one hour almost to the minute after the preceding text, made clear the young woman's growing exasperation over my lack of a single response throughout the day:

I'm staying in, tonite …

She would have to grant a text-etiquette novice absolution from unintended sins, I thought. My ignorance of her missives were on account in large part of business, in lesser part a simple newness to true engagement via text on the phone. I kept the sound, the buzzer off but for incoming calls. I found the buzzer settings and turned it on, now. I opened the truck's door and, turning my legs to the opening, tapped out something I hoped might make up for my silence.

Watch your TV Saturday night, little lady. Got a feeling we'll win this one under the lights

Call it a sense of destiny or a high feeling I'd been getting from Tacklebox and Peerfoy and even Turner himself. Typically tight-lipped and determined on these days, and somewhat characteristically so today, the driver was beaming here with the main event in his half-hometown not only of choice—he was one of just a few high-profile cup circuit drivers who actually spent any of his childhood in the Charlotte area, which before the banks and racing and pro wrestling was once dominated by the fruits of North and South Carolina loins. You could tell he wanted to win, and five spots off pole wasn't a bad place to be, considering scarcely a tenth of a second separated Bascombe's time from the leader. Fellow North Carolinian and serial Bascombe nemesis Montuck Jr., too, came away from his qualifying laps with a time well back in the pack, plenty of early wiggle room out of head-to-head rival-firebrand competition for Bascombe.

The Montuck team's haul rig and garage spot was 10 or so down the line from our own. On my way to retrieve my dinner suit from Tacklebox's little loaner Ford, I passed the team boys' party out back of the rig and turned my gaze out and away to the grandstands when I was surprised to hear "Yo Cash!" belted out from the little knot of bodies around a grill. Burgers sizzled, and I locked eyes with the hateful gaze, among the now somewhat familiar faces of Montuck crewmembers, of none other than a just positively plastered Chuck Huggins. Anyone familiar with the deleterious effects of alcohol could've guessed it, Huggins' eyes not quite focused but nonetheless filled with seething anticipation of a reckoning, comeuppance long overdue. Turner's personal dislike of the boy got me my spot on the crew, nonetheless.

I attempted a poker-faced turn back on my route to Tacklebox's Ford and my new black, positively non-iridescent suit and the coming night of God-knew-what. I attempted to pretend I hadn't heard, didn't have the time or inclination, I attempted haughty disdain whose best satisfaction in course of action was deliberate ignorance—this all flew like a lead balloon in the two or three steps I got in before Huggins repeated his "Yo Cash!", the entirety of the Montuck team now watching. I couldn't well ignore it, could I…

I stopped long enough for Huggins to weave his way around the grill and between the bodies of two somewhat alarmed-looking members of the crew toward me. When he got within five feet his eyes shot wide as if he'd come awake from a long sleep, been startled by a vision whose veracity he couldn't quite trust. And then he laughed long and hard. I kept my own gaze as skeptical as I could manage before he finally spoke.

"You're a goner. Just wait, little shiny man," he said. The crew at his back, I'll say, looked as skeptical as me.

"Oh, I don't know, Hugg," I said, using the diminutive typically reserved for his father. That got his attention.

He positively scowled.

"You a part of this team now?" I said.

The boys at his back now all either shook heads or raised their palms high as if to disassociate themselves, but Huggins couldn't see that, nor I imagine would he have been convinced, had he.

"We're gonna get us a little piece of Turner Bascombe this weekend, you can be sure of that."

"Godspeed," I said, "though I'm not sure what the hell exactly is going through your little head." I attempted a laugh, a bone to the guys at his back who then surprised me by going all poker-faced themselves as Huggins turned and glared at the lot.

I moved.

"Watch yourself, Cash!" he yelled after me. "You just watch yourself!"

The sponsor's dinner was at a joint in near-South Charlotte clear across town from the racetrack. I arrived before anyone else and waited out the racecar driver and whatever entourage he'd have in tow at the bar, texting him to tell him I'd arrived. The place was somewhere between urban café and old-style casual bar and grill a block from the high-end mall in town. The bar was all polished concrete and mismatched stools, but the dining room was dramatically, sparingly lit as if for quiet, private, important conversations. The clientele seemed to reflect the divergence — the women at my left could have been at a sports bar, judging by the football jerseys they were wearing, but at least a couple of the tables' diners, whom I could make out in the gloom back across the open space of the place, were in shirts and ties, jackets, maybe even a few suits not unlike my own.

Not exactly nursing a beer, then another, feeling uncharacteristically polished, buttoned-up, hidden from view in a rather enticingly comfortable way in my new suit, I listened to the conversation ongoing between the women at my left, in their mid-30s, maybe early 40s, about a sort of activism quite unlike the ragtag core of Bridget and the nameless faces downtown and on Wall Street and surely by now camped out in various locales in and around Chicago. Oddly, I thought, considering the venue, the $10 I'd just spent on a bottle of Miller High Life, the two were, it became clear, talking about an upcoming government-health-care-handout protest.

"Are you bringing your sign?" asked the woman farthest from me.

"Not this time. I've kind of gotten away from the signs."

"What does Darryl think?"

"Uh huh. He's big on the signs." They laughed, the woman next to me continuing, air quotes raised high either side of her head, "'Obamacare is elderly genocide.' It's just too weird, you know. I was on TV holding that damn thing one time and I like to never live it down at the office."

Life was protest, anticipation, shame, regret, the stuff of quotidian chit-chat for just-folks out at the bar for a Thursday night. I thought about my rats, their grind, the search for food, fighting-chewing their little ways through whatever flimsy barriers we erected against the prize of sweet sustenance. I almost laughed aloud at the vision I half-expected to greet me upon arrival home in the evening—under-sink cabinet doors open rat-wide in spite of my barriers, beer cans empty and strewn around the kitchen, a 16-beast-long drunken parade of vermin carrying miniature signs of their own emblazoned with slogans decrying humans' hedonistic tendencies and urging solidarity for the greater good.

WE NEED YOUR WHITE BREAD TO LIVE, ASSHOLE
TOGETHERNESS = COMMON SURVIVAL
WE ARE OUT HERE

...

My phone buzzed.

"Let's eat," Turner's voice behind me, an identical message now lighting up my face. I turned to find two big guys in blue polo shirts with floppy collars unpopped and windbreakers looking positively out of place with Turner, who wore a dark-red dandy-ish suit with embellished pointed lapels and tight silver pinstripes. The

208

black fedora atop his head had to make him the only race driver since the year 1960 to wear such.

Maybe it was Turner and I who were out of place.

"Incognito," he said, as if reading my mind, on our way to the table after the appropriate introductions. "You know any other drivers dress like this?"

Our tablemates were Bill and Bob of the famous Cheeter Farms of Northern Indiana corn country, as Turner put it. Their business was milk, cattle. More importantly, the pair were industrializing sustainable practices via a fleet of natural-methane-powered tractors to pull company milk tankers utilizing—none other than—the bubblin'-crude cow turds on the property there as fuel. With the fleet: an outreach initiative to boost their prominence nationwide, and they were rolling out a dairy-exclusive protein-power drink that would be hitting the grocery markets next season as healthy energy for the masses, commensurate with the company's own on-farm practices.

"If we want a winner," said Bill, the bigger of the two huge guys with about six inches on his maybe 6-foot-2 brother, "they told us you were it, Turn. And we want your damn hood and team, don't know what it would take to get it—we know you've got your daddy's money propping everything up here, but we aim to outdo it if we can."

Turner nodded.

"You might not get *wholesome* with us, exactly, but you'll get real exposure, that's sure. We do well this season, and we are, and we will, next season should be good too is my guess."

Then he got down to real business. "Speaking of *wholesome*, you boys like to drink? Qualifying done, I got almost 48 hours before I absolutely have to get behind the wheel again. I feel like getting hammered tonight. Y'all in? My treat."

They all laughed and nodded their affirmations and Turner summoned Pappy Van Winkle all around and the Cheeters interrogated the sad legacy of their family name with further tales of marketing-worry woe, which needed, for the farm and protein drink's sake, if not an injection of the kind of image-reversal that Beaver Cleaver as a pitchman might have engendered in the 1950s, certainly some kind of official sanction in the U.S. imagination. They'd landed like a shitbrick on the pop landscape this year with an investigative piece in *Esquire* of the "Shady origins of the latest biofuels pioneer." The writer told the story of their now decade-old migration from Southern California, where the land of their onetime cowfarm there was now a massive half-empty platoon of subdivided subprime real estate and sad-as-hell living they'd made a fortune punting off on current and former owners during the exurban Los Angeles real estate bubble.

True, all of it, was the trouble, Bill said.

"We're getting no help from the national newspapers, neither. It's like those New York writers are clairvoyant."

That wasn't the chief problem, of course, given the *Esquire* set would be just a small part of the power beverage's ultimate customer base, Bill said. "You're talking 80 percent well-meaning Republican dad types—road-warrior salesmen, truckers, maybe. Hell, Turn, we just need the prime hood exposure more than anything else. Lots of tight TV cameras on a leader."

He wasn't talking to me. I felt OK about it, my place here that of an unfortunate student's, in the end. I'd been more or less quiet up to now. Listening, I still was mystified by why exactly Turner sought to involve me in this charade. But for Turner's weird get-up (he looked more like Chicago Carl than the driver I'd come to know), it'd been simple, too simple, four guys sitting around a table, two of them, mostly, talking shallowly about current business and deep on personal-biz background. With the too-expensive-whiskey rush to my head, I felt on the verge of overflowing.

But "Big Bill" broke through every lull in conversation before I rose to whatever opportunity existed. Yes, Bill offered, he used the famous Chicago politician's moniker. His dad, from whom he and Bob had inherited the Cheeter brand, grew up in the Big Windy in the time of the last mayor's father's ascendancy. Big Bill busted the latest lull with a question aimed squarely at me, though he spoke it in Turner's general direction.

Why didn't "the quiet guy here seem to have much to say about it all?" he wanted to know.

Because the quiet guy thinks the both of you might as well be from Uranus, I thought, then looked questioningly to Turner (poker-faced, staring straight ahead over the shoulder or at the forehead, I wasn't sure, of Big Bill, who sat across from him) before half-stammering, "Not sure why Turner brought me out here tonight, y'all. Clearly I don't have much to add—uh, a fascinating story, you guys. I'll say that."

And Turner didn't so much as look at me, but he smiled. "I'll tell you why I brought him here."

"Uh-huh, uh-huh," Big Bill urging him on, drinking, Bob half-heartedly echoing the grunts.

"Same reason you brought Bob here." Across from me, the shorter Cheeter had been near equally quiet up to now.

"This man," Turner said, thumb wagging in my direction, "had absolutely fuck-all to do with Team Bascombe up until just how many weeks ago—how long's it been?"

I scowled inside, but held up three fingers, then thinking better of it and popping up the pinkie.

"Three-four, maybe more—he's been carrying tires for several weeks, let's say. But for my money he's a perfect example of what you get with us good-natured and fun and just in-fucking-visible boys—a yellow-and-black-damn beehive of a uniform through which the hopes and desires of generations flow. And fearless, too."

Bill and Bob Cheeter both turned level stares my way. I shrugged, all raised eyebrows, and belted back my glass.

"Another," Turner said, raising an arm high for the waiter. When waiter arrived: "Hell, give us the bottle."

The room seemed to hurtle around an axis somewhere between the bodies of the four of us, hanging lamps above the tables describing arcs of light suspended in midair in my periphery. Turner didn't know how wrong he was—or how wrong I suspected he was, *hoped* may be the better word.

"I've been criticized in the past for team drama, for lack of a better way to put it, boys," the man went on. "Too many hotheads on the crew, quick to smart to any perceived slight, all plotting their petty little ways into the spotlights of this racing business, the place behind the wheel, you know. We prided ourselves on that fact for a long time. It served us well, it did—nothing better for press than a bunch of assholes fighting with each other and everybody else out there all the time. If you follow racing, and I think you do, you know what I'm talking about."

"I do follow racing, Turn," said Bill, pointing then at me. "But I'm not sure I'm following you. So this guy's what—better mouse-trap over your past guys, something like that?"

The bottle arrived.

"Drink up," Turner commanded, and Bill laughed a little, Bob utterly stone-faced. But they did drink. "It's more than just my no-tion of where the team needs to be or who's a better tire carrier or jackman or chief. Let me tell you how I met the guy."

And he launched into a part-manufactured tale of Birming-ham night, the room steadying a bit with my concentration on the scene, my own recollection of lived events, what I took for the growing Cheeter horror but which was more fascination than any-thing else, given the ultimate outcome.

"I was coming off a knock-down drag-out absolute damna-ble veritable war," Turner told, "and I mean immediately coming off—hauling ass the hundred miles up back Talladega way from Tuscaloosa fresh off an argument with Hugg about his son. If you've never met the boy, know he's about the worst of the hot-heads we've ever had. Got a problem when the whiskey flows, too, know it. Picking fights, making everybody around feel like he thinks he's some kind of saint Godalmighty gived to their pres-ence. Not a good thing to feel. So seeing as his dad's my crew chief, and a damned fine one he's been, getting rid of the kid wasn't exactly easy.

"And not that we settled it that night, even, so I took it up I-20/59 and was doing probably 80-85 blowing off some of the steam when I had to ease back on the tight curves through down-town Birmingham and I came round one when I seen this light down at roadway level"—and here he kept his eyes locked on Big Bill, but pointed across his body direct to me. "This little man here was the light. Some kind of light, too. In your damned face!"

He couldn't even make out that the light was in fact a man in a reflective suit, he said, until he'd slowed considerably and passed. I remembered the down-shifts, the brake lights, Turn's turn into the breakdown lane half down the ramp to 17th and shuddered, recalling it as in a series of photos captured from a little black car passing by in the night.

Turner poured another glass in front of me.

212

We ordered what we would eat.

A tropical fish in a bowl under hot lights and without at least the courtesy of a concrete coral replica to hide behind. At McIntyre + Feldman, at least one could disappear in plain sight among the crowds. A minute later I had trouble recalling what prescription for the evening's mastication had come out of my mouth.

"Finish the story," I said. Bob got up to go to and then came back from the bathroom. We all fiddled with our drinks. Big Bill smiled and smiled.

Turner, turning to me. "You finish it."

He had a look in his eye I'd seen before. It was the one he gave the television cameras, the reporters, when he leveled a dare at one of his competitors, or his team, a dare to perform. The look was mischievous, a cocked-eyebrow kind of thing that said, Hey man, I mean this sincerely but I do also want you to know that I am hopeful for a gut-busting laugh just thinking about what you're going to do with it. It was an invitation to give it what you had, put on your best show, in essence—c'mon Cash, take advantage, brother.

But I didn't know how to begin to continue on before the men here, so I turned it on them, or at least the quieter of the two.

"So what's your story?" I said, nodding across the table to Bob and taking a crisp cold cleansing draft of the glass of ice water the clairvoyantly sympathetic waiter had brought round.

Bob didn't answer. His brother did.

"Bob here's the brains of the whole damn thing," said Bill, laughing and, again, not speaking in my direction. "I don't know what you've heard, Turn, but Bob's got a whole hell of a lot to do with everything."

"I haven't always," Bob said. It might've been the first words he'd spoken. He started to continue, "But—"

"But he's the reason we moved from Chino," Bill cut in. "He saw it coming, all the development, the environmental regs that make it let's say more than difficult to operate most any kind of business outside of solar panel installation in the People's Republic of California—don't even think about manufacturing the things, I could go on and on and on."

"Long time ago," Bob said. He had his head down like indeed he didn't want to go on.

213

"I think—" Turner started in but this time I stopped him.

"So why does Turner here, I wonder, seem to think that you equate to a man who's been on his job less than a month and whose primary accomplishment or uncommon ability or whatever it is is the need or want to stand out in the middle-of-night freeway traffic—or on pit road, whatever..." As I said it the room spun momentarily before stabilizing again, all eyes now shifting from me to Bob like they watched for a tiger to jump from its cage. The two brothers had probably 15 years on myself, maybe a decade on Turner, though, and I quickly saw that Bill's anticipation was less alarm than earnest interest in how exactly his clearly uncomfortable brother would deal with these two racing yahoos.

"Probably a temperament thing," Bob said. "Nothing more. My guess, anyway."

"Aw hell," Bill roared, "Bob's just being modest, he's like that."

Turner wouldn't take up my story again, as the elder Cheeter then spoke as much for Bob as Turner had for me, the younger giving the table this kind of hopelessly strained grin through it all like it was everything he could possibly muster to enjoy it. The story from garrulous Big Bill was all contrast, Bob the brains, Big Bill the glad-handing muscle, the younger Cheeter a veritable chemist and philosopher and heavy-duty-powertrain engineer at once guiding the farm and transport operation "like Dr. Claw, you know, in that cartoon"—*Inspector Gadget* I'd never have figured these guys to be the right age to remember, or misremember, as it were, but there it was—"except he never gets blowed the hell up in the end."

Big Bill Cheeter held his brother up as "the very reason we're here," he said.

Turner jumped at his chance, and as he spoke of me again in similar fashion, drawing out a most definitely strained comparison—"this man is holding this team together at this very moment, man, it's true, no telling where we'd be without him"—I exchanged an apologetic little eye-rolling with Bob. Bill and Turner were near tears with joy, toasting to their own good fortunes in exceptional cohorts.

By the time we'd finished eating I was in fact overflowing, every even small swallow of water bringing with it the sensation that a dam at the back of my throat could at any moment spill the partially liquefied pork-barbecue-filled pseudo-quesadilla, fried black beans and overly salty rice it held back. Turner collared me with his right arm around my neck in what I hoped was an affectionate headlock, when finally we'd gotten free from the Cheeters.

"Fucking brilliant, man," he said. "Just – fucking – brilliant!" Sarcasm? I couldn't be sure, but I certainly expected the worst. I wobbled upright when he let me go and said a little prayer to myself that everything went—and would continue to go—well enough. He waved to the valet outside and asked for a cab, which the valet made sure he knew would be no small miracle in this town, this late. Turner was all business with him, responding only with an affirmative nod, before he tossed his fedora way up into the air in a twirl, positioning himself under it all happy-go-lucky drunk to let it fall square on his head. He whooped when it landed, backward.

"You turned that shit around perfect. These kind of guys, farmers, truckers, man they respect that aggro stuff. I didn't think you had it in you."

Positivity—most I could hope for, given my precarious state. I nodded and thanked him. "Best a tire carrier can do," I said.

But Turn Turner further surprised me.

"Maybe elevation," he said, eyes wide, arms raised high with middle fingers pointed to the sky, "is your damn destiny in this business." Turner painted a picture of a path to the office for the Shining Man, sign inked permanently on the door for the "Futurist Shitkicker Seducer Extraordinaire, $F - S - S - E$," he said.

"Gotta say," I said, "they didn't really strike me—"

"OK, hold on, that's the one place where you fucked up," he said, reaching out and grabbing my left shoulder and shaking. "You're reading 'em wrong, you're reading Bob wrong anyway. He ain't no different from his loudmouth brother, just quieter. Those guys are Type A as they come, pretty much like me or you."

Type A? Me? Who's fucking up the read on whom? I wondered, but Turner had moved on before I could wrap my own bombed head around the appropriate rebuttal to the thrust of the man's argument. He was asking about "the women in your life"— the boy was looking to score somehow, some way. He was drunk, more so even than myself, I then saw or rather truly comprehended for once and all. He'd probably put back the bottle of Pappy virtually by himself. In the same instant, his eyes filled with the unfocused haze of the middle distance out across Sharon Road somewhere between the mammoth old Methodist Church there and halfway to his Martinsville, Va., short track favorite in his mind or somesuch, filled full of the glory of his own existence.

Who could tell? "You'll think differently about it in the morning, man," I said, a reference to all and nothing, and to which I expected no response.

But Turner was still razor-sharp: "I won't," he said. "So your sex life's as bad as mine, huh?"

The cab arrived and saved me from the necessity of a reply.

"Tell 'im where you live," Turner said. "Got any beer there?"

Next thing I knew we were fast en route to downtown and Turner was planning on crashing on my couch. I told him about my rats. Even better, he said. "Hell yes! Couch surfing in a rat's nest! Love it, Cash, love it."

I kept my mouth shut for the majority of the remaining short haul back downtown, until the cabdriver overshot the turn and, three blocks down, I realized it. The circle-back route put us past the thinned semi-encampment outside the AB tower. Turner, in a haze-gaze zone, I saw, next to me in the backseat—*don't pass out, bro, don't pass out*—perked at the sight.

"Well well well," he drawled. "Those motherfuckers are having a good old time."

He rolled down his window.

"Get out and get something for your damn self!" he yelled, then "Whooooo!" about as loud as a single human voice could get, then slapping on his knee and laughing.

I pretended to laugh along, apologized to the cabdriver, then said, "Well hell, that might have been me out there if you hadn't come along, you know. And the boys and girls damn well have a point, you ask me."

"They don't," he blurted.

I guess I thought about it. Nobody made much sense in all the mess of our lives.

"Yeah, nobody does," I said.

Before he passed on to the drunk's netherworld, he looked

216

me square in the eye, the intensity of his focus not unlike the ram-rod-straight blasts of my father's more inspired moments. Turner, ultimately, had a much more direct style.

"You're wrong, Cash," he said. "Some of us know what we're about. Nobody likes a loser."

⏳

I paid the foreign cabdriver—African, likely, what country I'd no idea—double for helping me get the man into the foyer of my building. But only after a length of time debating what exactly to do with Turner, who after showing his true colors had simply leaned his head back, tipped his hat down over his eyes and passed out cold.

"He's not waking up, man," I said.

The cabdriver, in absolutely crisp enunciation: "Shit." An exasperated sigh, some fiddling with his meter that shot the total up $20.

I didn't ask what that was for.

He sighed again.

"Gimme a minute," I said, and pulled out my phone to call Tacklebox, maybe the only guy I figured I knew and trusted well enough to ask just what the hell to do.

He didn't answer. I searched my memory file for recollections of exits and street names to Turner's place in Mooresville but ultimately came up empty. I got out of the car, handed the driver then all the cash I had on me, started to say, "Could you—"

"I will help you, yes."

"Do you know who this is?" I asked him.

He just shook his head no. "Good thing," I muttered, and we dragged Turner Bascombe out of the car, then into the foyer. I got my hands under Turner's shoulders, then, bidding adieu to the driver, and took a deep breath and started dragging him toward the elevator. I was within maybe five feet of it when the bell dinged. Shit.

The Nazi materialized, staring at his phone, and got two steps out before catching sight of me and stopping.

"Hi," I said over my shoulder, then heaved Turner a couple

feet to the right to get him closer to the wall to allow the Nazi past what I'm 100 percent certain had to look like a damn murder scene. But he didn't pass.

"Need some help?" he said.

I took him up on it.

"Go on and grab his legs," I said and he did and in no time we got the racecar driver comfortably on my couch looking doornail death in pinstripes, his ridiculous hat tipped down over his eyes, mouth wide.

"He ain't dead yet," I said, laughing experimentally. A snore erupted from the drunk. "Big thanks. I owe you. Bill me."

"That's Turner Bascombe, isn't it?" he said.

"You got me," I said. "I'm on his pit team." I held an index finger to my lips. "Shh."

"Very good, very good," and he laughed. "I'm mum."

On his way out he got the door nearly closed, then poked his head back in. "I'm up in 619, name's Chris."

"Appreciate it, Chris," I said, and I did, truly. "Call me Cash."

I would a few short minutes from that moment check my rat traps—no kills!—but first things first. I smoked a cigarette on the balcony and got woozy from the rush to my soaked mind, vision stuttering and shaking so that I had to close my eyes and hold tight to the railing for balance.

On the wobbly way in, I picked up Bridget's DOWN WITH DEBT sign and clumsily stuffed it in the back of my closet behind the Shining Man's suit.

Chapter 16

It was to be a beautiful morning in my humble abode, sun angling through the framed windows of the doors to my southeast-facing smoking porch and falling on the veritable specter of the still-crashed outsize racing personality on my couch. The light was on the move slowly west to east across the room and had just hit the man's fancy-oddball fedora, still propped up over his face where Nazi Chris and I left it the evening/early morn prior. I watched it hit the tight, dark weave, watched it move then for five minutes finishing off the last of my cigarettes with the morning's coffee and aspirin, watched the hat then move, almost imperceptibly, at which point I turned back out into the street and, before I could fully form a plan of greeting, Turner appeared behind me, coughing.

"Good goddamn, Cash." He leaned on the railing at my right.

"Yep," I said.

"Got another one of those smokes?" he said.

"Good thing you don't smoke," I said. "My last one."

Five minutes of silence may have passed, during which time the events of the day prior loudly screamed through my own hazy head in that kind of paranoia unique to such occasions, hungover backtrack-cycling worry for the integrity of your world. A kind of disbelief, too: Did any of it really happen?

"You want coffee, maybe? Aspirin?" I said, finally.

He did, and he wanted his car.

"Valet parked it at the restaurant, I think," he said. "Damn, I hope we didn't fuck that up."

"What's the last you remember?"

"I sort of remember sending you a text that we were there."

Wow. I nodded.

"Listen, I didn't tell you yesterday, or I don't think I did, but I ought to go ahead and do it. Hugg," I said, and I turned to him.

His eyes went wide, or as wide as the eyes of a man in his deracinated and wrung-out condition could go, which is to say he opened them the width of a needle beyond a slit. He massaged his temples with thumb and middle finger of his right hand and shook his head.

"In spite of the prevailing opinion from some of my A-1 haters, Cash, I ain't gay," he said.

Oh.

"Hugg, Huggins, I meant," I said. "As in crew chief Eddy, and Hugg Chuck the younger."

"I wouldn't call him that—wouldn't call Charles that, I mean. Few of these guys out here really want the whole follow-in-the-father's-footsteps thing, you know, one of the main reasons I knew it'd never work out with his drunk ass."

"Too late," I said. "I ran into him yesterday. Or he ran into me, with the Junior team." I went on and told him what happened, young Hugg's threat.

"Idle drunk bullshit, probably," Turner said. "Remember: I got your back."

He pulled out his overly elaborate cellphone and looked at it. My own was back in the house in a pocket of my suit, probably dead from its long, neglected night. I made a mental note to check for messages from Bridget.

"Must not have gone too-too bad last night," he said.

"All in good fun, man," but I was far from sure whether it was. In what little time I'd had to digest the previous night's events, my brain kept turning back to the bigger, louder of the two brothers, the sense of being played like a guitar destined for a cathartic smashing at the end of the set.

"Nah," Turner said, holding up the phone. "Just got an invitation from them out to a place on Lake Norman—'wine and whisky and women,' he says." Turner chuckled.

And he was shortly off, after he asked to see and I proudly displayed for him my solution to an infestation, as yet unsolved. The peanut-butter-baited snap traps sat in the dark of the cabinet as if entirely uncontemplated by sentient life form, delectable dollops turned to a crust after nearly two entire days in the not-so-open air.

"Well shit," Turner said. "You got no luck, Cash money." He put a hand on my shoulder and got all serious-like. "I predict utter and complete carnage in your near future," Turner laughing high and wild. "See you at the track, brother."

It was junior-league race day, prior to tomorrow's big event,

Turner and the entire team always on hand for it up in a spectator's box given the fairly recent, Turner told, tendency for so many of the top series' drivers to participate in the race as a sort of warm-up for the main event. Turner never bothered running in it himself for various reasons, he said, chief among them a lack of appropriately tuned equipment, concentration on a single car for the main event rather than a multiplicity—"we'd have to hire on a whole set of new design men, mechanics types, et cetera et cetera." Low cash potential, essentially, minimal return. Payouts for winning (which is to say nothing of next-to-zero TV exposure outside of only the most hard-up or focused of cable channels) and advert dollars had been on the decline for years. All the same, he never missed the opportunity to scope from on high so many of his competitors' styles and performance and strategy at the track, looking for vulnerabilities. As a tire carrier, I wasn't any kind of judge of this stuff. Only really the chief and one of three sometime spotters were truly engaged with all the goings-on. And by no means was I paid or required to be there, but over the weeks my interest had been piqued by the sort of working-party nature of the endeavor, like I imagined say a rock recording session in a band's hometown could be. Hangers-on, plenty of beer for the crewmembers, shit never really totally getting out of hand, unlike what I imagined the skybox looked like on race day packed with sales types from sponsor entities.

But when I got to the track late afternoon for the evening race, Turner was nowhere to be found. Tacklebox hadn't seen or heard from him all day, neither Peerfoy. I told them what I knew, or rather that I'd talked to him this morning, leaving out the fact that the rap was in-person. When I mentioned the Cheeters, Lake Norman, the two rolled their eyes.

"He ain't gonna make it," Tacklebox said between chews on his straw.

I laughed, but Tacklebox, now fiddling around with his phone, shot raised eyebrows in my direction.

"You know what I'm talking about," he said. "You guys hung out last night."

I hadn't told Tacklebox about meeting the Cheeters, but they all knew, somehow.

"He tell you that?" I said. The room heaved with disdain. Maybe it was some kind of gearhead professional jealousy, maybe there was more to it. Tacklebox, no doubt an ally to this point, or if not an ally, a friendly partner (I was still driving his little Ford, after all), huffed a bit as he stood, pinching his nose and moving past me to the other side of the room. He sat next to Chief Hugg and stared out the window of the little box, high above the grandstands. Tomorrow it'd be filled with five times the beer and liquor and no doubt Big Bill holding court, not to mention other dignitary blowhards who would probably do nothing for any attempts I might make and/or have made to this point to cop a dead serious attitude, if this business with Turner didn't kill it all by itself. Tacklebox sat next to Chief Hugg and spoke to him in a voice low enough that it was out of range for me. I stared out the window now to the stands on the other side of the mammoth structure and sighed, visibly.

"Down in the shit, Mr. Cash?" None other than Bob Cheeter stood now in the doorway off my left shoulder. "Myself, I feel like a Chicago dog somebody licked the celery salt off and threw in the gutter."

"Give me a minute to think about that," I said. Bob wore a three-piece black suit, a clownish apparition in a horror movie standing there, self-satisfied smug grin on his face. "You seen Turner?"

"Saw him earlier, yes," he said, his attention now moving across the room where Huggins had heard the exchange and was rising, turning, severely unsmiling, and moving to Bob. For just a moment, almost infinitesimal in duration, Bob quite actually seemed like he was about to turn and run, screaming, from the box, but then Hugg was in front of him with his right hand stretched out for a shake, stern mask covered over by a shiteating grin.

"Where's our driver, Bob?" he said. "You know this tire carrier, I see," Hugg waving dismissively in my direction. Before Bob could compose himself enough to answer, Hugg had led him by the shoulder out the door and off away from prying eyes into the greater American public beginning to file into the stadium.

I pulled out my phone and let it light up the, I hoped, distracted expression on my face. No word from Bridget since my response to her messages from yesterday, in which I'd put off all possibility of connection, of interaction. I read back through her messages,

222

and my translations this time veered toward a not-so-disengaged tack on the whole enterprise, the view less one of minor curiosity than of obvious invitation to a seduction, or of a seduction in and of itself, parceled out in 160-character bits of verbiage. You stupid motherfucker. I shook my head, remembering the visceral nature of our encounter among the bread-thief rats. Our chances were then helped when I paused my second reading of her messages midway through and looked around the room. There were—count 'em—zero women in attendance this night, and I shortly tapped out my own series of messages to Bridget telling her I had some time, would she allow a humble tire carrier to repay a debt, or better yet given the emphatic nature of the young lady's protest sign, to present her with such a situation in the aftermath of which she might be willing to forgive a debt, and debt was recognized, Ms., very much so, and could the young lady be genteel enough to accept the humble apologies of a highway-standing tire-carrying hill dweller-descended lowlife such as myself…

And I was off, wading through growing crowds along the stadium corridors, no sign of Hugg and Bob Cheeter, only Charlie Peerfoy (and Tacklebox, who got off a scowly "When do I get my damn car back, old boy?" as I walked out the door) with the immediate benefit of knowing I was gone for the night and would be back on-hand tomorrow—that is, until he told the rest of the crew, the look in his eye not quite all business, more uncertain skepticism he was being told the truth, suspicion of ulterior motives.

Hey Peerfoy, I said, I could use a recharge, my man—headed home for the night: He'd spill his guts all over Tacklebox and Chief Hugg and whoever else before sooner or later the entire rest of the team would be on board to reinforce what I couldn't help but see as a growing certainty that I was proving out Hugg's contention I was a nonentity, at best, at worst a long-term liability or a liar, that Turner was probably crazy and, while there was little they could do about that, other than decamp to another team, the former reality would make for a stressed rest of the year for my part.

I found my known traffic lane out of the facility blocked off to allow the oncoming deluge of junior-league race spectators, got lost somewhere on the far northeast side of the city on the way back to my apartment. By the time I got there hours had passed and dusk was near upon us, or me, I should say, as I had yet to hear word one from Bridget. A parade of drummers led by protesters carrying signs was passing by the front of my building very politely keeping to the sidewalk as I pulled up outside to turn into the underground garage.

My window down, waiting out the walkers, a guy pushing a bicycle painted with tiger stripes pointed my way and shouted, "Fight climate change! Turn the car off!"

I smiled and nodded. He just kept walking.

But I didn't leave it at that. First mistake.

"I'm with you, brother!" I yelled and then hit the gas hard into the turn, the sea—or, rather, thin rivulet of mostly single-file walkers—parted in horror. I couldn't punch in the entry code to the parking garage quite quickly enough to escape something hard thrown at the back of Tacklebox's car. (That'd leave a dent—*strike two, sorry Tacklebox*.) As the gate slowly rose and I wheeled the car under its bottom, I glanced in the rearview to find the cyclist now on his bike and right on my bumper, something that looked like a skinny brown straw between his teeth, following me down the ramp and around the turns through the basement cavern. As I cornered toward the bank of spaces where I typically parked, a rat crossed the path in front of me and I instinctively hit the brakes hard. It scurried out of sight under a car and the man behind me yelled a stream of curses echo-amplified by the space, his bike still, stopped, mere inches off the bumper.

I rolled up my window, hit the doors' auto-lock, pulled into my space, and leaned across the car over the passenger seat to grab a giant, heavy black Maglite flashlight Tacklebox left in here when I took the keys. The cyclist was by my door, now, kneeled over, mouth moving and dark-ish green eyes peering through a mask all acne scarring, five-day mid-20s stubble, Tacklebox-esque septum piercing and sweat. I nodded, raised an index finger and the flashlight in the other hand, cut the engine.

He was talking through it all, and only now could I half make out what he was saying. *Apathetic scum, what the [garble garble] dick it's because of you we're all going to hell in a handbasket [garble garble] the hell you think you are [garble]*. I cracked the window about an inch and a half.

"Can I help you?"

"What's your problem, man? You about killed three people

224

out there!"

"Looked to me like they moved well before I even got close."

"Using that damn machine as a battering ram is fucking criminal, not to mention…" It was now that I noticed as the scent hit my nose the guy was waving around a stick of burning incense—patchouli, maybe sandalwood, I always had trouble telling the difference, as the stuff made me sneeze, which I did forthwith, one of those multiple-sneeze attacks I used to get when a kid playing around in Eula and Ralph Cash's dirty backyard.

"Bless you," he said when it was done, and tried the door of the car.

Trying to fight off yet another sneeze attack, my personal danger-sense went from a mild anxiety to off-the-charts as the guy pulled hard as he could on the doorhandle and, flustered, then stuck the smoldering end of his incense stick through the crack in the window straight at my left eye. It was too short to make a connection, frankly, but the stink of the thing filled the car immediately and my eyes really began to water now. I leaned away into the car as far as I could and still be able to reach the automatic window controls on the door, which I hit, rolling up the window and catching the stick before he could remove it. It bent in the center, forming an arrow whose point aimed to the sky. This made him madder than all hell. He threw down his bike and pounded on the window, then moving around to the hood, yelling all the while, but first things first: I grabbed a half-drunk cup of black coffee wedged in between the seat and the parking-brake lever to douse the foul stick. Dude was standing on the hood now and looking like he was going to start jumping up and down when I turned the key, still in the ignition, and popped the shifter to D, jolting forward just a few inches and slamming the brake. I lost sight of the guy under the front bumper as he fell with a thud so profound I could hear it over the running car. Visions of manslaughter charges, the battered men in my wake (that poor drunk sap off Fullerton those months and what felt like infinite moons ago), danced through my head and I said a little prayer for his skull, opening the door, Maglite at the ready—just in case.

"You all right?" He was making his way slowly to his feet, cradling his left arm in his right. "Get the fuck out of here," I said, punctuating each word with a thrust of the light. I hit the auto-locks, slammed the door and stepped back slowly. He just stood there now, wide-eyed but with the hint of a grin on his face.

"Go!" louder now, Maglite gesturing toward his bike. "Get out."

But he just stood there.

I was far out enough into the garage lane to see now the big dent on the trunk lid, not to mention whatever condition the hood was in.

"If I see you around here again, look out," I said. "This is a shared car, guy who owns it is going to be A-1 pissed about this dent here."

He still didn't speak.

"What, did you hit your fucking head or something?"

"So you're in a car-sharing program?" he said.

I'd lucked into the right word choice—yes, my unwillingness/lack of real credit to actually purchase a car (I'd inherited the previous Ford and all other autos I'd driven from my mother) were bona fides enough to make me a responsible member of society, sure, my environmental cred secure with the idea that I was involved in some kind of do-gooding programmatic urban collective for such a sharing, that I wasn't just some selfish Neanderthal of a citizen. I walked around to and up along the passenger side with the flashlight raised high and far enough to see the colossal dip in the hood.

"I drive often enough," I said, "but I'd wager it's less than most. I doubt you'd be too happy if you knew what I did for a living, all the same, but we all have to get to work somehow, don't we. If where you work is clear on the South and West end of Charlotte and you live downtown, the one dinky rail line isn't going to cut it."

He winced and stared down at his feet.

"Are you OK? Talk to me, man."

He moved to pick up his bike and said he was sorry.

"Next time you want to yell at somebody, consider we all have tempers, man. Some worse than others. Like the guy who owns this car." I wasn't exactly sure of that, but after today it seemed real.

"And you do what for a living?" he said.

I hesitated to tell him—things were going well here—actually thought about making something up, despite the fact that it was at least abundantly clear at this stage in our affairs who held the

226

upper hand. I had the Maglite. All he seemed to have of anything that could be used as a weapon other than the doused, piddly little stick of incense still stuck in the window was the bike—from his position, he wouldn't get up more than 3 mph worth of speed before he hit me with it. Picking it up and heaving wasn't an option in the tightness of the space.

What use could be duplicitousness in the dark reality of the garage, surveillance cameras in every corner? The eyes of none and all were upon us. I opted for the truth.

"I'm a tire carrier."

"What, like for a tire shop or something?"

"Or something. Look close and you might see me on TV tomorrow."

"Tire commercials?"

"Few elections ago people were putting what I do in front of the word *dads* to describe a certain kind of middle-aged white guy, probably code for *Neanderthal* in your book."

"Racing."

"I've heard it called something like 'the most egregious waste of good gasoline on the planet,'" I said. "Think a guy out at the protests the other night said something like that. Pretty good description."

"And you ..."

"I don't know, I guess it doesn't serve any beneficial purpose other than as spectacle, something to do with your time, though I've heard tell of no small bit of fuel-efficiency-type tech to come out of the big push to win. Ever hear of Microblu bearings, coatings? Racing tech, currently being put to use to revolutionize the wear parts in big diesels, squeeze every last drop of fuel-mileage possible out of a gallon." True, care of the conversational expertise of the Cheeters.

He didn't speak. He moved like to swing his leg up over the top bar of his bike's frame and I took a step back, raised the flashlight instinctively. "Sorry," he said. "Maybe I owe you for the car."

"Yeah," I said, "just get out of here and we're square." For the first time in my life, I could afford the repair, I guessed. I'd worry about what to tell Tacklebox some other time, maybe just this, the truth. It seemed to be doing me good.

"Watch your back," he said as he pedaled off.

I'd heard that one before.

When I turned into the corridor from the elevator toward my apartment, I saw Bridget down the hall against the wall under a soft lamp outside my door, looking up now from her phone and smiling. A beautiful thing, the smile, my own brain reeling from the less invitingly affable encounter with the rats of the parking garage.

"Hey there, cowboy," she said, still smiling, grabbing my right wrist as I smiled myself and moved to put my key into the lock. She pulled then, hard, and planted a kiss on my face. I stumbled into her as she pivoted her back to the wall and grabbed my hips, then my shoulders, jumping and scissoring me with her legs.

I fumbled with the keys and we moved in tandem, my other arm around her back and our faces connected, into the apartment.

I hadn't exactly prepared for her arrival, expecting a less-driven Bridget to further engage in textual back-and-forth toward a possible later meeting, maybe days ahead, even. The couch was half-dissembled from Turner's night on it, backrest cushions all a shambles, some on the floor, even. We crashed down onto it, regardless, Bridget as far as I knew oblivious to any concern for tidiness that might have crossed my mind. That is, until a less-than-discreet noise emanated from the kitchen, a loud *! thwack !*, a muffled scuffling, followed by another *! thwack !* Then silence.

She opened her eyes, as did I, and we both sat up and laughed a little. Her t-shirt, with a cycling emblem touting the glorious invention of the bicycle and the contraption's city and highway mpg—∞—was cockeyed across her chest, her left arm out of its confines, right arm still stuck firmly within it. My pants were undone so that when I stood, they fell halfway down my thighs.

"What the fuck was that?" she said as I pulled them off, threw them aside and shrugged my way back down on top of her. We were stark naked and her lips had just brushed the tip of my cock when yet another *! thwack !* emanated from the kitchen. I well knew the source of the noise, of course, but had willed all trepidation, all concern whatsoever, down somewhere into the lower reaches of my stomach or brain, wherever such things go to die in such a moment. Bridget now sort of choked on her next words, sitting up on the couch, coughing.

"What – the – fuck is that?" she said. "I damn near bit you," and I almost laughed, but held back before she cackled with a glance down to the space between us, filled with my erection. She struggled to keep a straight face and look me in the eye. I grabbed for my shirt, cast off down on the floor beside the couch, and placed it over my lap.

"OK let's talk."

"I mean come on! There's not, like, somebody else here, is there?"

I had another idea.

"Hold on, stay here," I said then and moved, shirt dangling from my cock, to the kitchen, where the beer box held its standing vigil hard against the under-sink cabinets. No penetration there. Fear of the unknown always gets me doing things I know better than to indulge—a mark of the Stupid Man you might not look long to find evidence of in these pages. I had no special cognizance of it in that moment, but I know I prayed a little prayer there, and it wasn't to the God of the Bible or the Torah or the Koran or even a more heathenous version, a being you might find in Tolkien or taken in vain by any number of Faulkner or Algren protagonists—I prayed to my mother and the women of the beauty parlor, *Oh please keep me warm in your waiting seats and cozy in your blissful ignorance of the attention I paid to what you said.*

Ridiculous, maybe, but appropriate given the finality of the undersink scene I was to encounter.

I grabbed a paper towel from a roll by the sink and with woeful absurdity used it to keep my fingers from touching the cabinet's outer handle, gingerly pulling back the door, then the other door, and crouching from a distance so that the overhead lighting could reach the inner recesses of the low space. Three traps were upset, two rat-less right by the doors—I saw that first off—and back by the hole in the far right, rear corner lay a dark further shape bisected midway by sharp shadow from the light, the gray-brown body and surprisingly textured strand of tail extending from it, tail's tip just touching the edge of the closest upset trap. The motherfucker was bigger than I'd expected, nose to tail a fair foot and a half, maybe. Could be the imagination of recollection playing tricks on me, but the shock of size was real, the trap itself lay upright on its side, perpendicular to its normal positioning, the beast too turned on its side in its death throes so that its pale little feet and tiny claws stretched out to me, beckoning. I crouched, still, mind reeling to

229

replay the decidedly unmonstrous vermin's evening trajectory to death and destruction. I felt sorrow, elation, profound curiosity and, yes, fear of coming retribution all in the single instant before a shuffling sound behind me provoked a heart-pouding déjà vu and I wheeled round, shutting the doors in the same motion.

Bridget. Now down to business, still wearing absolutely nothing. My shirt lay now on the floor between my knees.

"What the hell are you keeping under that sink, cowboy?" she said.

I hesitated, and she read it spot-on.

"Show me."

"I don't think you want me to…"

"I can take it," and she could. She launched off into a story there crouched naked in front of the open cabinet of a similar under-sink infiltration at the house of a boyfriend when she was a wee 19, a few years back. I spent the odd colloquy, this meeting of the house-pest-riddance minds, with my hand over my crotch as Bridget gesticulated wildly through the story, an odd little double-fold of flesh at the place where her breasts met her armpits, like she wore some sci-fi invisible bra pushing the fat back over itself, disappearing, reappearing with every flourish—I tried to commit, told her my own tale, or that of Rob Rene's Brooklyn friend and the months-long commitment to total annihilation.

"How did your friend get rid of them?" I asked, and she raised her right pointer finger and looped it around, chest following the motion.

"First," she said, "look here," middle and pointer fingers now separated and directed toward her brown eyes, "not here." She cupped her breasts with both hands. I leaned down and picked up my shirt from the floor and hung it back up, and she laughed and sort of fell down to a crouch the emotion was so strong. Happiness, I hoped. Hilarity at least.

I picked up the half-empty beer box and moved to put it back in front of the closed cabinet doors—the dead could wait—but Bridget pulled my arm now, "I want to see it again," and so I let her and we crouched there and stared in the silence, the vaguely sweetly sick, dirty scent of rathouse, dander, sweat, whatever just strong enough to reach the tips of our noses, mine anyway.

"Here's the thing," she said.

"Shit stinks. Can I close it now?"

"Go ahead," and I did, returning the beer box to its rightful position, "the thing is you have options."

Her buddy's place, "his under-sink trenchline warfare-potential-type situation, it wasn't all that. They're not that fucking smart, no matter what people say, refuse to believe it. They don't have all the answers to our problems." He walled it off, she said, with two-by-fours and plenty of steel wool, expanding spray foam the bedrock to fill the old scurry-hall and any space behind the paneling, and they never came back. "I did only date him for a couple weeks after that, which maybe doesn't say much for your prospects, but there you have it."

We got it on, then, loud and breathy and sweaty—"Turn your air conditioner on much?" she said at the terminus.

"Poor does as poor is conditioned. Hell, I'm protecting the environment."

"You ain't poor, race man. Boor, maybe, prude, hand over your dick..." and she laughed and I laughed and reflexively gazed out through the open bedroom door to my pants, boxers, well out of reach, self-consciousness on high alert no doubt due to the somewhat stone sober nature of this encounter, the few beers I'd had at the track long having lost whatever potency they brought to the party—I couldn't remember the last sex I'd had under such conditions.

"Feel like a beer?" I asked.

"I'd drink one, or more, if that's what you mean."

So we remedied the situation, and on the way to the refrigerator I hoisted my jeans and put them on.

"I saw that," she called from the bedroom, then she sat across my thighs, facing me on the bed, and we talked and I told her about the enviro cyclist, about my car-sharing program.

"You lied to G-man Gerald?" she said. "Oh my God you are dead!" Yes, Bridget might even—gasp, no surprise—know the guy whose head I'd bumped on the hard concrete of the parking lot.

"If he's who I think he is—sort of a dude to know around here. Has this crew of bike thugs, hardcore environmentalist-types. Bet there's plenty of those types in Chicago."

We ought ultimately to get along, I said, he and I. I thought of bitter Billy, wanted to take the confrontation as evidence of

231

something more than just tempers flaring, more than the stupidity of the kind humans have engaged in for millennia.

"You'll see him I bet if you come out Wednesday," Bridget said.

Days hence would see the biggest movement toward disruption the late protest actions in town had seen, the rumored occupation of the ground floor of the AB building. I could be there, if I skipped out on the team a little early—it was a shop day, doable. I didn't know if I wanted to, yet.

"Will you come?" she said. "I called off work already, we could go together."

"Our first date and we'll both end it in jail, quaint," I said.

"It's romantic." She smiled. "This is our first date, anyway."

"Among the sink rats."

"Among the *dead*," she said. "C'mon, it's worth it, cowboy, if for nothing than spectacle. These Charlotte cops don't have the manpower to round up everybody and I got slippery hips."

There was little in this business for me other than the self-satisfaction of being another body in a possibly misguided effort, one whose energies might best be put elsewhere toward achievement of the same goal. More time with Bridget, though, was more time with Bridget—she ground a wet spot with her crotch into my jeans before laying back now, pulling the bed's sheet up to her shoulders and smiling, eyes to the ceiling. I smiled with her, but at once my heart fell a little with a vision of myself that hung there in relief. I'd moved somehow further forward along the straight-line continuum between a life of purpose, maybe, and the opposite, one more befitting the standard semantics of my surname, however ironically situated it had been to the reality of the lives of the generations before me.

"What do you want from your time out here?" I asked Bridget. "What do you want out of all this?"

"I ain't a prostitute, if that's what you're asking." But she laughed. She understood. "So from you then?"

"No no not necessarily from me. I didn't mean ..."

"Listen here, I'll go all relationship grandiose with it—it's a fucking grandiose question, race man. From you," she paused, looked straight up from her prone position, left hand above the sheet going down to her stomach. "From you I want only love and

232

respect. How's that for grandiose?"

Love—I could at least intellectualize it, sitting on the bed in front of her in that brief moment, Bridget's eyes alight with reflections of the floorlamp bulb in the corner of my bedroom, mouth smiling, head back on her pillow below me, mop of hair splayed out behind her like some kind of dark flower, if I couldn't exactly feel it, I guessed. Infatuation, though, proved itself with a falling away of the low-grade fear of my existence.

I sighed, and she said, "Too serious, Cash, too serious. Damn, you look like I just conked you in the noggin with a baseball bat." She laughed and sat up now, quickly, sheet falling away from her chest, then stood up on the bed and wobbly-tip-toed her hips toward my face. "I also want more of what we just had."

She got it, and we came damn near to finishing the beer box off before the end of the night—routine: open two, two more put in the freezer to chill quickly—its weight so depleted that before sleep took me I grabbed one of the living-room chairs to hold the under-sink cabinet doors fast, but not before I reset the two disturbed traps, baited further with fresh peanut butter.

I called out to Bridget then, still in the bedroom, close to sleep herself: "Do you think the rat will start smelling if I leave him through the morning?"

"Hell if I know. The damn things already stink. You said it yourself." Good point. "Save it for the morning—he'll be your raceday rat, forever enshrined in your memory in association with a big win." I got it, I got it, though perhaps she didn't mean what she said, or at least how a small part of me felt like interpreting what she said: associations appropriate to spur me toward the next thing.

233

Chapter 17

But raceday was exciting, lucrative stuff, all the same, a small city's worth of cars and humans and RVs and old elaborately painted school buses with big platforms built on top of them and big trucks and small trucks and big coolers full of beer on trailers and pop-up mobile bars and much else all pointed in one direction for the chance to spend the day in celebration of humans' technological excesses—these affairs were bacchanalian for many of the attendees, wrecks on the way home were legion as folks raced their vehicles to the safety of homes or hotels primed with speed-lust and alcohol. For team members, too, or at least those still young enough not to have fallen into the sort of jaded workaday attitude of middle age (and that was certainly the large majority of us), they represented fun, performance time, game on. And with Turner and the team's above-average efforts of late, of course, my bank account was feeling quite positive about it all, too.

I got to the track early—Charlotte was home time for almost everyone, and the race-team car parking lot was positively massive here, unlike other tracks. We all showed up separately. I caught sight of a lone rig among the four-wheelers in a nearby spectators' lot, bobtail (minus the trailer), its bright yellow cab rising heads above the sea of low hoods. From a distance it was the spitting image of Stonefly Sanders' banana-yellow Peterbilt, in whose cab I'd made my journey to Birmingham. I walked up for a closer look. The name on the doors was McCall, however, and I figured the unit as some race devotee among the highway haulers taking his vacation for the week at the track, probably camped out or cohabiting with one of the RVers inside, among the infield revelers.

I walked through the turn-three tunnel into the infield here for the first time in absolute awe of the raceday crowd gathering. The past couple of days out here had been low-key, though some of the revelers had been on hand since Tuesday—hell, some even earlier than that. The infield space was packed, tight lanes scarcely wide enough to accommodate two side-by-side Toyota Prius and cordoned off with chain-link aluminum fencing by which to walk, eyeing the tight turns up ahead for the careening golf carts of drunken spectators or pissed-off crewmembers in search of whatever want or need. I roamed through it incognito in jeans and a tight, too-small two-button knit. My race digs I'd get in time enough from the hauler's storage spaces.

I found my way through the infield maze to our breakfast team pow-wow, spent most of it amid a haze of musings over the girl who hadn't gotten away, yet, but who wasn't lying next to me when my alarm buzzed off this morning. No note, no text, nothing— she'd told me the prior night she would be out early, work by 6 a.m. at the supermarket deli counter. "Save a man some fried chicken, maybe I'll see you tomorrow night." That was doubtful, but I was hopeful. The only message she left was the DOWN WITH DEBT sign, telling me that yes sometime in the early morning she'd been rooting around in my closet looking either for it or God knows what all. She'd taken it out, placed it back where we'd originally left it, by the doors to the smoking porch. My fear-ridden mind might normally have been tee-totally alarmed over such an intrusion. But today I felt quite good about the woman.

The late team weirdness wouldn't get to me either, it was sure. It's raceday, I'm in love.

The boys around the back of the hauler were grim, I could tell when I bothered to attempt an interaction, two, three.

Finally, Tacklebox, "Nobody told you, man?"

Turner continued AWOL.

"Check with the Cheeters?" I said.

"Nobody really knows."

"Bob was up in the box yesterday."

"Apparently he says Turner wasn't with his brother when he got back, or when he called to check. I'm not sure. Hugg was pretty tight-assed with him yesterday." Meaning he was probably a total asshole about it.

Apparently "Turner left the lake and the Cheeters with a lady," Tacklebox said. "Hugg said." And here Tacklebox's eyes shot wide and he scowled. I wondered if he'd gotten a look at the dents in his Ford on his way in this morning—I beat him here, he could easily have seen the car in the lot.

Mention of Hugg got me looking down the line of my post-qualifying walk from two days back toward the little crowd behind the Montuck trailer, too far to tell who was just whom, what was what, really. I left Tacklebox to his discontent and briskly strode off toward the Montuck boys, no Hugg, just four of the team all in Montuck red and what could have been their haul driver off a small distance from the crew and standing over a smoldering grill. "What are you cooking?" I said, walking up to him. "All we had was catered fast food."

"These here'd be cowboy pancakes," he said, picking up the pan that sat on the grill-grate for show before flipping two of the four rough-edged disks sizzling in the oil there. "What makes 'em cowboy is the fire, the smoke—it seeps into the flavor a bit, see. And," he paused for a big show of inhaling the sweet scent coming up from the pan, "you smell that?"

I couldn't place it—smoky, sure, but rank, sweet, meaty at once.

"They're cooked in bacon grease." He shrugged.

Puke.

"I love the shit out of 'em. These kids," pointing back over his shoulder, "not so much."

They all of them stared my way now, the gent closest to me smiling through a mouthful of the bacon that created the grease when I caught his eye.

I spoke to him. "Y'all seen Hugg? Er, I mean, Chuck, of course."

"What you want with him?"

"He's not around?"

"Ain't seen him yet."

The guy stood up. "You Cash with Bascombe, right?"

I wore no team colors, the white knit and jeans. "I am."

"I want to apologize for him, man. We were pretty messed up the other day. He was the worst off. I'm Jason, by the way." He put his hand out all businesslike—he couldn't have been more than 20.

"All right, then," I said, and we shook. "Let me ask you this— is he actually on the team with you guys?"

"Tire carrier," Jason said. "We've all known him a long time. Had a guy leave, well, get fired. Needed somebody, and quick." He

236

left it at that, but the boys behind him didn't—they laughed openly, one then smacking the other hard on the shoulder and prompting an adolescent pretend scuffle.

"All right, then," I said again, something of a question creeping into my diction as I backed away. Jason just did one of those head-up nods I was well familiar with from the dudes who hung around in the high school parking lot smoking cigarettes, the guys on the Chicago corners selling dope: *I see you there, brother,* it said. *I see you and I'm prepared for the worst. Watch yourself.*

Back at Team Bascombe central, we sat through our typical morning team meet driverless, not exactly unusual—strategy: as always on our part, speed and precision, little else. If nothing went wrong with the car, no cut tires, involvement in on-track incidents, mechanical issues, Turner would run close to the front if not in the lead given his strong qualifying performance, and we'd pit when the other top cars did until it got down to the end. Depending on track situation and caution laps, we might then bargain on tire performance and play the fuel mileage game at the end to take the win, or we might just keep on keeping on, pitting with the other leaders. It was fairly simple job, in the end, absolutely cell-vibrating thrilling for the seconds you were in motion in tandem with the in and out, up and down of the jack under the car, competitors' racers flying by your back, otherwise a spectacle quite similar to what the audience in the stands saw, with the addition of more technological windows on the actions via your headset and the various broadcast feeds (though some of the hardcore fans had all that for every team, too) but—damn—minus the copious beer until the end was had. Hugg and his lieutenants had a solid handle on what was happening on the track. I stayed close and listened in on their conversations from time to time, but since Turner's warning to me to take things seriously, I'd stayed back from them, adopted the appearance, at least, of focus on my immediate surroundings, *my* tire stack, *my* helmet, *my* teammates' positions around me, *my* spot atop the wall prepping for the car's hard-brake slide into the pit box. The good graces of the team seemed to be shot to hell with Turner's disappearance and, in the team's hive mind, my involvement in it. But before all that, such good graces had been getting more, well, good.

237

We set up a few things. I rolled out tires for inspectors, stacking them back on a rolling rack and positioning them in our pit box. I inspected my spot on the wall, stood atop it and peered over the teeming mass of "Hot Pass" spectators milling around on pit road and the track proper, toward the near-empty stands. When I chanced a look down at the pit-road-facing section of the wall, I found a fan had inscribed a message for the team—one of goodwill, I guess you could say. *God bless this team and keep these men in safe stead. The Lord giveth.* Scrawled on the white paint of the wall in black Sharpie or other marker. I shuddered, stood tall, got woozy and sat down on the wall and put my head in my hands, heart pounding. I thought about my mother, tried to imagine her here lurking among the crowds up ahead of me. A guy came up and took a picture of eight tires we'd laid out in two rows still with their Bascombe-yellow aluminum dividers over the important parts of the wheels—meant as protection from damage, of course, of the mechanical variety. I watched him snap three-four shots, then turn his camera just slightly so, I assumed, I was now in the frame. I looked off beyond him into the stands and tried to envision Eula Littlejohn putting a black Sharpie primly into her purse.

"What are they for, those yellow things?" the guy said now.

"Keep people from touching them," I said, nodding solemnly.

He raised his eyebrows quizzically, then nodded himself. "Thanks, man."

Car inspections came later in the afternoon, after more fans arrived, all of it played out to the spectation of those with garage passes. The lot of the crew gave up blood for the race officials, samples that would be sent off to a lab and returned the following week. I crossed my fingers against a dope positive culled from too-close association with Bridget as I pissed.

Eleven a.m. rolled around and, since this was a night race, the first such I'd been a part of, Chief Hugg sent all personnel nonessential—for guarding the pit box from fans milling about the track through the afternoon, for instance, or moving the car through inspections—to home or that "special place, wherever it is, somewhere in the vicinity of the track where you've got some friends or, hell, you can take rest in the rig's trailer or at the team headquarters. Go where you need to," he said, "just get some goddamn sleep.

Some of you haven't experienced this before, it's hard to sleep in the daytime for you kids, but you've got to. We need fresh eyes, fresh heads, quick hands, we need them all tonight, and you're it."

I made a point of being the first out so as to beat Tacklebox back to the lot, and when I got back home I smelled a rat. I'd forgotten to do my duty and throw the beast away, so I turned a kitchen-size plastic trash bag inside out over my hand, lined with a paper towel between hand and plastic just in case, and I dove under the sink. I clumsily got my protected fingertips around the hard end of the tail and stood, held the beast and connected trap at arm's length. The trap's spring-loaded arm caught him right across the neck, but as I'd seen earlier he was sideways, a dried rivulet of blood diagonally across the top of the beast's head from eye to ear that I found upon closer inspection was in fact more of an abrasion itself, like one of the prior traps had caught his head at the wrong angle and just knocked him silly, whereupon crime scene analysis would lead one to suspect he'd jumped, scurried woozy back toward his hole to fall hard right into this snare. War, crime, whatever this was, proved gruesome business, but if it was to be here it were better it were well done, I figured, recalling the words of a Confederate dignitary spoken just blocks from here on his way South as the short-lived nation fell.

Bridget's options be damned, I thought, I was in this for the haul.

Down the garbage chute he went.

I then did what Hugg advised and tried my brain at sleep, mind on the race, mind on the race, mind on the race, task at Bridget's hands in mine and legs entwined, eyes closed and as if floating, here, in not out there, in here, we are, with more than mere professions of sweet love but acts on which to base them, carrying signs and marching for something, marching for togetherness toward a battered house that needs sweat look at the paint peeling on the steps up to the porch, porch deck boards peeling up from the frame, back at my mother's house, my door, my basement its walls covered in the Shining Man's suit shot through with light from a single candle rendered invisible in its base atop the table atop which rests Carl's laptop, cursor blinking, invisible fingers typing $4 - u - i - w - o - u - l - d - d - r - i - v - e - f - i - g - u - r - e - e$

239

$-i-g-h-t-s-4-u-I-w-o-u-l-d-t-e-a-c-h-o$
$-l-d-f-o-r-d-.d-r-i-v-e-r-s-e-d-4-u-i-w$
$-o-u-l-d-s-p-e-n-d-t-h-e-m-o-n-e-y-t-o$
$-f-i-x-t-h-e-d-a-m-n-t-r-a-n-s-m-i-s-s$
$-i-o-n-o-n-c-e-a-n-d-a-l-l-t-i-m-e-n-o$
$-t-s-m-o-k-e-n-o-t-d-r-i-n-k-n-o-t-p-r$
$-e-t-e-n-d-t-o-b-e-a-s-h-a-m-e-d-o-f-m$
$-a-l-e-a-n-a-t-o-m-y-o-r-o-u-t-r-a-g-e$
$-d-w-h-e-n-r-e-n-s-a-u-l-e-r-o-r-r-i-n$
$-c-k-o-f-f-f-o-l-l-o-w-s-m-e-o-r-y-o-u$
$-t-e-l-l-m-e-i-'-m-w-r-o-n-g-o-r-f-u-l$
$-l-o-f-s-h-i-t-o-r-l-i-t-t-l-e-m-o-r-e-t$
$-h-a-n-a-m-e-m-o-r-y-o-f-a-h-o-p-e-h-$
$e-l-d-f-a-s-t-l-i-k-e-a-p-l-u-s-h-t-o-y$
$-f-o-x-b-y-a-l-i-t-t-l-e-g-i-r-l-s-l-e-e$
$-p-i-n-g-s-o-u-n-d-l-y-s-w-e-e-t-l-y-c$
$-u-r-l-e-d-u-p-m-i-d-d-a-y-i-n-b-e-d-a$
$-n-d-b-r-e-a-t-h-i-n-g-j-u-s-t-b-r-e-a$
$-t-h-i-n-g-v$ sending a love note to a man far away, telling
him to wake up, goddamnit and smell the coffee cooking in your
kitchen Tim Morton's not not Will Theron not Annie not Bobby
Cash making it this time it's Turner Bascombe and your phone a
buzzing freakout and making for quite a nice sensation nestled in
the front left pocket of your jeans and god why do you wear jeans
when it's this hot out man got to be 467 Shining Man suits-type
hot out worn at once, 467,000 bodies cramped into a space meant
just for you and a family of rats your phone, Cash, your phone…

A text awaited my waking from a number I didn't recognize,
area code 312, Chicago.

Where are u

Almost an hour had passed but it was like I hadn't slept at all.

Home. Charlotte.

b there in 10

Followed by:

Need shower, ride to the track - got coffee?

Turner. Had to be.

"I dropped my goddamn phone in the lake yesterday," he said
as he barreled into the apartment 15 minutes on, still wearing the

same suit from the morning prior, fedora too. "What the fuck is that?" He pointed off across the space to the I-might-as-well-now-have-called-it-my-own DOWN WITH DEBT sign. "Don't tell me you've been out there. Nobody likes a loser, Cash."

"You already told me that, asshole. Where the hell have you been?"

"Changing the subject. Goddamnit, I know they've got to be worrying their petty little silly asses silly willy," he said, and laughed at himself to cap it. "I'm a little drunk. Coffee on?"

I put it on, and he downed six glasses of water in quick succession.

"Truth is," gasping, he said, "I couldn't go home, bet Hugg's got the damn National Guard posted up there by now and man I don't want to deal with his shit. I tell you, goddamnit Cash, I may have fallen truly in love this time around. Sounds stupid coming from a drunk racecar driver, I know, but those guys are just going to have to understand it and deal with it. Now can I use your shower?"

Who's got whose back? After his shower we sipped coffee and smoked cigarettes out on the porch, well into the afternoon shady period, and I told him the provenance of the sign, of Bridget, truncated version.

"Well you certainly make her sound nice," Turner said. "Good for you. Now, give me your cellphone, Hugg ought to have it in his contacts is my guess."

I didn't like the sound of that. "Wait a second—what are you going to do?"

"I'm going to tell him—or you are, technically—text him, that I saw me and everything's cool, 'I'm on my way to the track with Turner now.' Something like that."

No way. "I don't want to be wrapped up in this shit," I said. "Can't I just take you out there, drop you off, you say you took a cab from some place of *your* sole invention, instigation, or whatever—I don't even want to hear about it. You don't know how those guys have been acting since that whole thing with the Cheeters."

Turner stood up now and looked out into the street, thinking.

"They sulking around and acting like you're an asshole or something?"

241

More or less.

"I'm sorry, man. They know the drill, I guess. Remember, I got your back in all this, whatever happens."

"And what the hell does that mean, 'whatever happens,' and what fucking drill?"

"Say Hugg wants to boot you off the team, hell, I don't know. He can't do it without me. None of them can do shit. These people can be hardheaded as hell, though. You know that. Or should. You're one of them. Me too."

I didn't feel like reminding him I'd only been one for several scant weeks, less.

"You hear me, then," I said.

"I hear you, I'm listening—your idea sounds workable, or hell I could just take a cab myself, keep you out of it further."

I wondered aloud what the chances were of actually getting a cab in downtown Charlotte on a Saturday.

"Not good, but your girlfriend's buddies are out in force up the street, chances are some of the cabbies will be prowling, hoping for a fare from that. Come with me in case it doesn't work."

I did, and it didn't—post-3 p.m., Turner really needed to be there now, and if I didn't leave fairly soon myself I'd get caught in the non-tailgating crowd's mad dash-crawl to the race's start under the lights.

"OK," says Turner, "you'll just let me out in the team car lot and I'll walk on in, you can sleep in the car for a bit or just chill, whatever, or maybe come in shortly after me and pick a spot in the hauler."

I ultimately chose the latter, passing the Montuck trailer on the way in—all quiet but for gawking fans taking chintzy little pictures with their phones. I found Pete Kimball playing his guitar among the melee of race-fan humanity, though shielded from them by the narrow space between our rig and the next one. He was seated on the tractor's step, body poised to face away from the humming garage to the chain-link fence separating this area from pit-road central. The song was about love and death, the speaker lamenting what he had to do, kill his lady, after a love so strong it struck him blind in the abstract, blind to self-promotion and -preservation, cut down to peanuts and jilted by an act of petty flirting.

He grabbed your ass
Right there on the grass
And I knew my better sights was gone.

It worked better in performance, trust me. A Robert Johnson with all the appropriate vulgarity for the day, for a race in particular, if you ask me, which he did, ask, and I told him just what I thought.

"That's high praise, young man," he said.

"Be happy."

I got the blues…

Peerfoy materialized from around the hauler's front grille.

"I love talking to him," he said as Pete Kimball picked and wailed on. "Reminds me of my uncles. They were all into that old country shit." Peerfoy grew up in the city himself, Oklahoma, spent most of his childhood and adolescence turning wrenches with the white boys in voc ed, dreaming of race driving, finding aptitude in related pursuits. He'd been doing the shop/pit-crew thing for a decade, the most senior team member but for Hugg and a couple of his guys.

"No sleep for you either," I said, though I'd gotten that half-hour-or-so half-sleep.

"Wicked," he said, "nope," and he caught my eyes with an oddly scared sort of expression. "You're all right," he said. "I'll go ahead and say I'm sorry. I mean, I wish all these motherfuckers were better people."

Kimball kept it up eight feet off, chording taking a crescendo that underscored the truly perplexed "Well what do you mean *sorry*?" that I put back to the tire changer.

"It's nothing, really," he said. "I know how they treat the new people. Little guinea pigs for psych experiments and shit. It's stupid, and …" He didn't go on, but his pursed lips, deep breath in, out in a huff through the nose, told me he had more to say.

"People are weird," I offered, and Trey Olden was as if standing in front of me 20 and more years younger, skin several shades darker.

I slept no more. The week, the events of the day itself, conspired to breathe more anticipation than I'd ever known into my bones. My earlier faux-nap would have to suffice. I was alone in the rig's sleeping quarters, at least, alone with Anthrax and my thoughts. I banged my head on the little bed till my neck hurt.

The final pre-race team meet came a couple hours later, the lot of us, despite whatever differences sat like so many impenetrable bricks in the spaces between our bodies, buoyed by the arrival of our leader, though Peerfoy was noticeably stony-faced throughout the whole thing, not exactly unusual for him. Turner led us through a rousing invocation of the task at hand.

"I'm going to drive like there's no tomorrow left for me," he said. "Do your jobs just the same, and I promise you a win tonight." It was unusual for him to be so brash, so confidently full of platitudes, in private. He sounded like he was talking for the television cameras, but here we all were, no reporters, no bullshit, no cameras at all, and Turner for once looked less than the clean-shaven racing dandy of old—he'd skipped the shave at my place, his two-day love bender shown in the slightly more than five o'clock shadow gracing his chin. His hair, though clean, he'd not bothered to slick from a left part over the crown of his head. Lack of pomade, I surmised, in my bathroom. Here was Turner haggard and disheveled and in love and fired up for the hometown race.

We took our places, bad country music (fatass Toby Keith), national anthem, yadda yadda and the engines roared to life and the boys were off on the pace laps. It was no doubt my favorite moment of any race. I held on to the earplugs Tacklebox had given me that first night out as the green flag came down and the stands lit up with phone flashbulbs and that sound, my God, the sound of 43 high-performance engines at full throttle and the crowd up above and in front of and behind you just roaring right along with them—it was something beautiful, I thought, and I wanted to hear it straight, no muffling.

"I'd put those in if I were you, old boy," Tacklebox said to me soon as the cars had made it around turn one and the possibility of actually hearing someone talking at volume south of a shout was a reality. He always said it, and I always did it, eventually, until I put my helmet on, through which came the radio "clear", "car on your left", "clear" chatter of Turner's spotter, high up above for a window on the entire track. If a pit stop was called, I'd hear that, too, with directions as to what exactly would be done—fuel fill only, splash of fuel only, two tires (driver/passenger side), four tires, wedge/track bar adjustments, etc. ... If Turner spoke, too, I'd hear that, but he rarely said a word over the radio, his focus on the track was intense, until something he did paid off (cf the Talladega turn-turn near-lap-lasting scream of unadulterated joy).

The race started out routine, no cautions, and the first pit was smooth with four tires and fuel—Turner ran in the front till then, as several teams, some at the top of the pack banking on a caution soon enough, came in for fuel and two tires, saving time and jumping out in front for several laps before the fast portion of the field with fresher rubber all around made up the difference. One of the drivers taking advantage to move up was Montuck, who stayed out till he was running virtually on fumes, long enough to take the lead for a lap, after which he pitted, took two tires and fuel and emerged somewhat amazingly in spot three, meaning he'd gained 27 spots from his position in the back half of the pack. Racing well, back in it early in the game.

As we scoped the action, with Turner sitting in 8th position and gaining ground slowly as the two-tire-pit-stop rabbits ahead of him lost muster, Tacklebox collared me and pointed to his ear. He wanted to tell me something. I worked off my helmet. "You're jumping back too far!" he yelled over the noise.

I had no idea what he was talking about and told him so.

"Your left foot! Remember what I taught you—keep the foot in. That last stop you were clear out of the box!"

Was I? I couldn't know. I felt like I was in the groove of the race, body humming with adrenaline. I nodded quick, fast. I'd take his word for it. I kneeled down on and out over my spot on the wall and caught sight of the legend inscribed there. *God bless this team and keep these men in safe stead. The Lord giveth.* Some asshole had inscribed "and he taketh away" in red Sharpie to sort of finish the thought. Red. Tacklebox was watching me.

"What do you think? Montuck team?" he said, reading my mind as I examined the inscription. "Assholes," he went on.

We put our helmets back on and heard Turn over the radio as he passed red runner to take 3rd. "Hot damn good to see a little red in the rear view, such as it is." There was a reason for the spotter.

Too soon. The spotter: "Look out, red on your right, red on your right, he won't give up, on your right, on your right," then they came hard out of turn four into the front straightaway—"clear"—and roared by in front us. Turner had put at least a car length between them and was closing in on the leaders, round turn one, and the second-place car lost it just out of sight around turn two with a down tire, they said over the radio. Turner missed hitting him on the wall by a foot. "Four tires and fuel, boys, full stop, four and fuel. He'll stay out one lap, boys, out one lap."

Turner came round the first caution lap and feinted like he would follow the first-place car into the pits, then turning back out onto the track to keep another lead lap from Montuck, who remained behind him.

"Poor redboy!" he cackled over the radio.

I sat poised, foot atop the wall, listening intently.

Halfway round the next lap, the radio crackled to life with the spotter: "Look out, Turn, red right up on your bumper."

"What the—" Turner said.

We all jumped up to the broadcast monitor to watch it happen, Montuck actually bumping Turn at 60-and-some-odd mph, black-flagged for it, too, as Turner kept radio silence around the track and now down pit road and roaring into a stop in the box. I went over the wall, following the changer, squatted to seat the tire, the hand-off, and shot my left leg back to then spring right out around the front of the car, poised there and seeing, then, self-consciously, that selfsame left foot straddling the white pit-box marker line, heel out into the lane, thinking *Damnit Tacklebox you're right as ever*, sensing movement then off to my left all in the same instant, the red Montuck Chevy barreling this way. The stall just behind our own was occupied by Briggs Patton (yeah, a letter or two away from the small-engine manufacturer), whose team had been working over a misshapen front bumper for the entirety of the last caution lap—I was cognizant then, frozen in time, not only of my own mistakes but of just how long Briggs had been there, how long the car had sit to come out just at the perfectly wrong moment, just as Montuck's tail was about to clear its nose and Briggs screeched his tires and shot out into the lane, clipping the rear left corner of Montuck's car like the collision was immaculately preconceived, and Montuck's car now angled straight at my left leg, foot planted too far out, just as Tacklebox had long cautioned against, my one mistake, momentum in process, suspended, thigh muscle and calve contracting to push off rightward, laterally, with the cast-off front right tire back to safety at the wall. Not time enough to get it done. The left front of the Montuck car missed Adam Stant's ass by inches and plowed through my leg—a pain so terribly immense I can't do it justice with words, side of my helmet and head banging hard on the hood and the windshield flipping me up into the air, whereupon I hurtled over the rear spoiler and down on my helmet's face forehead and chin guards on the ground, coming to numb from the waist down with strong arms under my armpits, Tacklebox upside down overhead, night sky, lights, Peerfoy at my feet shaking his head, sad long-and-away look in his eyes as he stared straight into me, mouthing something I couldn't make out. Turner's voice on the radio through my helmet, "Is he all right, somebody fucking tell me he's OK—is he all right?" Chief: "We'll take care of him. He'll be all right." Pain in my left arm, vague, uneasiness in my chest, the sensation of needing to cough. My left legs might have disappeared could I not see them—I was laid over the wall, next to the broadcast monitor, Tacklebox talking to me and shaking his head when I didn't respond. I must have lost consciousness again, and this time I awoke in a hospital room on a hospital bed, left leg propped up, bent at the knee, over which I was afforded a view of a pair of wooden crutches upright against a chair next to the figure of Bob Cheeter dressed in jeans and a blue blazer and standing at a window offering a suburban-Charlotte vista. It was daytime. Must have been on the north side, near the track—you could just make out the downtown skyscrapers, something I knew virtually impossible from most spots south. I didn't talk. Cheeter heard me stirring, for he looked back at a certain point. He didn't say a word either, just looked. I gave him whatever version of the corner-boy head-nod I could muster—my neck wasn't in restraints, but man did it hurt.

"You awake?" Cheeter said after a time whose length I couldn't quite conceive.

"Of course," I croaked, clearing my throat, coughing a boatload of phlegm. "Get a man a cigarette?"

Cheeter smiled, ducked out into the hallway, popped back in.

"Pretty well deserted," he said. He wheeled the bed out into the hall all business, into an elevator back somewhere in the recesses of the place, down and out again through doors that led on to a patio before a big lawn. He passed me his pack, Lucky Strikes, unfiltered.

"Where the hell do you find these?" I said.

"Pretty well available in Indiana," he said. "Here too, I bet, if you look in the right place."

I smoked. Cheeter smoked. My leg wasn't propped up, I'd figured out by now—just encased in that bent-knee cast extending about halfway up my thigh and holding every bit of my foot. Shit.

"It's Sunday," I said.

"Correct."

"Who won?"

"Turner."

Just like he said he would.

An engineer filled in as tire carrier, Cheeter said. "Did a bang-up job on the short notice, apparently—I've been here much of the time. Racetracks aren't my thing, really."

Turner hadn't been by, nor Tacklebox, nor Peerfoy or Chief Hugg or anybody from the team but for the contract team doc, who said I'd be eight weeks in the cast, at least.

"My mother?" I asked. He shook his head no. I now remembered filling in the emergency contact phone number with my dad's apartment number in Chicago. Call it the self-preservation instinct tuned toward self-immolation, or another species of that willful isolation that'd taken hold of me since Chicago. True colors showing vividly? I loved my fellow man, I really did, especially guardian angel Bob Cheeter.

But, as always, there was a problem, could have been a problem. Might I trust him?

"A group of girls came by—one said she was your girlfriend."

Bridget.

"They were working on your leg then. I don't know what happened to them."

"What did they say?"

"What could they say?"

"Eight weeks, huh."

"At least."

We smoked another couple cigarettes under the NO SMOK-ING signs, or I did as Cheeter looked on. Back up in the room I rose woozy with painkillers and nicotine and tried out the crutches, got a prescription from the doc on call who gave me the clear to hit the road—"No driving on those things," he said—and filled it at the in-house pharmacy on the way out, the copay on Cheeter's dime. None of my personal stuff—wallet, phone, etc.—but for my keys, which I kept on a little clip inside an elastic pocket on the interior of the firesuit, was on hand.

"They're in the back of the hauler," I said, which now would be back at the team shop where Kimball typically parked it for the week.

"I got nothing but time today," he said. "Flight out tomorrow. Tell me where to go."

I'd put back on the white tee and jogging shorts I wore under my firesuit, cutting a three-inch slit up one side of the left leg to get the latter over the cast. They'd shed the firesuit at the track. I loaded up barefoot in Cheeter's SUV and struggled even to put my right shoe on once I'd fought my way into the back-seat, cast propped lengthwise along the bench. I got Cheeter's help with the left before we took off, scooted by the racetrack—Tackle-box's loaner Ford, gone. The key to it was gone from my key ring, too, I discovered with closer inspection. We ran by my apartment, then—no kills!—and I put on a recently acquired denim jacket, a front coming in overnight having cut temps by 10-15 degrees, fall at hand, cut most of the left leg off of the biggest pair of pants I had, black corduroys I then worked my way into.

Through it all, Cheeter didn't say word one about my DOWN WITH DEBT sign, still propped in its now more or less permanent spot. I contemplated taking it with me on the way out the door. Cheeter caught me staring at it.

"Been doing some demonstrating, have we?" he said.

I told him the story in brief on the way out.

He strolled silent, nonjudgmental, through it all.

Maybe I'd cased the character of trusty Bob Cheeter well, and maybe I wasn't the only one, I thought as we hit the freeway south toward team headquarters.

"Have you heard from Turner?" I said.

"Not since the track."

"Goddamnit Bob, don't lie to me."

"I'm serious," he said. "I offered to hang there in the hospital. Nobody else was. I thought somebody should be there, at least. Doc said your emergency number was ringing off the hook, no voicemail, no nothing. I know he probably wasn't supposed to be telling me or anybody else that. I overheard it. I'd come down from the box up top when the accident happened, just to see if I could help out—Bill, several others came as well."

I almost cried, then, at the specter of Pop's old rotary phone in that empty Chicago apartment once again screaming for an answer, Eula Banks standing over it struck dumb by indecision, chest pounding out the slow piano roll of Nina Simone's "My man's gone now." Something wasn't right, furthermore, with this picture, the extended team silence.

"Where'd Montuck finish?"

"Toward the back. Black flag for that caution bump, then the involvement in the accident. Put him laps down. He never recovered."

"Briggs?"

"Who?"

"The guy that hit him before he nailed me." Cheeter had no idea. Nobody paid a whit of attention to Briggs Patton, serial loser. His team probably spent another several laps working over the dent his front fender took in the possibly not-so-accidental accident with Montuck that put me here. I quickly re-formed my plan of action.

"I want you to drop me at the supermarket right off the freeway. I'll show you the one. Then go to the shop. The hauler will be parked around the side by the service bays is my guess, and Pete Kimball may or may not be with it. My guess is not, and if so, try the side door—driver's side—to the forward compartment on the trailer. It should be open. If it's not and Pete's not around, don't worry about it. Just leave and get on with your business. I'll need to borrow $20 if you have it."

Cheeter was tight-lipped through this, but here he piped in

with circumspection.

"Why the cloak-and-dagger routine? Nobody's going to be there, right?"

"If Pete Kimball is in fact with the rig, he may be asleep, in which case go on and try to wake him up—bang on the truck's sleeper, I guess. Tell him you're here to pick up my stuff. If he asks, or anyone else who might be there asks, I'm still in the hospital."

Cheeter didn't speak for a long moment.

Then: "OK," he said, simply.

"If you do manage to get into the trailer compartment, there'll be a black shoulder-type bag stuffed in I think either the second or third compartment from the driver side, top row, on the inside front wall of the trailer. Pretty simple to see." Nobody ever used those compartments as far as I knew, not even me, though yesterday was special.

"Bring it back to the grocery for a hand-off and you're on your own from there. You can tell them whatever you want, long as it eventually includes leaving me at the hospital and coming back to find me gone."

It was almost 10 a.m. by now. If I knew the team, the big win meant only the elder among them would be awake, and home, taking the day easy with family and such. The rest of them would be sleeping off the night's debauchery, Turner included most likely. I held out hope, at least, that I was reading him right and that he wouldn't in fact show up at the hospital sometime between us leaving and whenever Cheeter eventually told him he'd returned. If I'd been picked off by an unholy alliance between Chief Hugg, his son and loser Briggs Patton, I'd need more than Turner to prove it, but having the racecar driver on my side, if I could count on that, would ultimately be bedrock for whatever cause was to emerge from all of this.

"The grocery?" Cheeter said.

Bonus: 10 a.m., I also knew, was when the first fresh batch of fried chicken of the day came out of deli counter's big grease vats. By 10:15 I'd crutched my way to the counter to find an unfamiliar face behind it. I picked up an eight-piece, grabbed a baguette and fended off offers of assistance in carrying them. I could manage.

"Is Bridget working today?" I asked.

She was not. Should have figured. She was never around Mondays either.

"Is there a way I could get a message to her? I lost my phone. We're supposed to meet later but I don't think I'll be able to make it, all things considered." I gestured to my leg, crutches.

The woman produced another woman, a manager, who handed me her cellphone with Bridget's contact open.

"Thanks," I said, and dialed.

"Happy to help," she said, and backed away as the number began ringing.

"Hello?" Bridget's voice on the line shot a wave of relief through me and my heart wanted to skip a beat, pardon the cliché. I couldn't speak for enough time that she repeated her greeting, with a triple question mark and an exclamation point or two appended at the end of it, then:

"I'm at your work. Can you come get me?"

"What the fuck, Cash? Are you all right?"

"Just come get me, quickly as you can. I'll be out front eating a chicken leg."

"Ten minutes."

I thanked the manager, paid for my chicken and sat outside to await the workings of fate. It would take 20 minutes, at least, for the errand I'd sent Bob Cheeter on to run its course and for him to return. Half of that time was gone.

I devoured a leg, then a wing, opened the 20-oz. Coke I'd also bought with Cheeter's $20 and gulped half of it down at once. I was starved. I'd swallowed the first half of the mini-baguette when Bridget pulled up, no sign of Cheeter's SUV.

"Let's go," I said, and she sort of huffed as I begged off a hug and directed her to pick up the food. I crutched over to her foreign compact and wedged my way into the backseat.

"Where to, race man?"

"My place," I said, but as she scooted across the lot in the direction of the exit, "hold on," I said. She stopped the car.

"You want to tell me what the fuck is happening here?" she said, but I was halfway up the block, my eyes, mind out farther with whatever Cheeter found out there. Was this the right move? Would justice or retribution, revenge tragedy or whatever sort of tale was

252

destined to play out from this set of events not be better managed from the inside of the monster's mouth? I'd not exactly thought through the consequences and was now at least somewhat cognizant of my drug-addled state—I'd yet to feel a piece of pain but for some stiffness of the neck and arms. I'd need remediation in the coming days. The pain of moving around was sure to get worse before it got better. Bridget was looking back over the armrest of her little Toyota's driver seat. A smile had emerged from inside the outraged tone of questioning she'd hit me with before.

"What?" I said.

She laughed, shook her head no.

"Listen," I said. "I'm going to have to lean on you next several days, probably longer."

She winked with her left eye.

"I got you propped, Cash. It's OK." She reached back and placed a hand gingerly, tenderly, on my cast. I couldn't feel a thing. "I know fear when I see it. We'll be OK."

"To my place," I repeated, and there we went, no sign of Cheeter's SUV on the route to the freeway. I watched the road behind us intently for most of the way, then on the freeway too, for a trail car, painkiller come-down beginning a somehow familiar paranoia infection, maybe. Downtown in my rat-infested apartment, we didn't exactly repeat the scene from two nights prior but fell into each other's physical presence nonetheless out on the smoking porch, smoking, the two of us, as she went to work on my sore neck and shoulders, gently, and I told her my story, told her my fear.

I couldn't know, ultimately, if Turner was complicit in all of this or if any of it was really real, this growing feeling of certainty in the notion that an attempt had been made on my humble little life. There was the matter of Cheeter's only mildly-surprised-at-the-team's-absence nonchalance, and Turner's exhortations over the radio at the final moment came back to mind, I told Bridget, *Is he all right? Tell me he's all right!*, and the alarm in his voice had been real, or as real as anything he said could be. At once, the competitive reality, the disabling of the Montuck team for once and all, gave him as much motive as the Huggs' revenge desire—and Briggs Patton's luckless team could no doubt benefit from whatever off-the-books payout might be or was in fact coming their way.

As could I—at least I hoped I could.

"Ah fuck, my bank card!" I said.

"... ?" Bridget.

"My wallet was with my stuff," I said, "the stuff I sent Cheeter off to get before I called you and ditched him."

"Cheeter?"

"I told you about the milk-shit fuel guys, right? The energy drink? He drove me down to your store and was going to pick up my stuff—or I'd sent him to pick up my stuff with the intent of ditching him, or getting my stuff back, whichever came first."

"The workings of fate have brought us back together," she said, deadpan. "You should have just gone with him don't you—"

"I couldn't risk seeing Hugg or somebody else," I said, and I was afraid, it was true, afraid as I'd ever been and without an escape hatch short of hiding in plain sight here or at my mom's or somewhere else.

"Just go to the bank tomorrow and get a new one," she said. "The card, I mean."

"My ID's gone, too."

"If you know your address, account number, etc., it won't matter. You can close the account if you want to and pull out all the money." In a past life (summer of the prior year), she explained, she worked the teller lines at a branch in South Charlotte. I wouldn't close any accounts tomorrow. With any luck, we'd see an early payout on Tuesday from the Saturday night race, Wednesday more likely, and it'd be a big one. And who knew, I thought, but that Bob Cheeter would make his way back here after not finding me at the grocery. Maybe he'd begun to lace the indistinct pieces of the puzzle together from what blurry edges I'd laid out and would feel something like empathy, goodwill necessary enough to take it upon himself to return my belongings—if, that is, he found them.

It wouldn't happen tonight. I fell asleep midsentence at a certain point midafternoon in Bridget's arms, on the couch, and woke up with my head propped up comfortably on a pillow, busted left leg in its massive cast propped itself on the far arm. Bridget was out on the porch, smoking, and came in when she heard me stirring, every little movement an excruciating affair. Somehow, I managed to sit up.

"What time is it?" I said. Had to be going on 7 p.m. She'd been thinking all this time, you could see it in her furrowed brow, the slight frown, though she tried out a less-than-convincing smile when she came around to sit next to me, ignoring my question.

"How can you be so sure of all this?" Bridget said.

Chief Hugg had had it in for me from the moment I stepped out of Turner's plane in Tuscaloosa. His son: likewise. I'd gotten Tacklebox's car all messed up, pissed off the entire team by being the odd object of Turner's affection, for whatever ungodly reason. Peerfoy and that final resigned sadness, his weird-ass *a priori* apology—was *he* complicit, did he know the full import of what he was saying?

Ultimately, "I can't," I told her, wincing hard when I raised my left arm to put it on her shoulder. The stiffness was just in-fuck-ing-credible.

"Did they give you any painkillers?" she asked.

They did, I thought, but I didn't know where I'd left them.

"Check in your car for me?"

She did. Nowhere.

She rooted around the apartment when she returned, as did I, such as I could, slow-going.

"Beer," I said when it was clear the pills were gone, either in Cheeter's car or who knew where. "Maybe a bottle of Evan Williams or something. Accompaniment to a dinner of cold fried chicken, how bout?"

She sighed. "I'll make the run," she said. "You stay."

"Lock the door on your way out."

And she left. I think I was falling in love with her—a love borne of a desperate condition, I guess, or more of gratitude for sticking with, for someone to help you through—and I wanted to tell her. I cried when she shut the door, one of those silent, shuddering sob sessions full of primal fear, elation and grief at once for the prospects of tomorrow. I knew not what to do, or what I could possibly have done to deserve all that was under way. With my likely $500 hospital-bought wooden crutches, I creaked and groaned and hobbled my way up and on out to the smoking porch, where I stayed till my eyes dried and Bridget returned for the remainder

255

of the cool night, unable to muster the courage to stand and face what I had coming, maybe. We cuddled around the cast in blankets, sort of. She further kneaded my shoulders and back. We smoked.

There would always be tomorrow, I said at a certain point, drunk through and through. "Is there a chicken leg left?"

"I don't know," Bridget said.

God bless her, I thought, she's still here.

"What time is it?"

"I've got to get going soon," she said. I sipped the straight whiskey in my hand, unsure how it got there. She pulled out her phone, hit a button and her face lit up.

"It's 11. Time to go," she said.

She stood.

"Don't look so sad," she said. "It'll be all right."

I drank and she disappeared into the apartment, came back with the box of chicken.

"There's one leg left, maybe a thigh," she said and smiled. "I'll bring more tomorrow when I get off. Six o'clock."

Bless you, love, bless you. I was all silent smiles, but for: "Make sure you lock the door on your way out."

"10-4," she said, and was gone.

I didn't cry. I ate the chicken, then fell further into the hard porch chair and let my head fall back on the top of the backrest.

Next thing I knew I was staring up through the murky downtown night to the image of Nazi Chris up above, dressed for whatever he called work, fedora and all like a mid-century Madison Avenue sort, leaned way out over his porch railing and looking right at me. "You're going to get eaten alive by mosquitoes out here," he said.

"It's not mosquito season," I tried to say, but only really got out a few ratlike squeaks and felt a twinge on my right arm, which I slapped with my left—my neck was numb and I struggled then to sit upright, coughing up an excess of phlegm. The night was cool, the night was clear. Chris was all wide-eyed concerned.

"I'm all right," I said.

"I saw what happened to you on the television," he said. "Damn shame. Sorry."

"So am I," I said, more clearly now, "and you don't know the half of how sorry I am."

"Need anything, let me know."

I leaned over and picked up the bottle of Evan Williams Bridget left next to my chair and held it out for him.

"Want to help me put a bigger dent in this?"

He came down and I found out Nazi Chris was a lawyer and there were warm vibes radiating from him in spite of his cold-steel gray suit. I put to him the scenario I was contemplating. I tried to sell it as paranoid fantasy, tried to laugh at and believe the hilarity of it to dissuade myself. I would probably have done the same in that moment had Turner Bascombe appeared at my door. But Nazi Chris saw through my efforts at charade. He was taking it seriously.

"That would require some very handsome money," he said. "Traceable. How much would Briggs Patton stand to win from such a showing as yesterday?"

I was too new to the circuit, and Turner's team had been too good, to know much about what was gleaned by a team at the bottom of the barrel.

"But we could find out," he said.

We. Another member of a support team in a battle plan—on to the next thing, I thought, when the now unmistakable *! thwack !* emanated from the kitchen. "Holy mother of God," I said.

Chris: "What the fuck was..."

! thwack !

Sheesh.

! thwack !

A veritable bonanza of death radiated from the kitchen in waves of feral stink too subtle to case unless you'd experienced it before. Chris surprised me. "Did you just kill three of those motherfuckers?"

"How did you ... ?"

How did he? He just laughed. He was having the selfsame problem.

Into the kitchen merrily we went—or not so merrily, as it were, cautiously, really, on my part, hobbling on my crutches into the space to find Chris pushing back the chair and grabbing at the door to the under-sink cabinet before I could even think about getting a plastic bag over my hand.

"Holy shit you did it! A fucking three-in-one!" I was petrified in the kitchen's center afraid to look, Chris turned my way just totally ecstatic, face lit up, big white smile through his close-cropped beard—grown man as child. I couldn't help but smile myself.

"Look at it, man. Just look at it!" he war-whooped and danced a little jig in my rat-infested kitchen.

The impossible: a commotion of metal wire and wood, fur, scaly rat tails and crushed heads, three bodies crossed in a six-point star. A strong blast of that earthy, feral stink hit me with the sight, and I nearly swooned and fell flat. I held hard to my crutches.

"Go on and shut it up, my God," I said.

"You can really do this!" he said. "A natural. Hey," and here he was taking out his wallet, "I'll pay you $300 to set up my place like this. I think they're coming in under my refrigerator, but I'm not exactly sure."

"Hold on a second," I said. Let's back up, I told him, back to the smoking porch, where I eased my broken body into the chair and lit one and poured another and looked him dead in the eye with all the ferocious sincerity I could muster. "What do I do?"

"You got 'em covered, I'd say," he said. He drank, unblinking.

"Turner Bascombe," I said. "Fuck the rats."

"Of course," he paced a little now between the porch and the couch as if lost in thought, in fact lost in thought, muttering a little, whistling between mutters.

"You can kill my rats," he said, "I'll get your story into the public."

My services would go miles. *Pfft.* I didn't want my story in the public, I told him.

"I think that's your best bet. Get the journalists working on it, if they're not already. Free country, free services. Seems on its face like an accident, but ultimately it's too convenient. It's all fishy enough to spark some attention. And where there's journalists, and money at stake, there's lawyers, be certain. Somebody sues you, I got your back."

"That sounds familiar," I said. "Not in a good way."

"You'll have the world on your side. In the case against the money, everybody loves the poor son of a bitch fighting for his take."

Chapter 18

Until he loses. One need look no further than the network news to see such in action, though in America it was never much the reality until there was an obvious fight to be won, which the year 2008 had delivered again to the unwashed, teeming urban masses in spades, the election of the first black president and his health-insurance giveaway to the big national insurers later delivering the target to the other side—for my part, I guess if I hadn't exactly picked sides, I'd determined at least to be there with Bridget in the bank lobby Wednesday, bank card or no, mind made up there in the early morning electric light floating up from below from the streetlights of Church and the bulb of my couch-side table's lamp that shown on the face of the Nazi in my apartment, adding clarity, both, to the blue glow of Carl's loaner laptop, on which the Nazi typed. The result[11]: the details of my situation as I'd outlined for the not-exactly-a-stranger, laid out for a supposed friend of this stranger, who also happened to be a sports journalist with a knack for investigatory stuff—he'd previously worked on the local paper's

---

[11] *Dear* [NAME REDACTED TO PROTECT THE NOT-EXACTLY-INNO-CENT], *I might have something for you. You'll know of the incident out at the racetrack Saturday, involving the Bascombe pit crew member now with a broken leg after a collision with Montuck Jr.'s front-left fender. Facts we know are thus:*

**Briggs Patton was in his pit box for an entire lap preceding his exit into pit road, during which he collided with the Montuck car, causing the mishap.

**Montuck and Bascombe had been primary competitors at the top of the standings in the final 10-race playoff—until this race enshrined the latter at the top of the pack and put the former near the back.

**The pit crew member injured also happens to be the replacement on the Bascombe team for the son of the Bascombe crew chief, who in the Charlotte race was a tire carrier on the Montuck team (the son was).

**Over his night in the hospital following the race, the injured crewmember was accompanied only by a team sponsor (potential sponsor, mind you) representative—the crewmember has not seen a member of his team since, as of this moment.

**Crewmember also reports some negativity coming his way from the Bascombe crew chief, perhaps sour grapes over his son's firing from the team, perhaps there's more to it,

reportorial staff, now doing contract work on the sports side after being laid off following the 2008 crash.

In the light of day the next morning, after Chris emailed the doc to himself, promised to circle back with me by noon, and called it a night with a shared couple shots to finish off the bottle, I still wasn't convinced publicly enacted revenge on the group was my best tack, though the scheme fed well into my natural instincts, more akin to those of rats who dig their way into your sanctuary under cover of darkness and take what they want. The downside was such beasts' ultimate fates when their presence met the concerns of the day-to-day of those who lived in the light. To walk away with my life in my hands—if revenge was in fact to be had, if I was not just some paranoid drunk in psychotic painkiller come-down—I'd need to remain a daylight dweller, a top-side operator. Nowhere near certain I could continue that life, I yearned here again to break all connections, disappear with the girl to an island and hunt wild boar, drink coffee only when it was available, cultivate my own tobacco. It was a familiar feeling, but never had it hit me so hard as this.

Then I made my way down to the bank, where I gave them what I had: name, social number, address, sufficient for information on the balance of all accounts—Monday morning, no recent deposits—but for a withdrawal they also wanted the account number confirmed, likewise to issue a new bank card. Exasperated, I crutched back to my apartment to root around for the checks they'd sent me when I opened the account, some piece of mail with the number printed on it. I nearly choked at the stench of the place when I opened the door to the connected series of drywall

---

threats from the son, now a member of the Montuck crew (cf earlier mention).

The preponderance of all of this in my mind is pointing to collusion between: Briggs and Bascombe teams, perhaps Montuck himself and his new crewmember, with Montuck's operation and the injured Bascombe crewmember on the receiving end.

Further contacts: I doubt you'll get the injured crewmember to talk, but if things change I'll let you know. Do not under any circumstances use my name or the firm's name in any association with this. I might suggest calls placed to the three teams' representatives and whatever investigative body with the league typically follows up after these incidents, such as it may be. Happy hunting.

Respectfully yours,

...

boxes and it hit me full-blast. It wasn't the smell of death, exactly, rather of life: dirty, ugly subterranean rodent life, acrid and raw, the smell of the earth, decaying leaves and soil, four floors up. *The bodies*, I thought.

I managed to get to the level of the kitchen floor in front of the sink with the help of the counter. I held hard to it as I eased myself down, left leg in its cast unbendable and laid out in front of me in its brittle glory, a burnt-crisp sausage. My fingertips got about an inch away from opening the cabinets' doors to the rat-death trap when I realized I'd neglected to take appropriate precautions. I spied the plastic garbage bags clear across the kitchen in a corner and pushed myself in my seated position all the way there, grabbing four bags for good measure. By the time I got back to the cabinet, I was huffing and puffing and a sharp pain bloomed in my forehead as well as both wrists.

Here comes the hangover.

Heart pounding, I closed my eyes, breathed, then, with my hand safely inside two layers of plastic garbage bag, I dared open the doors.

The six-pointed star had been disturbed by a fourth body, exhausting my supply of snap traps. I studied the beasts, of varying sizes—two relatively large, two about half/three-quarter-size, little-league vermin. As before, I double-bagged the lot (traps and all—*mental note: ask Bridget, bless her, to pick up replacements*) and knotted off the top of the bags. The surprisingly hefty cargo I placed on the kitchen counter where I'd be able to reach it, and I now popped open the four square glue boards and arranged them to make a larger square situated in the corner the hole let onto. I struggled upright from the floor again, slid the chair into its position against the cabinet doors and delivered the bagged cargo to its final resting place at the bottom of the chute.

I would not find my checks—I half-remembered putting them in the glove box of Tacklebox's Ford, but couldn't be sure—nor any relevant mail showing the account number, no matter how long I shuffled from room to room to drawer to unused drawer. I tried to get into the bank's online system, but having never used it before, I needed the account number to register. Wedged into the double or triple bind, access to my own money barred, I resolved to continue the search at a later time and clicked over to my email inbox to—*surprise, surprise*—find a note from the impresario of fixed-gear bikes and cattle prods and late-night emo ouzo sessions. He'd sent it last night.

Money man! I hear you are in Charlotte [How exactly he didn't say—TV news, had I told V.?, Trey?, fucking Rinckoff? no way]. *This is a dispatch from the Great White North* [translation: Chicago, Billy's way] *from yours truly, requesting colloquy in a wayward barroom of your choosing* [I would not tell him that I knew of but one, more or less, the sports joint down the way, though I guessed I might get him or Bridget to drive us all to Henry's]. *They are teaching us to ride horseback. Or me, anyway. In two-three days' time we shall be riding down your Main Street (again, they tell me) at the lead of a great quad/bi-pedaled convoy of weird hipster types* [… a Chicago contingent in town for the AB occupation—safe bet, guess…]. *The band will be playing* [skeleton suits and all?]. *I'll be there a day early, or tomorrow, by the calendar* [Timestamp on the email: 1:09 a.m.]. *It'll be daylight, but perhaps a Shining Man on crutches is in order—fit a suit over whatever shell they've got you in? I hope you're all right, man. Hit me back. —Silly*

    P.S: Carl misses his laptop, he tells me, though if he really misses it my guess is you well know it. Fuck him.

And so I might have given Billy Jones less credit than he deserved for being a Southern boy through and through, in spite of what his lady Elsa might say about his time spent cooped up and hating life back in the hot and smelly craw of the great South. He paid attention, kept up with those of his own heritage. Or more simply: He watched car races and thus knew what had happened to me, because the boy was a closet race fan—the time away from Charlotte, perhaps, put the yearning in his bones for the pastime of all Southeastern pastimes, outside maybe college football. Billy wasn't a football sort, was he. Or maybe he was, I just hadn't yet encountered the circumstances for it all to reveal itself. Billy was in transportation, bikes, things that rolled and carried humans here and there and/or in circles… *Take him to the sports bar*, I thought.

    I wrote him back: *I know just the place. No phone, however. Here's my address. Hit me with email if you have an ETA and let's walk down to the bar from here.*

I typed out the apartment's digits and left at noontime warily, canvassing the streets as I exited the building only to be surprised from behind by Nazi Chris bursting into the daylight after a lunch at home.

"Yo Cash!" he beamed, and I positively gasped with fright. "Geez, man, sorry—hey, he's on it."

I lit a cigarette. "Who's on what?"

The journalist on the scent like a bloodhound. Chris then did something that annoyed me stone sober here in the daylight. He winked repeatedly like he wasn't 100 percent serious in the least.

"Dude, gotta ask," I said. "What's with the winking?" I'd noticed it was something of a tic of his last night but was too drunk to really give it full account. It lent everything he was saying an olfactory quality redolent of bullshit.

Chris just smiled. We've all got our issues, peculiarities, I crutched away thinking, Chris striding confidently ahead of me at twice the pace (though the man had to be hurting after how late we were at it last night). He disappeared right around the corner among my father's many streets up ahead and, when finally I reached it, my body was shot through with gasping trepidation for the second time in as many minutes. A sea of humanity filled the sturdy blocks ahead, no sign of Chris, starting just 40 feet beyond the corner, all gathered with signs around what I knew not.

"I have a right to my bad health," read one of them.

"Don't tread on me," another, less-original, as it were.

There was a Confederate flag or two or three, anti-abortion signs, anti-*Brown v. Board of Education* signs, anti-pretty much anything you can imagine associated with liberal democratic society signs, a crowd of humans who yearned for hunter-gatherer times, I thought. I fought the urge to turn back, burrow deeply into my rat hole in the air.

"What's the occasion?" I asked a guy who looked more or less like he ought to be back over on 5th and Tryon holding vigil outside the bank: stocking cap, long curly hair, motorcycle boots.

"Some 'patriot' group," he said, shrugging and using his fingers for air quotes. "Anti-tax, that sort of thing."

"Why here?"

263

"Federal building," he pointed out over the crowd toward a low-rise gray monstrosity in the near distance before walking on. There was nothing going on other than folks milling about, far as I could tell. No chanting, so speeches, no cops to speak of. I ambled a crutch stupor, slow hump through the crowd on the sidewalk. At a point about halfway through the bodies, I caught a familiar face among the teeming overweight masses. This one was lean, an expression more hardened, skin showing evidence of age, than I remembered from the night I first saw it with Bridget out by the bank.

"Well goddamnit," I said. "What the hell are you doing here?" and leaned hard on my right crutch as I thrust my hand out like a businessman before self-consciously pulling it back in. "Sorry," I grinned.

Knox the drug dealer grinned himself, then rejoining with those downhome-hick inflections.

"This man does not discriminate, I'll have you know," he said, the devil. "Equal opportunity and all that." And he leaned in close—"this crowd's got more money," he whispered. "Not a whole lot more, but I'm happy to charge 'em more."

He took it this wasn't my speed either, he went on: "Long as we're making assumptions."

"You got it," I said. Where was my DOWN WITH DEBT sign when I needed it? Not that I could actually carry the thing with the crutches. The sign would fit in well here, given the state of the U.S. government's financial coffers, just as sickly as the lot of the rest of us.

"I see you have been injured," Knox nodding, eyebrows high.

"I take it you don't watch the sporting news." Bridget had not divulged my occupation to the drug dealer.

I filled him in, short version, then: "How's dope for pain?" Though it was slowly dissipating with the passing hours, I was still feeling it with every knock of the unwieldy cast on a hard surface, every engagement of the thigh muscle whatsoever required to swing the thing, my leg, along with the crutch-walk. When he quietly motioned for me to follow him I made clear I hadn't the money for a deal today. He nodded, don't worry, don't worry, and we moseyed out of the crowd, around a corner, down a tight alley.

"Here's a dime or so," he said, "and this stuff is for real, no kidding," producing a joint unbelievably close to twice the width of a cigarette. "Enjoy, my fine friend. Sounds like you deserve it."

And he turned to leave me to my devices. I struggled to stash the joint in the pocket of my jacket and follow, but he moved fast and disappeared onto the street, into the crowd, I saw when I emerged from the alleyway finally and lost sight of him among the bodies. Another familiar face then locked eyes with mine from a distance of no more than 30 feet. Truck-driving Pete Kimball, recognition all over his face before he quickly looked away, then back, then delivered a meek wave. He was holding a sign that read simply IMPEACH—really, bluesman? He put on a tight grin and walked toward me now. I thought about running, seriously (such that I could with the crutches). Could I trust Pete Kimball? We were about to have a conversation, no way out of it …

"Goddamnit Cash, I would have figured you for a Democrat, I guess," he said, offering me the sign in a sort of half-heartedly jesting manner.

"That might be close to right," I said, "but who knows, in the end." I meant it. He pulled the sign back a little. Mainstream politics was fuzzy business—sort of like football in the two-party reality. Though the sport remained a prime entertainment for most, the sides commonly taken no longer looked as wondrous as they once had. The kids were fed up with their parents' choices for allegiance, the adults perhaps even more so with those of their progeny, who were shiftless and noncommittal. Saturday sit-downs around the boob tube, as Ralph Cash might have called it, to pull for the home team shot through with the despair not of loss or ineffectual mediocrity or hell even the pride of excellence, if your team was winning, but of the impenetrable gray area. Whether your team was even worth pulling for was too easily questionable, given the brains being destroyed on the field and at the bar after days spent in the conference rooms, and no matter if you hung around with a sign and maybe a tent outside the federal building or the bank. There was always another option that might fare better, too.

"For what?" I said, pointing to Kimball's sign.

Kimball looked around like to see who was listening.

"How you feeling?" he said, nodding to my leg.

"Oh I'm OK," I lied. I thought about the joint in my pocket. "When'd you get out of the hospital?"

Was he truly interested?

"So impeach for what?" I said. "I'm interested. I want to know." Really, truly, I wanted to ask him if he'd seen Turner, if I'd been missed, if my bag was still in his truck, if he'd even looked through the compartments back there, but I figured he mightn't have a single answer to any of those questions himself and in my haste to keep up my side of the exchange I just motored on. He probably wouldn't hook back up with the team before Wednesday, Kimball. I waited for him to do much the same—a pained look coming across his face, eyes averted left, then right, then he did this funny thing with his fist, like he was wiping a stray bit of spit from his mouth but had decided the best way to do that was to hit himself in the face.

Finally: "He has not upheld the constitution," Kimball said, "plain and simple."

I struggled to find a rejoinder.

"To serve and protect," I said, "or what?"

"He's not a pig," Kimball said, betraying his age. "All representatives of the U.S. government are bound to uphold the laws of the United States, to keep sacred the Constitution."

"You quoting from something?" He didn't answer, averted his eyes. I kept up the line of inquiry, genuine as it was. "Well if he hasn't, how not?" I was less sure than most of the reality behind any of these arguments, cognizant of moving into dangerous territory, or if not dangerous certainly uncharted, in my case. The bluesman wasn't exactly in his element when it came to conflict-laden rhetoric, borderline political fantasy, either. To his credit, he tried to bring it down to reality.

"Making us buy stuff," he said. "Off-the-charts reckless there. I mean the health insurance. Bank bailouts, all of that, too. And not just him, of course, the Congress is complicit, the entire Democrat party and most of the Republicans, for that matter."

"Wasn't that under his predecessor's watch?" I said. "The bailouts, I mean."

"Well sure. Same stuff applies," and he held his sign higher, "were he still around."

That was to say nothing, Kimball narrated onward now, back in comfortable territory and sensing a small kind of common ground, I imagined, with his race-team compatriot on crutches—I didn't object. Cue the recent melee in the Middle East, not just neverending U.S. combat but the hardening of the masses in their moves for liberty in the so-called "Arab Spring," Tunisia and Egypt, Libya and Syria and God knows where else to follow any day now. A kind of raucous awakening, maybe. Maybe not. Kimball shrugged. The bluesman offered a metaphor.

"Their daydreams made real like some guitar pickers I know—maybe a tire man or two. We really ought not to be fucking with that," he said. "Get out of there already and let them all sort their shit out."

I nodded in agreement, honestly now again, but the bluesman's rhetorical attack wasn't going to hold to my level for long, as he veered now into new world orders, something called the Trans Pacific Partnership he described as a kind of NAFTA on steroids veering beyond the realm of sanity, our leaders on the verge of giving away the house to the far east with its hard, heavy currency, its regulatory advantages.

"Longtime truckers know a thing or two about price controls and how they work," he said, "what happens when you take them away." In the 1980s, Kimball said, "we got an education in deregulation. China's thing isn't exactly the same, but in a lot of ways it rings familiar. They at least understand what they're in for should they choose to go the route of the rest of the world. Smart moves for self-preservation might mean they're unlikely to do so."

President wanted a free-trade deal regardless of what they did way over there. Congress was bent on insisting China let its currency value be determined by the world market, whatever that was, and I really tried to center on the certainty of an image in my brain around which to reason it all out. I couldn't, however, get the fluorescent interior confines of a particular big-box super-store out of my head.

"If you look at how this president, and the last one to a lesser turn, goddamn," Kimball continued on, "look at how they do their business and it's clear that Congress matters little less than a god-damn, here. President wants to give away the house, president will give away the house."

Impeachment wouldn't do much to change all that, would it, I said more than asked. I was engaged, at last.

"Probably not," said Kimball. "But hey," holding up his sign, "gotta stand for something, something real people can hold on to, something that demands action."

I thought of my own sign, back at home, its attack on a notion. *Debt.* Things owed, money owed. Abolition of all human appreciation of things come before, of influence, of help, of history. Down with the house! While Kimball might've agreed in general terms with such sentiment around back of his hauler, independent of mind as he appeared to be, it wouldn't pass muster ultimately, I knew, had I been holding it. I nodded dumbly and made a move to gaze back over my shoulder far and away from this place.

"See you at the shop this week?" Kimball said. "Load out for Texas Thursday, I think," which all told me less than I might have hoped. He tried a smile that came out more like a grimace, and I returned one of my own. I thought again of Turn Turner Bascombe and what the next days might hold, relieved though I was that Pete Kimball at least seemed enough out of the team loop to exist beyond the boundaries of the paranoia that gripped me, if not the paranoia of the political right. As I crutched away I again pictured the joint in my jacket pocket, jostling about with my keys, the last vestiges of a real life within the common structures.

I picked up my pace beyond the edges of the crowd. I could keep up with the other few walkers out on the street if I really worked at it, though by the time I'd fired up the joint on my smoking porch my armpits were rubbed raw and throbbing with the effort. I hit, blew, hit again, again, again ... until the thing was ash. I could almost see the bank from here if I leaned way out over the railing and craned my head around like this ... Not really, but I could imagine it, could imagine the people in there, likewise in the federal building, people with faces and names. I needed nothing from the latter, but Misty—"What is your last name, Misty, if you don't mind my asking?"—Misty Burlingame—"Are you from Carolina or somewhere north, say Vermont?"—migrated to Charlotte from New York City several years ago with a man whom she thought was the *veritable tits* (my words) and that she could help but

268

was ultimately helpless herself to do so. He's still there, in New York—Misty typing away in Charlotte at her overcomplicated typing machine, her ultra-complex database-access point—shacked up with a thin Jewish puppeteer who spends long nights in her studio courtesy of his long days within the famous confines of an infamous investment outfit.

That's a shame, Misty, such a shame. You have my money. I have empathy. I am shacked up with brown/gray vermin who are benefiting from my particular culinary style—they love my taste for cheap, fortified white bread and peanut butter, food of the gods and small children the world over—as much as I am benefiting from a sense of purpose in destroying as many of them as I possibly can. So, show me the money, Misty, show me the money.

I was hungry with nothing but a supermarket chicken box full of bones under the seat on my porch to sustain me. There was beer in the fridge, so I drank for my calories. Two beers in and I was hungrier than I'd started and woozy with all the stimulation. I laid on the couch and propped up my cast, my leg, and clinched my eyelids tight over a wave of nausea that crept horizontally to my stomach from my toes. I breathed, I breathed, to pass the time.

A knock on the door. Time? Nearly dark. Bridget. I struggled to get up, headache, dry mouth, urge to spit the fattest, juiciest loogie in human history, dry mouth.

I knocked my cast on the arm of the couch as I crutched around it. Pain. Hunger. I could smell fried chicken before I even opened the door.

"Damn it's cold as hell in here," she said as I waved her inside, to the coffee table, where I dug into the box.

"Oh sweet manna," I mumbled through greasy half-chewed leg meat.

Bridget closed the porch door—temperature was dropping fast, she explained.

"There goes the summer in fall. You, my stoned friend—yes I can smell it—are more famous than you thought."

When I didn't look up from the chicken: "Seriously, race man, and don't freak out on me or anything—but yes, that's right, look up from that chicken box, chicken man—seriously I heard a bit about you on the radio coming this way."

Nazi Chris was good as his word. I guess I was surprised, despite the assurances of the previous night. And I didn't appropriately react, couldn't, just looked blankly at her. I didn't know what to think, whether to really be happy or scared to death.

She went on, "It's just like you told"—air quotes danced about above her head—"'Some watchers are calling for an investigation into the circumstances around front tire carrier'—"

Pulse quickening, "OK, OK, OK. Where'd you hear it?"

"In the car, where do you think?"

"Let's go, catch the news at the bar." On the way, Bridget pulled out her phone and searched around for a clip, which she found. She stuck the phone up next to my head as I winced my way down the sidewalk, careful not to put too much weight on my armpits—both my hands were starting to cramp with the effort.

"League officials are denying knowledge of any wrongdoing at present but are not ruling it out. An initial investigation revealed involved teams' safety procedures seemed to be in order. Whether a criminal investigation is taken could depend on many factors, but chief among them may well be a preponderance of the so-called evidence of the targeting of front tire carrier—"

I couldn't keep listening. Full dark now, streetlights ablaze, we'd reached the bar, intruding through its rotating door and picking a spot at a table in back next to the Matt Caudill/Rob Rene team posted up in a couple high chairs along the rear wall. Both men inquired after my condition. Neither of them had seen any of these most recent news reports as yet, nor had I seen them since the accident—they had at least been aware of it, they said.

We ordered beers and I was giving Rene-Caudill the short version of the story when Rob piped in: "Hey, isn't that you?" He pointed over my head and out over the space to one of four TVs behind the bar—or two of four, as it were, tuned to the same channel, national sports news. It was indeed me in a team portrait from a month or so back, shorter hair, before the broadcast cut back to a reporter on location right downtown Charlotte here—you could just make out the encampment in the dim background outside the AB building.

"Bartender!" Rene called out. "Hit the sound on two and four."

Within seconds he had—"...what would be attempted murder and conspiracy if charges are actually filed, Charlie, though police claim no official involvement in the probe as yet and the Bascombe, Briggs and Montuck teams had no official comment to make. Cash himself—" *cut to my image, again, a buzzing bee of a man in firesuit, helmet at his side* "—could not be reached for comment. I guess we'll have to wait and see where this goes. The investigation wasn't initiated by the tire carrier, as far as anyone knows at this point."

Though I should have expected all of it, my mind reeled, turning in on itself as the bar buzzed in excitement around me. Bartender, Matt, Rob, Bridget, several patrons I recognized, all eyes on me. Somebody bought me a beer, another called for picking up the next one. Questions came in due course. That is, they came quickly, and I focused all attention on the beer in front of me as the chatter rose to a level so loud as to go virtually silent in my single-minded concentration. Bridget in the middle of it tapped me on the shoulder. I looked up, the cacophony hitting my ears again. "You all right?" she mouthed. I tipped back my beer and nodded.

Caudill and Rene were staring at me. I attempted a meek smile, shrugged my shoulders.

"Yes," I said, and they nodded.

Bridget pulled out her phone and tapped on it for a while. I turned my eyes back to my beer and tried not to look up. The TV sound had been turned down and a Lynyrd Skynyrd number transformed to an indie-rock jingle I recognized from the Sparrow ... *if we can call them friends then we can call them on their telephones / and they won't pretend that they're too busy or they're not alone / and if we can call them friends then we can call / holler at them down these hallowed halls / just don't let the human factor fail to be a factor at all...*

I breathed, looked up. Bridget banged away at her phone, and Matt and Rob were still standing close, the latter talking, but I couldn't hear it over the music, and both of them looking directly at me, their faces cycling between an expression I can only describe as a kind of trumped-up amusement and another, more familiar one: worry, concern, will-this-guy-like-keel-over-dead-any-minute-now-or-what...I closed my eyes...*don't, don't you worry, about the atmosphere / or any sudden pressure change / cause I know / that it's starting to get warm in here / and things are starting to get strange…*

"Chicken," I said, and stood, steadying myself carefully against the table.

"What the fuck, race man?" Bridget, not looking up from her phone.

"Let's go."

Caudill and Rene were positively horrified. Matt throttled Bridget's shoulder and pointed my way. Her own expression when she saw my face was less alarmed than all that.

"I know that look," she said. "Cash is messed up. He needs a rest." Fake smile, phone shoved in her purse. And we wobbled out of the bar, Bridget brushing off my protestations that we probably had a tab to settle up: *Let those dudes get it.* She pinned me against the brick of the building once we were on the sidewalk. She punched my chest.

"Are you fucking OK? You look like you're going to die on me here or some shit."

I was lightheaded, confused, heart racing a mile a minute.

"I might," I said.

"Fuck you," and she grabbed my shoulder and attached crutch and turned me down the dark sidewalk. I gripped the crutch handles as tight as I could, most of my weight again on my bruised and battered armpits.

"Motherfucker," I said, "I don't know what's wrong. Maybe I'm having a heart attack" and at the very thought of it I seemed to grow weaker, sweat popping out in odd places that could not be seen but felt—the insides of my legs, encased in half cut-up jeans, in cast, the soles of my feet. I stopped again. Good thing. We were at a red light. I turned to look down the street perpendicular into the oncoming traffic, a one-way street, no idea which street, but there, coming on fast on two wheels but getting passed by automobiles and pumping his legs furiously was none other than …

"Ah, your buddy G-Man," Bridget said gamely, and I just shook my head no, no. The look of horror that passed across her face when she caught my eye sent another little nauseating attack of dizziness through my head. I steadied myself on the crutches, and here the bicycling enviro-thug must have cased my identity.

"Race motherfucker!" I heard clearly, but only could make out a motion-blurred version of his form as he zoomed by. "I'll get you yet, jackass!"

"Ah fuck him," Bridget said, "yeah," grabbing my arm and pulling me forward with her. The world was a motion blur with that, and I told her so. "Should I get you to the hospital?"

"Dunno," I tried.

"What the fuck did you just say?"

My sensory engagement with the world was sharp in an auditory sense—I could hear, at least—but the rest was a fantastic muddle.

"Just get me home," I tried to say.

"I think I heard *home* in there, c'mon, pick up the pace."

I went through the motions, keeping it all together fairly well, considering.

"I don't want to alarm you, race man," she said when we were at the door into my building from the street, "but G-man is up at the corner staring at us."

I could sort of make him out, a two-wheeled silhouette against the cars at his back passing one after another with bright, trailing peels of headlight flash.

"I'll wave hello to him," she said.

I reduced my speech attempts to affirmative/negative-sounding grunts here, issuing one of the former and pointing to the door with my key card. In we went.

"OK, he's not following us," she said.

When we bumped off the elevator: "You're just like too high, right?" she said—*olfactory sense, check*. I too could smell the weed with just two steps toward my door.

"I should have known," she said as we entered. "Can't handle your dope. You're not stealing mine, are you?"

I didn't speak, opened my mouth and closed it again.

"Water," she said, and got me some. "So you're mute. Good, after what I heard earlier. Listen, I think you need some sleep, something."

I closed my eyes and the little lightning bolts on the back of my eyelids as I rubbed them rotated just as quickly as they appeared, disappeared. I felt like I might puke.

"Lay back," said Bridget, as if reading my mind. Wrong

move—the world tilted on its head, spun in a perpetual rotation away from center. I grasped at Bridget and the back of the couch and pulled myself upright. Mind reeled. I breathed, thought again about Knox, about what he could have given me. Hash? Some kind of acid-laced weed? I'd never tripped acid, but I'd heard stories. Delayed-reaction trip, time for the strychnine to lodge itself wherever it went to block receptors, increase electrical flow between other connections. Brain as computer, as machine with problems to be troubleshot with an Indian man over a phone to a call center in Delhi, Bombay.

"Fuck fuck fuck," I said, head between my hands.

"*Fuck fuck fuck,*" Bridget said. "OK I get it, got it."

"You can understand this," I said, deliberately.

"I can. A little slurred, as it were, but understandable. You're mending."

"I saw your pal Knox," I tried.

The otherwise keyed-up Bridget now just stared, not dumbly, more wise to the cause-and-effect of what was at hand, her face a blank slate slowly chalking up with recognition.

"You got the chronic—the good shit, or maybe not exactly good but the— *Powerful* is the word I'm looking for."

I told her everything, then, about the past days, about Nazi Chris upstairs, about the well-placed letter of scoop tip, about my own—*paranoia*, was it? I wasn't absolutely convinced of my own story in total, if I ever had been, and it helped that she wasn't either. I never moved from my position on the couch with her through our maybe hour-long exchange. I slowly returned to some semblance of normalcy, broken leg going numb propped up as comfortably as was possible considering the circumstance. Through all the chaos came ripping that overwhelming gratitude, too, undeniable affection.

"I love you, Bridget," I muttered to her, though I don't think she heard me in my severely compromised state, my fear still plenty contagious.

"The one problem with this is you are thinking wrong about the endgame. If I was you, on the TV and all that shit, I might disappear while I had the opportunity."

She didn't think they'd come after me here, did she?

"I do," she said. "I doubt they're into assassination or anything like that, but goddamn you know old tophat will be paying a visit."

"Turner?"

"Yeah, didn't you say he wore some kind of funky hat if he wasn't racing?"

Fedora, tophat, whatever, she spoke truths I guess I'd assumed the high-profile nature of what I was doing would trump over all. No way they'd risk being seen with the likes of me, their accuser.

Then again maybe I was just a rube, and dead wrong.

"Don't worry over what I've done," Bridget said. "You'll have plenty opportunities to repay. No doubt." She winked, then told me a story that had been told to her by Knox Garp, apropos of explaining the wild mental and physical effects of his special "chronic"—a particularly high-THC weed whose nomenclature I was well familiar with from decades of pop hip-hop. This stuff apparently had something else in it, too.

Bridget, resplendent and loud out on the smoking porch, to which I'd managed to hobble: "He told me about this puppy Great Dane—it wasn't his, just some dog, I don't even know if he ever saw it or if he was passing the shit on to me third- or fourth-hand. They called it Hamlet, the scientists running the experiment." The goal of said experimentation on newborn-to-juvenile-to-grown-adult Hamlet involved the ghost of the pup's dead father, or at least the wispy image of a dog that may or may not have actually been the pup's sire, projected in hologram form and backed by a doomsday soundtrack embedded with all manner of "that super-high-pitched dog-whistle-type noise that we can't hear but that apparently rings all kinds of five-alarm bells for dogs," Bridget said. "The ghost of the father, Hamlet, you get it."

The intent, she said, was to make the ghost live, real, to the dog, and to test long-term sensory effect, auditory suggestion of hallucination, memory. After locking the pup up with the hologram for hours a day for the first year of its life, anytime the audio used with such sessions was heard from there on out, the growing dog would bark and growl something fierce.

"So the whackos conducting this little test—and remember the source of who told me this, grain of salt, all that—they realized they'd programmed the pooch to totally like *hallucinate* the ghost, and the interesting thing, during the hallucinations prompted by the sound, the dog's hearing shut down."

How did the esteemed whackos know this?

"The barks—the dog wouldn't stop barking, and it was like he would start barking louder and louder and louder until he couldn't bark anymore and was hoarse like a fill-in auctioneer for the effort. And they tested with their instruments, I guess. I don't know…"

"That's terrible stuff," I said, but as soon as I said it I felt it, something of an urge to bark, a compulsion akin to what led my rats back again and again in droves to the scene of their compatriots' deaths. I stood up as I could, I told Bridget I needed sleep and would she please bring me eight more rat-size snap traps, in order that I might at least make some headway on fulfilling my part of the bargain with Chris, when she returned. When would it be? Wednesday? Yes Wednesday, another day and a half, no shift then, big occupation around the corner. "I'll be here by noon," she said. "You don't need anything else?"

I forced a smile, pointed across the room to the half-finished eight-piece, the fresh bottle of Evan Williams next to it.

"As always," she said. And when she was gone I hobbled into the kitchen and opened a beer and checked on the ocean of glue traps before the primary hole—no snares. I barked my way through the beer, so to speak, then barked the next one open, then barked a smoke afire and hobbled my way to the porch to think it through.

My own hologram was as if before me there, on the extra unused chair across the porch, here in the rarefied air above the streets that bore his eternal imprint. The man, now dressed in his present-tense surrogate of chances Turner Bascombe's own black fedora, never gave me a bit of advice I couldn't leave to the side, of course, the extra-lean way I tended to deal with adversity and Pop and Turner Bascombe more like nodding your way through a conversation than truly taking the reins of the ideas or narrative or emotion offered by the human being across from you—I dare not claim to be chosen, exceptional, elect. Pop wasn't one to give much advice directly, in any case, directive a matter of interpretation in most interactions. Yet, there it was, there he was, conjured with his foot propped on the railing with that ridiculous hat pulled down to his eyebrows and staring out away from me into the street. I barked another pull from the beer. "Know who your friends are," he said, always said, as close to direct as he ever was outside of baseball, back in the old day whenever the situation his son presented seemed to suggest less control than was to be desired in a fully functioning human. The time me and ninth-grade Schuyler got our asses kicked by the older straight-edge skinhead guys for pal'ing around with the black boys on the football team smoking weed, the hellish despair that came with the tenth-grade dopehead girl who first broke my heart.

Best he could do. I blinked, fast, three-four-eight times and rubbed my eyes and fought the urge to cry. I turned my gaze into the apartment, wobbled upright, grabbed the bourbon and returned to the porch.

I was a quarter way through it when I heard a half-cocked wolf whistle emanate from the space above my head. Chris was leaning out over his railing looking right at me.

"You've got visitors," he said quietly, and his right eye took to its trademark spastic winking. "Or one, at least. If that's who I think it is." He nodded out across the street, still winking. At the corner I could see from here stood none other than Turn Bascombe—ballcap pulled down close to his eyes. Definitely him, the way he held his head cocked back evermore full of himself. I wondered for a second just how Chris had cased him through the streetlight's shadows, the night, but no doubt he'd seen more than a few pictures of the man these last couple days.

Turner didn't appear to actually be looking up, so I skulked back farther from view and breathed quietly until I was sure he'd had time to make his way across Tryon and between me and the building, by which his view would be blocked. Chris remained leaned out, eyeing the edge of the building where Bascombe would have disappeared.

"You want me to come down?" Chris said. "We can start up that legal relationship whenever you want, friend."

I didn't need a lawyer, though, not for this, I thought. I could handle Turner alone. But there were second thoughts—and second sights—to contend with. At that moment out there, as I gazed up the street down which Turner had apparently come, none other than G-Man Gerald came flying up on his bike to the same intersection. I watched, tantalized, as he continued on the same route Turner had taken. He was got up all in black like the Chicago anarchist shock troops.

"You sure?" Chris said to my demurral.

"Hold, please," I said, but I didn't move. "They won't even be able to get in."

"They?" Chris said.

But less than a minute later the knock came—I looked quickly to the door to confirm that Bridget, yes, had indeed locked it. It was one of those institutional-type flat, slate-gray jobs with a pull-down handle like a public bathroom door, the lot of it no doubt framed in steel and heavy as hell. I figured it would be a beast to knock down, break through. Fifteen seconds turned to half a minute. Another knock.

I looked up at Chris. "Are – you – going – to – answer?" he half-mouthed, half-whispered.

I said nothing, didn't move.

"Yo Cash!" Turner. I raised myself off of my seat slowly. "It's Turner! Can we talk, man? It's not true, what they're saying, or I don't think it is."

I managed a standing position, grabbed my crutches from their spot against the railing and stood silently.

"I know you're in there, Cash. I saw your crutches propped on your porch on my way in from outside. C'mon, man, wake up!"

I fought the barking urge, instinct railing in my bones to do as told. The fear was there, though, fear of whatever chain reaction would follow. My mother would be proud. What were the chances Turner meant well? Here's a man whose cynicism was as complete as his daredevil nature on the track. Did that mean he was likely to take press vilification by someone who was arguably one of his better friends of late as an unforgivable affront? Was he so used to this kind of stuff that he didn't even give a damn? There was also an undercurrent of thought making its way topside that said I didn't need him on my side as much as I thought I might.

Or: was something else going on entirely? I heard the door to the building's seldom-used stairwell, just 15 feet down the hall from my door, open and close. Turn now was talking more lowly, presumably to someone in the hallway—I couldn't make out the words, and took the opportunity to move a little more quickly, just as quietly, to the door. The peephole yielded only a small sliver of a view of Turner's right shoulder, a portion of his neck and the side/rear of his head, turned to his left and indeed trained on another something/someone back down the hall. I couldn't make out his whispering.

Then his head began to move and I shifted to the side away from the hole.

"I saw that!" he bellowed. "Let me in, Cash. I'm not going to bite, for fuck's sake. I got your back, remember, I got your back. Your bank account ought to see a hefty hit tomorrow, my friend. It's going to look great!"

"Hey, cut it out, man!" This was Rob Rene from down the hall—I'd recognize the hippie-dippy inflections anywhere, down South Carolina hometown pothead through and through. The door to the stairwell opened, closed again. "Obviously he's not there, man. Leave the guy alone, all right. And shut up! I'm trying to sleep here!"

Turner didn't speak. I heard footsteps retreating down the hallway, and when I looked through the peephole again Rob was raising his fist to knock.

"Jesus H, man," he said when I opened the door. "What the hell is going on? I could hear the guy like he was in my front room with me."

I took him out onto the porch and called to Chris upstairs. Rob was going on and on with his outrage. Who barges into an apartment building and just starts raising hell like that? Who does the guy think he is?

"Turner Bascombe," I said.

Rob hadn't figured that out yet.

"Well damn," he said. "The guy who tried to…"

"Kill me? That's up for debate, I guess."

Rob kept talking. Chris wasn't coming out onto his porch. I watched for Turner to emerge from around the edge of the building back the way he'd come, but he never did.

"Chris," I hollered up, "what do you make of it?" I guess I wanted confirmation of my own fear, my own confusion, and then he stuck his head out over the railing and Rob went quiet. Chris was wearing his downtown fedora, now. I felt a chill in my bones, the weather was turning colder, no doubt.

"There was somebody out there with him in the hall," I spoke up to Chris. "Any ideas who it was?"

Chris shrugged, winking again.

"Let's talk more later," he said. "Gotta get some sleep."

I looked over to where Rob had been and he was gone, back inside the apartment. He was blank faced, like he'd seen a ghost. He motioned me inside, didn't speak until I was almost touching him.

"It was him, dude," he said very quietly, nodding his head up.

I had no idea what he was talking about and told him so.

"It was that guy, up there," now pointing up, "out in the hall. I know him, pass him every day in the hall, man. It was fucking him. He was out there talking to your racecar driver. And you didn't know that. Dude, you're in it, you're in the shit. This is weird."

No kidding, I said.

I shut the door to the porch.

"You're sure."

"Hell yes I'm sure. You wanna go up there and kick his ass?" Rene said. He was drunk. The look in his eye was dead serious.

"He's a lawyer," I said, like that made any difference. I needed time, I told him.

"You got it," he said. He raised a fist in solidarity on his way out. "Bedtime for me. I'll be around if you need me."

10 p.m., probably later. I checked the clock on the kitchen stove. 10:20. Good time of day for a smoke. I smoked out on the porch, stretched out, head on the chair back, eyes locked solid on Nazi Chris' porch above. I checked my email at a certain point. All junk. I opened my eyes and it was light out and I was freezing and had close to no idea what I was doing there, first instinct being to listen for my mother's footsteps somewhere high up above, evidence that all was right with the world. Other than to seek refuge from the cold indoors, I didn't move through the entire morning—a couple emails from Bridget about Wednesday plans, inquiries from press people that I was so stupefied by I had to ignore. What could I possibly tell them? Halfway through the day I was convinced I'd screwed up by running. I remembered

Turner's words about elevation, about sliding fast up the ranks, his team's move on from the long relationship with Chief Hugg, who despised me. But why would Nazi Chris lie about his association with Turner? Because Turner is directing all of this, including the hit on me, I thought, but just as quickly I backed away from it and began to see circumstances for what they may more likely have been, or would be to any less-paranoid person. Capitalization on a true accident by more canny, more savvy men than me and their damn near clairvoyant sense of what they were dealing with—another dog barking at familiar stimuli.

I needed to act. Midday I hobbled up the stairs—harder than I thought it would be—to Chris' place and tried to beat the door down, you'd figure as a casual observer, I knocked so hard. I didn't know what I wanted, a confrontation at the very least.

But nobody answered, no demure conservative wife, no Chris, no tenant. I resolved to wait, then resolved against that resolution. I set out to prove what little Turner had told me, such as I could. I crutched through the encampment outside the AB building and took my cause up with sales representative Jenny Brock, considerably more helpful than Ms. Misty Burlingame. I told her my situation, told her I had no proof of residency, no proof of identity, no bank card, no account number but that I could at least confirm my name, address, phone number and some of my most recent activity.

I struggled to remember the last time I'd used the card, and lucked out on memory of the cab ride from the restaurant. "OK," said Ms. Brock. "Now tell me what the charge was?"

"Double," I muttered, an unconscious racecar driver the premium. I hazarded a guess, pulling out $83 from the recesses of memory.

"Close enough," she said. "Yes, there is an electronic credit processing into your account right now in the amount of $23,956."

I figured it was worth a shot with her: "Do I have enough information to issue a new card?"

No such luck.

"I've got an idea," I said. "Turn on a sports-news TV station. I'll be on there," pointing down to my leg. "Journalistic confirmation?"

She laughed at me. She hadn't heard my story, she said.

Not a race fan?

Not hardly. Come back in the morning.

"Manager on duty is a huge fan. Maybe he'll make an exception."

It would be worth a shot—I'd by god be there anyway.

I crutched back outside and surveyed the headquarters of the unwashed—a couple of the tents closest to the door were half-dismantled from the chaos of last night's festivities, whatever they were, I guessed, and were being cleaned out by cops. Few people were around, otherwise. Hanging on a tree farther afield, near the corner around which I'd done the deal with Knox Garp and Bridget that first night here, I noticed Garp's beads, or a set just like them, 10 feet above the reach even of a human of above-average height, like the pair of shoes strung up on the dealer's corner Smitty pointed out to me that night so long ago.

I reveled in the good feeling that the predictable nature of this lent to my bones. I was feeling good, today, despite all. I had no commitment other than holding on for dear life as time marched. Nazi Chris still wasn't answering when I got home, so I posted up on my porch, ate two chicken legs, washing them down with a pull from the Evan Williams bottle as insurance against the slight chill in the air, then another against the dull but growing pain that was my left leg. Another. Another.

I woke late-afternoon to the sound of the on-street buzzer. It was Billy.

"You alone?" I asked him through the intercom.

He hesitated. "Yeah, well there's a couple guys waiting to get in, too, seeing someone else, I guess, but I'm by myself."

"Don't let them in, please," I said, and he grunted approval as I buzzed open the door. I could hear him offering apologies to whomsoever happened to be behind him. I didn't need any more intrusion on this space. I stood listening to the silence, for scuffles in the walls, for struggling beasts under the sink. Nothing.

Finally, a knock on the door. Through the keyhole I cased Billy, hair wild and ropy as ever, smiling for me, the camera, as it were, and indeed alone. I let him in and I didn't tell him all that I could have, but that was OK. As I knew from our last time together, Billy

Jones could be relied on to talk for hours uninterrupted if you got him comfortable. We passed the whiskey around awhile and then moved on to beers. Elsa had decamped for Europe yet again, he said, why he was involved in this.

"I may give the home place down there a visit, been ages since I've seen Albert Ledbetter," his father's old crony, he said.

"You have found your solitude," I said, but he was lost without the lady, as usual.

"But I think she'll be back," he said.

Was he sure?

"You know how it is," he said. (He wasn't.) A project, some film or other, took her out there. "Don't ask me what it is. Weird stuff, of course. I can appreciate it, but damn if I could tell you what it's about. Involves that fucked-up panopticon prison design. Foucault and all that. You know, guard tower set in the center around open cells," big sweep of his arms forward, then out and around his back. Fist raised in front of his face: "The all-seeing eye, right in the middle, that you know is watching you, that you can't see. You're never alone, Cash, speaking of solitude." Surveillance, the modern state, war come home.

I told him about my rats—prisoners or guards I wasn't sure. He nodded. Been there, done that.

The longer I stayed in place, the smaller the world became. Shedding methods of contact as I'd done to date had had an effect, but humans were humans and sought each other out, regardless. Armchair wisdom alert: The world intruded—what we were here for.

"Let's just stay here," I said. "The bar down the way is nothing special."

Periodically, Billy and I hit the porch, braved the creeping chill, though nowhere no doubt close to whatever cold he'd become used to his years in Chicago. I saw G-Man Gerald on his bike four different times on the street below over the course of the night. Perched high above, I could not be seen by the bike messenger, or at least I didn't think he could see me. The next to last time, maybe 11 o'clock, G-man rode at the head of a gang of others, the lot of them all dressed in black and heading, presumably, for the AB building. I pointed him out to Billy, finally.

"A messenger? Man of my own heart," he said, though he'd never donned the anarchist black nor could he really commit to the sensibility the getup implied.

I gave him Gerald's part in my story, at least, and all the while wondered what exactly he knew about the other bits of violence I'd engaged our mutual associate in on Birmingham's edge.

"There's a lot of types like that, like totally militant," Billy said of the G-man. "Day-to-day they might be no different than me and you."

"I tried reason on him," I said. "This guy's a total prick."

"Reason. What's that?" He laughed. "We're riding tomorrow—fucking horses, remember—we're riding with some messengers, I was told. May be he's one of us."

The Shining Man suit could use some modification, if not a complete blackout. At that moment, I was leaning against it, truthfully, leaning to further ensconcement in my personal prison here as an entirely passive actor waiting out whatever my fate was to be. But I pulled the thing out and Billy marveled at its quality.

"Where'd you get this?" he said. "It's like factory-made, almost. Fucking awesome."

"The Suited Man," I said.

Billy just looked at me.

"No shit," he said. "I wasn't going to bring it up, seems like a fucking dream." I watched him closely. He tugged on his beer nonchalantly, no manner out of the ordinary for a man remembering a night worth remembering, an outpouring of emotion rare in proper circles, even among lovelorn men.

"We're maximizing emotion, Billy," I said, "or we were that night, or maybe we should be now and always. It's a good thing. Hard to do." I furrowed my brow and nodded seriously.

It didn't get the reaction I expected—a smile, a laugh, something to deflate the sentiment.

"You know Trey is dead," he said. He got sick, compromised immune system turned in on itself, "something like that." I had no idea what to say, what even to feel. I wasn't sad, but I wasn't happy, either. I won't say the old man deserved what he got. I thought of the piles of photographs in my mother's basement closet, my basement closet. The undeveloped roll of film, the negatives, all in all a trove that well could have been the old man's salvation—was I responsible for his demise? I asked myself quietly as Billy continued to talk on Olden's unhappy funeral, the few people there, as if "none of it ever happened," he said, referencing all the work, the show, Trey's other projects. If only he knew the half of it, and I wanted to tell him about Birmingham, the Suited Man, about Rinckoff, but didn't for fear of complicating matters further than was necessary, than we had time for, maybe. I couldn't lie to Billy, either, I'd learned so long ago. My part in it was too hard to contend with—I couldn't approach it honestly, so I kept my mouth shut.

It was done.

And the loss was crushing, in a way. In part, I knew, I was responsible for Trey, felt it like a weight falling down on my head, his death a direct link to my angry late-night reclamation of my image, my shining form, from an uncalled-for usurpation. Mental justifications didn't make it all feel any better, and Billy, as if sensing my distress over the subject of Trey Olden, changed a subject.

"Have you seen or heard from V?" he said.

In some ways, Bridget and her constant presence had banished the Chicago Carolinian from my thoughts. I told him of my infrequent dispatches to her email address, none sent since the last one down in my mother's basement. I told him of Bridget.

"No better way to get over a woman than with another one," he said.

"Who told you that?"

"An old man five times divorced and remarried." Nobody in Chicago knew where the hell V had gone, he said, nobody he knew anyway. "Maybe back down here. It was like right around the time you left, she was kind of running around with Carl and all that— yeah, I know, sorry. But then I'd see Carl by himself down at the bar and he just shrugged it off, you know. He's 'busy' every time I call him these days. Or at least he pretends he is. I don't get it."

Armchair wisdom alert: People grow apart, I said, or something to that effect. "Elsa doesn't know where she went?"

"That's the thing: she truly doesn't, V just stopped returning calls, fell off radar."

And again: "People do that." I moved slowly to the kitchen

for some scissors. Most of the left leg of the suit would have to go—too skinny to fit over the cast at all, and I had no filler material with which to modify it, much less a needle and thread. When I moved back into the main room, Billy emerged from the coat closet, whose door I'd no doubt left open, caught in the act of pulling out a Team Bascombe pit-crew suit.

"Dude!" he said, positively joyful. "You've got to let me wear this."

I smiled, picturing Billy in the bumblebee colors atop a—"What color is the horse you rode in on? That you'll ride?" Brown, he said—horse of a different color out on Tryon. I was happy he was here, elated for the moment in anticipation of what came next.

"You got it," I said.

Chapter 19

Billy and the crew he was with—complete with Shining Band minus their shining suits, typical skeleton attire for this one, he said—had a permit for a 3:30 p.m. parade. Their quarry was staged north of town, he said, near the fairgrounds. Bridget showed at my door at noon randy as hell.

"It reeks in here, race man," she said. I checked the glue traps. Nada. Her hand was down my jogging shorts in no time.

Perched on top of me, she got hers as I struggled to overcome the discomfort in my broken-ass leg. She knocked the cast around, turning the top of it in fact into a thing more akin in stiffness to an overused cardboard box.

"You're fucking my cast," I said when her exhalations had subsided, though she continued up, down, forward, back, up, down… "It hurts."

She nodded and put her face between my legs and I closed my eyes and let it all happen.

I tried to explain to her the Shining Man suit, but she just waved it off when I got to the meeting with Turner on the freeway. "You're a piece of work, old man," she said. The occupation was set for 3, but when we got to the bank around 2—myself intent on making another attempt at a withdrawal—there was already a sizable contingent milling about the remaining tents, under Knox Garp's hanging beads, ready for the assault.

We milled around for a half hour or so. Did I know there was a protest of the protest going on over at the federal building? Bridget wondered. I'd heard of some recent such shenanigans, I said.

"There's going to be an action there," she said, this group disrupting the plans of that. I felt entirely inconspicuous in my reflective suit, bright yellow Team Bascombe ballcap, damn the negative media exposure that could well result, I thought. Entirely comfortable, I was, marred though the suit be by the dirty, off-white cast that was the bulk of its crooked left leg. Here was a man wearing

287

a Nixon mask, another as George W. Bush, hey a skeleton suit, my people. Anarcho-type guys—or gals, hard to tell—clad all in black now complete with G.I. Joe Snake-Eyes-type black masks, huddled around a pile of bricks it looked like they'd broken off a big planter for a small tree that stood just behind them.

I approached the group in black and asked them what exactly was going on. The guy who seemed to be calling the shots over the brick pile took off his mask and smiled.

"Got some incense?" Gerald said.

I turned to go, but he grabbed my shoulder and stopped me.

"Where'd you get that suit?" he said.

"Used to have a left leg, too," I said.

"Hard times," he said.

"This is my demonstration suit," I said. "I prefer the light to darkness." And he smiled, pulling his mask quickly back over his head.

"Whatever gets you off," he said, then knelt conspiratorially down. I bent over, such as I could.

"We need a couple pillowcases," he said. "Payback to those fuckers," gesturing back over the crowd to the cops on-hand, "for what they did to us last night." Gerald told of a mass clearing-out the night previous, the preamble to it the night before that, a damper on what would no doubt have been a bigger party today. The cops had obviously gotten wind of it all. Easy to see how they had, given I'd been hearing publicly about this on social forums online for weeks.

"I've got an idea," Gerald said. "You live around here, don't you? Can you make time on those things?" indicating the crutches.

"What for?"

He pointed to the bricks—"Pillowcases. Shotput, discus, dunno what you'd call it, stick a brick inside a pillowcase and fling it. Window-breaking time. I didn't say that."

Points for chutzpah, at least. I had biz in the bank, I told him, sorry, if he could wait—

He turned abruptly back to the rest of the blackout crew.

"We'll do without if Stinko doesn't show." He turned back to me. "You need something? Why don't get off and do your 'biz,' businessman."

"Nah, man, I don't need anything. I'm cool," and I tramped

back through the growing crowd, at ease despite the G-man's presence. I was just another weirdo here. That is, until I squeezed through two women at the other edge of the group nearest the AB entrance and was greeted by the phalanx of police.

"Stay back!" one positively shouted.

"I'm here for business," I said.

"We know what you guys are up to, just stay back," less emphatically.

"No, I mean I need to close a bank account."

He exchanged a look with the guy next to him, then the two parted to let me through. *Anything for a shining man on crutches,* I thought, my disability working for me.

Inside, the main lobby with its elevator banks was deserted but for some security. Only a single clerk was obviously on duty through double doors inside the branch. The bank had heard about it all too, it turned out, and only brought in a skeleton staff.

"Does that include the manager?" I asked the clerk who was filling me in.

She looked around the space warily and, I suppose, seeing nothing untoward outside of my shiny presence, disappeared behind a partition to the right of her desk, emerging with a middle-age guy.

"I heard you were a race fan," I said.

After having obviously gotten a load of my suit, he stared at my hat for a moment, then at my face, my busted-up leg.

"My God," he said.

"Jenny Brock," I said. "I confirmed my account details with her yesterday, aside from an account number. She said you might be able to help me get the money out, given my identity wouldn't be in question." I kept on with the explanation of my situation I'd given Jenny, Misty before her, and it worked.

"We don't have this kind of cash on hand," he said when I told him I wanted to close the account. "Best I can do is issue a cashier's check you can then deposit into the next account you open."

I wouldn't be doing that, I told him. We settled on $5,000 in cash, the rest in cashier's checks payable to me in $2,000 increments.

"Can I ask why you're doing this, Mr. Cash?" the manager, whose name I'd yet to glean, asked me.

I gazed back out into the lobby, empty, through big windows onto the crowd in front of the building—to my right, I could see through the two-story-high windows the back of the obviously quite small group of policeman on hand. Beyond them, the crowd swelled. The police spread out then to cover the perimeters of the crowd as it shifted and ballooned. A commotion at the center of the horde, I could make out through the gaps in the uniformed line.

"Let's just say I'm finished with banking—racing too, I guess," I said to the manager, who warily now followed my gaze back outside. Then: "I'll be right back," hurriedly disappearing behind the partition. The digital clock hanging from the partition read 2:42.

That was when the first brick hit, thudding hard on the plate-glass front of the branch and doing nary a bit of damage. "Oh my God!" yelped the clerk, who up to that moment had been sitting with her head in her hands at a desk behind the counter I leaned against. With the sound of the second, third and fourth then echoing through the empty place, she jumped up and disappeared where the manager had gone. The cops began to move forward toward the crowd as a unit. As the fifth brick was launched up from well within the crowd, I could see the blackout catapulters momentarily in a break among the crowd, Bridget too there among those providing a barrier between the cops and Gerald's crew.

The manager emerged then alarmed and empty-handed from around the partition.

"Get ready, Mr. Cash," he said. "If the window breaks it's gonna get loud in here."

They shifted tactics from individual throwing now—Stinko had arrived, I guessed, with his (or her) pillowcases. Two black-clad humans of indeterminate gender were now swinging bricks in pillowcases over their heads in accelerating circles, in time, makeshift slingshots. The cops were closing in on the small group (holding), encouraging visible resistance as they moved on the men/women in black. They didn't get all the way around before both bricks were simultaneously launched and came screaming like a couple baseball line-drive ropes out over their heads, trailing cloth comet tails, and the cops hit the deck. The projectiles hit the windows in a rising trajectory and the building alarm sounded with the crumble and spray of glass, one of the bricks coming to rest just shy of the clerk's desk. The outer noise now reached us full-bore. The crowd was chanting, simply, "Let – us – in!"

"You got those checks?" I said as the alarm bells screamed. "Gotta go."

But the manager was gone. I walked behind the counter, then beyond the partition to discover a set of stairs leading God-knows-where, up. I considered searching him out—I'd damn well need that money—but decided against it when a blackout guy who had to be all of 6'6" pushed past me with a gasoline canister in his hand and went on up the stairs himself.

With the police preoccupied by the small group of brick-throwers and their protectors outside, the more-whimsical bulk of the crowd danced its way into the building more or less unimpeded. A woman carrying a picnic basket, followed by another one, and another one, posted up by the counter where I stood and began laying out plates—brownies, earthy-looking cookies, tortillas, I don't know what all else. I balanced myself on top of the clerk's chair and looked for Bridget among them all, then out over their heads back outside, where the cops had several people in zip-tie cuffs. A security guy in a red uniform and holding a police baton threatened me with unknown levels of pain if I didn't get back out into the common area, out of the branch. The gals setting up the snacks then joined me where I was and dared him to do anything about it.

A guy on a unicycle came flying by and in a quick move swiped the red-clad security guard's baton and rolled on through the lobby twirling it like a pro, the fat guard giving waddling, ineffective chase.

Another big crash, this time from the lobby, where I guessed G-man had dispatched a portion of his crew. A woman in a harlequin-type bodysuit caught some incidental glass and was now screaming bloody murder at the brick-happy blackout, holding her head, blood trickling down the left side of her face.

Time to go. I motioned for her to come, and when she didn't pushed her with a crutch brandished like a cattle prod toward the door I'd come in. Loud music struck up behind me and I turned back once more to see several members of the melee dancing in the lobby. Among them, with his mask removed: G-Man Gerald, who then went stock still and stared right at me. I moved quickly behind the screaming woman toward a group of cops surrounding the small group of demonstrators who'd been the buffer between the police and the brick throwers. She retreated along past the group as I slowed to a crawl within 20 feet and tried not to look at them again—Bridget, wrists zip-tied behind her back, had seen me.

"Cash, goddamnit!" she yelled. "Hey Cash! Help me! C'mon!"

I kept crutching along, eyes forward, then turned behind me in time to see Gerald reaching out and grabbing my right shoulder, pulling me off-balance. I fell left, my cast catching no small amount of my weight on the way down. Tears came to my eyes.

"That's for my fucking head," G-man said. "Piece of shit." A cop from the group around Bridget saw the whole thing and was on his way toward us, but Gerald was off in a flash, running to his tiger-striped bike, onto which he jumped, rolled, bouncing deftly down a set of outdoor stairs in the same motion, and was out into the street before the cop ever even got to me.

"You all right?" he asked.

I shut my eyes now against the pain and held out my wrists for cuffs.

Bridget's voice through the growing cacophony: "Cash, tell these motherfuckers what's what! Cash!"

When I opened them, the cop who'd accosted me was leading her away by the arm. I struggled to my feet and watched her go, screaming the entire time, no longer defiant, tears in her eyes, on her face. At the final moment, across the street and next to a paddy wagon, she finally calmed down and just stared back. Her eyes spoke, nothing would be the same. She lowered her head as they pushed her into the box. And she was gone.

I crutched around the chaos aimlessly for a while. So much for Billy's permitted parade. I kept my head down when I mustered up courage enough to approach the wagon Bridget was in, until I came upon a cop.

"Hey man," I said. "My girlfriend's in there. Is there any way—"

"Oh yeah," he cut me off, sarcastic. "Nice get-up. We've got these people on criminal conduct, some of those black assholes with them, I mean, you know, wearing the black suits."

"We're peaceful types, man," I said, as if, *Look, I know she didn't mean to be involved with that.*

"She'll be booked at North Station. Take it up with them." I had no idea where that was and told him so. "Up Davidson," he said. Several miles, at least. I stood there a while. The wagon wheeled Bridget on, and a police-car blockade at the next corner parted for a fire truck, siren blazing. I turned back to see smoke billowing from a window of the AB building a few stories up.

The scene two blocks over was less dramatic, quite similar to two days prior, a conservative crowd rendered less so only by the garish lettering on a myriad of protest signs decrying abortion, taxes, government, civilization and polite society in general. I stood back from the primary crowd on the sidewalk at Trade, the crowd assembled ahead of a small, as-yet-unoccupied stage to my left, where a lone microphone attached to a P.A. and bank of speakers heralded entertainment to come. I started to ask somebody what to expect, looking for the traitors among them. Finding none obvious, I looked for the opportunists—Knox Garp. But then, way off in the distance, I heard faint, familiar strains of trombone, tuba, rollicking tribal drums. I peered off down the road to the east and here they came. Over the police cruisers stationed at Trade and Church, down the street from my apartment, skeletons, and behind them, horses, headed straight for the crowd outside the federal building. From here I could make out the yellow speck atop a tall brown horse, likewise. I crutched that way to get a better look, until I saw in the greater distance a positively horrific sight: black-clad anarchos on bikes spilling out from either side of the horse parade, passing the skeleton band in front and pushing forward at some speed for the small blockade. I was paralyzed by it all when G-man saw me, his tiger-striped bike recognizable from a distance. He was maybe 50 yards ahead and on a course directly for me, pedaling like mad. The commotion had gotten the attention of the counter-protesters by now, most of whom just stayed where they were and watched it all unfold if they watched at all, disinterestedly, really. Gerald continued to haul ass this way, leaving his compatriots behind. A cop with a baton tried to wave him down at the corner but didn't get the job done. I took a firm grasp of my right crutch and pointed it out in front of me. If jousting was what he wanted, today, jousting was what he'd get.

But he began to slow, stopping before he got to me. He took off his mask and smiled ear to ear. Billy.

"Traded getups with Gerald," he said. "That crazy mother-fucker's a horseman!"

"You mean he's wearing my suit?" The fact stuck in a little tight knot there in between my eyebrows as I seethed. But it took little more than a glance at my black-clad friend here to be reminded that I'd once been equally comfortable adopting whatever came before me as my own.

"I'll get it back, man, don't worry," Billy said.

"Forget it," I said. I would no longer claim the shapeshift-er's game as birthright. Transformation was a destiny so few could count on as a positive past their third decade of existence, another lesson I could thank my father's armchair proselytizing for, one obvious in the slow-and-steady predictability of my mother's day-to-day, Chief Hugg's manipulative conniving, Annie's addictions, even Trey Olden's high-flying gamesmanship, buried with him—he was who he was, surprise at duplicitous experimentation sits false with me to this day, the exact wrong reaction to the artist's sen-sibility. I could be any of them, I knew, but also something else, something of worth to somebody, to myself.

If, that is, I made it away from the spectacle storming around me with my body intact.

With Billy stopped, the cop had given chase.

"Dude, they're probably looking for Gerald—anybody in a black suit like that." I pointed back to the uniform and eased away. "They set fire to the fucking bank building. Think fast." The cop was closing in.

Billy pedaled on, and I moved slowly still, a little too slowly, out of the way in order to get my right crutch in front of the police-man's right foot. A hard shot as he sprawled across the pavement. I was all apologies, and he brushed himself off and reconsidered giving chase, posting back up to meet the parade at the corner with five other cruisers, each accounting for a pair of cops. I watched them from a distance. There were five horseback riders—Gerald, a guy I vaguely recognized from Chicago, three others I didn't. The anarcho-cyclists behind them, minus Billy, turned right at Church and rolled up past my apartment toward God knows where, a cou-ple of the police peeling off from this little blockade to follow. Gerald then rode right up to one of the lead cops and talked to him.

I walked closer to hear Gerald: "…with all the mess on Tryon, they told us to use Trade. And what is this?" pointing out in front of him at the mass of humanity outside the federal building, who remained, amazingly, mostly disinterested. No doubt the parade was the disruption Bridget talked about. I watched all approaches for the cyclists. A platform and podium back down the block, set up on the sidewalk out front of the building, was being occupied by several men in suits—among them I thought I recognized Nazi Chris, his hat, anyway. From a distance of 100 yards, I couldn't be sure.

A suited man took the podium, speaking through a PA system, and introduced himself as a member of something called "Carolinians for Communities," but what he talked about had all to do with the national health care law, of which he spoke with a vehemence a step in intensity or two well beyond that of Pete Kimball. He got some hoots when he called the president a Muslim and "terrorist sympathizer." Then he was done, and the man I thought was Chris took off his hat, and I crutched closer better to hear him pontificate. He wasn't exactly unreasonable—undeniably my upstairs neighbor, he made reference to the chaos a couple blocks over.

"It's a sad state of affairs that we find ourselves in today," he said, quite unoriginally. "Anarchists storming the temples of American finance, even some of the same group listening in on our little colloquy here," pointing off over his left shoulder and following with his eyes to Team Bascombe-suited Gerald, just beyond the police cars, and his horseback compatriots. Chris' gaze lingered there a little longer than seemed to be required by the oratory. I suppose he recognized the bumble-bee-yellow of the suit.

"Everybody is welcome," he continued, then, "that's quite all right. I'm here to tell you a little about what I do. I'm one of those dastardly types—you know, *lawyers*" (chuckles from the audience) "hard at work on bringing a case to court to hold the President guilty of not fulfilling his duty to uphold the Constitution of the United States." Big cheers erupting, even from some among the crew of paraders—truth to power an appealing notion, regardless of your political party.

"The case is complicated, but it reflects broader issues in what amounts to a crisis of leadership, the federal government's will-

ingness to run up debts that will bankrupt our children's generation, there is no doubt about it, and to continue to leave American troops in the lurch, fighting wherever they may be around the
world to secure our freedom."

Another cheer, applause, but it was muted by comparison.
He was losing me—and others of the less partisan among the
crowd—with this kind of rote sound and fury.

A commotion at the far end of the crowd, west down Trade
from where I was, with the cops and parade at my back. I spied no
shortage of black, and bikes, among the t-shirted masses.

"And in this election year, I'll also say, and I know there are
many among you who have been waiting for this, that I'm proud
to announce my candidacy for the city council in this district, to
represent the downtown residents of this great city. The district
also encompasses..."

Nazi Chris: A budding politician! As I was marveling at the
news, amid the far-off commotion I spied a pillowcase raised high
and being slung around in a tight circle. The combatant let the
thing fly now as Chris' monotone veered to the intricacies of his
district, then quickly stopped, the brick flying its high arc on quite
an accurate trajectory, Chris backing away quickly. It hit the microphone square—a *thwonck* followed by a big squeal from the P.A.
system echoed out over the space, and the dignitaries, or whatever
you'd call them, on the platform scattered—*waddled in a scatter*, you
might say for the more obese among them, a description that could
apply to several. Not so much Chris himself, who was off like a
shot, having taken the time at least to grab his hat, and headed this
way, home.

With the cops now streaming down the block toward the
brick's launch site, Gerald and company moved forward and got
between my position and that of Chris, Gerald laughing high and
wild atop his horse, which he seemed to control with the dexterity
of a jockey.

"Impeachment!" he scoffed down at the lawyer, who turned
and ran toward the alley behind our building, Gerald's horse giving
chase. I followed as fast as I could—not quite a run, but as close
as you could get on crutches. I was getting better at it, in any case,
and was spurred onward by desire for an answer, or if I had the
answer already a simple confirmation. Chris deserved a chance as

296

much as the rest of us. G-man was crazy as a bedbug, too, or sane beyond the sanity of the lot of humanity—anybody deserved help when faced with such an adversary.

When I entered the alley the horse was turning off down the next channel, which ran by our building's parking lot and out into the street to the main entrance. I followed, Chris, then the horse, reaching the street about the time that I took the alley entrance to the parking lot, the inner door then to the first floor and was standing in the elevator, nearer the lot that the main entrance, out of sight, holding down the door-open button, when Chris came running in. I let go the button as soon as he was in. "Did you get the door shut?" I said.

"It won't hold them long."

I'd punched the number to his floor—"we'll get off there and climb back down the stairs to my place. They'll be watching the floors to see where you get off."

I moved to open the porch doors when we arrived, but "No no no," he said. "They might see the doors opening." We heard a muffled crash of breaking glass, then, likely the building's front, followed by an annoying-ass alarm that would play soundtrack to the next 20 minutes.

"Good call," I said, and I smoked right there in the apartment. It'd cover up the rat stink, anyway, at least dilute it.

Once we stilled, Chris periodically standing and pacing as I smoked, I could hear another sound. A squeegee running across congealed bacon grease, a fork moving rapidly and repeatedly through a bowl of sauced-up spaghetti, a sickening sound. No fucking way was I going to finish this job. I needed his help, too.

The beast was caught between two of the big glue boards at the furthest-most point back in the cabinet—I got two bags over my left hand, kneeled down on my right foot with my left propped way out. When I got hold on the board that his forepaws were stuck in, I tugged slightly, and the little fucker howled. I let go and as quickly as I'd grabbed lost my balance, falling back onto the kitchen floor. Chris helped me up.

"I got it," he said. "Give me the bags."

The rat rolled around in the glue, digging his body further into its snare. When he got the thing out into the light, it was clear it'd chewed on one of its legs—a small pool of blood had gathered in the forepaw trap.

"Motherfucker," I said, woozy now and scooting toward the wall to hold myself up. It kept up a steady stream of squeaks and chitters as it writhed.

"Quick," said Chris, now getting the board wholly inside of one of the big trash bags, where the rat finally seemed to calm down, in the dark. "Something heavy, a hammer maybe?"

I thought. I went out into the living area and grabbed the laptop. "Use this," I said. Don't worry about breaking it, it's no big deal."

"You sure?"

"100 percent," I said.

He got down on his knees there over the bagged rat, smoothed the bag out over its shape and it renewed its wriggling, then stilled when Chris removed his hands. He raised the laptop high over his head and brought down a corner square on the rat's head. The screen separated from the body of the computer in the process, various chips of the plastic casing spreading around the kitchen. The rat moved no more.

"Goddamn you did it," I said.

Chris moved back and sat on the floor, leaned against the kitchen wall, eyes closed. He looked old, he did.

"Hell of a thing," I said. "Tell Turner to leave me alone next time you see him."

His eyes opened, surprised, a little, though it passed. He nodded, affirmative.

"You might be in over your head with the whole attempted-murder thing," I said.

"It'll never trace back to me," he said. "Besides, it's unprovable, as you well know. The shit was an accident." I searched his face for weakness, uncertainty, anything to indicate an outright lie. "I guarantee, though, Bascombe gets part of what he wants. Hugg is gone—within the month, whether the sponsors go with him or not."

He was telling the truth.

"Cheeters coming on board," I said.

"They are. Signed the deal Monday."

"Before Turner came here."

"Before Turner came here."

298

Noise in the hallway, a quick bang on my door, heavy footsteps running a quick pace on down the hall, more banging on more doors. I brought my index finger to my lips and smiled. Cloak and dagger—viewed from on high, I was in love with it, but this couldn't keep up.

Rob's voice, then, echoing down the hall—"get the fuck out of here, goofballs, before I call the police!"

"All right, man, all right."

Stair door opening, closing.

After a time, I took off my cap and gave it to Chris.

"You want out of here, right?" I said. I took off the one-legged suit and gave that to him, likewise a pair of jeans that fit him just a little snug, but "doable," he said. We were just about the same height—he had more middle. The hat fit without adjustments, too.

"We might have been two sides of the same coin in a prior life," I said. "Wear the suit and that hat out of here. Pull out of the lot like you own the place, keep the ballcap brim down low. Like me. Roll on. Now, give me your hat." I put on the fedora and it fit, as expected. I looked at myself in the mirror. Bags under my eyes, five-day stubble. I shaved, put the black suit and tie on. I looked again. Better. The hat wasn't a perfect match, but it'd do.

"I've got a long walk ahead of me," I said. "Be seeing you."

We stood by my apartment door. Chris pulled out his phone.

"I might call somebody to come get me," he said.

"You ought to just wait a while longer is my guess," I said. "An hour or two. I'd call you when I scoped the scene outside, but I don't have a phone. Fine to stay here. Take anything you like."

I was finished, though my odyssey made little sense but as a parable of how to transform human life into a cog to suit the needs of those around you while the self aimlessly searches, seethes, burns. This place would be no good to me, no method of escape from the people I couldn't be, much less those I might find something of worth with.

The thought of Bridget held the biggest disappointment. She would never forgive me, I knew, for not doing what was right or what I couldn't possibly do. I'm still not sure which, and never will be. There by the door I caught sight of the last chicken box—inside: two wings, quickly masticated before departure—and almost broke down and cried with the lawyer and would-be politician looking on as I ate. But the food bucked me up. I held it together, throwing the bones to the floor for the rats. They fell one after the next with a satisfying thump and clatter. I tipped the slightly alarmed Nazi goodbye with his own hat and locked the door on the way out. I took the stairs slowly, accosted once by a kid in messenger gear bounding up from below. "What the fuck, man?" I said when he grabbed my shoulder, looking right into his wild-ass eyes with my own best impression. I brandished my crutch threateningly.

"All right, all right," he backed away, a wave of incomprehension crossing his face, with a twinge of something else I recognized. Who was this suited man he was looking at? Fear was that something else. It made little sense to continue the confrontation. He bounded on up.

The building alarm wailed away. A fire was burning in a trash-can on the corner at Trade, where the cops had been stationed, a hydrant on the opposite corner spraying into the street. The black-out bikers continued to zip to and fro, Billy apparently one of them. I heard a window smash again and looked to see a second brick go flying into a second-story apartment window. I kept walking.

I had a long way to go the 10 to 15 miles back to my mother's. My armpits burned. Long after normalcy took hold along South Boulevard heading out of town, shit got weird as night fell. After all sidewalks came to an end, the boulevard poured out onto 51 and then U.S. 21 to Fock's Mill, my well-dressed presence on the grassy shoulders prompted a chorus of those too-familiar pitch-descending horn-honks, then some guy missed me with a bottle thrown from the back of a pickup truck. I was near McClendon's and thought about dropping in, though I had no way of paying for my beer. It was going on 10 at that point, and I hadn't far to go. The place was more or less empty, I saw. I recognized no one.

I smiled at my slight reflection in the windows out front, waved to the bartender inside, and kept on going, till I made my place, back where it began.

Epilogue

And there you have it, a revenge tragedy with a pathetic payoff in the contemporary sense of that word, *pathetic*—full of humiliating bile and embarrassment! You should sense something of what I mean already about the aftermath of the events described. After all, the end was in the beginning, though it may lie as far ahead now as it did then.

I have a long way to go, it's sure—I am far from death, lest a dump truck or drunk fuck plow me under. Employment is out of the question, and speaking of questions, it remains to be seen how a stupid man gets along with getting along in the churn of our cash-driven world.

But getting along by itself won't do. Bank floor managers under siege deserve some kudos, too, a measure of understanding, though on account of their errors my mother's basement is no nest with an egg in it. But it's more warm and cozy than all that—it is at least free of rats, free of unmanageable levels of darkness and humiliation, despite what so many of you will think a man past the terminus of his third decade in existence ought to be able to make of his time on this earth. I have light amplified, at least, and I can commiserate as I wish with the philosophers, not least among them the Pole Leszek Kowalkowski and his thoughts on the primed pump of religious reawakening—the need for it these past decades, in the wake of the "death of historical man," as he puts it, to save humanity from its attention deficit. History is now, in our current way of thinking. We make it as we go, the past be damned to nonsense—*it's all relative*, young Bobby Cash might say. I can hear Billy and Bridget saying it, too, in their less appealing moments. Turner Bascombe? No doubt about it.

I see the attraction of the perspective. My countervailing authority, however, will be neither god, real-estate shyster-turned-President Donald Trump, utopian political movement nor dystopian cynicism. The past does matter, I know. Combat-hungry anarchists will make you pay for forgotten indiscretions, nemeses and sometime friends relegated to dustbins of the mind will ride in on horses steel or otherwise waving batons or flaunting disingenuous personalities at your head. Hobble headlong into them waving your crutches as jousting sticks and you might locate a new method for bringing down the strictures that keep you from really knowing something of worth.

I am experimenting, at the least.

That may well make me more my father's son than I ever thought I could be. Back when, I vilified the old man for leaving me and my mother. I despised his peculiar workingman's erudition, his baroque sense for the dramatic. His departure from my mortal coil then drove the spike of recognition in further, you might say. Getting by, day to day, was not to be alive. The roar of train horn, screech of steel on the trestles of the old man's past, rip through my memory bearing an apotheosis of the proselytizing grind. We cannot help in our time but to be proselytizers, whether of a cutting-edge facial lotion or of our own bizarre or intensely humdrum routines, the worth of a man determined by the numbers of his followers, whether his online friends or those who subscribe to his particular version of truth. My father wanted me to know this, too, though it's taken me this long, putting it down, to figure it.

Work, stable family or stable of friends, it's not enough. But what is enough is not nearly so out of reach as you might think.

Oh so we should be happy with what we have? I can hear you mocking. *Yes be damned the injustice in how the money pie is divided up as the crooks walk free. He's just messing with us again! Be satisfied, think positive, all that bullshit.*

Indeed not.

Ask: Is it apathy or empathy that drives my days? As I've said before, I won't deny my own failings. I split the difference: Apathetic empathy, in my case, maybe, like I couldn't really give a shit if a connection is made, but if it is I'll take it all, for all it's worth, too. The former is the condition of every human existence at one point or another in any history. But the latter is over-rated, over-hyped. I experiment, trying to move beyond, with new ways to foster real connections with my fellow humans, and I'm happy for the opportunity. I like watching the cardinals and robins and little brown, black-faced European sparrows in the trees by the roadside, too, defending their territory from each other, from us. Honk if you agree!

And Bridget and Billy and Kimball and the sharpshooting Smitty are probably closer than we all might think on the spectrum of thrusts against power. Happy/emo-go-lucky Billy and personal-space-terrorist bicyclists share a common bond. If such forces find a way to put their disagreements aside for the greater salvation, we all might be in for a national fireworks show of an upheaval. They are experimenting, too.

Nobody really wants upheaval, however much they may think they do. As I'm sure Trey Olden would point out, unrequited/ unresolved conflict makes these days go by, provides a clear-cut and compelling reason for being without which the body gives in to its eccentricities, its maladies, calls it quits—the same can be said for similarly situated love and desire, of course, though I'll admit I do enjoy my affectionless peace, here, for now, interrupted at first only by the uninvited bursts of a certain racecar driver who heaped scorn on my pitiless little head. Thankfully, I suspect those bursts may be at their terminus, or at the least on the wane. As predicted, Turner has gotten the better part of what he wanted. Good luck in the new season, after season, after …

And I have taken to only occasionally pining after Bridget, after the elusive V, after the fumes of American-made automobiles, after my own shining creations—for a time I so pined that I amassed the fabric necessary to cover these basement walls with them, though I have yet to put their power to use in the outside world. I don't believe any of the pining will stand in my way—call me a veritable symptom of instant-gratification culture! Pass the bottle, brother!

I still don't really know what happened to Ralph Cash. But assuming his final note to me was more than just a game, I think I understand why he's gone, anyway. But first I had to understand that I was as stupid as the next man!

I will neither drink myself to death here in my hole, if I can help it, nor disappear off the edge of the I-77 bridge over the Catawba River, don't worry. I will not go the way of Henry's, a victim of the slow roll of commercial collapse, of easy spending money. My hideout here is no endgame, understand, nor prelude to a cryptic or hyper-emotional or deadened and depressed suicide note. I have plenty reflected natural light to keep me company before I re-emerge in another form, or in updated, less *buggy* form, in the parlance of our contemporary software-design professionals, replete with something I've yet to find.

I do know some things to be facts. That vanguard all-electric Nissan automobile is made somewhere in suburban Tennessee, and those ever-more-ubiquitous South Charlotte Mercedes drivers roll in care of the fine citizens of Nowhere, Alabama, where those machines are produced.

The foreign is native. I don't have a problem accepting that if you don't. And that brings to mind the truly amazing thing. It positively terrifies me to think of it, but in the process of putting this down it's become more and more apparent. As isolated and run-around as I am, who knows but that, up there in the highest screaming registers nearly out of the bounds of human hearing, I've been telling someone else's story.

Maybe, just maybe, that story is yours.

Nashville, 2016

Todd Dills grew up in Rock Hill, S.C., graduated from Winthrop University there (1998) and finished an MFA in fiction writing at Columbia College Chicago in 2003. He authored a prior novel, *Sons of the Rapture* (Featherproof Books, 2006) and a short story collection, *Triumph of the Ape* (2012), and was founding editor and publisher of *The2ndHand*, a literary broadsheet published from 2000–2013. *The2ndHand* continues as a sometime book publisher. Dills has been senior editor for *Overdrive*, a trade magazine for the small businesses in the long-haul trucking industry, since 2006. His feature journalism work there has earned several honors in business-to-business journalism. In 2014, excerpts from *Shining Man* afforded him the Tennessee Arts Commission's Individual Artist Fellowship in Fiction. He lives in Nashville with his wife, Susannah, and daughter, Thalia.